DARK MAFIA VOWS

AN ARRANGED MARRIAGE ENEMIES TO LOVERS ROMANCE

KAYLA MASON

1

GINEVRA

My knuckles are white as I grip my steering wheel firmly, trying to navigate the congested streets at 8:30 in the evening. The roads are packed with cars, their honking horns drowning out the music blaring from my car's Bluetooth speaker.

As I sing along to the lyrics of Pharrell Williams' "Happy," my stomach twists with nerves, trying to distract myself from the impending breakdown that's bound to occur any minute from now.

I hate being late. I hate being stuck in traffic, and most importantly, I hate it when my brother is pissed at me.

As if on cue, my music pauses abruptly, overridden by the shrill sound of my ringtone.

"Shit," I mutter under my breath as Lorenzo's name flashes on my phone screen.

I place a hand over my racing heart and clear my throat, forcing a strained smile as I answer the call. "Hey, big brother—"

"You're this close to getting a security detail and a nanny,

Ginny," Lorenzo's impatient voice booms through the speakers. "Where are you? The event started already!"

My smile wavers, and I let out a sigh. It's not the first time he's made this threat. We both know assigning a security detail would be pointless. I've managed to evade every bodyguard and infuriate every nanny since day one, much to Lorenzo's consternation.

"I know, I know! I'm on my way," I reply, trying to keep my tone light, but my frustration bubbles beneath the surface. "I've been stuck in traffic for almost thirty minutes now."

His exasperated sigh fills the car's interior. "You wouldn't have been stuck if you'd left the house earlier. Or, hell, if you'd let your fiancé pick you up."

I roll my eyes as he continues. "Rinaldo is already here, and he's getting pissed. He wanted to introduce you to some important people."

"I got held up discussing ideas for the bakery. You know how it is."

"Discussing ideas?" he scoffs. "What the hell, Ginny?"

I steal a glance at the dashboard and huff. "Relax, I'm right on time. The party doesn't really even start until eight."

"Ginny, the event started thirty minutes ago," he informs me. "I must've told you the time a hundred times, but then again, you've always had selective hearing."

I groan. "It's not my fault today."

"Hmm," Lorenzo hums sarcastically. "Where and when have I heard that before? Oh yeah— from you, every other day."

His tone makes me bristle. Lorenzo has never fancied the idea of me starting a business of my own. He's always taken pride in taking care of me, and now that the family business is facing challenges, he's more determined than ever to keep me under his wing.

Rinaldo Sanchez, my fiancé, hails from a family of affluent politicians and is one of Lorenzo's business associates. According to my brother's grand plan, Rinaldo is supposed to ensure I'm well taken care of.

So, the idea of me starting my own bakery? It drives him up the wall.

"I've been out with the people who can help me." I try to make my tone light. "Small business owners, locals, exactly the kind of people who know what works. You know that."

"Is this really necessary, Ginny? You could just focus on socializing with Rinaldo, keeping up appearances for the company, and maybe your upcoming marriage," he huffs, and I roll my eyes again. "Why do you even need this bakery?"

I can almost hear him pacing on the other end, his over-protectiveness almost suffocating. I don't take offense, though. It comes from a good place. We've been on our own for so long, separated from the rest of our extended family, that we're all we have for each other. I'm just as protective of Lorenzo as he is of me.

Okay, maybe not as much. My brother can be a bit over-bearing, but I still love him.

Lorenzo loves me too, that much I know. He's the best big brother anyone could ever ask for, and if there's a next life, I'd definitely want him right back in his role as protector, pseudo parent, and sibling. He's been my only family since our parents died, and I wouldn't trade him for anything.

If only he didn't still see me as that five-year-old with missing teeth, pigtails, and a jean romper. It's frustrating how he treats me like I'm made of glass, something fragile that needs to be handled with care.

I can't even tell the most important person in my life about my passion because he thinks I don't need to make money, that I should be devoting my time to broadening my social circle and prepping to begin my role as a trophy wife.

"It's a passion project, Enzo." I feign a chuckle, trying to lighten up his mood. "And how many times do I have to tell you I'm doing this for myself?"

"Passion project or not, you're late. You need to prioritize family over... whatever this is."

"I promise I'll be there in no time. Just give me a moment," I tell him. "The traffic is clearing up."

I hear his heavy exhale before the goes dead.

"Rude," I scoff, pressing the gas pedal as my car inches forward.

The song resumes right where it left off, and I hum along, feeling the tension in my shoulders ease just a bit. I'm finally ready to launch my bakery, and I won't let anyone— not Lorenzo, and certainly not Rinaldo—make me feel guilty about it.

I merge onto the main road, the city's tall buildings rising against the night sky, their glass shining with the city lights. Each one feels alive, showing the energy of the city, and for the first time in a long while, I feel like I'm in sync with it.

As I drive farther, the street opens up with fancy shops and nice cafes, their glowing signs lighting up the evening. I glance at the time again, and...shit, I'm running late. I hope I can still make a grand entrance with Rinaldo if I hurry. Otherwise, he'll be pissed, too. Not that I care all that much, but having a grumpy fiancée by my side all night will definitely be my thirteenth reason.

Finally, I arrive at the luxurious hotel, its bright entrance looking inviting. The valet area is busy, and I decide not to use it. I don't want to hand over my keys in this casual outfit.

My faded blue jeans and a simple white top feel utterly inappropriate for the fancy party and the high-profile guests inside. I can already picture the glances I'll receive from the socialites if I'm caught wearing this, or worse, if any photographers or paparazzi take pictures and they end up online.

Lorenzo would be livid for sure. Rinaldo, too. I can just imagine the scandalous headlines. I shudder slightly at the thought. The last thing I want is to attract any more negative publicity to me or my brother. The best plan is to drive inside myself and change into the clothes currently sitting in the backseat of my car.

The cool air greets me as I pull into the underground parking garage. White lights flick overhead, illuminating the sea of already parked flashy cars. The concrete walls are designed with sleek artwork, and the lighting is soft, creating an inviting atmosphere. I quickly scan the space, relief washing over me when I spot an empty space near the back.

The overhead lights cast a soft glow on the polished concrete floor as I maneuver my car. I signal and steer into the spot, my eyes again glancing at the time. I exhale in relief when I realize I may not be as late as I thought.

Just as I'm about to put the car in park, a sleek, tinted sedan suddenly swerves into my lane and cuts me off. My heart races as I slam on the brakes, the tires screeching loudly against the pavement. I grip the steering wheel tighter, irritation bubbling up inside me.

"What the hell?" I hiss as my car comes to a stop.

Seriously? Who does that?

I take a moment to steady my breath, frustration

coursing through me like hot embers. After everything I've gone through today, this is the last thing I need.

I throw the car into park and fling open the door, my heels clicking sharply against the concrete as I step out. The air is sharp and cool, and adrenaline courses through my veins.

The driver of the tinted car remains inside, seemingly unfazed as he scrolls through his phone, my presence not appearing to matter. My annoyance is growing.

"Excuse me!" I call out, raising my voice to cut through the low hum in the garage. "Do you mind? You just stole my spot!"

Silence. The driver doesn't even glance my way. My frustration intensifies, and I take a step closer, my heart pounding in my chest. "Hey! I'm talking to you," I shout, my hands on my hips, feeling the heat rise to my cheeks.

When he doesn't budge, I go red in anger. I raise my hand and bang the inside of my fist against his window.

That's when the driver opens the door.

"How dare you—"

My words are cut off when the culprit emerges from the car. A man steps out, tall and imposing. The familiar sharp features—high cheekbones and a strong jawline—are striking.

A deep scowl etches his handsome face, the same face gracing covers of various business magazines and news articles, giving him an air of arrogance. Dark hair frames his piercing green eyes, which seem to hold an intensity that commands attention. Dressed in a tailored suit that fits him perfectly, he exudes a stinking level of wealth.

Dario De Luca.

The name hits me like a punch to the gut, bringing back

a flood of memories I'd rather forget. Me, a little girl with a silly crush, and he, my brother's former best friend, who only saw me as that and nothing more. Over the years, he has turned into the man about whom I've only heard bad things. His reputation precedes him like a storm cloud.

What is he even doing at an event like this? Last time I checked, he never socializes or attends parties like this. Lorenzo claims he sees everyone as beneath him, and now, judging from the way he's looking at me, my brother's right.

"Yes?" His tone is dismissive, as if I'm nothing more than an annoyance.

And that's when I realize that he doesn't even recognize me. I can't help but feel a mix of anger, embarrassment, and disbelief.

"Are you serious?" I reply, incredulous. "You just cut in front of me and act as if it's no big deal? I could've hit your car if I hadn't seen you in time."

He shrugs, a faint smirk tugging at the corner of his lips. "If you'd been paying attention, this wouldn't have been a problem."

I recall some of the things I've heard about him—cold, arrogant, condescending. And now, he stands before me with that smirk, proving the rumors were indeed true.

My blood boils at his words. "What?" I choke. "Are you seriously suggesting this is my fault? You're the one who—"

"It is your fault." He cuts me off sharply. "I don't insinuate."

I inhale deeply, trying to calm myself down.

"I can see that acting like an arrogant jerk comes naturally to you," I shoot back. Calm down, my ass. I'm fucking pissed.

His eyebrows raise slightly, and so does my voice. "You

think you can just do whatever you want. Who the hell do you think you are?"

His green eyes harden, and I spot a hint of anger in them.

"Look," he bites out, his eyes sweeping over me dismissively. "I don't have time for this nonsense. Doesn't the staff have a different entrance?"

His voice drips with condescension, and my eyes twitch at the insult. I stand there seething, my fists clenching at my sides.

"Staff?" I splutter, staring down at my body, wincing. "I'm not the staff, I'm—"

"When I care, I'll let you know."

He turns away from me and heads to the elevator as if I'm not even worth his time. I can't believe he has the audacity to treat me like this. "You're not used to being called out, so you're walking away like the coward you are," I call after him, my voice louder and sharper than I intended.

He doesn't respond. The nerve of him!

The last time I saw Dario, he was with my brother, his aloofness and cold demeanor always getting under my skin. Memories of his dismissive remarks flood back, and I realize just how much I loathe him, especially since he doesn't even remember me.

Before I can even think it through, I find myself walking toward him, determined to catch up before he reaches the elevator.

"Hey, I'm talking to you," I call out, grabbing him by the arm to halt his movement.

He freezes, his gaze dropping to my fingers wrapped around his arm, his face twisting in disgust, as though I've just hurled a pile of excrement at him.

"Get your hands off me." His voice is cold and forbidding. If I had any brain cells in my head, I'd pretend this was an accident, laugh it off, and hurry away. But I didn't get where I am by running.

"So you're not going to apologize?" I snarl.

My heart pounds against my chest, each beat resonating like a warning bell, urging me to stop. But I ignore it.

"Apologize for what, exactly?" His tone is casual, almost bored.

I raise an eyebrow, feigning thoughtfulness. "Hmm, let's see. For starters, how about what I just told you? You clearly saw me going for that spot, and now you're playing dumb as if it never happened."

What are you doing? My inner voice screams at me, but it's too late to back down now.

On a list of stupid things to do, confronting Dario De Luca—the man who was once my childhood hero but is now a name synonymous with danger—tops them all.

Dario's eyes narrow and if possible, they get colder. I can't help the shiver that courses down my body, and I resist the urge to take a step backward. I'm not going to give him the satisfaction of showing him I'm scared of him or that he intimidates me.

"You have no idea who I am, do you, or you wouldn't make the idiotic mistake of laying your hands on me," he drawls, his voice dripping with disdain.

"I'm not by any means a professor of English, but I don't think that combination of words meant *I'm sorry*, so let's try again, shall we?" I retort with a bright, mocking smile. His jaw ticks in response.

I've seen countless photos of Dario online and in the newspapers our butler likes to read, but seeing him in person, tight-jawed, eyes narrowed, makes me pity the poor cameras that struggle to capture his true essence.

Dario is a stunning man. Even as a teenager roaming the halls of our house, he was an angel to my too-young eyes. How wrong I was. From what I've heard, beneath that perfectly sculpted face and full, red mouth, Dario is nothing but pure evil.

"You can't just treat people anyhow you want and think you can get away with it." I throw my hands into the air, releasing him. "That's an asshole move."

"And you assume I have a problem with being the asshole?" His brow arches in a way that's far too sexy for my liking. Everything about him is sexy, from the way his navy three-piece suit molds to his impressive physique to the way his dark hair falls over his forehead in messy waves.

His face remains impassive, and I wonder for the millionth time what happened to Dario that changed him so much. I don't remember a lot about him, but what I can remember is the dimple that used to peek out when he occasionally smiled. Now, he looks as if he hasn't smiled in years.

Suddenly, he reaches inside his suit jacket. I let out a startled sound and jump back, half-expecting him to pull out a gun and shoot me for bothering him. Instead, he withdraws a wad of cash and holds it up.

"You can have all of it if you get out of my way and forget this conversation ever happened."

I glance down at the money and then force a stiff smile. "You couldn't buy me if you tried."

"I'm not trying to buy you," he replies coolly. "I'm trying to get you out of my face."

I grit my teeth. "I wouldn't even be here, if you'd just say you're sorry, which, by the way, is the right thing to do. No. It's the least thing you can do, and—"

"You seem to enjoy the sound of your own voice far too much," he says, cocking his head. "But I don't. You're clearly a child, and I've had enough of you wasting my time," he bites out, tossing the wad of cash at me.

I flinch as it flies toward my face, and by the time I remember to catch it, it's too late. The money scatters across the floor between us.

I look up from the notes strewn about the floor, a scathing comment on the tip of my tongue, only to see that Dario is already across the garage. I watch helplessly, seething with indignation, as the elevator doors slide closed, sealing him out of view.

I stand there, fists clenched, staring at his car. For a fleeting moment, I consider doing something crazy like denting it, but I decide against it. I'm not that suicidal, and besides, I refuse to prove Dario right by acting immature.

Taking a deep breath, I try to calm the storm of emotions swirling inside me.

"What a jerk," I mutter, heading back to my car. I feel like such a fool, and I'm grateful no one was around to witness that.

I slip back into my car and find a new parking spot, and as I start maneuvering into my dress, one thought dominates my mind. Is Dario headed to the same event as I am? Will I run into him again?

I shake my head to clear the thought.

I may not know what caused the rift between Dario and my brother, but I do know that the teenage boy who used to lift me up so I could reach the Lucky Charms from the top shelf is long gone. In his place is the most gorgeous but infuriating man I've ever met.

Well, as far as I'm concerned, this entire encounter never happened. We don't run in the same circles. I'm sure I'll never see him again.

I won't let him ruin my night; I remind myself. Not at this event. Not ever.

Good riddance.

2

DARIO

Such a brazen little spitfire.

A low, amused chuckle escapes me as the cool metal elevator doors slide shut with a soft thud. As I press the button for the tenth floor, her voice lingers in my head, replaying her sass and biting sarcasm. The memory draws a grin to my lips.

I can still see the way her eyes, an intriguing blend of brown and hazel, sparked with boldness as she stood her ground against me. *Who is she?* I wonder.

She's beautiful, no doubt about it—with thick black hair pulled into a ponytail, high cheekbones sculpted to perfection, and porcelain skin that looked almost ethereal under the lights. But it was her audacity that truly caught me off guard.

Most people would know better than to speak to me that way. But it was evident in the way she spoke that she didn't give a fuck about who I was. It almost seemed as if she knew exactly who I was and hated me for it. That makes my grin widen.

Ordinarily, I wouldn't let anyone speak to me like that

without facing consequences. But today? Let's just say I'm feeling generous.

The elevator pings softly, breaking me from my thoughts. The doors glide open, revealing an opulent foyer. The lights from the chandeliers above shine warmly, reflecting off the polished marble floor. Faint music drifts from the ballroom ahead.

I stride across the gleaming floor, the quiet click of my shoes echoing in the spacious hall. To my left, a pair of double doors stand open, offering a glimpse into the world of luxury inside—elegantly dressed guests laughing, sipping champagne, and mingling. With a quick adjustment of my suit jacket, I make my way toward the ballroom.

It's extravagant, as expected, filled with rich colors and bright lights. Glittering chandeliers hang from the ceiling, casting a warm glow over the crowd. The air is filled with practiced laughter and the sound of glasses clinking together. Men in tailored suits and women in exquisite gowns parade their status as if it were a badge of honor.

I hate events like these.

They're a cesspool of pretense and false pleasantries, with envy and rivalry cleverly hidden behind fake smiles and raised champagne glasses. But then again, I've long since grown used to it.

With my wealth, vast connections to countless businesses—including those I control—and my covert ties to the mafia, these gatherings serve as constant reminders of just how far I've come from nothing.

Still, there's a purpose to nights like this. They're perfect for gleaning information, catching tidbits of loose lips fueled by too much champagne, and cornering slippery business partners who think they can outmaneuver me.

That's exactly why I'm here tonight.

My eyes sweep the room as a waiter passes by with a tray of champagne flutes. I snatch one, the bubbling liquid fizzing against my lips as I scan the crowd. It doesn't take long to spot him.

Across the room, standing by a grand piano, Esteban Torres holds court, surrounded by four men. As always, he's dressed in overpriced dark clothes, looking smug as hell. He says something that makes the others laugh, and a familiar wave of anger pulses through me. The spineless bastard wouldn't even be in this room if it weren't for me.

As I make my way through the crowd, a few heads turn, watching with curiosity. My eyes stay locked on Esteban, the conniving snake who thinks he can cheat me and walk away unscathed. Men like he reminds me why I don't trust easily.

The moment he spots me, I watch his smile falter a bit before he manages to cover it up with an obnoxious grin.

"Dario De Luca," he greets, his voice slick and oily, as if he's trying too hard to mask his nerves. "Didn't expect to see you at one of these events."

I flash him a cold smirk. "Ah, Esteban Torres. I didn't expect you to have the balls to try and outsmart me, especially after last year."

He grimaces but keeps that cocky smile on his face. "You can't hold last year over me forever, Dario. Sure, you helped my business during a rough patch, and I thanked you for it. It's just business. Dark days come with the territory. Not everyone's walking around thinking they're some messiah. The underdogs have to rise too, don't you think?"

I take a step closer, my voice dropping to a venomous growl. "Helped your business? I *saved* your entire family from being swallowed whole. You were bleeding out, circling the drain of bankruptcy, and I poured money into your sinking ship. And what did you do? You had the audacity to rewrite our deal behind my back like some rat scurrying around in the dark. You don't fuck me over, Esteban. Not if you want to stay breathing."

His jaw clenches, the bravado cracking just a little. The men around us exchange uneasy glances before retreating like the spineless sycophants they are, eager to avoid getting caught in the fallout.

"How dare you embarrass me like this?" He chuckles bitterly, trying to mask his fear. "Did you think I'd grovel at your feet just because you threw me a lifeline? You didn't even help me. It was all just business to you. You, Dario De Luca, are a selfish bastard. You only invest in what serves you in the long run." His lips curl into a smirk again, as if there was something he knew that I didn't.

I look down at his shorter stature, a dark satisfaction curling in my gut.

"You should know better than to toy with me, Esteban." I click my tongue, pressing down on his shoulder with an iron grip. "I built you up from nothing, and I can tear you down just as easily. You know exactly how ruthless I can be."

"You can't do shit to me," he spits, trying to shrug my hand off his shoulder. "The new contract terms are already in place. There's nothing you can do now."

I can't help but chuckle. He really doesn't know what's coming to him, which is only going to make this more fun for me.

I tighten my grip on his shoulders, my blunt fingers digging through the material of his tuxedo until I feel his shoulder blades tense against my hand. For a brief second I see a flicker of fear in his eyes, and satisfaction flares up in me.

With a dark smile, I lean in closer, enjoying the moment. "You have until the end of the week to fix this, or I'll make you pay in ways you can't even imagine. By the time I'm done, you'll be begging me to just kill you."

My threat hangs in the thick air between us as I grab a hold of his other shoulder with my free hand, squeezing hard enough that he winces in pain. There's pleasant chatter and soft music in the background, and to other people watching, we might just look like two friends having a conversation.

"Do we understand each other?" My tone is calm, but my eyes blaze with rage.

Despite the beads of sweat forming along the creases of his forehead, he spits, "Do your worst. I'm not backing down."

I chuckle at his bravado. Surely, money is a confidence booster for fools.

"Good. I prefer it that way. See you soon, Esteban."

With one final, mocking pat on his shoulder, I turn to leave. My steps halt abruptly when I spot my old friend Lorenzo. Standing right beside him is my spitfire.

I'm unable to turn away. I don't *want* to turn away. With them standing side by side, I notice the resemblance in their facial features. It's unmistakable. They've got that same jawline, chin, nose, and lips...

That's when it clicks. Shit. How did I not recognize her sooner? Of course, it's Ginevra Bianchi—Ginny, Lorenzo's little sister.

I chuckle softly in disbelief.

The last time I saw Ginevra, she was barely five years old with mischievous hazel eyes, trailing after me and her brother with futile pranks, dressed in cute bows and dresses. She's grown up now, far too grown. If I didn't know any better, I'd think she was still that same Ginny from childhood. But now...fuck.

She's changed from her simple blouse and jeans into a tight-fitting sequined dress that hugs all her curves. Her hair, now black and not the blonde I used to remember, falls down to her ass in soft waves, framing her ethereal face.

A slow, sinister smile spreads across my lips as a wicked plan begins to take shape. I've been plotting to humiliate Lorenzo for years, and now, it seems my revenge has presented itself on a silver platter.

I observe Ginny politely laughing at something the man beside her says. They form a small group with Lorenzo, Ginny, and another man I recognize as Rinaldo Sanchez, a business associate of Lorenzo. But as I watch, I see Rinaldo's hand resting on her waist, revealing he's more than just a business partner.

A mix of annoyance and amusement churns within me. Lorenzo has certainly found an intriguing match for his sister, even though they look like a pair of mismatched socks together. His hand around her is not possessive or protective in the slightest. Rather, it hangs there awkwardly, and her smile looks forced as he drones on. Observing them is as thrilling as watching paint dry.

If I had a woman like Ginny in my arms...

I let that thought trail off because I know it leads nowhere good.

Instead, I slip my hands into my pockets and look at her for one more moment, etching her features in my brain. Then our eyes meet.

Even with the distance between us, the air between us feels charged. Her eyes widen slightly as she takes me in. And then, when I think she'll look away, she holds my gaze. Something flares in her eyes—something sensual. Curious. Fierce. Primal.

Heat coils up my spine as we continue our silent, intense

little staring game. It feels as if we share a hidden secret to which no one else in the room is privy, and my hands clench into fists, the thought of exploring the more forbidden territories between us becoming disturbingly appealing.

For reasons I can't fully understand, the idea of corrupting her in the most twisted ways I can imagine is starting to sound tantalizingly irresistible.

In that moment, I realize I've found the perfect opportunity to set my plan in motion and bring the Bianchi empire to its knees. And Ginny may be the key to making it happen.

3

GINEVRA

The morning sun spills into my penthouse, warming the hardwood floors as I glide through my yoga routine. I let out a contented breath as the cool morning air hits my sweat-soaked skin. It's been a hectic few days, and I couldn't be happier to finally have some peace. What better way to spend a lovely morning than with some yoga?

Soft music plays from the TV, a morning talk show featuring cheerful hosts discussing the latest beauty trends among women. One of the male guests on the show says something about how he didn't know women had body hair because he'd never seen a woman with any before.

I roll my eyes, stretching my body into another pose as the show host laughs heartily. The annoying show continues, their conversation becoming louder and more obnoxious. They are now arguing about whether or not makeup is just a mask for ugly women and that women who know their true beauty don't need it.

I try to tune them out by breathing deeply and slowly. But when the loud conversation continues, I sigh in irritation before breaking my pose and grabbing the TV remote off the coffee table before switching to the news.

As I prepare to return to my stretching, the headline on the screen grabs my attention:

"Shocking Murder: Mutilated Body Discovered in Abandoned Warehouse Linked to Organized Crime."

My hands freeze over the remote, my entire body stiffening at the sight of the crime scene photos being shown on the screen. As I watch the news unfold, the anchor's voice steadies, but the words send a chill down my spine.

"Authorities have identified the victim as Vincento Torres, a cousin of prominent businessman and millionaire Esteban Torres, known for his lucrative real estate investments in. The body was found in an abandoned warehouse on the outskirts of the city at early hours of the morning, prompting an investigation into possible organized crime involvement..."

I feel a pang in my chest as a clip of Esteban addressing the press appears on the screen. Esteban and my brother were business partners at some point, though they hardly talked much anymore.

"I will get to the bottom of this!" he exclaims in anger and pain. *"I will get justice for my family!"*

I turn the TV off, my morning already ruined. I can't shake the feeling of dread that rolls through me knowing that Lorenzo is tangled in business dealings with the cartel. Everyone knows that the cartel runs this city like a well-oiled machine, their influence seeping into every corner of life. They control everything—from high-profile businesses to the underbelly of illegal activities that thrive out of plain sight.

I've heard stories of their hierarchies, with powerful

figures pulling the strings in politics, business, import and export, illegal trading of drugs, and even the police force.

Everyone dances to their tune, and it's terrifying how many wealthy men are likely part of this shadowy world. They wear their suits like armor, blending seamlessly into the upper echelons of society while participating in the darkest of operations. Investigations come and go, but nothing ever sticks. Their power is formidable.

And then there's Dario.

I've seen the way people shift in their seats when Dario enters a room. There's an undeniable chill that fills the air, a mix of fear and respect that commands attention. I can't shake the feeling that he holds immense power, both in the legal world and in the realm of organized crime. Lorenzo doesn't reveal a lot to me about stuff like this. He only tells me that Dario is an arrogant, conceited prick who thinks he's hot shit because of his money.

But oh, hot he is.

My throat hitches at the memory of him looking at me across the ballroom two nights ago. I remember the way my body shivered at the way his gaze travelled from head to toe, drinking in my curves until I felt naked. My whole body burned from desire, and then mortification. I was in the arms of my fiancé while feeling hot and bothered by another man across the room.

He was not only hot. He was handsome in a way that made my heart flutter. I can't help but remember the boy he used to be—the one who played basketball with my brother, the one I had a crush on when I was just a girl. Back then, I thought he was the most beautiful boy in the world. That opinion hasn't changed much in over fifteen years.

My stomach drops as I recall the way his heated gaze hardened the moment his eyes met my brother's. I wonder what exactly came in between them. They used to be inseparable when we were younger.

Back then, Dario was just the son of one of my Papa's henchmen, not the powerful man he is today. My parents always disapproved of him, especially my mother. Yet Lorenzo kept hanging out with him. I wonder what changed.

The memory of Dario's smile surfaces, and this time around, I push it away. He didn't even recognize me when we spoke the other night. Although I don't blame him. I was just a kid the last time he saw me, and I've changed so much since then—my hair color, my body, the fact that I'm no longer a fucking kid.

No longer motivated to continue my routine, I feel the need to go grab some coffee from my favorite cafe. Going on a short drive this morning would definitely brighten my mood.

Just as I'm about to head out of the door, the intercom on the wall buzzes.

"Ms. Ginny, you have a package waiting. Would you like us to bring it up?" the lobby attendant asks.

I'm already slipping into my shoes, so I wave them off. "Leave it by my car, please! I'll grab it on my way out."

I assume it's the car seat covers I ordered two days ago, and I'm surprised at how fast it arrived. Usually, it takes me a couple of days to receive my deliveries, but I guess I'm just fortunate this time around.

Grabbing my car keys from the magnetic key holder on the wall, I leave my apartment and head for the elevator. The doors open with a soft ding, and I make my way to the outdoor parking lot where I left my car last night.

I step out of the building and walk towards my car. At a distance, I spot my package in a brown box beside the

Porsche Macan Lorenzo got me for my twentieth birthday. It's been two years, and yet it still looks brand new with its sleek exterior gleaming under the morning sun.

A small frown appears on my face as I see how small the box is. It's much smaller than I expected, and confusion washes over me. Did I order something else? Or did the delivery driver mix up my order? A car seat surely wouldn't fit in such a tiny box.

I feel myself getting pissed again. It's too early in the day for this. I'm temporarily pulled from my anger as I bask in the sun, bright yet not too hot, against my skin. Ugh! What I wouldn't give to lounge on a beach somewhere right now.

Speaking of beaches, I remember suggesting to Rinaldo that we go to Santorini, Greece, for our honeymoon. He dismissed the idea immediately, claiming that the term "honeymoon" was meaningless. According to him, every day of our marriage should be special, and we didn't need any pointless vacations to mark our union.

I roll my eyes at the memory.

'Way to ruin your entire day, Ginny,' my inner voice mocks.

Just then, as if on cue, my phone buzzes in my pocket. I pull it out and see that it's Rinaldo calling. I answer with a sigh.

"Did you not get my text?" he snaps as soon as I place the phone against my ear.

"No, I didn't," I sigh, already fed up before the conversation even unfolds. "I must have missed it."

"What were you busy with this time around? Doing Yoga?" he taunts. He knows I do yoga almost every morning, and it's another of my interest he thinks it's pointless.

'If you want to get some movement in your body, get a gym membership or something,' he'd said the last time he stayed

over. He was irritated when he woke up expecting morning sex and found me doing yoga instead.

I feel my eyes twitch in irritation.

"I know you're still mad about that night, but I don't appreciate you talking to me like this," I say, trying to stay calm. "I've apologized, and it's been two days."

"You apologized, yet there's always something silly distracting you from more important matters," he retorts. "Like, I don't know, your fiancé's texts and missed calls."

Pinching the bridge of my nose, I sigh.

"What did you want to talk about?"

"We've been engaged for two months, and you're still not wearing my ring, Ginny. Do you know how that makes me look?"

I try not to dwell on how he's more concerned about appearances than about genuinely claiming me as his fiancée. I nod along, half-listening as I continue walking towards my car.

"Fine, I messed up your ring size, but I've been asking you for weeks to find time for us to get it right. We should go ring-testing later this week. Please make the time. I'm a busy man with the elections coming up, and I want you by my side as we start the campaigns. Our wedding will be here before we know it…"

I tune him off as a chill runs down my spine. Something feels off. My heart races, but I push the feeling aside.

"So, what's it going to be, Ginny? Will you be free, or does this clash with one of your…activities?"

"Yeah, I'll call you back later," I mumble distractedly before ending the call.

Just as I take another step forward, a blinding light erupts before me, followed by a deafening explosion. I'm thrown backward, and my body crashes against a far wall behind me. My mind is a mess, the world spinning, the ground shaking beneath me. My heart pounds in my chest as I fight to comprehend what just happened.

Smoke fills the air, and chaos erupts around me. I struggle to sit up as panic claws at my throat.

The package exploded on my car.

Someone just tried to kill me.

4

DARIO

"Today, we need to discuss our upcoming launch of the new electric SUV. This model is designed to combine luxury and efficiency, and I want to ensure we position it effectively in the market."

The sharp click of my watch echoes in the quiet of my office as I place my hands on the table and glance around. My business partners sit across from me. My business partners are seated across from me: Tom, the anxious finance guy; Lisa, the astute marketing director; and Marco, the head of operations.

Sunlight streams through the large windows, casting a bright glow over the room. The air is thick with the kind of tension I'm used to. Despite having worked together for more than a year on this project, I can still smell their anxiety whenever they're in my presence—it's palpable, lingering scent of cheap perfume, that refuses to dissipate.

Tom shifts nervously in his seat, adjusting his glasses. "We're projecting a 15% increase in sales, but we'll need to adjust our marketing budget to achieve that."

His hands tremble slightly as he hands me a report detailing the figures.

I nod, scrolling through the report on his tablet. "How much are we allocating for the marketing campaign?"

"Approximately two million dollars," Lisa replies confidently. She's always been the most self-assured, or at least the best at masking her apprehension. "I believe we can make the most of that by focusing on social media and targeted ads. Our last campaign yielded great returns, and I'm confident we can replicate that success."

"Social media is crucial," I agree, leaning forward. "We need to generate excitement for the launch. While partnering with eco-friendly influencers can help spread the word quickly, we mustn't lose sight of our primary targets—the elite."

We're not just launching an electric SUV; we're creating an exclusive logistics service for the wealthy.

Tom leans forward, adjusting his glasses again. "What's your vision for building that exclusivity? We need to differentiate ourselves from the competition."

I nod. "First, let's implement a limited membership model. We cap the number of clients and require an application process. This creates a sense of prestige, like being part of an elite club."

Lisa's eyes light up. "Marketing it as an exclusive service will resonate well. It's not just about getting from point A to B; it's about status."

"I-I also think we should form partnerships with high-end brands—luxury hotels, upscale restaurants," Tom says. "We can offer complimentary rides to exclusive events or discounts at partner establishments."

"That's an excellent idea," I respond gruffly.

"Oh...it's nothing," Tom chuckles nervously, shifting in his seat before writing something down in his notes.

Marco, who has been quietly absorbing the conversation, speaks up.

"Is there a way to encourage current members to bring in new ones?" He asks, looking thoughtful.

"A referral program could work well," Lisa chips in. "Existing members can invite others to apply, and we offer incentives like complimentary rides for successful referrals. It builds a community around our brand.

Tom raises a finger, and I hear the excitement in his voice. "What if we offer gated access to high-profile events? Members could have special drop-off points at galas or fashion shows, making them feel even more exclusive."

Hums of agreement surround the table.

"One important thing," my voice booms across the room. "We should engage with local charities. Positioning ourselves as socially responsible will appeal to the philanthropic nature of wealthy individuals. It enhances brand loyalty."

They all note down the points I've made as I continue to speak, my voice hardening.

"We can't afford any hiccups. I want you to coordinate with the suppliers and make sure they're ready for the increased demand."

"Sir?" Marco interjects. "What about competition? They've been aggressive lately, especially with their new line of hybrid vehicles. We need to stay ahead."

Elysium Rides.

When I launched Stride, my elite logistics company, a little over a year ago, Lukas Braun, a prominent German businessman in Manhattan, quickly followed with his own venture. They tried to replicate the services Stride offers, bombarding the market with aggressive marketing and advertising campaigns.

But all they did was prove that they were a knock-off version of Stride, a cheaper alternative that people who craved the elite experience but couldn't afford it went for.

I smirk. "Let them come. We have an edge they don't. Our quality speaks for itself, and the technology we're integrating is unmatched. Plus, they know that there are invincible lines that cannot be crossed."

The implications hang in the air. The others exchange glances, and I can see the mix of fear and intrigue in their eyes.

Tom clears his throat again, ready to speak.

"I think we should also—"

A loud commotion erupts outside the conference room door. Voices rise, sharp and urgent. "Let me in! I need to see him!"

"What the hell is going on out there?" I mutter in irritation.

"I need to see that bastard!" The voice booms, loud and clear.

The tension in their air thickens, and my fists clench as I relax into my seat.

"I'm sorry, but this meeting will have to continue some other time," I hiss through gritted teeth.

Without sparing a second, they scramble to their feet and nod at me before leaving the room.

I call my secretary.

"Get whoever it is in here."

Moments later, the door swings open, and Lorenzo Bianchi storms in, his face flush with rage. The atmosphere shifts instantly, thickening with tension. His presence is electric, crackling with anger. "Dario! You think you can just do whatever the fuck you want?"

Behind him, I spot Emily, my secretary, closing the door with a nervous expression on her face. She knows she's in deep trouble.

"Lorenzo, what a pleasant surprise, seeing you in my office this early in the morning," I chuckle, focusing my attention back on the man before me.

He's now standing directly in front of my desk, with the large mahogany piece of furniture being the only thing separating him from me. Satisfaction rolls through me as he releases a low growl from his lips. Idly, I wonder idly if he would punch me if he could, or if he's still the coward I remember.

"How dare you involve my sister in our issues?" he roars, his face now a deep shade of red.

I lean further into my seat, trying to remain calm as I watch him bang his fists against my table.

"You tried to kill Ginevra to make a stupid statement!" He continues, his voice getting louder at my lack of a response. "How could you bring her into this?"

I smirk, loving where this is going. "Kill? Why, now this is a very serious accusation to make, Lorenzo. Plus I think it's quite too early such a commotion, don't you think?" I keep my tone light, but the underlying tension is palpable.

His eyes flash as he leans into the table. "I saw the way you looked at her at the party. I've hidden her from you and this sick world all this while for a reason, but the moment you saw her, you decide she was the perfect pawn in your little revenge game!"

"Did you ever stop to think that I was looking at her because she looked so damn hot in that dress?" I snarl, a surge of satisfaction warming my spine at the mix of shock and fury in his eyes.

"She's grown into a gorgeous woman," I continue. "I'm sure everyone in that room wanted a piece of her—myself included."

Lorenzo slams his palms against my table. "You bastard!"

"Okay, that's enough," I cut him off, my voice hardening. "I've indulged your theatrics long enough, and my patience for this disrespect is wearing thin. Did you ever consider that one of your enemies might be behind the attempt on your sister's life? Maybe an old friend you stabbed in the back for your selfishness," I continue, unfazed by his rage. "You're quite good at making them, after all."

Lorenzo's eyes narrow, his jaw tight. "Since you want to talk about stabbing in the back, let's cut the games, Dario. I know you're the one who supplied counterfeit goods to my company under a fake name."

I can't help but smirk, relishing the moment.

"Ah, that's one I can't deny. It's one of the things that still pleases me to this day. One simple move brought an entire empire crumbling to the ground—literally."

His eyes go red, his body almost shaking from the heavy emotions.

"Business is business, Lorenzo. You should know that by now." I lean forward slightly, enjoying the way his anger radiates from him.

His temper flares, and he leans even closer; the distance between our faces is charged with unspoken threats. "Trying to harm my sister is crossing a line too far, Dario."

My voice drops into a low growl. "You deserve every fucking thing that's coming your way, Lorenzo. And I'm afraid, this is just the beginning."

"You're a sick and evil man. I regret having you as a friend." His face contorts in disgust.

My anger flares. "Something we both agree on. Now get out." I spit.

I see the thick emotion in his eyes as he glares at me for a short moment. Anger, pain, and a slight flicker of regret. But I don't care. The misfortune of the Bianchis is one of the things I live for.

"This isn't over."

"Oh, it is. You're lucky I'm letting you walk out of my office on two legs," I hiss. "It's the least I can do for my old friend."

Lorenzo's face burns with rage, the muscles in his jaw twitching. "I'll never beg or be at your mercy, Dario. You're mistaken. Stay the hell away from my sister."

As he storms out, I feel a flicker of satisfaction. His anger is almost entertaining, like blood flowing through my veins. I watch him leave, the door slamming behind him, and the silence that follows is thick.

Once the room settles, I lean back, letting the memories wash over me. There was a time when I called Lorenzo a brother. We were inseparable, thick as thieves. Even though he was a year older than me, some people thought we were twins.

I saw him as my family—until he turned on me without a second thought.

The memory of his betrayal stirs something deep inside me, igniting old feelings of anger and resentment. I thought those emotions had been buried under the satisfaction that came with my revenge. But they were still there, and in times like this, they threatened to eat me whole.

This confrontation set the wheels in motion for phase

two of my revenge. I would make Lorenzo pay for his betrayal, until I am both tired and satisfied. But until then, I need to find a way to see Ginny again. This game is far from over, and I intend to play it to the end.

5

GINEVRA

A groan escapes my lips as I slam my phone a bit too forcefully onto the side table beside me. I never realized how maddening boredom could be until I started staying at Lorenzo's house.

After the incident three days ago, Lorenzo put me on house arrest, swiftly packing up most of my things from my apartment and moving me here, to his penthouse in the upper reaches of Manhattan.

My army of bodyguards has doubled, and while I'm permitted to go out, it's always under heavy escort. Mostly, I just linger in my assigned bedroom. Occasionally, like today, I wander through the vast house, but it feels like I'm trapped within these walls.

I know the real reason I haven't left is fear. I'm terrified because someone out there wants me dead. Sometimes, I still hear the explosion echoing in my mind. I remember how the blast threw me to the floor and the sharp pain from the scratches on my arms. Luckily, I wasn't seriously injured since I stood far away when it happened, but it still feels like a nightmare I can't escape.

So I stay put. Even though it makes me want to suffocate sometimes, I don't leave.

Lorenzo has been trying to cheer me up these past couple of days. I notice he comes home earlier than usual, most times with my favorite ice cream or desserts he knows I like. But beneath his smiles, I see the worry in his eyes. He looks even more stressed now than he did when the tragedy that befell our family's architectural firm happened.

Today, I tried to do something different instead of moping around all day. I attempted making lunch myself. I tried following a recipe I found online for grilled chicken salad, but I ended up burning it badly. I ate a cold sandwich because I was too lazy and sad to order some food, then I watched the most boring movie ever.

It's still 2 p.m., but the day has felt so long already. I'm sitting in Lorenzo's living room, the heavy drapes of the curtain drawn tight against the world outside. The house feels like a fortress—solid and imposing, with its dark wood paneling and ornate furniture that seems to whisper of old wealth. I used to love Lorenzo's house so much. It had a certain dark charm to it —the perfect mixture of old money and modern luxury.

Now, it feels like a gilded cage.

But living here now has made me realize how depressing the constant dark colors and minimalist decor makes me feel. It's very different from my apartment, which was light and spacious, with colorful artworks hung on walls and plants in every corner.

God, I miss my house and plants. Lorenzo didn't bring them, and tears spring in my eyes as I realize they must have withered by now.

I startle slightly at the sudden ring of the doorbell and the sound of the key code being entered. Wiping my tears harshly, I wonder why Lorenzo is back so early. I grab my phone again and pretend to be scrolling through messages when I hear the sound of his footsteps approaching.

"Sweet Pea?"

I turn, a little surprised to see Rinaldo walking towards me. He's the only one who calls me that, a nickname I loathe but can't escape.

"Hey," I mutter as he gets to the sofa and leans in to press a kiss to my forehead.

Rinaldo visited me two days ago after he heard what happened. He didn't stay long, claiming he had a very important meeting to attend. I wasn't shocked, and honestly, I didn't care. I was too shaken to care.

The plush sofa sinks under his weight as he sits beside me, gently cupping my face.

"Have you been crying?" he asks, his brow furrowing.

"No," I lie, the word slipping out easily.

He observes my face for a few seconds before saying, "You're lying."

I sigh as his hand continues to cradle my face.

"Move in with me, Ginny..."

"Rinaldo—"

He leans in, pressing a kiss against my lips. I sigh again, and he takes advantage of that, his tongue slipping into my mouth. I respond eagerly, ignoring the way his tongue moves like he's unsure of what he's doing.

I run one hand through his blonde locks while the other holds his shoulder tightly. My fingers tug at his hair lightly as if I needed something physical to ground myself in reality.

"Slow down, Sweet Pea," he murmurs against my lips, placing his two hands on my waist to keep us steady.

"I want this, Rinaldo," I murmur against his lips, leaning towards him.

We don't have sex very often. Rinaldo is always busy with work, so a large percentage of the times I spend the night at his place is spent with him playing video games or going straight to bed the moment he eats dinner. The few times we do have sex, it's always a letdown. Rinaldo orgasms and goes right to sleep while I have to finish off with my hands.

I don't miss Rinaldo himself; it's the intimacy, the physical connection that I long for. The sensation of being touched, the pleasure of being truly satisfied, and the raw, exhilarating release of being thoroughly fucked—these are the things I've been without for too long.

In truth, they're things I've rarely had the chance to experience.

I lean into him and begin pressing open-mouthed kisses against his neck.

"I need to forget everything, baby," I murmur, throwing one leg over his waist until I'm straddling him on the sofa.

He grunts as I roll my hips against his erection. "Fuck, Sweet Pea."

"Make me forget."

Grabbing my face, he smashes his lips against mine. I feel the slightly awkward clash of tongue and teeth as his tongue swirls around inside of my mouth. Instead, I focus on the sensation of his hardness rubbing against my clothed clit as I rock against him.

He plants his hands on my waist, and I whine against his lips as he stands to his feet.

"Someone might walk in," he leans back to give me a small smile.

In that moment, I'm not sure I would care. Yet, I blow out

a breath before directing him to the guest room. The moment we get in, I try to push him down to the bed and straddle him again, but he carries me to the middle of the bed instead.

No words need to be said. I already know Rinaldo hates it when I try to stay on top. He begins to unbutton his shirt, and I take that as a cue to pull off my simple sundress and panties.

When we are both naked, he slips on a condom he brought, like he planned to come have sex with me, positions himself between my spread legs, and slips into me.

"Fuck, you're so wet," he grunts, burying his head in my neck. "I could do this forever. Just let go."

I close my eyes as he begins to thrust. I know exactly how this will go, and I regret kissing him back in the first place. His thrusts become faster, and he plants his hands at the sides of my head to hold himself up. Soon enough, he's grunting and moaning loudly.

"Do you love this, baby?"

My gaze shifts from the ceiling to his face. "Yes, baby," I let out a high-pitched moan, the one that usually makes him pound faster until he comes.

And that's exactly what happens.

As he pulls off my body, I cover myself with a blanket, suddenly feeling hollow and empty.

As he slips his clothes back on, I close my eyes, waiting for him to leave.

"I brought you something, Sweet Pea," he suddenly says.

When I open my eyes, I see he's holding a velvet box.

"It's high time you wore my ring on your finger, don't you think?" He asks, flashing me a smile.

He hands the box over to me just as his phone rings. I

place the box and place it on the bedside table without opening it.

"Sure, I'll be there very soon," he tells whoever is on the line before ending the call.

When he starts telling me how he has to go attend to something important, I don't say anything. He says something about how I should try to relax and how I should think about us moving in together, but I can't help but feel more isolated than before.

The room feels colder now, the plush fabric of the blanket pressing around me like a cage. I watch him leave, the door clicking shut behind him, and I'm left in a silence that feels suffocating. The ticking clock on the wall seems to mock my restless thoughts, each second more dreadful than the last.

I lie back on the bed and stare at the ceiling, the weight of the day pressing down on me. My fears return. Who would want to kill me? The question spirals in my mind, tangling with the fear that refuses to fade. I close my eyes, trying to block out the thoughts, but they come rushing back—the smell of smoke, the panic, the screaming.

I lose track of time, lost deep in my thoughts. The next time I hear heavy footsteps in the house, I know it's Lorenzo. I quick throw my sundress back on and step out of the bedroom. I meet him halfway down the stairs.

"What's wrong?" I ask the moment I see his face.

It's very obvious that something happened. His face tells a story of distress: bloodshot eyes, missing suit jacket, several buttons undone on his shirt, and his hair tousled as if he's been running his hands through it all day. A faint smell of beer lingers around him.

When he doesn't deny that something is wrong, my heart thuds. This has to be bad.

"Talk to me, Lorenzo," I grab his hand. "You're scaring me."

He takes a moment, as if he's gathering his thoughts. As he walks back down the stairs to the kitchen, I follow him.

"It's Dario," he finally says, his voice thick with frustration. He slips his hands into his pockets as he paces the length of the large kitchen.

My stomach drops at the mention of Dario. The name feels like a poisonous fruit—sweet yet lethal. A part of me still hasn't stopped thinking about that night, even though I know he's bad news.

"What did he do?" I swallow hard.

Again. What did he do again?

"He's gone public with some damaging news about us. Claims we can't pay our debts. It's chaos."

As Lorenzo buried his hands in his hair, I let the message seep into my skin.

"Why is he doing all this?" I finally speak.

Lorenzo hisses, anger blazing in his eyes. "Apparently, he's behind one of our creditors. He released a slanderous statement claiming that the Bianchi Empire is unable to pay back their debts, and now other creditors who were previously dormant are demanding their money back. It's...fuck! This is a nightmare."

His voice cracks at the end, and I feel my heart clench at his pain.

I feel a fresh surge of anger and hatred towards Dario. What the hell does he want from us? Why won't he just stop?

My blood boils in desperation to know exactly what happened between them. How did they go from being best friends to being sworn enemies? Why did Dario make it his mission to attack our family and everything we've built?

As I watch Lorenzo, weighed down by the thought of losing everything, determination ignites within me. I can't let Dario destroy our Papa's legacy. Lorenzo's legacy.

My eyes dart to where his phone lays on the kitchen counter, right beside where Lorenzo stands. I step towards him and pull his into a hug.

"Hey. It's going to be okay," I whisper as I discreetly grab his phone from the table, my heart pounding in my chest.

When I lean back, the hand holding the phone is hidden behind me.

"Why don't you go take a shower? I'll order us some Chinese."

With a tense nod, Lorenzo heads upstairs. I wait until he's out of sight before I turn the phone over in my hands. His password is my birthday.

The soft glow of the screen illuminates my face as I scroll through his messages and contacts, searching for anything I could find on Dario. His number. His address.

I sift through sparse chats and Lorenzo's work emails until I come across a file labeled with details about business associates and prominent businessmen in Manhattan.

I know Lorenzo well enough to understand that obtaining such information isn't unusual for him. Our family business, while legitimate, often intersects with less savory elements to maintain its status and relevance.

My Papa used to say, *'Sometimes, you have to do bad things for the greater good.'* I suspect it was more of a mantra to justify the questionable practices that contributed to his empire's growth.

As I continue scrolling through the names, almost ready to give up because the list isn't arranged alphabetically, I finally spot it. I found it.

Dario's address stares back at me, making the wheels in

my head spin faster. My heart races, not just with fear but with the thrill of what I'm about to do.

When Lorenzo leaves the next morning, I steal the keys to the Audi he hardly drives and climb out through the fire escape. Luckily, he didn't assign any security detail to that side of the building. They'll still think I'm inside all day.

It's time I confronted Dario De Luca. I won't let that asshole ruin my family.

6

DARIO

"The next shipment arrives later this month, boss." Anton's voice fills my car. "If we don't want a repeat of what happened the last time..."

"It won't happen again." I grit my teeth, turning the steering wheel to the right and entering the quiet street that leads to my house. "I made sure of it."

Our last shipment of blow had been intercepted by Customs and Border Protection. After our insider in the agency was arrested months ago, a long legal battle ensued. He was eventually released but was stripped of his position. Then the new commissioner in charge made the silly mistake of thinking he could mess with the cartel. Mess with me.

Law and order don't exist here. Or as far as I'm concerned, we are in charge of what goes and what doesn't. Unfortunately, he didn't get the memo and tried to play hero, so I sent him a little gift in appreciation. It was no coincidence that before the case could hit the news, his residential home in Upper East Side was burned to the ground.

With him in it.

That served as both a punishment and a warning to the next appointed commissioner who dared to mess with us.

"Keep your eyes and ears open for any new developments," I order as I pull into my driveway.

"Yes boss."

The call ends with a beep before I turn off my phone. It's a Friday evening, and even though I don't normally take breaks from work due to the nature of what I do, I just need a little breather.

The familiar sight of my suburban home greets me. Under the evening sky, the house stands tall and modern, its dark glass windows reflecting the fading sunlight. The manicured lawn stretches out like a green carpet, bordered by perfectly trimmed hedges. The environment here is a stark contrast to the chaos of the city.

My penthouse apartment in Midtown Manhattan is at the center of the bustling city. Although the location is perfect for my line of work, sometimes I just crave some peace and quiet.

This is my true home, the place I escape to for a taste of normalcy. I haven't even installed any security here as not many people know I stay at this location. Unless we've had business dealings in the past or share a mutual business partner, this house probably operates under an alias— belonging to an immigrant Asian family just off the boat, courtesy of my efficient assistant.

It's my way of keeping a low profile and drawing less attention to myself.

As I pull into the driveway, I notice something feels off. That's when I spot a strange car parked outside my fence— an Audi, glossy and black, its curves sharp and inviting. My curiosity piques. I come to a stop right outside my gate and step out of my car. The gravel crunches under my feet as I approach the Audi, wondering to whom it belongs and why the person is parked outside my house.

My heart quickens when I see her, and I can hardly believe it. She must have gotten my address from her brother. I wouldn't be surprised—he's likely been keeping tabs on me over the years, ensuring I don't catch him off guard.

When you make a lot of enemies on your path to success, paranoia can kill you faster than people ever could.

He's obviously tried to ensure that I never cross paths with his precious sister. Well, it's too late for that—his efforts to keep her away from the big bad wolf have been in vain.

Because she's here. It's Ginny.

An inner excitement stirs within me, slowly traveling from my pounding heart and rushing through my veins. She doesn't know I'm here yet. Or if she does, she's doing a very good job of pretending. I wouldn't be surprised. Ginny is someone who would never give me the satisfaction of acknowledging my presence.

But I don't give a fuck about that. She's here, and I can't help but relish the anticipation of what this encounter might bring.

I take my time admiring her as she stands by the car, her posture tense and defiant.

She's in a short, light blue sundress with ruffles at the short sleeves and ends. The color makes her long, dark hair appear even darker. As usual, the soft waves frame her beautiful face.

My eyes trail down to her exposed legs, and I feel the arousal travel straight to my dick. My body heats at the thought of having soft flesh wrapped around my waist.

Her hair is the perfect length to wrap around my wrist as

she kneels before me and takes my dick in her mouth. Or to pull roughly as I take her from behind...

Fuck.

Pulling my thoughts from the gutter, I focus on her face. Her plump lips are pressed together into a firm line as if she's fighting back whatever words she wishes to spit out towards me, and I can't help but chuckle.

That's when she turns to look at me.

The evening air is a bit warm, wrapping around us like a blanket. Rays of light from a nearby streetlight catch her hair, making it glow with streaks of golden in it.

There's a fire in her eyes that makes it clear she's not here for games, and that only adds to my amusement.

"Is there something I should know?" I ask, letting the soft breeze carry my voice as I draw closer. "Your brother visited me earlier today, and now here you are." I stop directly in front of her, lowering my voice. "Am I in some kind of trouble? Or is this some sort of covert family invitation to join the Bianchi clan?"

Her nose flares as she raises her head to meet my gaze. Damn. She's making it hard to focus on anything but her. Her glossy eyes lock onto mine while she—

"You piece of shit," she spits, making the mistake of stepping even closer to me.

Now, I can see the sprinkle of freckles across her nose, I can smell her faint vanilla scent with a hint of lavender, and I see her hazel eyes, a perfect mixture of light brown and green.

"How dare you?" Her voice fills the air again, bringing my attention back to her angry face.

"How dare I do what, Princess?" I can't resist, I reach out, brushing back a strand of her hair. "You'll need to be specific."

She lets out a harsh chuckle.

"You think you rule the world, huh? You think you can just go about doing whatever you want to people—"

"Shouldn't you be hiding somewhere?" I interrupt, frowning as I pull my hands away and slip them into my pockets to avoid doing something foolish, like pulling her closer.

"Your brother told me what happened. What an unfortunate thing," I say, my voice dripping with sarcasm.

She glares at me, her expression a mix of anger and determination. I can't help but chuckle. It's amusing how she thinks she intimidates me.

"Why are you even out?" I continue, feigning concern. "Someone tried to kill you the other day."

If someone tried to kill my sister, I'd make sure she was kept safe within the walls of my home while I hunted down whoever the bastard was. But that asshole Lorenzo can't get anything right. He probably doesn't even know she's not home.

"You're behind that, aren't you?" she shoots back, her voice sharp like a knife. Her accusation hits me like a bullet.

I smirk, leaning casually against the side of her car. "Trust me. If I wanted you dead, you'd already be gone."

My smile widens as I watch her throat bob, her hands balling into small fists, as if she wants to punch me in the face and is probably second-guessing her decision to come here. I can see her frustration bubbling over. I thrive on her anger and the way it crackles between us. It's only a moment before she finally snaps.

After Lorenzo accused me of trying to kill his sister, my curiosity got the best of me. I asked one of my men to look into what happened. Apparently, someone had sent her a bomb package and it had been left beside her car. She barely missed it.

Amateur.

"I, for one, think the whole thing was handled poorly," I say, leaning closer to her ear to whisper. "Blowing up your car and causing a whole mess—just for what? You're still here, wearing that pathetic glare and interrupting my time off with your obnoxious presence. Maybe next time I should have a go at it myself."

I'm not surprised when my words make her even bolder. She steps closer, her face flush with anger.

"I'm not scared of you, asshole—"

"You should be." I cut her off. "I can be very, very dangerous, especially when threatened on my own property, baby girl."

Her chest rises as she takes in a deep, frustrated breath. My eyes drop to her chest. From my height, I can see the top of her cleavage—and the fact that she isn't wearing a bra.

Cold annoyance fills me. It's glaringly obvious that she didn't think this through. How could she be here, standing alone with and challenging the man who she thinks tried to kill her? Is she often this reckless?

The only thing reckless here are your thoughts, a voice in my head mocks.

I hate that my body wants her, that I notice the way her eyes twitch when she's angry, the way her throat bobs when she's thinking of what to say.

"Stop messing with my family!"

The fire in her voice thickens the tension already crackling in the air around us.

"No."

She opens her mouth to speak, but I interrupt her for the umpteenth time.

"Now, what's the fun in that?" I chuckle. "It's not like you can do anything to stop me, so why should I willingly comply?" I ask, my words laced with mockery.

I revel in how she gets worked up, how her cheeks flush and her eyes sparkle with indignation. It's a game to me, and I'm in control.

"You'll be shocked at what I'm capable of," she spits, and seeing the pure hatred in her eyes, I know she means it. She would do just about anything to get me out of the way.

I feign a chuckle. "What are you going to do? Send your limp-dicked fiancé after me?"

"Now I see you're just an unhappy man with no friends or family. You thrive on manipulating others to mask the fact that no one loves you." Her words strike a nerve.

On another day, she'd be dead, but I'm not that careless. Her last known location would trace back to me, and covering up a murder involving a high-profile name in the city would take considerable time and resources.

For now, she should thank her fucking lucky stars.

"Don't test me, Princess," I warn. "You won't like the outcome."

"Do you genuinely think your threats scare me?" She chuckles humorlessly before speaking again. "Or that I'll fall to my knees and beg you to spare my family?"

"Oh, I'll get you on your knees if that's what I desire." I step closer, trapping her against her car. "If that's what I want, I'll have you lying wide open on your car right now. Anyone passing by can watch as I make you to beg me with your body." My voice drops to a whisper, and I hear her breath catch.

"Or with that snappy mouth of yours... But I'm not at all interested in immature kids who've just reached puberty. No matter how hard you try or how good you are, my answer will always be no. My taste is far better than wannabe politician's side piece."

My words hang in the air, heavy with intent, and I watch her, relishing the way she reacts. Her face goes pale for a heartbeat before it flushes a deep crimson. Her eyes, a mixture of anger and arousal, glare at me.

Then, before I can anticipate her next move, her hand lands across my cheek.

7

GINEVRA

A shocked gasp leaves my lips, my hand stinging from the hard contact with his face. I can't believe I just slapped him. I've never hit anyone in my life, but this man seems to bring out the worst in me.

I'm seething, my breaths coming in sharp, rapid bursts. My chest heaves, but I try to steady myself so he doesn't see the effect he has on me.

Ugh! The nerve of this arrogant bastard.

I hate his ridiculously handsome face, his mocking smirk. I loathe how his green eyes hold amusement and mischief rather than anger as I challenge him. I hate that my words have no effect on him, that his eyes glint in satisfaction at my distress. I hate that this is all a joke to him. While my family suffers because of his actions, he gets to live happily and flaunt his stupid money everywhere.

I hate that he makes me feel weak, stupid, and powerless. And like a common whore.

My hands twitch, ready for another strike. How dare he insinuate that I want to...fuck! I can't even bear to think about it.

I make the mistake of looking at his face before I swing again. His green eyes have darkened dangerously into a striking emerald shade. Anger simmers beneath them, swirling like a storm. His jaw ticks, threatening to give him away, but then he tries to hide it beneath that infuriating smirk of his.

"Oh, Feisty," he chuckles, closing the space between our bodies.

His gaze sweeps over me, sending a chill down my spine. He's so close I can count his lashes that are a little too long for a man, smell his expensive cologne, and feel his breath ghost against my skin as he speaks.

"Do it again, Ginny. Hit me again," he murmurs, the heat of his body radiating through the little space between us. "I. Dare. You," he adds lowly.

Damn it. That's hot.

And I hate it.

I hate it being told what to do, but what I hate more is the stupid smirk I want to wipe off his lips.

I raise my hand to hit him again, but this time around, he's faster. One large hand grabs my wrist firmly, twists my hand behind me, and the next thing I know, he's spun me around, pressing my front against the cold surface of Lorenzo's car.

"Did you really think I'd let you hit me again?" he asks, his voice deep and rough, vibrating along the length of my body.

His front presses against my back, and I can feel that he's built like a tank. Through the layers of clothing—my thin dress and his plain, black shirt—I feel every ridge and dip of muscle. I feel every hard line that separates us. I feel the thud of his heartbeat against my spine, and my knees go weak. It feels wrong, like everything I should never touch. Yet so right.

"Let me go," I demand. I need some distance from him to regain control and to remember the reason why I was angry in the first place.

He does the opposite, tightening his grip ever so slightly against me.

"Are you that brave, or are you just fucking stupid?" he whispers hoarsely against my ear. "When a man two times your size dares you to do something, what makes you think you can do it and get away with it?"

I blow out a frustrated breath and grit my teeth before struggling against his strong hold.

"I said let me go, asshole," I ground out, but it's all pointless. His body is flush against mine.

Still, I don't relent. I try to twist and turn in an attempt to break free.

"Careful, Ginny." His rough stubble brushes my cheek as he whispers. "You're turning me on."

That's when I feel it, his undeniable hardness pressed against my ass. My body heats up at the realization, and a pleasant shiver rolls down my spine.

I remind myself that I hate him. That he's the reason why our family business is on the verge of bankruptcy. That he's the enemy.

"Your attempts at intimidating me don't scare me, Dario," I bite out, and I hear a low curse escape his throat.

"Say my name again, Ginny," he rasps. "I love the way it sounds on your lips."

Every attempt at reminding myself how terrible this man is falls flat at the thick desire evident in his voice. It's my first time calling him by his real name since we met again, and I make the mental note to never repeat it. I have a string of more befitting nicknames for him.

"You feel it, don't you?" His breath ghosts across my neck, and goosebumps rise on my skin as his hot breath fans my earlobe, causing the hair there to stand on end. I bite back a moan when he secures both my wrists in one hand before sliding his free hand over my stomach. I gasp as the big hand comes to rest directly under my left breast.

"What the fuck were you thinking coming here without wearing a bra, Ginny?" he rasps, and I swallow, feeling my insides clench and twist.

I clearly wasn't thinking at all. I'd been so eager to sneak out of the house that I didn't even realize I was only in a flimsy dress. And when I saw him earlier, the way his eyes zoomed in on my exposed legs, only then did I feel naked under his gaze.

"I was fucking pissed," I hiss, finding my voice.

"And are you still pissed, Ginny?"

My toes curl in my flats, and I feel wetness pool in my panties. He only calls my name when he's serious, and I can't decide if that makes this situation better or worse.

"Let go of me."

"That doesn't answer my question," he says before chuckling. "Perhaps I should take that as my answer, that you're no longer pissed."

"Fuck you!"

"Maybe later I'll let you do that, Princess. How would you like it? Gentle, hard... Rough?"

I groan inwardly. How does he manage to twist every single thing I say?

"Does overpowering people you're physically stronger than make you feel better about yourself? Does it make you feel like more of a man when you exert your power over others?" I say in a mocking tone.

I want to annoy him, to infuriate him the way he does me, but my words only earn me a chuckle.

"What do you think?"

At this point, I've almost relaxed into his hold. His hand is still under my boob, now tracing idly under the curve of my breast.

A low hum escapes my throat.

"Let's see. I think you should listen when a woman tells you to leave her alone. Can you do that for me?" I say it in a sickly-sweet tone, like I would tell a kindergartener.

As I expect, he laughs again. For a man as intimidating and dangerous as he, laughing comes easy to him. Or maybe he's just doing it to spite me. He knows exactly how to get under my skin.

"Is that why you're no longer fighting against me? Because you want me to let you go?" he mocks.

My body burns, and I remember why I hated him in the first place. I know it won't end well if I keep fighting, and I hope maybe that will push him into loosening his grip. But a part of my brain, the one that's dirty and unhinged, likes the way his fingers are dangerously near my nipples, the way his warm breath tickles my neck when he taunts me.

"It's getting late." I harden my voice. "My brother will soon notice I'm gone, and I don't want him to get worried."

"You should have thought about that when you decided to physically confront the man you think planned to kill you," he says through gritted teeth, and I hate that his words are true.

Coming here was a stupid mistake.

"Never try something like this again, Ginny." The warmth is now gone from his voice. Instead, he snarls coldly,

"If you were someone else, I would have made you pay heavily for stalking me--"

"I didn't—"

"Finding the address of someone you met once at a party and waiting for them at their house is exactly that, Princess," he harshly interrupts.

It sounds so bad when he says it like that, but that's because he's a master at twisting the truth. And twisting people.

My breath leaves in a sharp woosh as he pushes himself off me. I suddenly feel cold from the lack of contact. A shiver wracks through me, but I refuse to cover myself from his gaze.

"Go home."

A simple order, one that makes me want to do the opposite just because he tells me to.

But yeah, that would further prove to him that I'm stupid.

Huffing, I raise my head before looking at his face.

"Step away from my car, asshole," I hiss. "If you think you've succeeded at intimidating me, think again. Unlike every other person you've come across, I don't scare easily."

And then his smirk returns. He takes a step back for me to pull open my door. When I get into the car and turn on the ignition, the annoying tilt is still on his lips.

I make a show by revving the car's engine before finally pulling out onto the road. As I drive farther away from him, my hatred returns, burning hotter and brighter than before.

Nothing, not even a few heated touches and whispered words, can change the way I feel about him.

8

DARIO

I'm in a good mood today.

It's one of those days when everything feels as if it's falling perfectly into place. I've got exciting plans, and I can't wait to see how they unfold. Today, I'll be launching another phase of my revenge plan against Lorenzo. I like to think of him as a smart man, his ways unpredictable. But lately, he's been making things little bit too easy.

Holding public meetings, like the one I'm driving to, is a risky move. Every businessman knows that. It's a double-edged sword, and Lorenzo should know better. Maybe he thinks that addressing stakeholders and investors in such a public manner makes him seem trustworthy, transparent even. And for someone like him, that may work. He's always had a silver tongue, even when we were younger. It's what makes him such a good actor.

And a backstabber.

I'm almost insulted that he thinks this event will go off without a hitch. It's as though he underestimates me. He knows I'm indirectly one of his creditors, and still, he chooses to host this press conference, exposing himself to scrutiny and potential backlash.

Bold move, Bianchi. Bold and stupid.

Then again, it appears stupidity runs in the blood. The memory of Ginny's soft skin, the way our bodies pressed together, her sharp breaths and sharper tongue—it's been haunting me. I can still smell her perfume, feel the silky texture of her hair slipping through my fingers.

Stop thinking about her.

I grit my teeth and force my focus back to the task at hand. The Skyline Events Center looms ahead, a massive structure. I pull into a spot near the entrance and retrieve a file from my briefcase before stepping out into the midday sun. The heat is oppressive, but I adjust my suit and make my way toward the entrance.

Photographers and reporters swarm the front door. The moment they spot me, the clicking and flashing increases. As usual, they keep a reasonable distance from me, and the reporters don't shove cameras in my face and demand answers to their questions. The last man who did that...let's just say the rest have gotten the message. Today, I don't mind the attention. That's exactly why I'm here—to stir the pot.

With a confident stride, I push through the doors. The meeting is already underway when I slip in, the murmurs of disgruntled creditors filling the room like a low hum. Journalists and photographers line the edges of the room, their devices flashing, microphones poised.

Lorenzo's voice carries across the hall as he stands at the podium, his expression confident.

Perfect. I can't wait to watch him crumble.

I position myself at the back of the large hall, barely noticed by any of the several businessmen and investors who are currently focused on Lorenzo.

"Ladies and gentlemen, once again, I thank you for joining me today." He speaks into the small microphone on the podium. "I assure you, the Bianchi empire is far from collapsing. We are navigating through temporary challenges, and I urge you to dismiss any allegations of our impending bankruptcy."

His voice is strong, his face is relaxed, and he pauses to scan the room, making eye contact with a few of the stakeholders. The man is a good actor, but his immaculate performance doesn't fool me.

He gently adjusts his tie, a nervous habit I remember from years ago, before he resumes speaking again.

"Our recent setbacks, particularly with the Riverside project, were unfortunate but not unmanageable. We have already initiated legal proceedings against the contractors responsible for the substandard materials that led to the collapse. I have every confidence that we will recover our losses."

I almost laugh. Legal proceedings, indeed. He can't even afford the legal cost of such a rigorous lawsuit. Hell, he can't afford a legal lawsuit against *me*.

Two creditors raise their hands. I recognize the both of them. The first man, Taylor Johnson, is a seasoned Australian investor who just recently hit billionaire status. That's the thing about making money solely from investing. The market is volatile, and even if one is an expert, unforeseen events could still happen, leading to severe financial loss.

Who would have predicted that the almighty Bianchi empire would face such a severe crisis? No one but me. I almost feel bad for Mike. He was one of the biggest investors in the project. Now, it seems he won't be a billionaire for too long.

He leans forward, rubbing a hand over his jaw.

"Lorenzo, what specific steps are you taking to ensure that future projects adhere to safety standards? We need assurances."

Lorenzo nods, looking almost relieved at the question. "We've implemented stricter oversights and are working with new contractors who have proven track records," he explains in a firm tone.

Another creditor, a young owner of a tech startup, chimes in. "And what about the financial impact of the Riverside collapse? How are you planning to address the losses?"

"Rest assured, we are negotiating with several investors who believe in our vision, and we're exploring new financing options," Lorenzo replies, his voice clear and unwavering.

The crowd murmurs, some appearing convinced. I scoff inwardly. They're too placated for my liking.

I flick a glance at my Rolex and realize I can't wait any longer.

Clearing my throat, I step forward, walking down the aisle in slow, steady steps. Heads turn to look at me.

I keep my gaze fixed on Lorenzo, who has an unreadable expression on his face. But the eyes—the eyes always give them away. He tries to hide it, but even several feet away, I see the fear glistening within his black orbs.

"Is that truly the narrative you want to present?" I say, my voice smooth and confident. The room falls silent, all eyes shifting between the both of us. The tension in the air gets thicker. "Because I happen to have evidence that suggests otherwise."

Lorenzo's eyes widen slightly in a mixture of anger and

surprise before he masks it with indignation. "Dario, this is not the time--"

"Not the time?" I interject, a grin spreading across my face. "I think it's precisely the time. Would you like to see the financial statements from your own firm? The ones that clearly show your debt has accumulated beyond what you're willing to admit?"

A sliver of satisfaction rolls through me when his body stiffens ever so slightly.

"It seems your *temporary challenges* are far more severe than you'd like to admit."

A roar of questions erupts, capturing the unfolding drama.

He turns away from me to address the murmuring crowd. "As many of you are aware, Dario and I have a long-standing personal disagreement. This is just one of his ploys to sully my name and my legacy."

A harsh chuckle leaves my lips before I pull out a few pages from my file and hold them up for everyone to see.

"These documents reveal something far more alarming than just budget cuts. You've not only tried to siphon money by using substandard and counterfeit materials, but you've also misrepresented your financial situation to secure loans. I have copies of the fake financial statements you falsified."

That's when the room bursts into chaos. Cries of disbelief and anger mix with the sound of shuffling papers and fists slamming on tables.

Lorenzo stammers, trying to regain his footing. His fingers grip the podium like a vice.

"That's not true...that's fabricated. He's fabricated this to paint it on me!" he exclaims in exasperation. But of course, no one pays him any mind.

"The fact that you've used future projects as collateral without informing your creditors isn't just a risky move," I call out over the chaos. "It's outright deceitful."

Lorenzo's face turns red with fury as he steps away from the podium, coming to the edge of the stage.

"You can't just—"

"Can't just what?" I challenge, stepping forward. "Can't just reveal the truth? Your creditors deserve to know that the Bianchi family is neck-deep in financial ruin, and your assurances are nothing but empty promises."

"Dario!" he booms, stepping down from the stage and storming towards me. "This is... this has gone too far. You could have told me this in private!" He hisses, and I hear the desperation that has crept into his voice. I relish the distress I see in his face.

"Private?" I laugh loudly, crossing my arms and enjoying the spectacle. "You made it public the moment you decided to mislead these people. You've cost them millions, and they have every right to know every single thing that's happening and demand answers."

The tension in the room is so thick you could cut it with a knife. Anger and palpable emotions crackle in the air, buzzing right beneath all the ruckus. While some of them are hounding Lorenzo for an answer, some exchange anxious glances, and I can see the tide turning. They're realizing they've been played, and now they want blood.

"Mr. Bianchi," one of the older creditors speaks up, his voice shaky but firm. "Is this true? Are we really at risk of losing our investments?"

Lorenzo's facade crumbles further, his mouth opening and closing like a fish out of water. "I can assure you, we're working on a resolution," he stutters.

He must think these men are fools. His shaky tone and the doubt in his eyes betray him.

"Working on a resolution?" I echo, feigning concern. "You mean working on a way to keep your family's name from being dragged through the mud? That's rich, Lorenzo, even for a man like you."

The chaos escalates as the voices become louder, turning into full yelling.

"Give us our fucking money back! We made the mistake of investing in this cursed company," a random man booms across the room. Soon, the hall erupts with different shouts and demands.

"You've mismanaged our investments!" another adds.

"You scammer! You're an embarrassment to the legacy your father left."

I grit my teeth at the mention of Lorenzo's father, but I don't let my mask slip. Instead, I smirk as the clicks increase furiously, capturing the spectacle for the evening news.

Lorenzo is clearly panicking at this point, unable to calm any of the creditors down. Journalists are typing furiously on their laptops. Photographers are taking pictures that will circulate across the internet before the day ends.

I stand back, arms crossed, a sinister smile etched on my face as I watch the display. This is what I wanted—a front-row seat to Lorenzo's downfall. The people who once held power over me are now powerless, trapped in a web I carefully curated myself.

As the uproar continues, I lock eyes with Lorenzo, who looks like a cornered animal. His breath quickens and his nostrils flare as he glares at me.

I don't feel an ounce of remorse. The Bianchi's brought this upon themselves. I just helped hasten up the process of their doom. A smile graces my lips as I savor the moment. I don't care that pictures are being taken or that several stories and narratives will explode on the news by the time I leave here.

This wasn't just about business. This was personal. He never saw it coming, never realized that every handshake, every deal he made, was pulling him deeper into the web I was spinning. And now? Now, he's exactly where I want him. Desperate. Vulnerable. Helpless.

His expression shifts to full-blown rage, and I can almost feel the heat radiating off him.

"Get out!" he shouts, his voice cracking. "You have no right to be here!"

"On the contrary," I reply calmly and loudly over the voices. "I have every right. I'm here to collect what's owed, and trust me, I won't be leaving empty-handed."

He tries to storm towards me, but a few men hold him back, grabbing his shirt, tie, hand, or any surface of his body they can find.

And my job here is done.

Before I turn to leave, I flash him a wicked grin, the kind that promises more chaos to come. "See you at the top, Lorenzo. Or, you know, whatever's left of this when I'm done with you."

As I step out of the hall, the noise behind me fades, replaced by the rush of adrenaline coursing through my veins. The thing about betrayal is, it teaches you how to win.

I remember when we were kids, how we plotted and schemed against our enemies together. We dreamt of building empires together one day, sketching plans for skyscrapers on old exercise books.

Now, I'm the architect of his downfall, and every step I

take feels like a victory. The Bianchi legacy, once so secure, is now crumbling, and I'm here to ensure it falls completely.

After all, the Devil doesn't just plant the seeds of destruction. He watches them grow—and he enjoys every second of it.

9

GINEVRA

A small sigh of disbelief escapes my lips as I stare at the bold, red letters on the sign ahead. SOLD.

The word glares back at me, mocking the dream I had so carefully crafted. My breath catches, and I feel as if I've been punched in the gut.

Just last week, I was buzzing with excitement, my mind alive with visions of what I'd turn this space into—a vibrant hub for my bakery business. I could almost smell the buttery, sweet aroma that would fill the air, see the colorful walls, the glass cabinets filled with delicate pastries, the shelves stocked with baked treats.

But now, it's gone. All of it.

And I know exactly who's behind this.

When I got the news earlier today from my agent, I just knew I had to come see it with my own eyes. Maybe it was because I didn't believe it. The last time I checked, there were only two other people competing for the building—a middle-aged man who wanted to open a local bookstore and a married couple who were farmers and wanted to create a food market. I was the highest competitor, and my payment should have been finalized this week.

Then, this happened.

When my agent told me the final sale price, I didn't argue. There was no point—it was far beyond anything I could compete with. All I could do was nod and hang up, stunned.

A wave of betrayal crashes over me, confirming what I already knew.

Dario.

The name is like a sharp stab, deeper than I want to admit. I hate that I feel especially broken that he's the one who did it. It shouldn't hurt this much, but it does. If someone else had taken the building, it may have been easier to swallow. But knowing Dario—Dario, of all people—only acquired it only to spite me, to hurt me, knowing it would get to Lorenzo, too...it makes my blood boil.

My jaw tightens as I turn away from the building, my heels clicking angrily against the pavement.

Glancing at my watch, I remind myself not to be late for my meeting with Bakers United, the city's tight-knit group of bakers. Their support has been invaluable throughout this process, from business advice to helping me find my footing with the locals.

I cling to the hope that maybe, just maybe, they'll have some solution to this mess.

The sidewalks are bustling with people, their laughter and chatter very fitting for the clear weather. When I reach the familiar Audi—Lorenzo's spare car, which I've been driving—I'm painfully reminded of all the sacrifices I made to get to this point.

When Lorenzo faced his first major setback with the

construction company, I knew it was the wrong time to approach him for financial help.

First, he'd refuse, reminding me that I didn't need to work. And second, his hands were full, buried under mountains of debt and creditors. I had already burned through most of my savings, so I did the only thing I could—I sold two of my cars, leaving only the Porsche, which was now blown to bits.

I fumble with the keys, the metallic sound jarring against my mind. I can't shake the image of Dario's smug grin in my head—the way he always seems to orchestrate our family's misfortunes from the shadows. My pride won't let me confront him ever again. My reaction will only give him the satisfaction he craves, and I refuse to beg him for help or acknowledge his role in my downfall.

The car purrs to life, and I pull out into the streets. The coffee shop where I'm supposed to meet with a few members of the union isn't too far from here, so I don't bother playing any music. I can't wait to hear the solutions they're willing to offer when I tell them of my predicament.

Soon, I arrive at the small building situated in a quiet area of the city. After finding a good spot in the parking lot, I grab my purse before stepping out of the car.

When I enter the cozy coffee shop, the rich aroma of freshly brewed coffee envelops me like a warm hug. I quickly scan the room, searching for the familiar faces of my partners turned friends.

In a far corner, I spot the three familiar figures huddled together at a small table. Mark, a tall man with a scruffy beard, glances up but quickly averts his gaze when his eyes meet mine.

As I get closer, I see Lucy, with her bright red hair, but her usual warm smile isn't on her face. Instead, she shifts uncomfortably in her seat. Sophia sits beside Lucy, with soft brown curls framing her face and her lower lip between her teeth, biting nervously.

Something is wrong.

"Hey, thanks for meeting me," I say, trying to muster a smile, but it feels forced. They nod, barely meeting my gaze. The atmosphere is tense, thick with unspoken words.

As I settle into the empty chair, I notice their body language—hunched shoulders, eyes darting across the room. It's almost as if they don't want to be seen with me.

"What's going on?" I ask, my voice steady despite the unease creeping in.

Lucy plants a smile on her face as she gestures to the cup before me.

"We ordered your usual."

But I don't even glance at it. My stomach is tied into knots.

Mark finally clears his throat.

"Ginny, we...we need to talk." His voice is low, almost a whisper, as if he's afraid someone might overhear.

"That's what we do whenever we meet. We talk." I chuckle nervously.

Lucy bites her lip, glancing at Sophia for support. "With everything that's happened...it's just..." she starts, but her words trail off.

The weight of their hesitation hangs in the air between us.

I feel a lump forming in my throat. "You're scaring me. What is it?"

Mark shifts uncomfortably in his seat. "We've decided...it's best if we withdraw our support for your bakery." His words hit me like ice water, freezing the moment.

I had a feeling that this would happen, but still, it doesn't shake the shock that rolls through me.

"Withdraw?" I repeat before protesting in a slightly raised voice. "But I thought we were a team!"

"I know, I know," he replies quickly, his eyes darting around the café again. "But with the scandal, we can't afford to be associated with you right now. It's...it's just too risky for us."

Tears burn in my eyes, and I struggle to keep them at bay.

"Please just..." I pause to grit my teeth. "The situation with my family is only temporary, and it has nothing to do with the bakery--"

"It has everything to do with it," Mark says, then sighs. "Your family's name has a bad rep right now. Our own businesses will be affected if we proceed with this partnership with you."

"My family's problems don't concern you in any way," I say in a hard voice. "It's not as if we're opening a business together or something. I'll do my own thing while being a part of the union. I just need to be in a community."

I hate how desperate my voice sounds. I hate that they're right. This is going to affect their businesses, as well.

I grab Lucy's hand, grasping for the last straws of compassion.

"You know it's literally impossible for me to start my business here if I don't have support from a union," I tell her. She's always been kindhearted. She'll understand.

"Ginny." She doesn't look into my eyes. "I think it's really selfish of you to even argue with us on this. You come from a wealthy family. Though you're facing some mishaps, you'll be able to recover from this."

I pull my hand away from hers, her words chaffing at my heart.

"However," she continues, turning to look at me, "if we get dragged down into your mess, our businesses may never recover."

Her words sting even more than the betrayal I feel. I bite my lower lip till it draws blood. My frustration bubbles over, and in a moment of clumsiness, I knock over my coffee cup. The dark liquid spills across the table. Just what I needed. I fumble to grab napkins, my face burning with humiliation as I wipe up the liquid.

Sophia speaks up for the first time, her expression filled with genuine regret. "We're really sorry, Ginny. We wanted to help, but we have to think about our own businesses, too."

I look at them, feeling the sting of betrayal wash over me. I've always admired Lucy's passion and resilience, Mark's business acumen, and Sophia with her gentle demeanor was like a sister to me. But now, they're treating me like a pariah. "So, that's it? You're just going to leave me to fend for myself?"

They exchange glances, distress etched on their faces. Lucy leans forward, her voice barely above a whisper. "We wish it could be different, truly. But we can't be seen around you right now."

The weight of their words crushes me. I sit back in my chair, the warmth of the coffee shop suddenly feeling cold. I can't believe they're kicking me out of the community they promised would offer support.

"Fine," I say, forcing the words out between clenched teeth. "If that's how you feel, then I guess there's nothing more to say."

As I stand to leave, I catch a glimpse of their faces—

averted eyes, shameful expressions—and the anger hits me hard. They don't have any right to look as if they regret what they did. If they could do it again, they would.

I feel the anger bubbling up inside me as I walk out. I had trusted them and believed they would stand by me. Now, I'm left to grapple with the harsh reality that even those I thought were allies can turn their backs when things get tough.

As I step out into the bustling street, the sunlight feels harsh against my skin. My mind is racing, and I need someone to talk to, even if it's to vent my frustrations.

When I slip into Lorenzo's car, I dial Rinaldo's number, my heart pounding. I know he's not the most affectionate person sometimes, but he knows how much this bakery meant to me. I'd call Lorenzo, but he's been too busy, and I don't want to bother him.

The moment Rinaldo answers, I don't hold back. "Rinaldo, you won't believe what just happened. The building I was planning to buy got sold. I wasn't even informed that there was a new competitor. And now, the Bakers United kicked me out of their union." I chuckle humorlessly as a tear slips down my cheek. "They just abandoned me. I also think that asshole Dario is trying to sabotage me again. I hate him!"

"Ginny, calm down," he replies, his voice annoyingly calm. "Dario? Do you mean Dario De Luca? Why would he try to sabotage your little bakery business?"

"What?" I exhale a breath, a jaw in my head ticking at the genuine disbelief in his tone.

"He might be your brother's rival, but I don't think he has the time to involve you in their mess."

He says it so condescendingly that I'm genuinely short of words.

Taking my silence as acceptance, he continues, "You're going to be a housewife soon. You shouldn't stress over business matters."

His words strike a nerve. "A housewife? Is that all you think I'm good for?" I yell. "Before you met me, I'd always had plans to open my own bakery. Do you think I'm just going to sit around while you make decisions for me just because we're getting married?"

"Here you go getting angry again," he huffs, and I imagine him rolling his eyes. "Honestly, maybe this is for the best. The universe is trying to tell you something. Maybe you should have never bothered yourself with this in the first place—"

"This is not for the best," I scream. "I can't fucking believe you."

He blows out a breath, and I can hear his irritation through the line. "Fine. It's not for the best. It's just a phase, Ginny. You'll adapt," he snaps.

"No, I won't." I don't care that I'm shouting now. I'm so fucking done. "This is my dream! If you can't support me, then I'm done with this engagement!"

Silence stretches between us, thick and charged. I can almost hear him processing my words. "You're being unreasonable," he finally says, but the fire inside me won't be extinguished.

"You're so fucking selfish." I chuckle harshly. "I wonder why I've put up with this sham of a relationship for too long."

"Mind your words, Ginny," he warns, but I don't have it in me to care.

"Fuck you, Rinaldo. Fuck your condensation, your random mood swings, and your attitude. Fuck *your* selfish dreams for what's supposed to be *our* future."

"Ginny—"

"I'm done," I declare, the finality of my words crashing over me like a wave. I hang up before he can respond, my heart racing with mixed emotions. Anger, hurt, relief.

I drive home, the city whizzing by in a blur. The streets are filled with people chatting and laughing, but I feel like a ghost. Empty. Invincible. Alone.

"Dario, you think you can just ruin my life and walk away?" I mutter, gripping the steering wheel tightly. I think I'm going crazy. "I won't let you get away with this."

As I pull into my driveway of Lorenzo's house, the sun is slowly dipping behind the horizon, creating an orange hue that bathes a warm color across the lawn. The house looms ahead, stark and quiet, mirroring my frustration. I step inside and toss my bag onto the couch, the sound echoing in the empty space.

I hate him. I hate him so much. I'm desperate to show Dario that I'm not a pawn in his game. That I'm a player, and I won't back down. But the resolve is drowned by my sorrow. The only gripping need within me is a desire to just forget. To pretend he doesn't exist. To pretend like my life is as perfect as it was before he came.

And I know exactly what I need to do.

10

DARIO

T he low hum of laughter and the steady thump of bass ripple through the club's walls, cocooning me in a haze of smoke and cheap cologne mixed with the sweet tang of cocktails.

I swirl the whiskey in my hand before taking a slow sip, letting the cool liquid burn its way down my throat. Leaning back into the plush leather seat, I take another sip, savoring the moment.

Several ledgers are spread out on the table before me. I grab the nearest one and begin to go through its contents, skimming over each entry before moving onto the next.

There is something calming about this routine— tracking the flow of cash from my various underground businesses while music pulses around me.

The atmosphere makes it easy for me to lose track of time while I go through every single piece of paperwork. I have an office at the back of the bar, but I prefer staying here, my eyes occasionally drifting to the crowd below when I need a break from the numbers.

From the elevated booth where I'm seated, I have a

perfect view of the club. The dance floor, the bar, and the stage all unfold before me, alive with energy. The room is bathed in shades of red and blue from the pulsing lights, casting shadows that dance across the walls.

I'm about to dive back into the ledgers when something on the dance floor catches my eye—a woman.

She's dressed in a skimpy outfit that clings to her curves, the fabric shimmering under the flashing lights. The way she moves is magnetic—her body rolling to the rhythm of the slow R&B song blasting through the speakers.

My heart stops as she throws her head back, making her face come into my view.

Ginny.

A bitter chuckle escapes my lips. The one woman I haven't been able to stop thinking about ever since the last time we met, when I had her body pressed against mine...

It's been over a week since I saw her, and I wanted to take my time to gain some rein over my mind before I saw her again.

Yet here she is, right in my club, dancing as if no one else existed. The universe was playing one sick, twisted game by bringing her right into my territory before I'm ready to see her again.

Everything else fades into the background as I stare at the fluid, mesmerizing, and erotic way she moves her body. The light catches her skin, making it glow. The way her long hair falls over her shoulders, the way she moves unapologetically—it's intoxicating.

I feel myself grow hard in my pants just watching her. Every part of me craves to touch her, taste her, and feel her grind against me. But it's a line I shouldn't cross, not again. It's dangerous. I shouldn't want her the way I do.

She has no idea that she's captured the rapt attention of

every man in this room. I feel something hot and dangerous burn low in my chest at the realization that every other man is watching her body the same way I am.

Maybe I should have just stayed in my office. I'm about to make good on that decision when I see a guy inching closer, his hands finding their way to her waist. A surge of possessiveness washes over me, igniting something deep within. I'm on my feet before I can think, muscles tensed with anger and determination.

I don't even care how stupid or obvious I look charging over to them now. I watch people step out of the way as I make my way downstairs. Most of them turn to look at me warily, fear coloring their features. The music and noise fade into a dull roar as I storm through the crowd.

I reach her just in time.

My voice is hard and calm, yet it cuts through the pounding music.

"Get away from her."

It's a simple instruction, but it makes the guy stumble back, a mixture of shock and fear in his eyes. He knows exactly who I am and what I'm capable of. The thought fills me with dark satisfaction.

The guy wastes no time scrambling away.

"You," I growl, looking at her flushed face.

"What the fuck are you doing here?" she hisses, a molten fire burning in her eyes. Under the flashing lights, I see the hints of green in her hazel eyes.

"I should be asking you that damned question, Ginevra," I say. Her head reels back, as if she's shocked that I called her by her full name. Then her breath hitches slightly as I take a step toward her. "Why the hell are you here?"

She blinks, and the anger returns to her eyes.

"Leave me the fuck alone, Dario!" she yells, turning to walk away from me, but I'm not having that.

Ignoring her protests, I grab her arm and pull her away from the dance floor. Her heels click against the tiles angrily as I drag her down to the corridor at the back of the room. Her angry insults get drowned out by the loud music tries to wrench out of my grasp, but I only tighten my hold and pull her into the quiet hallway.

"Let go of me, you asshole," she spits just as a waitress bumps into us. Her eyes widen slightly before she bends her head, mumbles an apology, and scurries off.

"If you keep fighting me, I'll throw you over my shoulder," I warn, turning to look at Ginny.

She scoffs like the brat she is. "Is that supposed to scare—"

A loud yelp leaves her lips as I lift her body up and over my right shoulder.

She gasps in disbelief. "Put me down this instant, Dario!"

Her dress hikes up just enough for me to catch a glimpse of lace panties, and without thinking, my hand lands on the back of her thighs, right under her ass, shielding her from any wandering eyes.

Her body stiffens slightly, and I try to ignore how soft her skin feels underneath my hands as we continue our way down the hall, which thankfully is empty. I arrive at a restricted room and unlock the door with my fingerprint before stepping in and closing it shut. As I slide her body down my shoulders, my hand on her thigh moves upward until it's holding her waist.

"I asked you a question earlier," I snap. "What are you doing here?"

That's when she pushes against my chest, the fire in her eyes returning.

"Who the hell do you think you are to demand such answers from me? Who do you think you are to drag me away like some rag doll?" she seethes, pushing against my chest.

I take a step back, needing space to breathe, needing to stop inhaling her intoxicating scent. It's too much, too overwhelming.

"You're the one who walked into *my* club. You were the one dancing on *my* floor, drawing the attention of *my* patrons," I hiss, feeling my own anger simmer beneath the surface. "You're the one constantly stepping into *my* territory, Ginny. Always capturing my attention," I rasp, watching the way her chest rises and falls as she breathes heavily. "And now, dancing with some random guy like you have no idea how that drives me insane?"

Her nostrils flare. "I didn't even know it was your damned club, or I wouldn't have set foot in it."

"But here you are," I sneer. "Causing trouble like always."

"Fuck you, Dario. Do you honestly think you can waltz into my life and control everything I do?" she hurls at me, her voice trembling with fury.

She's not done. Her eyes flash with indignation as she continues. "Since you came back into my life, everything's been spiraling out of control!"

In that moment, everything else fades away, and all I can focus on is her. The way her breath comes in quick bursts, the fire in her gaze. It's infuriating and intoxicating all at once.

"Don't pin your problems on me, Princess. You can thank your brother for that," I bite back.

Her eyes narrow. "And today? All I wanted was a break, and you couldn't even let me have that!"

"A break?" I scoff, bitterness coating my words. "You thought dancing with a stranger was a good way to clear your head?"

She squares her shoulders, eyes boring into mine. "Yes. Maybe I wanted to. I don't have any reason not to. I called off my engagement. A year with my fiancé, and now, all I want is one night where no man tries to control me!"

Every other thing she says fades into thin air.

"You called off your engagement," I say, my voice low.

She pauses, her eyes drinking me in. The air between us feels charged, thick with tension. I step closer, feeling the heat radiating off her.

"That's the best news I've heard all week," I mutter, watching the way her pupils dilate at my words.

"You...you can't say that to me." Her voice falls into a breathy exhale.

"I can," I murmur, leaning in close enough to feel the heat of her breath. "I saw you with him once. At that ball. I remember thinking that surely he could not be the man you wanted to be with."

She swallows hard. "And what makes you think that?"

"He's not your type," I hum, our faces inches apart. "Your brother probably arranged it. A convenient alliance for the family business, right? Someone with influence, like Rinaldo."

"How dare you insinuate my brother would sell me off?" she hisses.

"Why else would you be with someone like him?" I whisper, leaning in even closer. "A man who could never satisfy you. Not emotionally. Not intellectually." My voice drops, dangerously low. "And certainly not sexually."

She lets out a forced laugh. "Now I know you're just

cocky. How bold of you to assume I'd stay with a man that long without him being amazing."

"Oh, so you're telling me he was a good fuck." I catch the flicker of discomfort in her eyes at my crude words, but she masks it quickly.

"Yes," she replies, her voice sharp.

I step closer, lowering my voice to a dangerous whisper. "Now, you're just lying, Princess. You don't look like someone who's ever had amazing sex. Not the kind that makes you feel alive. The raw, dirty, messy kind. The one with hair-pulling, biting, scratching—the kind that turns you inside out and makes you come so hard you forget about the rest of your shitty life."

Her breath falters, and for a moment she's silent. We stand there locked in a stare-off, daring each other to break first. To give in. To surrender.

"You're the most despicable person I've ever met," she finally whispers, but I can see the conflict in her eyes. "I want absolutely nothing to do with you."

"I think you're lying." My lips brush against her ear, making her gasp softly. "You think about me too, just like I think about you."

When I grab her exposed thigh, she makes a sound between a gasp and a moan.

"Dario." She lays her palms flat against my chest to push me away.

I bend down till our foreheads touch. "You know I love it when you say my name like that."

My body burns from her soft touch. And when she slides her hands over my shoulder to pull her body flush against mine, I groan.

"Fuck, Ginny." My hand hitches higher on her thigh, my thumb tracing patterns on her inner thigh.

She whimpers, her fingers digging into my back. When I lean down to press kisses on her neck, she moans, throwing her head back against the door.

"You have no idea how obsessed I am with your scent." I run my nose along the length of her neck to her shoulder. "Your taste." I lick the same path, traveling back up before pulling her earlobe between my teeth. "Everything."

She buries her hands in my hair, and I pull back slightly to look at her. The thick desire in her eyes, the way she's biting her lip and breathing heavily, drives me crazy.

We both wait. One second. Two seconds. Before I can risk it all by kissing her, a loud knock interrupts us.

The air instantly chills as she pulls away. I step back, and she slips past me, eager to escape the moment.

"I'll take you home."

Maybe because she knows I'll carry her to my car if I have to, she doesn't protest. The night air is chilly as we step out of the building. She shivers slightly, but when I take off my jacket and offer it to her, she ignores me.

When she slips into the passenger seat of my car, I know her scent will linger for days. I don't just know if it's a good or bad thing.

I turn on the engine and pull into the dark streets. At first, the silence was thick and uncomfortable. Before she starts fuming again, launching into an angry tirade about how I ruin everything and how she never wants anything to do with me.

My body is still tense from earlier, but she continues to mutter insults under her breath. I can't help but smile and steal glances at her. The fire in her eyes, the way her voice trembles with passion when she speaks—it's captivating.

"How do you know where my brother lives?" she asks as we pull up to Lorenzo's house.

"How did you know where I lived?" I shoot back.

She huffs before undoing her seatbelt. As I stare out the window, I catch a glimpse of someone lurking across the street, looking at the house. Before I can pay closer attention, they vanish into the shadows.

"Stay away from me, Dario." Ginny's voice pulls my attention to her. "I mean it."

She gets out of the car, and I watch her walk toward the door, a mix of frustration and longing bubbling inside me. I should have done more tonight. I should have kissed her, touched her the way I knew she wanted to be touched, and made it more difficult for her to stay away.

As she disappears into the house, I can't shake the feeling that this night has changed everything. The tension between us lingers like smoke in the air, and I know this is just the beginning.

11

GINEVRA

A tired yawn escapes my lips as I close the book I've been reading—or rather, trying to read. I've been stuck on the same page for over ten minutes, my mind wandering elsewhere while my eyes lazily skim over the words.

I've been cooped up indoors for days, and the boredom is driving me insane. The walls seem like they're closing in, and amid all this, my thoughts are fixated on my encounters with Dario. They play and replay in my mind like a broken record, especially our most recent run-in at the club.

It's almost absurd how he seems to be everywhere. Ever since we collided—no, *he* collided into me—at that event, it's as if I summoned some spirit that ensures he shows up wherever I am.

Okay, slight exaggeration. We've only met twice since then, but both times are permanently engraved in my memory.

His intense gaze, the way his touch lingered, the heat of his lips against my neck, his hands tracing slow, deliberate circles on my inner thigh. I still shiver at the thought. But it's not simply the physical connection. He's infuriating—his smug remarks, the way he gets under my skin with those crude jokes. He drives me mad in a way that makes it impossible *not* to think about him.

But then reality slaps me in the face every time Lorenzo comes home at night. I can't even remember the last time we had a proper conversation. He's been running himself ragged, desperately trying to save the company, but nothing seems to be working.

He's losing weight from hardly eating, and he looks more disheveled than ever, with his hair longer than usual, a scruffy beard, and those tired eyes.

Whenever I catch myself thinking about how perfect it felt with Dario pressed against me, I remind myself that he's the reason Lorenzo's life is in shambles and our family is falling apart.

This morning, though, Lorenzo mentioned he had a new idea that might turn things around. For the first time in ages, he actually smiled at me—and even ate the banana bread I baked. In that moment, a glimmer of hope flickered. Maybe things will get better.

My mood lifted even more when I remembered that there hadn't been any more assassination attempts against me. Dario has made it clear he wasn't behind them, which narrows down my suspicions to someone else who may have it out for my family. Papa made a lot of enemies in his time and while that's not exactly comforting, it does make me feel somewhat safer. At least I have private security now.

Rising from the bed where I've been lounging since breakfast, I decide to do something productive. And by productive, I mean taking a shower and changing into fresh clothes.

By the time I'm done, it's past noon, and I'm hungry

again. The little slice of banana bread and coffee from this morning didn't exactly fill me up.

I opt for my comfort food—pizza. Despite the belief that all bakers are good cooks (but not all cooks are good bakers), I have zero cooking ability. For some reason, every time I try to make a dish that doesn't involve flour or baking ingredients, it ends in disaster.

As I reach for my phone to place an order, I notice my battery is nearly dead, and my charger is nowhere to be found. I've practically torn the house apart looking for it. I haven't used it since that night at Dario's club, and even then, I didn't take it out.

Great. Just what I need.

I scour every nook and cranny of the house, but it's nowhere to be found. Frustrated, I toss a cushion aside and let out a sigh. I can't deal with this anymore.

With a sudden burst of determination, I decide to make a quick trip to the electronics store just down the street. My bodyguards have strict orders to keep me safe, but I manage to persuade them with a playful smile, reminding them it's just a quick errand. The two times I snuck out of the house didn't go unnoticed by Lorenzo, and now he's punishing me by tightening the security.

"You really want to walk with me just down the road?" I ask when one of them offers to follow me. "Don't you think that'll only draw more unwanted attention to me?"

The same guy offered to buy the charger for me, but I refuse to turn my bodyguards to my errand boys. Plus, after being indoors for days, I'm actually looking forward to the walk. It's maddening being cooped up for so long.

When none of them answers, I sigh. "I'll be fine, I promise," I assure them.

They still insist on coming along, so I give up and let

them. At least they're letting me leave the house today. I feel as giddy as a kid who just got free ice cream. I inhale deeply under the warm sun, craving a tan, and try to ignore the two men looming behind me. The walk to the gadget store is short, and when we arrive, I tell the guards to stay outside before stepping in.

The store is bright and filled with shiny gadgets, the fluorescent lights casting a cheerful glow over the rows of shiny screens and tech accessories. I weave through the aisles, admiring the latest phones and tablets. My fingers brush over the cool surfaces, and for a moment, I'm transported to my teenage years when I had an obsession with new technology.

Drones, VR headsets, gaming consoles— you name it, I had it. I was much happier back then, getting anything I wanted handed over to me. I was ignorant of how ruthless the business world was and how it negatively affected people's personal lives.

I shake the thoughts away and grab the charger I need. But instead of heading straight to the register, I browse the aisles, lingering at a display of headphones. I pause to try on a pair. The music is soft, soothing, and I close my eyes briefly, letting the sound wash over me. It feels good to escape, even if only for a moment.

But then, the atmosphere shifts.

A loud crash echoes from the entrance, and my heart drops like a stone when three masked, heavily armed men burst into the store.

Panic surges through me, and I stumble back, my breath catching in my throat. I glance around, but my bodyguards are nowhere in sight. Where are they? They're supposed to protect me! My eyes dart outside, and that's when I see them lying on the ground—unmoving.

Fear claws at me, and I know I have to act fast.

"Get down," I yell when the first bullet pierces through the air, instinctively shielding a teenage girl who stands frozen in shock. Her eyes are wide, filled with terror. "It's okay, I'm here," I whisper, trying to comfort her, even though my heart is racing. I can hear the robbers shouting, their voices a chaotic mix of demands and threats. The store attendant is cowering behind the counter, his hands over his head.

"Please, just take what you want," I hear him plead, and the desperation in his voice sends chills down my spine.

"We don't want your money. We want Ginevra Bianchi."

I freeze at the mention of my name, and my blood runs cold. They're not here to rob the place—they're here for me.

My mind races as I glance around for a way out, my pulse pounding in my ears. The exits are blocked, and the reality of my situation crashes over me like a wave. Desperation tightens in my chest as I slowly start backing away, scanning the room for any possible escape.

"Stand up, wherever you are, or we'll kill everyone in this room," one of the men shouts, and I know I can't hide forever.

I can't let these people die because of me.

I take a deep breath, my hands trembling at my sides. I can't let them take me. I need to protect the girl beside me. "Stay down," I whisper to her, my voice barely audible.

Slowly, I stand, and immediately, all eyes turn toward me. The door isn't far from where I'm standing. If I can just make a dash for it...

Before I can move, a heavy hand clamps down on my arm, sending a sharp pain shooting through me. The world starts to spin.

"Let me go!" I scream, my voice piercing through the

chaos, but it's swallowed by the other screams and shouts echoing around the store.

"Move it!" the robber growls, dragging me toward the entrance. I kick and struggle, but my limbs feel weak, as if they've turned to jelly. His grip is unrelenting, like iron chains pulling me forward. I can feel the adrenaline rushing through my veins, but it's not enough. I glance back at the girl—her face frozen in terror—and my heart cracks.

"Please, don't hurt her," I shout again, desperation thick in my voice. But my words fall on deaf ears. I can feel my legs start to buckle beneath me, and just as I'm about to gather the strength to fight back, everything blurs.

The last thing I see is the girl's wide, frightened eyes before darkness engulfs me.

12

DARIO

I adjust the weight of my gun in the waistband of my pants as the car cruises through the dimly lit streets.

Tonight, Esteban's getting a visit he won't forget. I warned him, publicly and clearly, yet the bastard thought he could outsmart me—tried to disappear into a shiny new house on the outskirts of the city. The fool should have known better. Now, he's made it personal.

The car screeches to a halt in front of Esteban's Mansions on the Upper East Side—his latest pathetic attempt at hiding after he tried to scam me. A bitter chuckle escapes my lips as one of my men swings the door open.

I've had a guy on the inside planted within his security team for months. Esteban, that clueless bastard, didn't have a clue that every move he made was my business all along.

I'm not one to boast about my street smarts, but in moments like this, I savor just how easily I play these games. He thinks he's been running the show. But I've been pulling the strings, waiting for the right time to cut him off for good.

It's a shame he's not even going to live to tell anyone how he tried to double-cross me.

I step out of the car, straightening my coat as the night air bites at my skin. My men surround me, ready for action, but the truth is I don't need them for this. I'm here to finish this with my own hands. The thrill of what's about to happen rushes through me, my fingers itching to grip the cold steel of my gun.

Like I said, I'm not proud. Just too damn good at what I do. And Esteban? He's about to find out the hard way that no one crosses me and walks away breathing.

My black coat flutters in the cold breeze as I stride toward the entrance, my mind locked on one goal. My men fan out ahead of me, shadows moving with precision. Each one grips a custom Glock fitted with suppressors, their sleek black barrels glinting under the dim streetlights.

A brief, almost inaudible *phut* breaks the stillness, just a soft whisper of death as the silenced rounds slice through the air. Esteban's guards don't even have a chance to react, their bodies crumpling to the ground with barely a sound. The modified pistols make quick, clean work of them. No loud shots, no alarms—just a quiet, professional elimination. Exactly how I want it.

I can't afford to draw any attention tonight. Not yet. At least until the moment I'm standing right in front of him.

When I reach the first door, I don't waste time knocking. I slam my boot into it, the wood splitting under the force. The door creaks and groans before giving way. My men flank me as we head straight for the bedroom.

"Wakey, wakey, Esteban! We're here for a little chat," I singsong, my voice echoing off the walls. The sound alone is enough to rattle the coward out of his sleep.

We reach the main bedroom door—locked, of course. I raise a brow at my men, and with a quick shove, they force it open. What greets me inside makes my blood boil, and a smirk curl my lips at the same time. Esteban's lying in the middle of a king-sized bed surrounded by five naked women of all shapes and sizes.

Amusement quickly turns to disgust. The man has a family—a cousin he's lost because of his own stupidity—and here he is, rolling around with whores as if his world isn't falling apart.

"The room's soundproof, boss," one of my men mutters, his teeth gritted.

I pull my gun from my waistband, taking aim at a ridiculously expensive lamp beside the bed. The shot rings out like thunder, and the glass shatters, sending shards flying. The bang jolts Esteban and his little harem out of their sleep. The women scream, scrambling off the bed in a frenzy of confusion and terror.

Esteban stumbles to his feet, eyes wide with panic as he locks onto me. Reality hits him like a bullet—and I'm the one holding the gun.

Esteban's voice trembles as he stumbles over his words, trying to pull a pair of boxers over his waist, his hands shaking. "What's going on?"

I step closer, the dim light casting shadows across the room. "Hello to you too, Esteban," I sneer, my voice low and menacing. "You really thought you could run? After I gave you a clear warning, you still made me come after you?"

He stumbles backward, his eyes wide with panic as I close in on him. He's already pleading, his voice dripping with pathetic desperation. "Dario, please, let's talk about this. I can explain—"

"Talk?" I cut him off with a growl, my patience gone. "I don't talk, Esteban. Not after what I did to your cousin to show I wasn't bluffing. I gave you one week. You're out of time. And yet, nothing. Not a single word about what we discussed."

He gulps, sweat beading on his forehead. "Look, Dario, it's not as easy as I thought. Retracting the contract—there's legal paperwork, processes—"

"Don't fucking piss me off further by lying to my face, Esteban," I snarl.

I flick my hand, signaling my men, and they begin tearing apart the house, searching every room and corner. I watch Esteban's panic rise as he sees them ripping through his belongings. He's losing control, and he knows it.

"What are you looking for?" he asks, his voice shaking, eyes darting around.

"Just making sure you're not hiding anything," I reply coldly, never taking my gaze off him. "You had some balls thinking you could con me, Esteban."

Before he can respond, I grab a fistful of his hair and slam his head against the bedside table. The sharp crack of his skull hitting wood echoes in the room. Blood splatters across the polished mahogany surface, and he grunts in pain, disoriented and stumbling. I pull him up, and he's barely standing—his legs wobble, one side of his face already swelling, blood pouring from his ears and nose.

"Perfect," I muse before shoving him into a chair my men have set up in the middle of the room. They tie him down, his body limp, and I unzip the bag we brought with us.

I pull out my switchblade—one of my favorites. Its blades gleam under the dim light, varying from curved to jagged, each designed to inflict maximum pain. When I approach him slowly and grab his hands, which have been tied together in his front, his eyes widen, and I can see the realization dawning on him.

"Dario, p-please," he stammers, his voice cracking. "We can negotiate. I'll give you whatever you want."

I let out a dark chuckle. "You had a whole week to do that, Esteban."

I grab his hand, his fingers trembling beneath my grip as I run the blade over his skin, choosing which one to slice first. His pleas turn into a desperate wail as I press the blade against his left index finger, cutting through flesh and bone. The finger drops to the floor with a wet thud, blood spraying across his lap.

"You know how ruthless I am," I snarl, the blade gliding over his pinky next. "And yet, you still thought you could play with fire."

"I'm sorry! Please, Dario, don't—" His voice is raw, choked with sobs as I sever it and move toward his thumb. Blood pours from his hand, soaking the chair beneath him.

"Dario, please," he cries, his voice breaking as tears stream down his face. "Don't kill me...please, for old times' sake."

I ignore his pathetic whimpering, slicing through his remaining fingers with precision, his cries drowned out by the sound of bone cracking under my knife.

"Be quiet," I say with a cold smile, "and maybe I'll consider forgiving you."

He's a broken mess now, sniffling and whimpering as I casually count the remaining fingers on his left hand.

"Seven left," I muse aloud. "I think I'm being too generous." I press down on his right hand. Another loud cry leaves his lips when I twist the middle finger of his left hand, feeling the sharp tip of my blade piercing skin and muscle.

Just then, one of my men bursts in, his face pale. "Boss, we found someone in the basement."

Esteban's eyes widen in terror, tears streaming down his face as they drag in an unconscious girl.

I laugh, a dark sound, until my voice dies in my throat. "You sick, twisted—"

It's Ginny.

My breath hitches. She's been tied up, her face bruised and smeared with dried blood. A slap mark streaks across her cheek, nothing life-threatening but still enough to make my stomach twist into knots. My mouth dries up with an odd, bitter taste as my eyes trace her body. Her head hangs low, her posture slumped. Defeated. I've never seen her like this before. She looks so small, fragile, and weak.

"Take her to the car and stay with her," I order Anton, my most trusted man.

As they head out of the room, my mind reels as I imagine what they must have done to her. My eyes go red in fury as I turn to Esteban and grab his neck.

"Did you touch her?" I hiss, tightening my fingers around his throat. His eyes widen in terror, shaking his head frantically, but I squeeze tighter.

His breath comes out in short gasps, desperate for air, while his face turns crimson under my grip.

"I didn't... I swear!" he rasps, choking out the words. "My men brought her in this afternoon. She wouldn't shut up, so they roughed her up a bit, but I didn't lay a finger on her."

I release him, and he collapses onto his knees, wheezing like a dying dog. Relief washes over me knowing she wasn't violated, but that doesn't extinguish the rage burning inside me. She was locked up, beaten like some lowlife criminal. It stirs something deep, something primal.

"You've just crossed a line even I can't save you from," I growl.

"I didn't think—"

"How and why did you find her?" I cut him off, grinding my teeth. "Of what use is she to you?"

Esteban trembles, desperation leaking from his every pore. "I invested in her brother's company," he sputters. "I lost millions of dollars. I was just trying to get back at Lorenzo."

The pieces start falling into place. "You're a creditor of the Bianchi Group. You screwed me, then dumped the money into their company..."

He nods frantically, words spilling out. "I lost everything. I could have paid you back, but Lorenzo's company bled me dry. I was just trying to survive! I just wanted revenge. He took everything from me."

"Survive?" I sneer, glancing at the luxury around him. "Yet you had enough to host your whore parties. You still live well." Then it clicks. My eyes narrow. "You sent her the bomb, didn't you?"

Esteban's face goes pale, his lips trembling. "It wasn't supposed to...I just wanted to...I didn't mean to hurt—"

Too late.

With a flick of my wrist, I snap open the switchblade and plunge it into his neck. Blood spurts out, drenching my face and chest as I pull the blade free and stab him again. His body jerks violently, a sickening gurgle escaping his throat as life drains from his eyes. He slumps backward, knocking the chair over, his lifeless body sprawling on the floor. Blood pools beneath his head, dark and thick.

I stand over him, my chest heaving with the rush of anger and satisfaction. Wiping my face, I clean the blood from my hands and swap my shirt before walking out.

As I approach the car where Ginny waits, something

gnaws at me. The anger that's been driving me cools into something more dangerous—uncertainty.

Did I kill Esteban for his betrayal?

Or did I kill him for her?

13

GINEVRA

The first thing that greets me when I wake up is the soft morning light filtering through the familiar curtains of my room, a stark contrast to the sharp pain coursing through my body.

My eyes feel heavy as they flutter open, and the first thing I see is Lorenzo, sitting beside my bed. His hands are buried in his hair, distress etched across his face, and a wave of panic washes over me.

I try calling his name, but it comes out as a weak croak. That succeeds in grabbing his attention.

"Ginny!" His head snaps up, and in the next moment, he's rushing to my side. His voice is filled with concern as he gently touches my arm. "Are you okay? Do you need anything? How do you feel?" he asks urgently.

"I'm fine," I force myself to say, trying to reassure him, but my throat feels painfully dry and irritated.

He instructs one of the maids lingering nearby to fetch me a cup of water.

"What happened? How did I get here?" I ask, struggling

to piece together the events of the past day—or how long I've even been here.

Lorenzo takes a deep breath, his expression shifting to one of guilt. "I'm so sorry, Ginny," he chokes out. "I'm so sorry for everything. I should have protected you better. I should have managed my business matters more responsibly, so you weren't dragged into my mess..."

I slowly sit up, pushing my hair away from my face. "You don't have to apologize, Lorenzo. The building collapsing was never your fault. Everything that happened afterward was beyond your control."

"It is my fault, Ginny," he insists, his voice cracking. "I've made many mistakes in my life, but the most painful one was putting you in harm's way."

"Enzo..."

"Contrary to what you think, I'm not a perfect businessman," he admits, his head bowed. "I've done some questionable things to cut corners. Even though Dario's involvement made things worse, I am no saint."

I swallow hard, looking at my brother's troubled face. The worry lines on his forehead are more pronounced. His eyes are sunken with dark circles underneath. He's lost a significant amount of weight since the scandal broke.

"I'm sure none of the things you've done were things you could have avoided," I finally say. He lifts his head to meet my gaze, surprise flickering in his eyes.

"Ginny, you don't understand," he replies, his voice trembling. "I've made choices that put you in direct danger. You were almost killed! I'm not the good person you think I am. Not to you, and not to some other people I've encountered."

I reach for his hand and squeeze gently. "Lorenzo, everyone makes mistakes. Being an influential and wealthy man like yourself means you have to navigate a world full of tough decisions. It's not just black and white."

He shakes his head, a mix of frustration and sadness. "But those choices have consequences. I never wanted to drag you into this mess."

"Stop saying that!" I exhale in frustration. "You didn't drag me anywhere. You were trying to protect us. Cutting corners is part of the game in your world. I get that."

Uncertainty flickers in his eyes as he looks at me. "There are things you don't know." He sighs.

"We're family," I insist, my voice firm. "We face whatever problems we have together. Just promise me you'll be careful moving forward."

Finally, he nods. "I promise, Ginny. For you."

I smile at him, and the room falls silent for a few minutes before Lorenzo speaks up again, his tone lighter.

"Also, I'm glad you broke up with Rinaldo. I know I sound selfish when I say this, but he was of very little help to you and to our family."

I can't help but chuckle at that. "Our relationship was arranged for business purposes. Both parties knew that, so you aren't selfish for recognizing we weren't gaining anything from him. If anyone is selfish, it's him," I say, and we both laugh.

"I don't think you even liked him."

I groan. "Honestly, I tried. He's just the kind of person who keeps giving you reasons to stay away."

We laugh again. But when the laughter dies down, Lorenzo's expression shifts.

"Dario brought you home. He dealt with Esteban," he says, his voice lowered.

My heart skips a beat at the mention of Dario. "Wait, Dario? He did?"

"Yeah," Lorenzo says, his eyes narrowing slightly. "He made sure you were safe."

And that's when bits and pieces begin to return. The kidnapping, the beating I received, getting rescued by strange men, and bumping into Dario in my kidnapper's bedroom. I'd refused to look at any of them, but I saw the blood...so much blood.

"When you say Dario took care of him, did he..." I choke, unable to complete the sentence.

Lorenzo clenches his jaw. "Esteban won't be a problem for you anymore."

A breath leaves my mouth as I sink back into the bed. My mind is a whirlwind of thoughts and emotions. I feel a confusing blend of gratitude and bewilderment. For someone who claims to hate me, why would Dario deal with my threat? Even if he had his own issues with Esteban, why would he go through the trouble to rescue me and bring me home? Why would he even care?

I'm not surprised by what happened, though. Personally, even though I haven't witnessed it firsthand, I've heard enough to last a lifetime. The real darkness that lurks behind men like Dario—businessmen with Mafia ties who aren't afraid to eliminate anyone who gets in their way.

In a world like theirs, only the strongest survive and remain relevant. Dario is a cold, shadowy figure with deeper secrets that I'm not sure I want to uncover. Whatever went down between him and my brother is undoubtedly part of that darkness.

Noticing the furrow in my brow, Lorenzo sighs.

"Just rest, Ginny. Don't worry about anything right now," he urges, getting on his feet.

I look at his face again, and I can't shake the feeling that there's something else he's not telling me—something important. I don't press the issue, though. I can see the sadness in his eyes, and I know he still feels guilty for everything that's gone wrong.

After Lorenzo leaves the room, I take a moment to collect my thoughts. After a few minutes, I retrieve my phone from the bedside table to send Dario a quick text to thank him.

"Hey. This is Ginny. I just wanted to say thanks for bringing me home. I appreciate it."

His reply comes almost instantly. *"No problem."*

It feels cold, distant. I don't know what I expected, but I can't shake the feeling of disappointment. I decide to push back, trying to lighten the mood.

"You know, you could be a little nicer. Do you think you can manage that?"

My heart races as I wait for his response.

A moment passes before his reply arrives.

"There are so many things I'd be willing to do for you, Princess. Being nice isn't one of them."

My breath hitches, and I pull my lower lip between my teeth.

"Why are you so crude?"

"Maybe I just like seeing you squirm."

I grin, feeling a flutter of excitement. *"Is that all? I thought you cared."*

"I thought you denied being a stalker. How did you get my number?"

A chuckle escapes me, and I have to remind myself that I shouldn't like Dario. Yes, he saved me, but that's all.

"My brother, obviously," I text back, adding an eye-roll emoji.

I wait for his response. One minute. Two. Five.

"I have to go."

I stare at my screen, disappointment snaking through my chest.

Yeah, no. I'm definitely reading too much into this.

Shaking my head, I decide to take it easy for the rest of the day. I get up from the bed and head to the theater room —a part of Lorenzo's house I rarely visit—hoping a movie will distract me.

An hour into the romantic comedy, my phone buzzes with a new text. I glance at the screen and see a message from an old friend. Well, I wouldn't exactly call her a friend. We attended the same private high school and run in similar circles. She's always had a competitive edge and enjoyed poking fun at others. Unfortunately, I bump into her often, and we just sort of have each other's contact information.

"Congrats, girl! Although I'll say this came as quite a surprise," it reads.

Confused, I try to reply, but more congratulatory messages start pouring in. My heart races as I scroll through my notifications, each one leaving me more confused and panicked than the last.

When I read one of them that congratulates me on my engagement, my heart drops.

"What's happening?" I mutter, sitting up and deciding to go online.

I already ended my engagement with Rinaldo. If that fucker tried something stupid...

All breath leaves my lungs when I see an article announcing my "upcoming marriage." Panic sets in as I read the headline:

"GINEVERA BIANCHI, SISTER TO CONSTRUCTION MOGUL LORENZO BIANCHI, ENGAGED TO CONGLOMERATE OWNER, DARIO DE LUCA."

"What?!"

This has to be a mistake. Who would spread false rumors like this?

I dig deeper, frantically searching for more articles. That's when I see the photos of Dario and me leaving the club together that night plastered all over the internet.

My mind spins, and I can't breathe. How did this happen? Why didn't anyone tell me?

Lorenzo.

I shoot up from my seat, rushing out of the room to catch Lorenzo before he leaves the house. My heart pounds with a mix of urgency and frustration. When I burst into the living room, I find Lorenzo, but my anger quickly fades when I see *him*.

Dario is lounging on the sofa, his posture relaxed yet commanding. His dark suit and coat highlights his broad shoulders and muscular build. His emerald, green eyes are sharp and intense, like polished gemstones, and his dark hair falls in messy waves over his forehead.

The slight smirk on his chiseled face adds to his cold, intimidating presence —an enigma that draws you in while warning you to stay away.

The tension in the room is thick. Every glance between us is charged. I can't shake the feeling that what I'm about to hear is something I'd very much rather avoid.

"Ginny," Lorenzo says, concern evident in his voice as he notices my expression.

Before I can respond, Dario's eyes meet mine, his smirk widening. "Ah, she wakes," he says, his voice smooth with a dangerous allure.

The way he says it, with that knowing look, sends a shiver down my spine. I feel a rush of anger, fear, and, more intensely, a deep, searing hatred.

"What the hell is going on?" I demand, my voice trembling despite my attempt to sound firm.

My breath catches in my throat as I turn back to look at Lorenzo, my heart racing with fear and anticipation. This is not going to end well.

14

DARIO

I lean back in my chair, relishing the drama that is about to unfold. Ginny's eyes lock onto mine, darkening with pure rage before she turns to her brother, her face a storm of disbelief and fury.

For once, her anger isn't solely directed at me. Well, that's not true. I can tell it's building up, set to explode once she grasps the full scope of the situation.

She's fuming, her eyes blazing as she storms towards Lorenzo. And she looks so fucking beautiful.

Her hair is wild around her face, and her body vibrates with energy as she gets in his face. Right now, her hazel eyes are a vivid green, flecked with hints of brown and gold, matching her intense fury.

"You arranged this, didn't you?" she snaps at Lorenzo, her voice sharp and filled with betrayal as she shoves her phone screen in his face. "You actually think I'll marry him?"

The mixture of shame and guilt on Lorenzo's face fills me with dark satisfaction. I have to bite my lip to keep from laughing. Last night, I offered Lorenzo a deal he couldn't refuse. I agreed to pay off all their debts and even lend them enough to get their company back on track, but there was a catch—Ginny has to marry me.

As Ginny stands before him, demanding an answer, I see the wheels turning in his mind. Regret, embarrassment, and remorse are thick in his eyes, but he knows he has no choice. There's no going back now.

The deal he signed is ironclad—if Ginny files for divorce before a decade elapses, I'll retract the funds, leaving them in worse debt than they ever were in. But after ten years, she's free to go. I also made sure Lorenzo signed over the rights of the Bianchi Empire, naming me the sole investor with the highest bid and effectively preventing any other company from legally intervening.

The plan was a strategic play, ensuring no escape for the Bianchi family.

Last night, as I dropped Ginny off, a flicker of guilt crept in. Yes, Lorenzo's greed was behind the kidnapping and the murder attempt, but I played a part in escalating things. If Ginny had been seriously hurt, I would have felt responsible, and that thought left a bitter taste in my mouth.

Yet, despite that guilt, I feel an unexpected protectiveness toward Ginny. Seeing her bound and hurt solidified my resolve to end the Bianchi family's torment, even though I still crave revenge. What better way to seek it than by marrying her, the one person Lorenzo would never let me be involved with under normal circumstances?

"Ginny..." Lorenzo chokes, unable to form a coherent sentence. "It's not like that."

"Oh my god," she gasps, her eyes glistening with thick emotions. "You actually arranged this. A part of me hoped you would deny it...that you'd say it was all his doing."

I roll my eyes as she points an accusing finger at me.

Lorenzo shifts uncomfortably, shame heavy on his face. "Ginny, you don't understand everything. I'm doing this to protect you."

"Protect me?" she echoes incredulously, her hands clenched at her sides. "I'm not a child you can lie to, Lorenzo. If this is your idea of protection, then...well, I don't know what to tell you, Enzo. This is a fucking prison sentence. You've sold me to him!"

"That's ridiculous, Ginny," Lorenzo scoffs, trying to save face.

I can't help but smirk at the spectacle. The tension in the room is thick, and I enjoy watching them squabble. Lorenzo, for all his bravery, looks cornered. He runs a hand through his hair, pacing like a caged animal.

"No! You're the one being ridiculous here," she screeches. "What did he promise you? Money? Protection? Did he blackmail you? Is that why you decided to sell your sister off like a piece of property?"

"Look at our situation," he says, voice rising. "We're drowning in debt, and Dario is the only one willing to help us."

"So it was for money?" She chuckles harshly. "I guess some things never change. Pimping me off to Rinaldo didn't work, so you found the next man willing..."

"You think I want this?" Lorenzo yelled. "We have no other choice!"

"Maybe you should have thought of that before making deals with the devil," Ginny fires back, her voice trembling with anger. "I won't be a pawn in your game, Lorenzo."

"Ginny, please," he pleads, desperation creeping into his tone.

I lean in slightly. "You know, Ginny, you don't exactly

have a choice in the matter," I say, my voice dripping with amusement. "The contract has already been signed."

She whips around to face me, eyes blazing. "I will never marry you, Dario!"

Her words send laughter spilling from my lips. The sound bounces through the walls, and her nostrils flare as her anger intensifies.

"Is that so?" I challenge, my smirk fading as I step closer, closing the distance. A rush of adrenaline courses through me as I feel her heat and inhale her scent.

She raises her chin, defiance and anger strong in her features. "You're a piece of shit, Dario. Forcing my brother into signing whatever this is? That's a new low, even for someone as despicable as you!"

Every sliver of amusement drops as I take another step toward her.

Without turning back to look at Lorenzo, I order, "Leave us."

The tone of my voice leaves no room for argument, and he hesitates before reluctantly walking toward the front door.

As the door clicks shut. I step closer to Ginny. "What did you just say? Repeat it," I demand, my voice low and intense.

She stands her ground. "You're nothing but a bully."

"Bully?" I scoff, stepping even closer. "I'm offering your shitty family a way out, and you treat it like a curse? This is the thanks I get? You should know better than to speak that way to someone who clearly holds your future—and your family's—in his hands."

"And you should know by now that I'm not scared of you," she hisses as I continue to advance toward her.

"Really? Maybe you should be."

A flicker of uncertainty crosses her eyes as she sees that

I'm not stopping. She moves back as I march forward. Her eyes dart to the wall behind her, and knowing that she's about to be cornered, she dashes to the corner.

That's before I grab her elbow and pull her right where I want her.

"Let me go," she fumes as I press her back against the wall and position myself directly before her.

"You know, you could be a little nicer," I snarl, repeating her message from earlier. "Do you think you can manage that, Princess?"

"Fuck you, Dario," her chest rises and falls.

I'm hit with a thick sense of Deja vu. How many times have I had her close? Felt her warm breath against my skin? Heard her heartbeat thumping beneath her skin, and resisted the urge to kiss every inch of her body? How many times have our arguments turned into heated conversations and restrained lust?

"You shouldn't say those words to me, Ginny," I rasp, brushing her cheeks with the back of my fingers. "It always gets me so fucking hard."

Her breath catches as her lips part slightly, but she says nothing. She says nothing, staring up at me with eyes filled with a mix of anger and something else—something deeper and more intense. It's a gaze reserved just for me, one that can only be found in the darkest corners of her eyes, hidden within the depths of her soul.

My heart pounds faster as I lean down, my gaze never leaving hers, watching each of the minute expressions flicker across her face, trying to capture them all on paper and memorizing their nuances so I don't forget a single thing about her.

The deep flush on her cheeks, the pink tinge to her lips,

the way her long eyelashes flutter with desire as my face hovers directly over hers.

A small gasp escapes from her parted lips when I slide my hands along her waist, pulling her closer to me. Her breasts brush against my chest, and I inhale sharply when I feel her hardened nipples through my shirt.

"You claim you hate me, yet you respond to my touch," I murmur, leaning down to kiss her exposed shoulder. "Your body always reacts to me," I add, sucking gently on the soft spot between her shoulder blades.

She shudders under my mouth, and the soft gasp that escapes her mouth sends warmth down to my dick.

The anger in her eyes is still palpable, but so is the undeniable lust and tension between us. My heart raves with the primal urge to press my lips against hers, taste the passion on her tongue, and hold her firmly while she trembles from the pleasure I could give her.

"You don't get to decide my future." She breathes heavily.

Gritting my teeth, I pull away from her, forcing myself to take several steps backwards and create some distance.

"Actually, I do," I reply, my tone firm. "Starting now, as a matter of fact. You're moving into my house tomorrow. Get your things ready."

Her mouth drops open in shock, her eyes narrowing as she struggles to find words. I tug at my tie, feeling the fabric constrict around my throat. The silence stretches, thick with simmering tension.

I can't shake the feeling that this isn't just about revenge anymore—there's something deeper at play. As I watch her, I see the fading bruises on her arms, and anger surges within me once more. The thought of Esteban's hands on her makes my blood boil, and I wish I could make him suffer endlessly.

"Since you have no objections—"

"I won't be moving in with you," she exclaims.

I pull at my tie again, the tightness serving as a reminder of my resolve. "And I won't repeat myself. Be packed and ready by tomorrow. Or I swear to god, I'll make you regret it."

The finality in my voice leaves no room for argument, but her eyes blaze with a mix of defiance and hurt. Her chest rises and falls with each heavy breath as I turn to leave.

I can't shake the feeling that what's coming next is going to be deeper and more intense. As the door closes behind me, I wonder what our next encounter will bring, knowing it could change everything.

15

GINEVRA

I glance out the tinted windows as the car glides through the quiet streets of the upscale suburb where Dario lives.

Large, modern houses with wide verandas stand in a row along the street, their owners' expensive cars parked outside. Tall oak trees shade the roads, adding beauty to the neighborhood.

Now that I'm really looking at it, the environment is peaceful and serene, away from all the noise and bustle of the city. I can't believe someone like Dario lives in a place like this. I always thought people—entitled brutes—like Dario thrived in the chaos and turmoil of the urban world. It makes no sense for him to live here.

The last time I was here, it was under very different circumstances. Just over a week ago, I'd come to confront Dario about a statement he'd released to the press. Now, I'm being driven to his house with all my belongings in the trunk. It feels like a nightmare.

After our argument yesterday, he stationed bodyguards around Lorenzo's house to make sure I didn't leave. Early this morning, he sent a car with his men to inform me that he wanted me and all my things brought to his house before noon. The man is a total psychopath.

My mind wanders as the houses zap past on either side of the car. The dull pain that has refused to leave my chest returns in full force as the memory of Lorenzo's betrayal returns.

It stings that my brother chose to save the company by selling me off to the very man he's been enemies with for years. I can't fathom how he thought this was a solution. With the business on the brink of collapse, he must have felt he had no choice or options. But selling me like this? It's a betrayal that cuts deep.

I stare out the window, watching the scenery blur into streaks of green and gold as I'm driven farther into the estate like a lamb being led to be slaughtered.

After hours of pleading and trying to reason with Lorenzo—begging him to back out or find some sort of loophole in whatever contract he signed with Dario—I reluctantly accepted my fate.

Soon, Dario and I will be married, bound by a contract that leaves me with no way out on my own terms. We'll be stuck together for ten years. This isn't just a marriage—it's a literal prison.

My heart feels heavy, and I'm not in the mood for the small talk the driver attempts. Instead, my thoughts spiral into the uncertainty of what lay ahead living under Dario's roof, at his mercy. I clench my fists in my lap, willing myself to stay calm.

When we finally slow down in front of the familiar black gates, I take a deep breath. Security lets us in, and the car slips into the compound. I look around, taking in the beautiful architecture and the well-maintained gardens surrounding the house.

The house stands tall and imposing, its modern design casting shadows in the bright afternoon sun. The car comes to a stop, and I am brought out of my reverie when one of Dario's men who followed closely in a car behind us comes to open my door. My feet land firmly on the ground as I climb out, following his lead toward the steps leading up to the front door.

As I approach, I realize just how big this place is. We enter through the large doors, and I notice three uniformed house staff standing by the door with their arms behind their backs.

An elderly woman steps forward, greeting me with a warm smile.

"You must be Miss Ginevra Bianchi. I know you prefer Ginny," she says softly. "Welcome, ma'am."

Even though I hate that I'm here, I can't deny the warm atmosphere surrounding the house. "You can call me Rosa," she says with a smile. "Don has told me so much about you. Come, dear, let me show you around."

I bite my tongue to prevent me from asking her what he told her or why she calls him Don. Instead, I follow her in silence as she leads me through the house. It feels even bigger inside, with soft lighting highlighting the elegant decor.

"This is the living room," Rosa says, gesturing to a large space filled with plush furniture and tasteful art. I can't help but admire the way the light plays off the surfaces. She continues pointing out other features as she leads me through the hallways, stopping at intervals to show me different rooms.

We climb the stairs, and she shows me three of the four

bedrooms in the house. As we reach a point halfway down the hallway, she points to a door at the end of the corridor.

"That's the don's room," Rosa says softly, her voice soothing, like a balm on my raw nerves. "I've been instructed to take your things there."

When I stay silent, she continues, a twinkle in her eye. "Don't worry. He isn't back yet. You know how busy he is."

I ignore her knowing look. Does she realize I'm being forced into this situation, or does she genuinely believe Dario and I are in a loving relationship?

"Don?" I ask, unsure what else to say.

"Yes, that's what we all call him." She chuckles, and I can't help but smile at her warmth.

"I'll leave you now," she says after a moment. "Call me if you need anything."

"Actually," I blurt out before she walks away, "I'd like my things taken to another room."

If Dario thinks being his fiancée means agreeing to everything he wants, he's in for a shock.

Rosa's eyes widen slightly, but she maintains a polite smile. "Of course. I'll arrange to have them moved immediately. You can choose one of the other rooms."

"Thank you," I say, returning her smile.

As she heads downstairs, I walk toward the room farthest from Dario's bedroom. I push the door open and stand in the doorway, taking in the simple but elegant decor. Soft colors and a large window overlooking a neatly trimmed garden greet me. I step inside and sit on the edge of the bed, staring blankly at the opposite wall, trying to process everything.

The thought of Dario marrying me as part of his revenge scheme feels twisted. Memories resurface of him and Lorenzo, once inseparable, laughing and playing football in our yard. I must have been five or six, while they were about seventeen. Back then, I imagined they'd be best friends for life. So what had happened? How had things gotten this bad?

Lorenzo refuses to tell me what went wrong, and I can't help but wonder what he's hiding. A low groan escapes as I fall back onto the bed, my eyes drifting up to the ceiling.

A knot tightens in my stomach as I replay our last conversation—the one before he left, and Dario's men arrived to pack my things.

"Ginny, we could lose Papa's company for good if you don't do this," Lorenzo had said, his voice heavy with pain and exhaustion. *"I'm heading to the estate in Italy next week to discuss this with the rest of the family. So far, they don't have any objections; as usual, they only care about their pockets and the family investment. But what about our young cousins, our elders? Are we really going to let those who come after us grow up without a legacy? They'll be a laughingstock, and Papa will hunt me down from his grave."*

His words echo in my mind, slicing deeper with each repetition. I want to scream at him, to tell him how much I resent the choice he's forcing upon me. But as much as I'd rather do anything else, I can't let the Bianchi legacy crumble—not when I have the chance to save it.

Even though I'm still furious with him for practically selling me off, I would do anything for my brother. He's all I have. He's struggled for years, trying to live up to the impossible expectations Papa left behind. He's taken the blame for every misstep, shouldering it all.

"I hate this, Enzo! I hate that I'm being sold off to that jerk like some pawn! You're not even considering what this will do to me!"

"I know it's unfair, Ginny," he'd replied, pain etching his

features. "But think of everything that's at stake. I can't shoulder this burden alone. You're my sister, and you're all I have left. We can't let our family name die because of this."

I'm beyond tired when I finally relax into the bed, closing my eyes in a futile attempt to escape reality. I pull the blankets tightly around me, but sleep evades me. My mind swirls with thoughts of what my new life will entail.

What will I lose if I go through with this? My dreams, my autonomy, my chance to choose love over obligation? The thought of surrendering to a life predetermined for me makes my heart ache.

Will I have any freedom? Will Dario attempt to control me the way Rinaldo did?

What do you think, Ginny? my inner voice mocks.

Of course he will.

A frustrated sigh escapes my lips. The man expects me to share a bedroom with him. We can't even be in the same room without arguing. The thought of sharing a bed with Dario makes me cringe, yet a shiver of intrigue runs down my spine. I wonder what it would feel like to have his body pressed against mine, his hands sliding over my hips, pulling my back to meet his front...

Okay, let's not go there.

I blow out a breath, turning to face the wall. A yawn escapes me. I'd gotten up early to pack my things from Lorenzo's house. Though Dario's men had come to handle the job, I'd insisted on packing my personal belongings myself before they'd loaded everything into the car.

Eventually, exhaustion wins, and I drift into a restless sleep filled with fragmented dreams of dark hair and emerald green eyes.

When I wake hours later, my throat is parched. It's dark

outside, and I wonder how long I've slept. I push myself up, rub my eyes, and decide to take a quick shower.

Like every other part of this house, the bathroom is lavish, with a marble floor that sparkles under the harsh fluorescent lighting. An inviting bath sits in the center of the room, and I long to sink into it.

Shaking my head, I undress before walking over to the shower. After a warm shower, I change into more comfortable clothes before deciding to go find some water in the kitchen. As I tiptoe down the unfamiliar hallway, I can't help the chill of fear that travels down my spine. I'm not necessarily scared of the dark, but I'm not used to this house, and the shadows creeping along the walls make me feel like I'm in a strange, unfamiliar world.

Soft light illuminates the staircase. I carefully descend and head toward the kitchen. The house is eerily quiet, and I assume all the domestic staff have retired for the night. A part of me wonders if they live here as is the case for most wealthy people.

I turn into the kitchen, and the sight before me stops me in my tracks. Dario stands there, his back to me, raising a bottle of water to his lips.

And he's shirtless.

16

DARIO

Leaning against the cool granite countertop in the kitchen, I try to calm the storm inside me. The faint hum of the refrigerator fills the silence as I take a sip of water, the cold liquid barely quenching the heat rising in my chest.

It's past 10 pm. I stayed at the office longer than I should have, trying to prepare myself for this moment—coming home to meet my new fiancée.

Being under the same roof with Ginny and having to see her every day will be more torture for me than I'd intended it to be for her. The few heated moments we've shared in the past haven't left my memory. How much more now when I can't avoid her presence?

I don't want to avoid her presence.

I want to make her squirm. I want her to feel every bit of discomfort that she causes me. I want her to spend her days unable to stop thinking about me and her nights sleeping right beside me, the man she hates the most.

Oh, I take pleasure in seeing her pretty face flush with anger, wishing I could be obliterated from existence.

I thought if I spent more time in the office preparing for this moment, I could control my reactions when she walked into the same space. But now, as she steps into the kitchen, I feel that control slipping away.

I feel Ginny's presence behind me even before seeing her. I hear the moment she enters the kitchen, her soft footsteps padding along the floor. I know the exact moment she spots me—her sharp intake of breath gives it away. I resist the strong urge to turn, to look at the face of the woman I'm going to marry, the woman who has consumed my every passing thought.

The faint scent of vanilla wafts into the kitchen, wrapping around me like a soft cocoon as she walks past me. I clench my teeth when her arm brushes against me.

And that's when I see her.

My breath catches in my throat. She looks as if she just stepped out of a steamy shower, her hair slightly damp, droplets glistening as they slide down her neck. The skimpy nightdress she wears clings to her curves in a way that makes it impossible to look away.

My pulse quickens, and I grip the water bottle tighter, trying to maintain my composure. The plastic crumples in my strong hands, the sound echoing in the silence between us.

Warning bells ring in my head as I watch her. It seems like each time I see her, she dresses skimpier than the last, except the day she was found in Esteban's house. The neckline of her nightgown dips so low that the tops of her cleavage are on display, the sheer lace hem resting just above her nipples. I see the outline of her medium perky tits, and I bite back a groan as they jiggle with each movement she makes.

Completely ignoring my presence, she heads straight for the fridge, her back to me, and pulls out a bottle of water. My eyes zero in on the curve of her ass as she bends, conjuring up dirty images of all the things I want to do to her.

I can't tear my eyes away, admiring the way her body moves, her nightgown hugging her in all the right places, leaving nothing to the imagination. It's infuriating...and intoxicating.

My throat suddenly feels dry again. I take another large swig out of my bottle, my gaze resting solely on Ginny as she unscrews the cap of her water bottle and mirrors my movement.

She tilts the bottle back, taking a long drink. The way her throat moves, the slight arch of her back as she drinks— it sends a rush of heat through me, straight to my dick. My control wavers, teetering on the edge of snapping.

When she's done drinking, she wipes her mouth with the back of her hand, discards the empty bottle, and starts to leave the kitchen.

"I haven't officially welcomed you to your new home, Ginny," I say before she exits.

I smirk when she halts in her tracks and turns to look at me. She's so easy to provoke. I know she's still fuming about the arrangement, so I'm sure anything related to it will get a rise out of her.

Her eyes come up to meet mine, and I see the anger simmering just beneath the surface. I fold my arms across my chest, and I see something flicker in her eyes as she watches the movement. The look disappears almost immediately, her steely gaze returning.

"I'm sure Rosa has given you a tour," I continue before

she can speak. "Very nice woman, isn't she? I hope you're comfortable with the arrangements I've made."

"Comfortable?" she huffs, and fuck, I missed the sound of her voice.

In this short moment, I realize I hate it when she's not talking to me. I hate it when she ignores my presence.

"Mm-hmm," I hum, slipping my hands into the pockets of my sweatpants. "Although you seem to enjoy making things difficult. I already arranged for us to share the master bedroom, but you decided to move your things to the guest room instead."

"You're sicker than I thought if you think I'll ever sleep in the same bed as you," she spits, her voice sharp.

I take a step closer to her, my smirk widening. "I'll remind you of this when you're finally sleeping on the same bed as me."

A humorless chuckle escapes her lips. "You're enjoying this, aren't you? You love making my life miserable so much that you'd force me to marry you, even though it's the last thing I want, and you know it'll make me completely miserable!"

Maybe it's the way she says it, her voice hard and thick with emotion, but it dissolves every atom of amusement in me, leaving only irritation behind.

"You know, you could show me a little more gratitude for saving your life," I say, taking a step toward her. She remains rooted to her spot, her unwavering gaze piercing into mine.

"Gratitude?" She scoffs, her eyes blazing.

"Yes. You know, a little thank you to me for the fact that you're still alive and standing here today talking back at me," I say sarcastically.

Her eyes flash. "Oh, so now I should be completely indebted to you because you took me from Esteban's house?

"Yes," I snap, my irritation bubbling over. "I saved your life, Ginny! Do you even realize the kind of man he was? Do you know what he would have done to you?"

She crosses her arms over her chest, her expression defiant. I'm almost distracted by the way it makes her boobs almost spill out of her dress.

"And what about what you're doing to me now? Coercing my brother into signing this arrangement? Forcing me to not just marry you but to also move in with you," she seethes. "This isn't saving me. It's a prison!"

The tension between us thickens as I step closer to her. "You don't get it, do you?" I say, my voice low. "I didn't bring you here just because I'm the villain you believe I am. I want to keep you safe."

"Safe?" she challenges, her voice dripping with bitterness. "Is this your idea of safety? Trapping me in a house with my captor?"

"As opposed to what?" I shoot back. "Living your whole life in fear? First, you were almost killed by a bomb explosion. Then you were kidnapped. Do you know what would have happened if I hadn't rescued you that night? What Esteban would have done to you?" I take a deep breath, trying to steady myself. "You could at least show some fucking gratitude. I didn't have to intervene. I could have walked away."

"Oh my god, Dario, you're my hero. Thank you so much for saving me from that scary man Esteban. I would have been dead if it wasn't for you." Thick sarcasm drips from her high-pitched voice, and I grind my teeth as my own anger builds.

"Is that why you're marrying me? So that every morning when I wake up, I will thank you for saving me and giving me the privilege to live before doing anything else for the day."

My hands are balled into fists as I try to control my anger. She continues, not caring that her voice is loud. None of my housekeepers sleep in my house, but Ginny doesn't know that. That only means she wants everyone in the house, especially my housekeepers, to hear whatever she has to say.

"You claim to be such a good person by rescuing me, but this single act of forcing me to marry you cancels out every good thing you think you've done," she screeches.

I remain silent, and that only seems to infuriate her.

"I've never known you as a good person, but going to these lengths just to get revenge on my brother is just inhumane." Her voice cracks slightly as she spits.

I feel a nerve snap in my head, and at this point, I'm livid.

"Go to your room, Ginny," I bark, done with her tantrum for the day.

But she's far from finished.

"Why? Is that how much you hate hearing the truth?" she spits, staring directly into my eyes before adding. "The truth, they say, is bitter."

I decide to ignore her. She's looking for a reaction, trying to hurt me as much as my actions have hurt her.

However, my patience snaps when I hear her next words.

"Your parents would be ashamed of how you turned out..."

In a flash, I'm right in front of her, cornering her against the counter.

"Repeat what you just said, Ginny," I snarl, my fingers twitching to grab something. "I fucking dare you."

I hear the slight hitch in her throat as I pin her with a heavy gaze. Her eyes waver slightly before hardening.

"I said your parents would be ashamed..."

Her words are cut off as I yank her roughly toward me and slam my lips against hers.

17

GINEVRA

The moment Dario's lips meet mine; every thought leaves my mind and my body. The kiss happens so fast that I barely register it happening at first. But seconds later, I feel him everywhere.

Every nerve ending in my body ignites into fire. My stomach flips, my head spins, and when one of his hands comes to circle around my neck, my control snaps, and I'm kissing him back as if my life depends on it.

His mouth moves over mine with such hunger and desperation that it has me clutching his shoulders. Our tongues glide over each other in an erotic dance. He tastes like whiskey, mint, and a hint of cigarettes that leaves me wanting to taste more.

I feel everything he does, the way his tongue flicks out over my lower lip, the hard pressure of his fingers pressing into my scalp, the gentle tugging on the hair at the nape of my neck as he draws me even closer. His free hand roams across my body. He brushes the side of my breasts and glides past my waist until it finds my ass. As he grabs the flesh and squeezes, I make a small sound in my throat.

When his tongue flicks out to lick the seam of my bottom lip, a whimper escapes me. He presses harder against me, pinning me against the edge of the countertop, and I can't help but groan.

He hisses as I slide my hands down to his chest, my palms flat against the warm skin.

"We shouldn't be doing this," I say in between his drugging kisses.

"Fuck no, we shouldn't," Dario breathes as he presses kisses down my neck. "Just like I shouldn't be this obsessed with you." He drags his teeth over the sensitive skin on the side of my neck, making me gasp breathlessly. "I shouldn't crave your body like I crave air."

I feel his erection digging into my stomach, and it makes me bite my lower lip to stop another moan. When his hands caress my sides and then slip under my dress, I know I have no willpower left to stop us. My panties are already soaked, and my pussy throbs in anticipation.

"You want this too, Princess," he whispers against my ear as he presses his hips against me. His voice sounds husky and raspy, almost unrecognizable coming from his own mouth. "Don't you?"

I'm biting my lip so hard that I might draw blood. I close my eyes tightly to stop the sensations coursing through me. But the desire, the wanton need...it's all too much.

Suddenly, he pulls back, and I almost whine at the loss of contact. Then he leans his forehead against mine, his breathing heavy and uneven. "I asked you a question, Ginny," he rasps.

I stare into his deep green eyes, and the lust simmering beneath his orbs makes them glow like polished emerald.

When his hand travels further to caress the edge of my panties, my breath hitches.

"Tell me to stop," he whispers, one finger skirting dangerously close to my drenched core.

My breath leaves my lips in a woosh. "And you stop trying to use reverse psychology on me," I hiss.

One side of his lips pulls up, and it strikes me how dangerously beautiful he is. He looks like sin, like every woman's dark fantasy.

When his hand cups my pussy fully, every thought of opposing him vanishes from my mind.

"Fuck, Ginny," he groans, his second hand digging into my waist as if he's restraining himself. "Tell me to stop right now."

I close my eyes and dig my fingers into his shoulders as one finger slips under my drenched panties, brushing over my sensitive skin.

"Don't stop," I moan.

At the simple command, he crushes his lips against mine again. A rush of sensation surges through my whole body, setting off fireworks inside my belly. A shudder runs through me as two fingers slip into my slick entrance.

"Dario," I moan, sliding my hands up to clutch his hair.

"That's it," he says against my lips, moving at a torturous pace inside me. "Don't fight it."

I kiss him hard, pouring all my anger, frustration, and desire into the dance of our tongues. Pulling his bottom lip between my teeth, I tug. "This does not change anything between us."

"No, it doesn't," he rasps as his fingers sink deeper inside me.

I roll my hips against his hand as his thumb brushes over my sensitive clit. "Fuck... look at you making a mess all over my fingers," he groans deeply.

I roll my hips again, not caring that I'm practically riding his hand. And he's watching me with hooded eyes, his face flushed with passion. His pupils are dilated, making his eyes glow even brighter. He looks like an angel, a devil, a Greek god.

I throw my head back as he curves his fingers inside me, hitting a different angle.

"Oh Dario," I grunt, pulling his hair tighter as I ride his fingers harder.

His other hand grabs one of my breasts and squeezes firmly, making my head burst with pleasure. "Yes, that feels good," I sigh, my hips grinding against him. "So fucking good."

I grab onto his shoulders and thrust myself against him faster and faster while he slides his fingers deeper inside me. "Dario...oh yes..."

"Mmm, fuck...are you going to cum all over my fingers, Ginny?"

"Yes," I moan as the pressure builds higher and higher and higher...

A sharp exhale leaves my lips as Dario pulls his fingers away from me. My eyes snap open, a retort dancing on the tip of my tongue. But then he slips his fingers into my mouth. Fuck. My pussy clenches as I suck on my juices, swirling my tongue over his thick fingers that were just inside me. His eyes darken to a dangerous shade, and I catch the flex of his jaw as he watches me. He pulls his fingers out of my mouth, making a pop sound.

And then he sinks onto his knees before me.

Just when I think he can't get any sexier, he looks up at me like a predator hunting its prey. "Grab the edge of the counters."

Somehow, the rough timbre of his command makes me

even wetter. My fingers grab the edge of the marble countertop firmly as he pulls one leg over his shoulders.

"I want to taste you, Ginny," he whispers, pushing my nightgown up to my waist and running his nose down to my soaking pussy. "I've wanted this since the moment I saw you at that ball. Those faded blue jeans you wore that night...they've been seared into my memory ever since."

A sharp, tearing sound cuts through the stillness of the room as he rips the delicate lace of my panties, the flimsy fabric giving way under his touch.

"I think about you obsessively, Ginny. I'm so completely consumed by you that I can't even sleep at night without losing myself in thoughts of you. Jerking off to the thought of you, imagining every single thing I want to do and say when next I see you," he confesses, his voice low and raw.

His breath hitches as it fans over my wet core, and I can feel my body responding, tightening, as my arousal intensifies.

"So wet for me," he murmurs, licking the wetness that slid down my thighs as he moves up to my pussy.

It's all too erotic, too dirty...I like it very much.

When his tongue finally meets my wet folds, I cry out loudly. The heat radiating from the center of my body, spreading throughout my limbs, fills me to my very core. He sucks on my clit, teasing me with his tongue, his hot breath tickling my inner thighs. His tongue laps hungrily, and one of his hands grabs my ass to drag me further into him.

Fuck...he's eating me out like he's been hungry for years. And it feels too good.

He alternates between licking and sucking until my thighs begin to quiver and I'm reaching down to grab the back of his head. I roll my hips against him, feeling tingles all down to the tips of my toes.

"That's it, baby. Ride my face like the dirty girl you are," he groans.

His rough voice sends me over the edge, and soon, he's holding me tightly as my body convulses uncontrollably. He doesn't stop his relentless licking and sucking until I'm completely spent, moaning his name like a wounded animal in its final throes.

Carefully placing my leg down, he stands up. The sight of my juices coating his smirking mouth will be forever imprinted in my memory.

"Are you okay?" he asks, his voice a low rumble. I nod, feeling a sudden wave of shyness. It's the first time I've ever been brought to orgasm like that, and the experience was astonishing. But I'd rather leap off a cliff than admit it to him.

"Tired?" he murmurs with a smirk, his finger trailing gently down my cheek.

I suddenly feel the urge to wipe that smug grin off his face.

"No," I purr, sliding my hands down the hard muscles of his chest.

His eyes dance dangerously as they watch me. And when I lean in to kiss one hardened nipple, he lets out a low hiss. I drag my teeth over the skin surrounding it, flicking the tip with my tongue.

One of his hands plants on my hip, squeezing tightly. I trail my kisses down to the center of his stomach, kissing his abs slowly until I get to a scar just by the side of his bellybutton.

"Stab wound," he grounds out as I look up at him.

Still looking into his eyes, I trail my tongue over the ridge and line of the scar, wondering if there were any more and confirming the proof that he was a man tortured by demons. Now, I plan to make him forget.

Sliding my hands to the waistband of his sweatpants, I slowly pull the fabric down, revealing a hard cock glistening with precum. My pussy throbs as I take his hard girth in my hands.

"Fuck, Ginny," he hisses, his fingers digging painfully into my hips.

"Did eating my pussy make you this hard?" I whisper, trailing my fingers over the sides of his shaft.

His breathing has quickened, his eyes glazed with lust as he slides his hand to the back of my head.

"Yes. Now, get on your knees and take my cock in your mouth."

I hate it when he tells me what to do, but somehow, his rough command fills me with exhilaration, sending shivers down my spine. Without sparing another second, I sink to my knees before him, taking his sweatpants down with me.

When they pool at his ankles, I wrap both of my hands around his length. It's so big, so long, and so warm. My mouth waters in anticipation of his taste.

As the first lick of my tongue to his tip, his arms flex and clench. I kiss the glistening tip slowly, lightly dragging my teeth along the smooth skin.

"Ginny," he warns, tightening his grip on my head. "Stop teasing."

I hum softly in agreement before taking him into my mouth. We both moan together at my first taste of him. Then, inch by inch, I take him in deeper.

There is nothing soft about his cock. It's blunt and hard, pulsating against my walls as he continues to tighten his hold on my hair. I pull back and take him back in, one of my hands holding his hip for support. I swallow him whole, reveling in every single delicious inch of his hot flesh.

"Fuck, Ginevra," he rasps, and I feel the heat of his gaze as he looks down at me. "Look at me, baby."

I obey his command, my body shivering at the nickname. I love all his nicknames for me, but my favorite is when he says my name with that deep rasp of his. My body feels as if it's on fire, burning from the inside as his fingers come down to stroke my cheeks. He pulls the tip of his dick out of my mouth before pushing back inside.

I moan around the fullness, pressing my thighs together to relieve the pressure throbbing in my center.

"Are you getting turned on sucking my cock, Ginny?" he asks in a low groan.

I moan my answer, pushing him deeper to sink into my mouth. I suck hard. Harder than I ever had before. His gruff moans make my toes curl. I love it when men moan. I love the power it gives me, the rush it sends through my veins.

But just when I think I'm in control, he grabs the back of my head with his two hands.

"I'm going to fuck your mouth, baby," he warns. Well, I don't take it as a warning. My pussy throbs even harder, and I feel my slick juices sliding down my thighs. "And you're going to take every inch of it."

I moan as he begins to move his hips, slowly at first. His girth stretches me, making tears pool at the corners of my eyes. As my hands come down to caress his balls, something snaps within him, and soon, he's thrusting into my mouth. Every time his cock hits the back of my throat, I moan, his salty taste making me crave more.

"Fuck, baby," he rasps, holding my face in place to keep me still as he drives into me. Each stroke is harder than the last. Faster. More forceful. "You love it when I fuck your mouth, don't you?"

I moan around him, and one of my hands travels down to play with my pussy. The gesture makes his eyes darken into dangerous slits as his hips begin to pump faster.

"Fucking beautiful," he growls as his cock pounds against my walls. "You're mine, Ginny. No one else gets to see you like this, touch you like this."

And then, his hips buck. I hold him firmly, sucking all his juice as his orgasm hits. His deep groan reverberates through my body, sending shockwaves of pleasure through my core. I never knew pleasuring a man could feel this good. Not until him.

When I've sucked him off completely, I release his dick from my mouth with a pop. His eyes glaze over, and he releases a tired chuckle.

"Come here."

He pulls me up and pulls my body flush against his. His fingers caress my mouth. "Sore?"

I shake my head as tiredness rolls through me.

"You'll be by tomorrow morning," he muses before carrying me into his arms.

Somewhere at the back of my head, the warning bells ring. I know this is supposed to be a one-time thing. I'm not supposed to let him carry me upstairs, touch me softly like I'm a porcelain doll just after fucking my mouth like a whore. But I love it. I close my eyes and lean against his chest.

And when I feel my body sinking into a soft mattress, his smell envelops me, and I know it belongs to him. I don't protest. When I feel his warmth beside me, I realize he won again. On his bed, I fall into a dreamless sleep with his body right next to mine.

18

DARIO

Ginny is still sleeping in my bed when I wake up. I glance at the time. It's 4:30 am. The last time I woke up this early was when I was still in my struggle to build my empire. Back then, late nights and early mornings were a usual occurrence for me.

I glance at the woman beside me, her soft body pressed against every inch of me as she sleeps. I watch the slow rise and fall of her chest like a hawk, unable to look away.

At some point during the night, our bodies became tangled together. Ginny is a deep sleeper, the kind who throws her hands and legs everywhere when she sleeps. And for some reason, I don't mind that. I love that she's all up in my space, that I can feel the heat of her body as it's intertwined with mine.

What the hell is happening to me?

I move to get out of bed when she makes a soft sound in her throat before snuggling deeper into me. I can't help the soft chuckle that escapes my lips. If I tell Ginny how she's practically holding onto my body right now, she'll bury her

head in shame. Or better still, she wouldn't even acknowledge it at all.

My eyes trail over her soft facial features. She looks very
peaceful when she sleeps—the most relaxed I've ever seen
her. Her dark hair spills all over my pillow, surrounding her
head like a halo. Her long eyelashes fan her face, her cheeks
are crushed into the pillow, and her mouth is parted slightly
open. Her soft snores fill the room, doing something mushy
to my insides.

My eyes trail down the column of her neck, and I work a
swallow in my throat as they travel down to her breasts. The
top of her nightgown has fallen dangerously low, revealing a
peak of one rosebud nipple. This fucking nightdress. I curse
low in my throat before reaching out to pull it back to its
normal position.

But now, the image of her nipple is engrained in my
head. It doesn't help that as my eyes roam over the curve of
her hips down to where her gown stops right below her ass,
I'm imagining her naked and writhing under me.

I've felt her warmth clench around my fingers and
have tasted her juices on my tongue. I thought that would
make my craving stop. I thought it would satisfy this
raging hunger within me. But it has only made me want
more. Now, I want to see her naked body. I want to run my
hand over the soft flesh as I slide my dick into her warm
core.

We only slept together after I brought her to my room
last night. I didn't want to assume she'd be up for sex just
yet. Not that I'd have had any trouble convincing her, but for
some stupid, unusual reason, I'm willing to wait until we
reach a better understanding through our frequent spats
and animosity.

The idea of her still hating me while I'm with her doesn't

give me the usual thrill—it would be different if I knew she didn't detest me quite so much.

Gritting my teeth, I pull the covers over my body before getting out of bed. By the time I get to the bathroom, I'm sporting a painful hard on. I quickly brush my teeth, skip shaving the two-day stubble on my chin, and head toward the shower.

The tiles are cool against my feet as I step in, a stark contrast to the heat coursing through me. I turn the knob, and the warm water cascades over my body, the rich scent of soap filling the air. I scrub my skin, working the suds into a thick foam, trying to wash away the heat, the tension, and the remnants of last night that cling to me like a second skin.

But as I rinse off, I switch to cold water, hoping to shock my system into submission. The icy spray hits me, sending shivers down my spine, but it does nothing to quell the fire within me. My thoughts drift back to Ginny, her defiance, the way she challenges me at every turn.

Then, my thoughts drift to her wetness, her soft moans against my ears, her wet pussy sliding over my face as she climaxed. I grit my teeth, the cold water only amplifying the turmoil inside me instead of doing the opposite.

Before I realize what I'm doing, my hands work up another lather, and I'm sliding my fist over my hard dick. My breathing increases as I move my fist up and down, the slick friction making me twitch with want.

I imagine myself sliding into her warm pussy, and I tighten my grip, imagining her wetness coating my cock as her walls clench around me. I let out a low groan, feeling my balls tighten at the pleasure, picturing her walls being stretched by my dick.

Her face flashes into my mind, flushed and panting with

desire, and I picture myself fucking her, slowly at first, then slamming into her before our bodies start shaking and we come apart together. A few more pumps of my hand, and I'm spilling onto the tiled floor, gasping for breath, my eyes closed. I can hear my heartbeat echo in my ears, and I can feel the water trickle down my body.

I rinse myself off and step out of the shower, my frustration now at its peak. When I return to the bedroom, she's still asleep. I turn away from her before I do something stupid like wake her up with my mouth between her legs.

Instead, I quickly get dressed in one of my expensive suits and shoes, slip my wallet into one of the pockets, grab my briefcase, and head out into the early morning air, hoping I can tuck all thoughts of Ginny far, far away.

I SIT IN MY OFFICE, the dim light from the desk lamp casting long shadows across the room. My eyes aimlessly roam across the wall opposite my desk, over the expensive art and various accolades lining its surface.

Right now, it all feels hollow. I glance at the ornate clock perched high above the other decorations on the wall. It's 9:46 pm and my third night away from my house.

I've avoided the house for days, unable to shake the memory of Ginny and the moment we shared. And like now, every second I've spent away from her has been exhausted thinking about her. About her body, her mind, and her soul, if possible.

This wasn't part of the plan. I'm supposed to hate her, to make her life miserable, yet here I am, stewing in my own thoughts, replaying every moment we spent together.

The silence is deafening, almost eerie, broken intermittently only by the soft ticking of the clock on the wall. I lean back in my chair, running a hand through my hair, frustration swirling within me. I shouldn't have fucking kissed her.

Even before I touched her body, I knew the control she had over me. The way her hazel eyes managed to completely suck me in, the way the mere sight of her body left me mesmerized. The only woman I've ever craved so badly is the one woman I should avoid.

But I didn't. I'd thought, *Just one kiss and I'll be satisfied.* Instead, that one kiss had turned into tasting her, letting her taste me, and wanting more.

And more...

For three days, I've tried and failed to purge her out of my mind. I've reminded myself of every possible reason why she should remain out of bounds. How her family brought me so much pain, how her brother turned his back on me when I needed him the most.

My mind drifts down memory lane, down to the memories I've tried to keep on a leash, the ones I only go back to when I need to fuel my quest for revenge...

The day my father got the job with Lorenzo's family, his excitement was palpable. I could tell from the way his voice practically buzzed with energy when he told my mother and me that we'd be moving to live with his new boss in the staff quarters assigned to us.

We took a taxi from the countryside into the city, heading to the grand house he'd been raving about for days. I remember staring out the window, watching the towers and skyscrapers soar above us.

When we eventually arrived at Bianchi's Mansion, it was even grander than I had imagined. The magnificent entryway still looms in my mind. The polished marble floors gleaming under the soft glow of the chandelier.

I stood there, a small boy feeling dwarfed by the opulence surrounding me. It was like I was in the scene of one of the movies I watch, the place I use to believe was only where that kind of wealth existed. The thick scent of polished wood and expensive perfume lurked in the air, making my stomach churn with nerves.

Then Lorenzo had appeared with a bright smile that instantly put me at ease. He was about my age, and his friendly face was a welcome sight in this intimidating new environment.

"Come on in, I have so many games you can play with," he'd said, pulling me inside.

Lorenzo was incredibly kind, and at just ten years old, I felt like I'd found both a brother and a best friend. As we grew older, our bond only grew stronger, even though we'd gone to different schools and led separate lives.

My father worked as his father's personal henchman for seven years, and during that period, we experienced a financial breakthrough. It was fortunate, especially since my mother had been diagnosed with stage II breast cancer and we could afford the treatment.

I remember the relief that washed over my father's face when he talked about his earnings for my mother's chemotherapy. The weight of fear lifted, even though it was only for a moment, grateful for the life Lorenzo's family provided.

Despite how close Lorenzo and I were, I couldn't help but notice the way his mother always looked at me—with a disdain so sharp it could cut glass. Even as we laughed and played, her eyes were a constant reminder that I didn't belong.

I tried to ignore it, focusing instead on the joy of being with Lorenzo and the news, a few years later, of his new sibling. I can still remember the excitement that bubbled through him. At twelve, he was finally going to be a big brother, something he'd always wanted.

When Ginny had arrived, Lorenzo was ecstatic, and I shared in his excitement, feeling a warmth bloom in my chest whenever we carried and played with her. And as Ginny grew, she became the light in our lives, her constant laughter and mischief blurring out their mother's hatred for me, which worsened as I became a teenager.

But then, my mother's cancer had returned, and everything had taken a dark turn. I was seventeen, Lorenzo was eighteen, and it was the summer before he left for college in the UK. Lorenzo invited me to their beach house in Italy, offering a brief escape from my troubles.

We spent a perfect day on the beach—sun shining, Ginny building sandcastles, and us splashing in the waves. But that night, everything had changed.

I remember the slap that pulled me up from my slumber, how harsh the fingers felt against my skin, and how I woke up startled and confused.

In the darkness, I was yanked from my dreams by a rough grip, dragging me down a hallway I had never known existed in that house. Each step felt like a descent into hell. I was terrified and confused. I could hear distant whispers from a room nearby. The air around me felt thick with tension, and my heart had raced with dread.

When I was pulled into that dimly lit room, the sight before me left me even more baffled. There was Lorenzo, his face stricken with guilt, while his mother looked on with disgust as usual.

But it was Antonio Bianchi, Lorenzo's father, cigar smoke curling around him like a predator, that sent chills down my spine. His expression was foreign to me—cold, menacing.

And then I saw my own father in a corner, beaten and bruised, huddled on the floor. My heart sank, and I rushed toward him, desperation clawing at my throat. But a henchman had slapped me across the cheek, sending me sprawling back.

"Dario!" my had father shouted, pain and fear mingling in his *voice, but all I could see was Lorenzo standing there, frozen, his eyes wide but unmoving. The betrayal felt like a knife twisting in my gut, sharper than the pain on my skin.*

My best friend hadn't lifted a finger to help me. Why?

I grit my teeth, blinking the memories away. They fade to the back of my mind, where they belong, but I can't get rid of the emotions. As always, they linger like a shadow in the corners, waiting for the right moment to manifest.

This is one of those moments.

Balling my hands into fists, I resolve that I'll never let what happened with Ginny happen again, even if it kills me.

19

GINEVRA

I wake up to the soft morning light spilling through the curtains, a groan slipping past my lips as the rays hits my face. It's day four of living in the enemy's house, and I'm already dreading it.

Enemy who made you come all over his kitchen counter, my inner voice mocks.

"Shut up!" I retort aloud, pushing that memory back into the dark, forgotten recesses of my mind.

The past three days have followed the same tedious routine—waking up, showering, having breakfast delivered to my room, meeting with the wedding planner, having lunch, napping until dinner time, and then either watching a movie or playing games on my phone.

Rinse and fucking repeat.

I didn't have many friends. The ones I did have were mostly for social events—school, extended family functions (which Lorenzo and I haven't really kept up with since our parents passed), and the occasional acquaintances from social media groups and mutual connections.

Being part of high society meant I wasn't allowed to go out much, invite friends over, or have casual meet-ups.

It was difficult to maintain friendships when those who tried to get close were assessed for their family background and their future inheritance. The friends I did make under such conditions were often snobs with communication issues, flaunting their wealth to solve every problem.

I couldn't deal with it, so I became more of a loner.

Today, I want to do something different. Maybe I'll take a swim in the lavish pool out back, or perhaps I'll go shopping —not for the wedding, but for myself. After all, there's no rule that says I can't leave the house. Besides, it's high time I take advantage of the unlimited card Dario left me three days ago before he completely vanished.

As I sit up, my eyes are drawn to the bedside table, and a breath leaves my lips when I spot it—an engagement ring, glinting like a betrayal under the streak of sunlight. Beside it, I see a white piece of paper. I bring it up to read the two words written on it.

Wear it.

ANGER WELLS UP INSIDE ME. His actions shouldn't shock me, given how despicable he is. But I can't help but be furious. How rude of him to leave the ring like this, without even a word in person. I know our engagement is arranged, and we're not truly in love. Heck, I don't expect him to get down on one knee and slip the ring onto my finger. But after everything that happened between us, I expected at least a proper acknowledgment.

One thing I should remind myself consistently is to never have any expectations when it comes to Dario.

I pick up the ring, feeling its weight in my palm as I swallow thickly. It is, without a doubt, the most beautiful ring I've ever seen. The band is crafted from lustrous gold, intricately woven into an elegant design. It's a far cry from any conventional engagement ring.

But it's the stone that captures my breath. It's a stunning shade of diamond, swirling with rich browns and hints of green that shimmer under the soft sunlight. Each movement catches the light, and the gem seems to glow from within, casting a warm hue that dances across my skin.

A part of me wants to put it on to see how it would look on my finger. But another part of me recoils the thought. Wearing this ring would mean embracing this facade. I don't want to be a pawn in Dario's little game.

Yet, as I sit there, I can't help but wish things were different. That night in the kitchen, with the heat of our argument turning into unrestrained passion. I close my eyes, recalling the way he looked at me, the way he kissed me, touched me as if I was the only woman in the world, the way he carried me to his room and put me to bed.

And the way he disappeared the next morning, my inner voice reminds me dryly.

I shake my head, trying to dispel the thoughts.

Dario has been avoiding me since then, and maybe that's for the best. I left his room and avoided being anywhere that I could mistakenly bump into him, even though I know he hasn't been home for three days.

I've also been planning our wedding, and it has kept me a bit busy, but it feels more as if I'm organizing a show for an audience. He's hired the best planner, making arrangements as if this isn't all a sham. I sigh, pushing the ring aside.

Earlier, I decided to do something different today. I'll start by having breakfast in the dining room instead of my room. After a shower, I slip into a fitted white tank top that hugs my skin and a pair of denim shorts with frayed edges. I want to look good, not for him, but because I want to feel good for the rest of the day.

Okay, that's a lie. With the ring he left beside my bed, I suspect Dario came back late last night. I'm dressed like this in the hopes that I'll see him, that I'll make it impossible for him to pretend I don't exist.

As I head downstairs, a rebellious spark ignites within me.

"Ginny," Rosa greets with a pleasant gasp as she sees me enter the kitchen. I return her smile with a genuine one, and when I offer to help her make breakfast, she tells me it's already done.

I insist on serving myself, and after a bit of back-and-forth, she shakes her head and heads toward the exit.

"Is Dario home?" I ask her before she leaves.

A knowing glint appears in her eyes as she turns to look at me.

"Yes, he is, thankfully. I wonder why that boy insists on putting his work above everything else? What man leaves his beautiful fiancée alone at home for three days?" She tuts in disapproval.

From the way she speaks about Dario, it's clear they have a long history, and she's like a mother figure to him.

"So terrible of him," I mutter, feigning anger.

"I'll go call him down."

"Don't tell him I'm here," I say, and she chuckles and nods as if she knows something I don't.

"As you wish, ma'am," she says before walking away.

Beaming, I pour myself a cup of coffee, the rich aroma filling the air. I set a plate of toast in front of me, the crisp sound of bread crunching as I slice it. I take a moment to relish the breakfast, savoring the idea of riling him up before work. I can already picture the look on his face when he sees me here.

Just as I take a bite, I hear his heavy footsteps. Dario enters the room, and even though I expect his arrival, my breath hitches at the sudden shift in the room's energy. I raise my gaze to him, maintaining a nonchalant expression on my face.

He looks sharp in a tailored suit, the fabric hugging his frame just right. The scent of his cologne—a mix of cedar and something spicy—fills the room, making my heart pound against my chest. His face. Fuck! It's so unfair for one person to look this sexy.

His dark hair looks longer than usual, falling over his forehead in messy waves. His emerald green eyes are narrowed into slits as he approaches me. His jaw is clenched, and I resist the urge to lick my lips at the sexy stubble sprinkled over his cheeks. I imagine what the roughness would feel like against my skin when his head is between my...

"You're eating in here today?" he asks, his voice snapping me out of my reverie.

His voice is laced with irritation, eyes narrowing as they flicker over my sitting frame.

"Thought I'd change things up," I reply, keeping my tone light, though my heart races. I enjoy the way his jaw tightens, the way he shifts his weight as he stands there like a lion ready to pounce.

"Right," he drawls, stepping closer, invading my personal

space. "You know, it wouldn't hurt you to act a little more...engaged. I have housekeepers and domestic staff. These people observe everything."

I roll my eyes, feigning innocence. "What exactly are you talking about?" I take another bite of my toast.

"Don't play games, Ginny. Why aren't you wearing your ring?" His voice deepens, and I can feel the heat of his stare boring into me, igniting a fire in my chest.

I guess the first thing he looked at when he saw me was my left ring finger. Controlling prick.

"What ring?" I ask, my voice steady, though inside I'm churning. "I don't know what you're..."

"I'm not in the mood," he snaps, his jaw clenching as he steps closer, his body towering over my sitting frame.

I hum, taking my time to sip of my coffee. When I place the cup gently on the table, I look up at him.

"Did you suddenly remember you have a fiancée after three days?" I ask coolly.

"Why? Did you miss me?"

His voice doesn't have its usual teasing lilt to it. Instead, it's hard and mocking. I bristle, but even though I want to return the energy, I decide to keep up with my facade, knowing it will infuriate him further.

"Never. I'm just...concerned. We don't want the house-keepers gossiping about us to others, now do we?" I say, fake concern dripping from my voice.

I know that isn't a possibility. Dario, like many other influential people, has his domestic staff sign nondisclosure contracts before they begin working for him. But even without the contract, I'm sure they would be terrified to run their mouths about him elsewhere, knowing how terrifying he can be.

Harshly, he drops his sleek briefcase on the dining table

before planting his palms against the surface and leaning further into me. My breath hitches, but I refuse to let him intimidate me.

"I don't have time for games."

"And who says I'm playing games?" I shoot back, staring right into his eyes.

Our faces are a few inches apart, and my eyes suddenly flicker to his lips, remembering the way he kissed me that night. My body burns with a wanton heat, and it's becoming increasingly difficult to pretend that he isn't the one getting under my skin rather than the other way around.

Feeling cornered, I abruptly get up and try to return my now empty dishes to the kitchen. I carry them in one hand, but before I move past him and reach the sink, Dario chases after me, grabs my free hand, and tugs me backward.

The ceramic plate and cup slip from my hand, shattering against the tiled floor.

"What is wrong with--"

A sharp breath leaves my lips as he swiftly lifts me up by my waist, the movement causing me to grip his shoulders for support. He takes three long steps away from the broken dishes before dropping me right in front of the kitchen counter. My head fogs up as the memory of that night hits me like a wrecking ball. We are in a similar position, the equally similar sexual tension thick in the air.

"We have an event tonight," Dario snaps, and the coldness of his harsh voice hits me. "You need to wear it."

"Gold isn't my color."

"You will wear the fucking ring, Ginny," he hisses, his eyes darkening with barely restrained fury.

I meet his gaze, my deep-seated hatred for him flaring up again.

"And what if I don't?" I challenge, lifting my chin up in defiance.

"The consequences of disobeying me are severe. You won't like them," he growls, his words sinking into me like poison. "I can end this contract whenever I want. It would be nothing for me, but for you? Your family will fall to ruin. It wouldn't cost me a damned thing."

His threat hits me square in the chest, squeezing out any breath I had left.

I feel my hatred for him intensify, clawing at my insides. My mind replays that night in the kitchen—every heated glance, every stolen breath, the undeniable chemistry that crackled between us. A stupid, foolish part of me thought that night had changed something between us.

Stupid, stupid girl.

"I fucking hate you, Dario," I spit, my voice trembling with raw emotion.

"The feeling is mutual, Ginevra," he says coldly, his emerald eyes hard as stone. "Just do what you're asked, and stop acting like a spoiled child. I won't be as tolerant the next time you defy my orders."

I want to scream, to push him away, to rip him apart with every insult I can think of, but deep down, I know that's what he wants. He's still the cold, ruthless Dario De Luca, and he's waiting for me to break, to give him the satisfaction of seeing me lose control.

I try to sidestep him, but his body blocks my path, the tension between us thick enough to choke on. "Move," I demand, my voice low, but the firmness of it barely conceals the storm of emotions swirling inside me.

A sliver of dark satisfaction flickers in his eyes, and he finally steps back, giving me just enough space to breathe.

"I'll pick you up at seven, Princess," he says, his voice dripping with condescension. "Be ready when I return. And, oh—wear something red."

With those parting words, he turns and walks out, leaving me standing there with a racing heart.

20

DARIO

She's wearing black.

We're both seated in the plush leather back seat of my car, the hum of the engine the only sound in the stillness. The stiffness crackling in the air feels palpable —so thick that it can be sliced through with a knife.

Ginny sits beside me in silence as we glide through the city lights, her presence all too electric.

When she stepped out earlier—thirty minutes late, just to spite me—I couldn't breathe for a second. Something in me twisted warm and tight. I felt all my breath leave my chest before something squeezed the dark hollow left behind.

Her defiance—fuck, it drives me mad. But it also consumes me.

That black dress, the one hugging every curve, made my blood run hot. It clung to her body like it was painted on. The V-shaped neckline plunged low, revealing the smooth, supple skin of her cleavage. The skirt hugged her hips, and the slit that ran up her midthigh revealed flashes of her smooth, creamy skin. She's a vision—deadly and beautiful.

I thought red was her color but seeing her in black made all my inhibitions fly out the window. Almost. My restraint is hanging by a thin rope, ready to snap at any moment.

And then there was the ring. My ring. Wrapped around her slender finger like a claim—a reminder she's mine filled me with dark satisfaction.

Balling my hands into fists, I cast her another glance suddenly overcome with a surge of possessiveness. The sequin fabric of her dress shimmers under the soft glow of the city lights streaming through the windows.

Her hair cascades in loose waves that frame her face perfectly, while her makeup highlights her striking features — smoky eyes that could pierce through me and red lips that make me want to ruin the distance between us, to crush my mouth against hers until she's breathless.

My eyes travel lower, to the slit in her dress that parts even further with each shift of her legs. Her smooth thighs tempt me in the most torturous way.

Grinding my teeth, I tear my gaze away from her before I do something reckless. My heart is pounding with a mix of desire and frustration. I want to talk to her so badly, and it takes everything in me not to reach out and touch her, to feel the warmth of her skin against my fingertips.

I want to close the gap between us, but I know if I touch her, even for a second, it'll ignite something uncontrollable.

The want—no, wanton need—I feel for Ginny is suffocating, consuming every part of me. Every glimpse of her makes me go wild, like a feral animal.

Memories from earlier today flash in my mind. The white, almost see-through tank top she was wearing, the way her nipples puckered out of the thin fabric. Her shorts hugging the curve of her ass in a way that had me cursing under my breath.

I'd barely been able to contain myself when I had her up close and cornered against the kitchen counter. The memories of the one night I'd tasted her linger in my mind, like a drug I can't quit. That night, she consumed every part of me, and I'd vowed to never touch her again, to stay in control. But it's useless. She's all I think about—at work, in meetings, everywhere. Her moans echo in my head, tormenting me.

When I couldn't stand it anymore, I locked myself in my office and gave in, my hand around my dick, pumping, imagining it was her slick, warm heat wrapped around me instead. Imagining how I want to fuck her moist pussy.

Fuck.

Now, I'm getting hard again just thinking about it.

I blow out a sharp breath and turn my gaze out the window, trying to calm the throbbing ache. I ball my hands into fists, trying to rein in the desire, the hunger clawing at me.

This night is going to test every ounce of restraint I have left.

Thankfully, we approach the venue for the event—a lavish hotel that stands tall against the night sky. The charity gala is not something I'd typically attend, but tonight is different. Tonight, I'm here to show off my fiancée —make it clear she's mine.

The car slows to a stop, and I step out to the blinding flashes of cameras. The cold air bites, but it doesn't compare to the heat roaring inside me. Adjusting my jacket, I offer my hand to Ginny as she steps out, poised and graceful, the perfect picture of control.

Her slender hand slips into mine as she steps out beside me. She takes a deep breath, but her expression doesn't give anything away.

"Smile," I tell her as we turn, ready for the events that will unfold.

We begin to walk down the carpet, and I feel the eyes of the crowd on us. Amongst the gushing and fawning, I hear whispers from some of the guests, their glances lingering on Ginny with mixed expressions of curiosity and admiration.

I tighten my grip on her hand as the lights flashes pop like fireworks, capturing our entrance. I can feel the warmth of Ginny's palm against mine, and I focus on her, trying to block out the noise.

"Just keep walking," I murmur, sensing her unease. Ginny glances up at me, and for a fleeting moment, I'm reminded of just how strikingly beautiful she is. She glows, even under the scrutiny of so many eyes. I don't think I can ever get used to her ethereal perfection. I don't want to.

We enter the ballroom, and I sense her trying to slip her hand out of mine. I tighten my grip, pulling her back towards me.

"We aren't done performing yet," I say quietly, my voice a warning.

The gala is alive with energy, and for a moment, it feels like just the two of us in this bustling sea of elegance.

People turn their heads as we approach, their eyes lingering on us, the new couple making their first public appearance together. I can feel the weight of their gazes, some curious, others judgmental, and I couldn't care less. I just want to make a statement. I want to claim her publicly.

The room is filled with tables draped in elegant white linens adorned with gorgeous centerpieces. The soft glow of candlelight flickers, casting a romantic ambiance over the space. A live band plays soft classical music in the corner, and the sound mingles perfectly with the conversations and laughter in the room.

I slide one hand over her waist, pulling her flush against my side. Her heat seeps through the thick material of my tuxedo, and I hear the soft hitch of her breath.

"You don't have to," she tells me through gritted teeth. "They already get the message."

I glance down at her, taking her left hand in mine, my thumb brushing over the diamond on her finger. "I want to." The words leave my mouth, heavy with meaning.

Before she can protest, I spot him—Rinaldo, striding toward us. My stomach tightens at the sight of that smug smirk plastered across his face. He's dressed impeccably in a tailored suit, but it's the mere sight of his condescending gaze that sets my teeth on edge.

"Look who it is," he calls out, his voice laced with sarcasm. "Our most recent power couple."

Ginny stiffens beside me, her body rigid at the sound of his voice.

"I would say your engagement to Dario sparked more interest in the public than ours did..."

"Back off, Rinaldo," I say sharply, my voice low but firm.

He takes a step closer, his eyes glinting with mischief. "Why, Dario? I never got the chance to say my congratulations in person."

People are starting to notice the small scene, and a few murmurs and whispers erupt around us. I clench my jaw so hard I'm sure my teeth will crack. Thank god it's a phone-free event, no photographers allowed inside—at least I don't have to worry about this being plastered all over the internet. But the way he's trying to humiliate her, to break her down in front of everyone, sets my blood on fire. I won't let him get away with it.

Taking another step toward him, I repeat the two words more firmly. "Back off."

Something sinister flashes in his eyes as he looks at me, and then, casting one last glance at Ginny, he adds, "Enjoy your evening," before sauntering away.

I immediately turn to Ginny, catching the slight tremor in her hands and the way her jaw tightens in anger.

"Are you okay?" I ask softly, my thumb brushing her cheeks.

"Yeah, fine," she snaps before exhaling a sharp breath. "Let's go. People are staring."

"Let them stare." The words slip out before I can stop them, and I tuck a loose strand of hair behind her ear. She blushes beneath the makeup, her cheeks tinged with pink, and I can tell that she hates the reaction because she clenches her jaw immediately after.

Slipping my hand into hers again, I guide Ginny through the crowd. She seems to relax a bit, but I still sense the slight tension in her shoulders as we navigate past tables filled with guests chatting animatedly.

As we continue to weave through the crowd, I spot Lorenzo across the room, his tall frame easily recognizable. He's engaged in conversation with a group of people, his easy smile drawing them in.

Ginny sees him as well, and she goes rigid again. She's still pissed at him. At this point, she may be pissed at me, as well.

She hates you, just like you should hate her, a voice whispers in my head just as Lorenzo catches sight of us.

His face lights up, and he breaks away from the group, striding toward us with an open smile.

"Well, I didn't expect to see you both here," he says with that trademark smile.

"We wouldn't miss it," I reply, keeping my tone cordial.

A flicker of emotion crosses his eyes as he looks at Ginny.

Lorenzo's eyes flicker with something—regret, maybe—as he looks at his sister. "Ginny, you look... stunning. That dress is perfect on you."

"Thanks." Her voice is flat, the one-word reply cutting through the thick silence that follows. It's brief, but it hangs heavy until Lorenzo clears his throat and continues.

"There's a silent auction starting soon," he says, forcing a smile. "And I hear there are a lot of bidders with money to spend."

I glance at Lorenzo, feeling the weight of the unsaid things between him and Ginny. The tightness in her posture, the way her hand trembles just slightly in mine. It's familial and unresolved and I can't but feel bad about causing it. Well, almost bad.

I suddenly feel like an outsider in a conversation I have no part in.

Ginny doesn't respond right away, her gaze focused somewhere beyond the ballroom, lost in a world I can't reach.

"Great," Ginny finally mutters, her tone sharp and curt. Her eyes flicker to her brother, a flash of something painful crossing her face before she masks it. "Enjoy the auction, Lorenzo."

Her words are cold, dismissive, but I can see the storm brewing behind her eyes.

Lorenzo gives a tight nod, lingering for a second longer than necessary before turning away, blending into the crowd. I can feel Ginny's pulse quicken under my fingers as she exhales sharply, as if she's been holding her breath this entire time.

"You okay?" I murmur, leaning down so only she can hear me.

She doesn't answer immediately, her eyes still locked on where her brother disappeared. When she finally speaks, her voice is quiet but firm. "Let's just get this over with."

We approach the table, and I pull out a chair for Ginny, dragging it closer to mine before gesturing for her to sit. I half expect her to roll her eyes or throw a sarcastic comment my way about being possessive, but she just sits down quietly.

Gritting my teeth, I try to focus on Lorenzo, who is saying something to the other guests seated at the table with us. He looks significantly better than the last time I saw him. That depressing air around him and the gloominess in his eyes are gone. I guess his company's success is doing wonders for his mood.

Ginny remains silent, and I can't ignore the hurt expression on her face as she glances between me and her brother. Guilt twists in my gut, but I push it down, telling myself she'll get over it. Time will heal things. The company's doing better, and eventually, she'll come around. But the ache in my chest refuses to go away.

After a few minutes, Ginny pushes her chair back abruptly and stands. "I have to use the restroom."

Without another word, she's gone.

I focus on the extravagant spread before me, taking a bite of caviar, savoring the rich taste while trying to ignore the inevitable conversation with my worst enemy across from me. Lorenzo is glued to his phone, typing away, the silence between us stretching thin. After a few more minutes, and the quiet departure of the other two guests, it's just the two of us left at the table.

"She's still mad, huh?" Lorenzo finally speaks, breaking the strained quiet.

I lean back into my seat, running a hand through my hair. "Yeah."

"She's probably mad at you, too."

"She hates me," I admit, and for the first time, the weight of that reality sinks in, sending a sharp, unwelcome ache through my chest.

I don't want her to hate me.

Lorenzo sighs, rubbing the back of his neck. "Yeah. I haven't exactly painted the best picture of you to her."

"I'll bet you haven't. Telling her that her precious brother's a backstabber doesn't exactly make you the good guy here either."

"I didn't betray you—"

"Right. You just stood by and watched while my entire world collapsed when you could have stopped it. No big deal. It's fine."

My words hang in the air between us, and the atmosphere becomes tense again. Past memories, betrayals, and pain flash through my memory, and I assume he's also thinking about the same thing.

I tap my fingers against my knee, a nervous tic from childhood I haven't fully shaken. When I grew older, that nervous energy morphed into a need for a cigarette or a glass of whiskey.

"What does she like?" I ask, breaking the silence again.

Lorenzo blinks, caught off guard. "What?"

"Ginny. What are the things she likes?"

His eyes widen just a fraction, and for the first time, I catch a flicker of surprise in them. It hits me—hard.

Maybe I care about Ginny more than I've ever let myself admit. When she's upset, it gnaws at me, infecting my mood.

And when she's happy... well, I've never really seen her happy around me. That thought stings in a way I hadn't expected.

A tightness forms in my chest, like a fist slowly closing around my heart. I want to see her happy. More than that—I want to be the reason she's happy. Not out of obligation or this twisted situation we're in, but because I actually give a damn.

Fuck. This wasn't supposed to happen. I wasn't supposed to care.

But now I do. More than I should.

21

GINEVRA

I slip into the bathroom, the noise and chatter of the gala fading into the background. Once I confirm it's empty, I push the door shut behind me and hear the soft click of the lock. The moment I'm alone, I lean back against the door, letting out a shaky breath as my body sinks to the floor.

The lights overhead are harsh, bouncing off the gleaming marble tiles and making everything feel too bright, too overwhelming.

Tears well up in the corners of my eyes, and I fight to hold them back. I feel stupid. Useless. Like some expensive accessory Dario brought to flaunt in front of everyone. The weight of their judgment and scrutiny had become unbearable, suffocating, until I had no choice but to leave the room.

Ever since this whole mess started, I've been trying to remind myself that I'm not just a pawn in their game—Dario's or Lorenzo's. I am my own person, and I'll make choices that benefit me and my career. No one else.

But sitting there with Lorenzo and Dario pretending everything was fine made me feel worthless. Like I was nothing more than an object. A trophy for their satisfaction. A means to an end.

The thought of it makes my stomach turn.

Judging by the pleased expression Lorenzo wore during those few minutes we spent together, the company must be doing well. I'm happy for him, but the way I was expected to stay there, acting as if everything was normal, felt like a slap in the face.

My hands ball into fists as I remember Rinaldo's mocking words. I shouldn't be bothered by him because he's an asshole, and I ended things with him before my forced engagement to Dario. However, he doesn't know that. The moment I broke up with him, my engagement to Dario was announced.

I take a few deep breaths, yet I don't feel better even the slightest. After a few minutes, I push my body off the floor and walk over to the sink. I have the strong urge to splash cold water on my face, but I remind myself that I'm wearing makeup and there's still a party going on outside.

My eyes glance up, and I catch my reflection in the mirror. For a moment, I hardly recognize the woman staring back, dressed in elegant black, but feeling so out of place.

I hate Dario for all the things he's done, but I also hate that I can't shake the frustration I feel when he's angry with me, like earlier today in the kitchen. I hate that he's unpredictable—hot this moment and cold the next.

I hate that I care, that it affects me. I shouldn't care about any of this, yet the conflicting emotions swirl in my chest, making it hard to think straight.

Feeling the need to get some fresh air, I push through the door and navigate the crowded ballroom, avoiding the curious glances of a few guests. I look toward Dario and

Lorenzo and see them in a conversation. A huff slips past my lips before I pull my gaze away from them.

Finding solace in a dimly lit hallway, the floor lights cast soft shadows along the walls. As I walk, the buzz of the party fades into a distant hum, my footsteps leading me aimlessly.

Eventually, I stumble upon a small corridor that opens onto a veranda. Stepping outside, the cool night air brushes against my face, a welcome relief. Leaning against the railing, I gaze out into the darkness, hoping to clear my mind. But just as I start to relax, heavy footsteps echo nearby, and my stomach knots at the sound of that dreaded voice.

"Ginny! There you are!" Rinaldo's voice cuts through the quiet, and I turn to see him striding toward me, his expression smug and infuriatingly confident.

I ignore him, hoping he would just go away, but knowing him, I know that's literally impossible.

"What do you want, Rinaldo?" I finally snap, crossing my arms defensively as he comes closer.

His footsteps don't stop until he's invading my space. "Is that any way to greet your ex-fiancé, Sweet Pea?"

The nickname sends shivers of disgust down my spine. I never liked it.

"I was looking for you," he continues, undeterred by my silence. "Do you think you can just end things with me over a flimsy phone call, ignore all my texts and calls, and then jump into the arms of another man?" His voice drips with disgust.

I take a deep breath, trying to calm my temper. "You have no idea what you're talking about."

"Don't I?" He chuckles harshly. "Then how do you explain the fact that just days after ending our engagement, your engagement to someone else was announced? Dario De Luca, of all people," he spits.

My throat burns with anger and humiliation. "I don't wish to talk to you, Rinaldo. Leave me alone."

But he doesn't listen. As he steps closer to me, I have to take a few steps back, but this only means he has me cornered against the wall. His eyes glint with pure evil, and my heart thumps with a mixture of fear, anger, and dread.

"Why? Are you ashamed, Ginny? Ashamed that you're such a whore?"

"Don't you dare talk to me like that," I finally snap. "Our relationship and engagement were a sham, and you know it. If anyone ruined anything, it was you. Selfish bastard."

His eyes flash, and in an instant, his grip tightens painfully around my arm.

"Is that so?" He smirks, his breath hot against my face as he lifts my left hand. My engagement ring catches the moonlight. A bitter chuckle escapes him. "Is that why you chose to proudly wear his ring instead of mine? Is that why you moved in with him?"

How did he find out about Dario and me living together?

"When you broke things off, I thought you were just being dramatic, as usual. Ignoring my calls and texts, trying to push me to do better," he hisses, his grip on my wrist tightening further. "Until I heard about your engagement to another man," he continues, his voice rising.

"The next day, I went to your brother's house, and guess what the maids told me," he barks with another loud laugh. "You moved in with him a day after your engagement became public. You wouldn't move in with me after months of dating and getting engaged."

"This has nothing to do with you," I say firmly, trying to pull my arm away. "I ended things. You need to move on."

"I guess my suspicions were true. Your brother's just

your pimp, selling you off to the best man he can get his hands on," Rinaldo sneers.

"The best? You think you were the *best man* my brother could find for me?"

His expression is one of surprise at my response. He's trying to rouse a reaction from me by dragging my brother into this, but I refuse to give him the satisfaction.

"We both knew our relationship was arranged from the start," I continue, unflinching. "You act as if you contributed anything to my life—as if I gained anything from you."

"You—"

"You're just the jobless son of a politician. The whole arrangement was to give you ties to a reputable business because you don't have the brains or guts to make it in politics."

"How dare you?" His face turns an angry shade of red, his fists clenched.

"If anyone should be mad, it's me! I wasted my time with you," I say, my voice rising. "Your influence did nothing for my family. You were a burden I couldn't wait to get rid of. And sex with you—" I laugh bitterly. "It's the worst thing I've ever experienced."

His eyes blaze with fury, but I ignore the pain searing in my wrist as his grip tightens.

"You think he's better than me? You think he actually wants you?" he snarls.

"Dario respects me," I retort, standing my ground despite the way my heart is currently racing. "Something you never did. You wanted to use me to satisfy your ambitions, not mine."

"Respect? That's rich," he scoffs, his voice dripping with disdain. "You're just a trophy for him, a prize to show off.

You're still the same girl I knew, the one who desperately craves affection from anyone who gives her any."

"Crave attention?" I scoff. "I was pretending with you, Rinaldo. Everything from the beginning to the end of it was a lie."

Then, lowering my voice into a whisper, I say in fake concern, "Maybe you should look inward and really ask yourself what's so miserable about you that despite all your money and status, no woman wants to be with you."

I rip my arm from his grip and try to push past him, but he grabs my hair and slams me against the wall. My back stings from the impact.

"Get away from me," I spit through gritted teeth, my voice trembling with a mixture of anger and fear. I try to shove him off, but his hold only tightens. "You can't control me anymore!"

His eyes darken, a cruel smirk tugging at his lips. "Maybe I should remind you what happens when you run your mouth around me," he growls, raising his hand to strike me.

I brace myself, my eyes squeezed shut and heart pounding, waiting for the inevitable blow.

But the impact never comes. Instead, I hear a sickening crack followed by Rinaldo's pained groan. I open my eyes just in time to see Dario, his face twisted with fury, holding Rinaldo by the neck and pinning him to the wall. Rinaldo's nose is bleeding profusely, and his eyes are wide with shock and fear.

Dario slams his fist into Rinaldo's face again, the sickening crunch of bone echoing in the night air. Rinaldo lets out a guttural groan, clutching his face in agony, his hand now visibly broken.

"Dario, stop," I cry, my voice shaking as my heart races,

fear mixing with relief. If he keeps going, this will turn into a disaster.

Dario exhales harshly, then shoves Rinaldo's crumpled body to the ground. The air between us crackles with tension, and I watch as Rinaldo tries to get back on his feet, only to stumble and fall back to the floor, his face twisted in pain.

Dario stands over him, his voice low and lethal. "The next time I see you near my wife—if you so much as lay a finger on her—I will kill you."

His words hang heavy in the air, a promise laced with a deadly finality.

Without another glance at Rinaldo, Dario grabs my hand and pulls me away. My heart pounds in my chest as we leave, the night air doing little to calm the storm raging inside me.

My heels click against the tiled floor as Dario leads me down the hallway toward the elevator. His hand grips mine tightly, his breaths heavy with restrained anger, but instead of feeling trapped or disgusted like I did when Rinaldo held me, I feel something entirely different—protected, special, safe...and...so fucking turned on.

The elevator doors slide open, and as we step inside, the tension clings to us. I can still feel the anger radiating off Dario's body like a live wire, the air around him charged with intensity.

The doors close with a soft ping, sealing us in the small space, and I tilt my head to look at him.

I should thank him for saving me. If he hadn't stepped in, I can't bear to think what Rinaldo would have done. But Dario still hasn't looked at me, his jaw clenched, eyes fixed on the elevator doors.

Earlier tonight, I wanted to escape his presence, wanted

to get far away from the weight of his gaze. Now, all I want is for him to see me, to feel how grateful I am for what he did.

Gently, I slide my hand up to his face, turning him toward me. His skin is warm beneath my touch, and for a brief moment, his eyes meet mine, blazing with something raw and unspoken. But before I can utter a single word, a low growl rumbles from his chest, and in one swift motion, he captures my lips in a fierce, possessive kiss.

The force of it knocks the breath out of me, but I don't care. All the fear, all the tension from the night, melts away under the heat of his kiss.

I kiss him back.

22

DARIO

Every single shred of control in me snaps the moment my lips crash against Ginny's. I've been struggling to rein myself in all night, but after seeing another man's filthy hands on her, touching *my woman, my wife,* I lose it completely.

But she's not really your wife—you feel nothing for her, remember?

The thought creeps in, a mocking voice in the back of my mind, taunting me. I shove it aside, burying it in the darkest corner of my head.

It doesn't matter what our arrangement is supposed to mean. Not now. Not when I'm holding her like this, tasting her, feeling the heat of her body against mine.

For now, all that matters is this moment, and the fire burning between us.

My hand slides into the back of her hair, gripping just enough to tilt her head as I deepen the kiss, my tongue teasing hers while my other hand pulls her body flush against mine. She moans into my mouth, melting against me, and the sound drives me wild.

I tug her bottom lip between my teeth, biting just enough to make her gasp—a sound that only ignites the fire already raging inside me. I've been craving this all day, burning with the need to touch her, to claim her since I walked away from her this morning.

I feel her nails digging into my skin through the fabric of my tux, her body trembling under my touch. The sensation sends a thrill through me, pushing me to the edge of control. I want to mark her, to leave a reminder for anyone foolish enough to come near her. I need everyone to know she's mine—no one else can have her.

"Dario," she gasps, her breath hitching as my hand slides over her exposed thigh, slipping beneath the slit of her dress.

"I've been dying to do this all night," I growl, gripping the soft flesh of her thigh and letting my thumb glide over the sensitive skin of her inner thigh. "This fucking dress..."

She lets out a choked gasp, her hand tangling in the hair at the nape of my neck, pulling me closer, her need mirroring my own.

"Someone could come in," she breathes, her voice shaking with desire, but there's no conviction behind the words.

As if on cue, the elevator pings, signaling that we are approaching the ground floor. I trail my eyes over her face, which glows with pure desire. Her eyes are dark pools full of lust as she looks up at me, her lips red and swollen from our passionate kissing, her lipstick now smudged.

The sight only enhances the arousal burning low in my belly and stokes the heat coursing through my veins.

The elevator comes to a stop, and with our hands still firmly intertwined, we step out. The lobby is almost deserted, save for the receptionist, who looks up at the sound of Ginny's heels clicking against the tiled floor. But I don't care who's watching. I'm not letting go of her tonight.

Outside the main entrance ahead of us, I can still make out the small crowd of reporters and photographers standing there, probably waiting to capture the guests that are arriving late.

Grabbing her hand tighter, I pull Ginny toward the side exit which leads to the back of the garage. She stumbles along beside me while I quickly text my driver to meet us by the valet entrance.

The short journey feels longer, and all I can think about is how I want to kiss her again so badly and how much I need to be inside her. Just thinking about it is enough to get me painfully hard.

As we step through the side door, the cool air of the garage envelops us. The faint hum of fluorescent lights casts a sterile glow that illuminates the rows of parked vehicles. Just ahead, I immediately spot the Lamborghini Urus parked ahead, the polished exterior gleaming under the soft light.

I squeeze Ginny's hand as we approach the car, and on spotting us, my driver, Timoteo, pulls open the door.

The moment we climb into the luxurious leather seats, I take Ginny's face into my hands before leaning down to devour her lips like a starving man. This time, she eagerly returns the kiss and wraps her arms around my neck, her fingers gripping tightly at my shoulders.

The kiss is heated, hungry, and utterly desperate. I slide my hand under the slit of her dress again, feeling the familiar warmth between her legs. She moans as she tilts her hips, urging my hands higher.

"Fuck, Ginny," I groan before pulling her roughly across my lap over my throbbing erection.

The sounds of our heated breathing echo off the walls of the car. Timoteo, who is still standing by the car, can hear us by now, and the thought of him hearing the sounds of Ginny's moans fills me with feral possessiveness.

I want to ask him to get out, but when Ginny rolls her hips over me, I can't form coherent thoughts anymore. All I can think about is the feel of the sleek curves of Ginny's ass under her dress and how I want to get her naked.

My dick strains against my pants, begging me to unzip the fly, slide her panties to the side, and fuck her with her dress on. I want to be rough. I want to rip her clothes off until I can see every inch of her smooth porcelain skin. But it'll be our first time, and a part of me that deeply cares about her wants it to be special.

"We should head home," I groan against Ginny's lips.

She makes a low sound of protest in her throat before rolling her hips again.

"Shit, Ginny," I groan, grabbing the back of her neck to keep her still. "Keep doing that, and I'll fuck you right here without caring if anyone sees or hears us."

The rough edge of my voice has an opposite effect on her. A blush spreads across her face and throughout her entire body until I am absolutely sure she is completely flushed.

"But the drive home is long," she whines, her soft breath hitting my face.

And she's right. I don't think I can wait thirty minutes with Ginny right beside me while Timoteo drives us home. At some point, I'll end up fucking her with my driver right in the front.

I grip her hips tightly, my fingers digging in as I weigh my options. An idea sparks in my head, and I press a short kiss against her lips before lifting her body off me.

"I can take us somewhere."

Stepping down, I shut the door behind me and grab the car keys from Timoteo. Nearby, there's an old property of the Bianchi's, one of those that collapsed and is now sealed off under my control.

I slide into the driver's seat after sending Timoteo away, pull the car out of the garage, and out the back of the hotel. I grip the steering wheel firmly, my body almost shaking due to the pent-up arousal and tension in the car.

Ginny remains quiet behind me, but I can hear the sounds of her harsh breathing in the rear compartment. After five torturous minutes, we arrive at the gate to the estate located in the quiet residential quarters of the city.

The two security guards on duty recognize me immediately and push the sliding gates open. I order them not to let anyone in before moving forward.

The car's headlights cut through the dim light as I drive in. My gaze is drawn to the side of the building that has collapsed; debris strewn across the ground in huge blocks. I maneuver cautiously through the quiet garage, navigating potholes and uneven pavements before finally finding a spot near the edge, away from the wreckage.

The moment I shift the car into park, I quickly get down from the driver's seat and rush into the backseat. I pull the door open, and Ginny's hands grasp tightly onto my clothes, pulling me in with her. I try to climb her body by pushing her into a lying position, but she has other plans.

Her hands grip my shoulders as she pushes me back against the seat before climbing over to straddle my waist. There is no patience, no restraint as our mouths find each other, our tongues dancing in frenzied passion.

All thoughts of taking it slow disappear to the back of

my brain as she licks and bites my neck, our hands fumbling with the several layers of clothing between our bodies.

She pushes my tuxedo jacket down my shoulders, and I quickly slide it off before fumbling with the zip at the back of her dress. Our gasps and moans intermingle as she unbuttons my shirt halfway before undoing the buckle of my belt.

When her zip gets stuck, she slips her hands out of the sleeves and pulls the dress down her front, leaving it around her middle.

I suck in a sharp breath at the sight of the red lace bra that covers her perky breasts.

"You said I should wear red," she murmurs, staring at me through her heated gaze.

I slip my hands between her thighs and cup her clothed pussy.

"Is this red, too?" I growl, slipping the flimsy material to the side and rubbing my thumb over her wet, swollen lips.

"Yes," she moans, her fingers biting my shoulders.

I press my mouth directly on top of her soft breasts, opening my mouth to take one clothed nipple between my teeth. She grabs my head roughly with both hands, rolling her hips over my fingers as I suck her nipple.

"Fuck, Dario," she gasps. "I want you now."

I let out another growl when she slips her hands into my briefs and grabs my dick. That's when I turn feral.

Grabbing her panties, I roughly tug the fabric. She lets out a soft gasp as it snaps before I discard it on the ground. My dick stands out proudly as I completely pull it out, its tip pointed up towards my chest. I take pleasure in watching Ginny's eyes widen a fraction at it before she positions herself above me and slowly slides down.

She moans, and my hands dig painfully into her hips as

she takes me in, inch by inch, until my cock is completely buried inside her. I lean forward to pull her lips into a kiss, giving her a few seconds to adjust to my size.

The kiss turns frantic in seconds, and soon she's gripping my shoulders to push me back.

Taking her lead, I watch with hooded eyes as she lifts her hips up before slamming down on my length. I grab her hips to support her as she gets into a steady rhythm, rocking, grinding, and thrusting.

Pleasure shoots through my entire body, spreading warmth throughout my veins and making my heart race. I focus on her face, the sheen of sweat on her forehead, her wild, dark hair cascading down her waist, and the sweet moans falling out of her lips as she continues to ride me.

Her soft sounds drive me absolutely insane, the sound of it only heightening the arousal pulsating within my veins.

My fingers dig into her hipbones as she picks up her pace, thrusting and grinding. My hands gather her hair to the back of her head before wrapping it around one wrist.

"Dario," she moans as I tug her head backward to kiss her neck.

My tongue traces along her pulse point as my free hand grabs one of her breasts and squeezes firmly. Our moans mixed with grunts fill the silent garage as we rock faster, harder, deeper until...

"Oh fuck, I'm going to come," she moans out loud.

My fingers clutch her waist even tighter as I thrust upward to meet her in the middle. Soon her body trembles as the wave of her orgasm crashes over her. She lets out a cry that is torn from her throat, and I feel my body tense up, my orgasm coursing through my veins like liquid fire, burning all the way down to my toes.

"Fuck," I grunt as she comes down from her high, rolling her hips slowly as I ride out my climax.

Then she looks down at me, her cheeks flushed, her hazel eyes still glossy with lust. I stare at her for a moment, our breaths both heavy as the reality of what we just did comes crashing down on us.

"We didn't use protection," she says a bit shyly, biting her lower lip.

"I'm so sorry...I didn't think. But I'm clean." My voice comes out harder than I intended.

She swallows and nods. "Me, too. And I'm on the pill."

When I crafted my revenge plan that involved marrying Ginny, pregnancy and children never crossed my mind. But now, the thought doesn't seem as bad as it would have a few months ago.

And that is bad. Very bad.

Something is happening between Ginny and I, and if I don't nip it at the bud, it's going to eat the both of us whole.

23

GINEVRA

The air around us is thick with a different kind of tension as Dario pulls the car out of the quiet compound. The cold breeze from the AC vent bites my skin, making me shiver.

I sit in the passenger seat, stealing glances at Dario. His jaw is tight, and his hands grip the steering wheel with so much force that I fear he'll break it.

We are both fully dressed now—sans my ripped panties that he slipped into his pocket—but the evidence of the past ravenous minutes is very much evident in his wild hair and flushed skin.

The night outside is dark and heavy, the streetlights casting bright lights that illuminate the winding streets. The car ride home feels like an eternity wrapped in silence. Each second stretches painfully long.

An unpleasant feeling pools in my stomach, and a heavy weight, thick and suffocating, hangs in my throat.

Memories of our heated moment in the garage flood my mind, and I wonder if he's replaying it, too. I wonder if he liked it. Or if he's filled with regret. I steal another glance at him—his brow is furrowed, and I can't help but wonder what's going on in his mind.

I pull my gaze away from him, my stomach tightening again. My gaze remains outside the window until we approach the familiar, luxurious street of his house. As we pull into the driveway, I take a deep breath, steeling myself for the awkwardness that's sure to follow. The car stops, and the silence feels deafening.

He opens the door and steps out, the sharp movement sending a jolt through me. I quickly follow suit before he crosses over to the passenger side, my heart pounding as we walk side by side toward the entrance.

The night is still and cold, the only sound being the crunch of gravel beneath our feet. I want to say something, anything to break the silence, but my words hang thick in my throat.

Dario unlocks the door and steps aside for me to walk past. As I move in, the faint scent of his expensive cologne hits me, and I'm reminded of how I kissed and licked his neck earlier.

The atmosphere seems even more tense and awkward as we both make our way up the stairs with Dario behind me. I feel his hot gaze slither down my exposed back, and my whole body is up in flames.

When we get to the top corridor, I'm reminded that we don't share the same bedroom, and exactly why I left his room on the first day. The irony isn't lost on me. I didn't want to share a bed with him, but now I've done even more than that.

I've had sex with the man.

I hesitate for a moment, searching for the right words, the right line of action. After the first night I spent on his bed, he basically hadn't spent the night here until late last night while I was already asleep.

I wonder if he expects me to follow him to his bedroom since I've spent a night there before. Does he expect me to sleep in his room regularly now because we've had sex? But if he doesn't, it would be weird to just ignore the man I've just had sex with, right? But why do I have to be the one to say something?

Exhaling a short, frustrated breath, I manage to mumble a whisper of a greeting.

"Goodnight."

"Goodnight," he says firmly.

His eyes meet my gaze for just a moment, and there's a flicker of something in his eyes—frustration, perhaps? Reluctance, maybe? Heat...yes.

Then he turns away, walking toward his room. The door clicks shut behind him, leaving me standing alone in the hallway feeling a mix of disappointment and confusion.

What the hell just happened?

Shaking my head, I head over to the opposite wall, push the door open, and enter my room and lock it shut behind me. I take a shower, scrubbing my body to wash his touch and smell from my body.

It's all pointless. And when I eventually fall asleep moments later, I slip into the dream world where the events of earlier repeat over and over again.

BRIGHT SUNLIGHT STREAMS through my window as I rise from bed the next morning. It warms my skin, but it does little to chase away the unease lingering in my chest. I remain in bed for a few minutes, just gazing at the ceiling. When I'm sure Dario must have left for work, I take a shower, change into fresh clothes, and head to the dining room. Hopefully, a good breakfast will clear my head.

I step into the kitchen and make my way toward the dining room. The table is set in preparation for the meal, but the sight of Dario already seated at the far end catches me off guard. His dark hair is slightly tousled, and his clean-shaven jaw is sharp and clenched. He is dressed in a fitted black shirt that accentuates his broad shoulders with his usual black pants and black leather shoes. He looks impossibly handsome, and my heart skips a beat at the sight of him.

"Morning," I say, my voice barely above a whisper, suddenly aware of the flimsy, short romper I'm wearing.

"Morning." Dario doesn't look up from his coffee, his expression as cold and unreadable as it was last night. I feel a rush of embarrassment flood my cheeks.

Rosa enters the room, her bright smile cutting through the tension. "Good morning, you two. I hope you're ready for a delicious breakfast!" She chirps, bustling around the kitchen.

I take my seat, trying to ignore the quiet intensity in the air. Dario remains focused on his coffee, his demeanor unchanged, and I'm getting more pissed by the minute. I'm thrown back to two days ago when he acted exactly like this. His hot and cold attitude is giving me a fucking headache.

"Did you sleep well?" Rosa asks no one in particular, as if she can sense the tension in the room.

"Yes, I did," I reply with a forced smile, trying to keep the warmth in my voice.

But my stomach squeezes painfully again, and I fear I've lost my appetite.

Rosa sets down a plate of fresh fruit and a basket of bagels at the center of the table. She leaves and returns almost immediately again with a kettle and a teacup for me. This time around, my smile is genuine, as I find it so sweet that she remembers I don't like coffee.

"You both should eat. It's important to start the day right."

Her voice is overly cheerful, and I know it's a deliberate attempt to dispel some of the tension in the room. I try to engage in a casual conversation with her as she places more plates before me.

The weight of Dario's silence is still heavy opposite me. As I take a single grape into my mouth, he stands to his feet. I crush the grape with my teeth as I catch his gaze briefly, and there's an intensity in his eyes that makes my heart race. It's a mix of frustration and something else I can't quite place.

I focus my attention back on the food before me just as he steps away from the table. Just when I think he'll walk away without saying a word, Dario surprises me by leaning over and pressing a soft kiss to my forehead. My breath catches, and warmth rushes to my cheeks. The gesture is so unexpected and tender that I forget about the tension for a moment.

"See you later," he says, his voice low and rough, like a promise, before heading toward the door.

I sit there, stunned and blushing, and I feel Rosa's eyes on me.

"Well, that was cute," she teases, a playful smile on her face. "You should see your face, Ginny!"

"Rosa, stop it," I murmur, trying to hide my blushing face, but I can't help the smile creeping onto my lips.

"That's how he is," she continues in a breathy voice as she pours herself a cup of coffee. "The don has a tough exterior, but he's a softie underneath. He treats all his workers well. Paolo, the gardener, had a sick mother. Before she died, the don paid off all their debts and paid all her hospital bills up until the moment she died. He let Paolo keep his job even though Paolo missed work on many days due to taking care of her."

I feel a strong pull in my chest at her words. It's almost as if she's talking about another man, but I've seen the way she acts comfortable around him, and I know she might be telling the truth.

"When he learned that I lost my only son on my birthday, he started bringing me flowers and gifts every year," she says, her voice thick with emotion.

A soft gasp leaves my lips, and I blink repeatedly, suddenly feeling teary-eyed.

"I'm sorry about your son."

"It's okay. It happened several years ago." She chuckles, but for the first time, I notice the pain in her eyes. "He would have been around don's age now."

Leaning in, her voice softens as she tells me, "Your fiancé has had a hard life. He lost his parents young, and he doesn't talk about it much. All I know is that they died when he was young, leaving him all alone. He can seem so closed off, but he's had to fend for himself his whole life. That's all he knows."

A pang of sorrow strikes me at the thought of him being alone in the world. "What about his family? Does he have anyone?"

"As far as I know, no," Rosa replies, shaking her head. "It's just him. That's why he carries himself the way he does. Imagine being all alone, Ginny. It's a heavy burden."

The revelation tugs at my heartstrings. I try to know if I can recall his parents from the hazy memory I have of him, but I don't remember a thing. It was mostly just him and

Lorenzo. I can't help but feel an overwhelming desire to understand him better, to know what shaped him into the man he is today.

To know what exactly happened between him and my brother.

"Just be patient," Rosa advises gently, as if she can read my thoughts. "He'll open up when he's ready."

And just like that, I have a new assignment—to unravel the mystery that is Dario.

24

DARIO

Ginny's arm is intertwined with mine as we step into *Maison Luxe*, an exclusive designer boutique known for its one-of-a-kind pieces.

The air smells faintly of fresh flowers and new fabric, the sunlight streaming through the tall windows casting a warm glow over the elegant gowns and tailored suits on display.

We already have designers handling our wedding attire, but with upcoming public appearances, Ginny suggested we add a few fresh additions to our wardrobes.

The serene ambiance should be relaxing, but my focus is elsewhere—on Ginny. She's been tightly clutching my arm and leaning into me ever since we got out of the car. It wouldn't feel strange if we were a normal couple, but we aren't. This is still new territory for us both.

"Welcome to *Maison Luxe*! I'm Camille, your style consultant for today," a woman announces as she approaches, extending her hand to me first. Her gaze lingers a little too long, her eyes bold and assessing as if she's calculating how much I'm worth before even getting to know me.

"Thank you." My response is curt, not because I'm unfriendly but because I'm not interested in whatever game she's playing.

Camille's smile widens a fraction. "We're thrilled to have you here. I've heard you have quite the discerning taste." she chuckles softly, leaning in as if she's about to share some inside joke meant only for me.

Ginny's arm tightens around mine, her hand sliding up to grip my bicep. The engagement ring glints under the boutique's bright lights, catching Camille's attention. Only then does she finally glance at Ginny, her smile faltering ever so slightly before she asks, "And you must be the bride?"

"Yeah, that would be me," Ginny replies, her smile wide, though I can sense the subtle edge beneath it.

Camille's focus drifts back to me, her polite smile never reaching her eyes. "Right this way." She gestures toward the fitting area. "We have some stunning pieces for you to try on."

There's a flicker of irritation in me at how dismissive Camille is toward Ginny, but I decide to overlook it—for now.

"Make yourselves comfortable," Camille says as we reach a plush seating area. "I'll bring you some refreshments."

As she walks away, I barely notice her leaving because Ginny nestles into my side, resting her head against my arm. A rush of warmth spreads through me, a comforting sensation that momentarily eases the tension simmering beneath the surface. Despite everything, having her so close feels... right.

After we had sex three nights ago, I've been trying to keep a reasonable distance from Ginny. But it's almost impossible. Whenever I'm near her, I lose all sense of why I'm doing this in the first place—to punish Lorenzo. This isn't supposed to feel good. I can't let it.

I don't want to get too comfortable with this arrangement, and I don't want Lorenzo to get too comfortable, either. Either he gets his family business back on track and sacrifices his sister's happiness in the process or the other way around.

He can't have both.

But Ginny...fuck. She makes it so difficult to stay distant and maintain my nonchalance around her. And this is my default setting--I've always been cold and detached from people. It was deliberate at first. It's how I've survived, especially after my parents died, and in the business I'm in, being emotionally unavailable isn't just a tactic—it's essential.

But now, Ginny's warmth is slowly seeping into my veins, literally and figuratively...it's getting to me, working its way through my defenses.

She's changed. She's been...kinder. Softer. She smiles more, her voice no longer sharp or argumentative, and there's a look in her eyes—one I can't afford to fall for.

I shouldn't like it. I shouldn't revel in the sparkle I see in her eyes or the way she feels more comfortable around me.

"You seem to be getting pretty cozy with our arrangement," I lean in to whisper in her ear. My lips brush her skin, and she gasps softly, so softly that I almost miss it. And that's all it takes for my dick to get instantly hard.

"Maybe I just want everyone here to think we are the most loving couple on earth," she breathes, a mischief glint dancing in her eyes as she looks up at me.

I want to kiss her. I want to taste her again, and she knows it.

Her gaze drops to my lips, and I'm holding on by a thread, fighting the urge to pull her into my lap and kiss her until she's breathless. My mind flashes back to three nights ago, and despite my best efforts, I can't forget it. I've been trying and failing to forget.

"Careful, Princess," I murmur, brushing the back of my hand over her cheek. "You're making me hard."

Her cheeks flush a deep red, and I can't help but chuckle. It's like a ripple effect—the color spreading across her face, betraying the cool façade she tries so hard to maintain.

"Ginny?" Camille chooses that exact moment to appear with a clipboard. "It's time for your fitting."

She gestures for Ginny to follow, and I watch as she stands, smoothing down her simple dress, a mix of nervousness, excitement, and something else on her face.

"It's *Miss Ginevra* to you," she says sweetly, her voice dripping with mock politeness. My girl smiles sweetly at the consultant before gesturing for her to lead the way.

Camille stiffens, her forced smile barely hiding her annoyance. "Sure, *Miss Ginevra*," she mutters before leading Ginny toward the fitting stalls.

As Ginny follows her, she shoots me one last glance, her lips curving into a secret smile that only I can decipher.

I settle back into the plush sofa in the waiting room for less than a minute before another consultant appears—Jennifer, the same woman who fitted me for my suit at my company's grand opening ceremony. She's middle-aged, professional, and one of the few people here I don't feel like throttling.

"Lovely to see you again, Mr. De Luca," she greets warmly. "I've arranged everything for your fitting."

I glance over to where Ginny disappeared, hearing faint instructions to take off her clothes.

"I want us to stay here," I say firmly.

The space is luxurious, with mirrors lining the walls. I hear Ginny's pleasant gasp and imagine she's just been shown a dress. Yeah. They could fit me here. I want to hear more of her voice.

"Of course." Jennifer nods, excusing herself to bring everything into this room. Two assistants return with a rack of suits and tuxedos. They begin their work, adjusting the fit of a dark suit on my frame, but my focus is on Ginny's voice filtering through the wall—soft, nervous laughter and the sound of fabric shifting.

It's a sound that fills the space with an odd kind of comfort, and before I can stop myself, I realize I'm smiling.

"Let's see how this looks on you." Camille's voice drips from the fitting stalls, laced with the kind of casual venom you'd almost miss if you weren't paying attention.

A few beats pass before she adds in mock curiosity, "You know, I couldn't help but wonder—what's it like being engaged to such an influential man?"

Excuse me?

"Excuse me?" Ginny's incredulous laugh mirrors my own thoughts, but it's brittle, a crack in her usually unshakable confidence.

"Oh, no offense intended. I just meant...first, you were practically Mrs. Rinaldo, right? I mean, that man has connections. Politics, isn't it?" She pauses as if she's genuinely considering her next words. "And now, you've upgraded to De Luca. A billionaire? You must have a knack for landing influential men."

She delivers the jab casually, as if she's commenting on the weather.

Rage boils under my skin as I grip the fabric of my suit. Camille is talented, one of the best—that's why I specifically wanted her to fit Ginny personally. But her lack of basic human decency? That's a line crossed. I hear Ginny's laughter falter, and the warmth I felt moments ago evaporates into cold fury.

"I don't think that's any of your business."

Camille actually has the nerve to laugh. "In today's world, influence and power...well, they're everything. Women have to be smart about it, you know? Use what they've got to get what they want."

I ball my fists, willing myself to stay calm. But my patience is razor-thin, hanging by a thread that Camille seems determined to snip.

"Is there something you're trying to say?" Ginny asks, her voice deceptively calm. Ginny snaps, her voice cracking under the strain. I can hear the hurt she's trying so hard to swallow.

"Not at all, I was just saying with Rinaldo, you had the politics card. And now with De Luca, well..." She waves a hand in the air as if to encompass all of Dario's wealth and status. "Let's just say it's a good move. He's a very powerful man."

"I'm not marrying Dario for his money."

"Of course not," Camille replies. "Finding someone who's both incredibly rich and, well, willing to overlook all the...past complications isn't easy."

That's it.

Without hesitation, I rise sharply from my seat. Jennifer and the other designers flinch, clearly startled, but I know they've all heard Camille's cruel words. Fury pulses through me as I stride toward Ginny's fitting room. Each step seems to throb against the silence of the shop, the air growing heavier with every second.

I reach the door and push it open without knocking. Camille's face snaps toward me in surprise, while Ginny turns to meet my gaze, her expression torn between disbelief and anger.

"What did you just say to my fiancée ?" My voice is low, threatening. I close the distance between us, stepping into the room, unbothered that it's a private fitting space. I plant myself protectively in front of Ginny, shielding her.

Camille squares her shoulders, her initial confidence wavering. "Excuse me?"

I lean in slightly, my tone dropping to a dangerous growl. "Don't make me fucking repeat myself."

Ginny tenses beside me, her eyes darting between us. She gently places her hand over my clenched fists, a silent plea for restraint. "Dario, please..."

I pull my hands away from hers, my gaze still fixed on Camille. "Stay back, Ginny." I can't—won't—let anyone tear her down like that. Not now. Not ever.

Camille's voice shakes, though she tries to maintain her composure. "Y-you think you can just walk in here and threaten me? This is my workplace!"

A bitter laugh escapes me. "I can shut down this whole place with one call."

The room buzzes with tension, heavy and suffocating. From the corner of my eye, I see the other employees watching from the open doorway, their faces frozen in shock as they witness the escalating confrontation. This could very well mean their jobs, as well.

"Apologize to Ginny," I growl, venom lacing every word, "or I promise you, your career will be over. I don't care how high you've climbed recently. Nothing will protect you from what comes next. That's not a warning—it's a fact."

Camille's face flushes, her pride struggling against the fear rising in her eyes as I reach for my phone. The red creeping up her cheeks only sharpens my anger.

"Dario," Ginny whispers, her hand brushing my arm, desperate to diffuse the situation.

I ignore her plea, my fingers already dialing the number. Camille's bravado falters instantly, her confidence evaporating as she senses the shift in the room. "I didn't mean it like that," she stammers, her voice wavering. "I wasn't trying to insult her."

"The line clicks as Roberto Mancini picks up. "Dario De Luca," his familiar voice comes through, steady and professional.

"Roberto, I need something handled," I say, cutting straight to the point, my tone leaving no room for discussion. "Your manager at the Fifth Avenue branch, Camille Waters. She needs to go."

A pause follows, and Roberto exhales slowly on the other end. "Camille?" he repeats, clearly surprised. "She's one of our top performers. Is there an issue of which I need to be aware?"

"There is," I reply coldly. "She insulted my fiancée. That's all the reason you need."

Another pause, and then a resigned sigh. "I see. I understand. Consider it done."

I hang up without another word, turning back to Camille, who's visibly paling just as the area manager steps into the room. Her name escapes me, but she's calm, composed—and likely summoned by Roberto himself.

"Camille," she begins with a carefully measured tone,

her gaze steady. "I'm afraid I'll have to dismiss you. Effective immediately."

The color drains from Camille's face as she stares in disbelief. "What?" Her voice cracks. "You can't be serious. I have qualifications from top fashion schools. I'm the best in this store!"

The manager remain unflinching. "It's already been decided."

Whispers ripple through the room, quiet murmurs filling the charged silence. Camille's eyes dart around, searching for some kind of support, but no one speaks up. No one moves. They know better than to.

"This is an abuse of power," she hisses at me, her voice trembling as she struggles to regain control. "You can't just—"

"I'm sorry, Camille," the manager says firmly, cutting her off. "Please collect your things."

Camille's defiance crumbles, replaced by a stunned silence as the weight of what's happening fully sinks in. She turns, walking away without another word, her colleagues exchanging uneasy glances.

The murmurs around us grow louder, uncertainty flashing in the eyes of her colleagues as they exchange uneasy glances. But I don't care about their whispers—I'm still seething, my anger rolling in waves beneath the surface.

I raise my voice, letting it boom across the store with authority. "I'll be buying out your entire dress collection. Every. Last. Dress."

A collective gasp sweeps through the staff, their stunned reactions palpable in the thickening air. Disbelief spreads like a ripple, but I ignore it, my gaze locking onto Ginny.

Her eyes meet mine, wide with concern and something

else—a flicker of uncertainty, maybe? Her voice, barely a whisper, reaches me. "Dario. This is...a lot."

I step closer, taking her hand in mine, feeling her warmth ground me. I give it a firm, reassuring squeeze. "No one will ever disrespect you, Ginny. Not while I'm here."

My words come out like a vow, unshakable and fierce. I feel the possessiveness rise in me, sharp and undeniable. "You are mine now," I murmur, leaning in, my voice dropping lower. "Mine to protect, mine to worship."

I see the effect it has on her—the hitch in her breath, the way her lips part ever so slightly as I close the distance. My gaze darkens, focused entirely on her as I utter the final word.

"Mine."

25

GINEVRA

The car ride home stretches in silence, thick with unspoken words. Soft music plays from the speakers, yet it does nothing to calm my racing heart. My throat feels heavy with unspoken words, and I struggle to control my heavy breathing.

My fingers press a button on the window, making the tinted glass slide down. A gentle breeze blows over my face as the car drives down the familiar road, but it does nothing to make me feel better.

We both sit silently at the backseat of Dario's Lamborghini, and I can feel the heat of Dario's anger simmering beside me, still charged from what happened at the boutique. It's not directed at me, but it still makes my stomach churn with anxiety...

And something else.

There's a strange comfort in knowing he's upset on my behalf. I can't quite grasp why that makes my heart flutter, but it does.

Dario hasn't said a word for several minutes, only shifting his attention between his phone screen and the bottle of water in the cup holder beside him. My fingers twitch on my lap as I look outside, trying to ignore his presence beside me.

The tall buildings and bustling city streets blur past the car window as we drive past them, the mid-afternoon sun casting long shadows across the road.

But after a long minute, I steal a glance at him. His jaw is set tight, and his eyes are now fixed on the road. Part of me wants to thank him, to say something...anything, but the words are stuck in my throat. We sit in the silence that is wrapped around us like a heavy cloak, heavy and awkward.

I look outside the window again as we approach the familiar, quiet, luxurious neighborhood of Dario's house. When we get married, it'll become my house, too, whether I like it or not. When I think of home, his large duplex is what will appear in my head.

The almost identical houses, large and extravagant, with their immaculately groomed lawns, blur past my eyes. The car slows down as we approach the gates of Dario's house. Most houses here don't have gates, but it doesn't shock me that Dario is private to that degree.

The gates are opened by the security guards, and we slowly pull in. When we finally pull into the driveway, the air feels electric, charged with awkwardness and a mix of something new and uncertain.

The car engine stops, and I push the car door open almost immediately. The bright sun hits my skin as I step down and head toward the front door with Dario's heavy footsteps behind me.

The tension floats in the air between us. I climb up the stairs with him right on my tail. I feel the heat of his stare warming my body, and a strong sense of Deja vu hits me.

When I get to my bedroom door, I notice he's stopped and is now watching me.

I don't turn to look at him, scared of what I'll do if I saw his face.

"Um...I'll see you later."

"Yeah. Later." I hear his gruff response behind me as I twist the doorknob and enter the walls of my room, the only place I'm safe from his heated looks and the intensity of his presence.

But not safe from thoughts of him. I'm never safe from that.

It's a weekend, and Rosa had told me earlier that Dario was taking this particular weekend off. It's not supposed to be a strange thing, but Dario works every single day. It's something I hope will change as time goes on.

Once inside my room, I feel an overwhelming urge to cool down. I head toward the bathroom and turn on the shower knob, letting the water warm up while I strip off my clothes.

The steam fills the bathroom, wrapping around me like a comforting cocoon. Except it's not comforting. It reminds me of every heated touch and kiss I've shared with Dario.

As I stand under the cascading water, I let my thoughts drift. I replay Dario's rage as he defended me earlier, how his voice had practically vibrated with anger when he confronted Camille.

There's something intoxicating about knowing he cares so fiercely, even if our situation is complicated. Something runs down my spine at his unabashed protectiveness, at the passion in his voice. It makes my stomach flip and warmth flood through me. My heartbeat quickens.

I scrub my scalp a little too harshly as I wash my hair, the scent of shampoo mixing with the steam. Thoughts of him continue to race through my head, and the feeling of heat floods through my body.

I switch the shower to cold, and a certain restlessness fills me as the water slides down my skin. When I'm completely rinsed off, I grab my towel and slowly dry off my hair and body. With slightly shaky hands, I wrap the towel around my chest before stepping out of the shower.

I catch my reflection in the mirror as I walk past. It shows the aftermath of the day—red cheeks from the heat of the water, eyes still wide with lingering excitement.

When I get to my bedroom, I change into a pair of cotton shorts and a tank top. I decide to try and take a nap, hoping to escape the whirlwind of emotions swirling in my mind. With the towel still wrapped around my head, I crawl into bed, pulling the covers around me, but sleep doesn't come. Instead, I toss and turn, my mind racing with thoughts of Dario. The way he looked at me, the tension in the air when we were close...all the times he's touched me, kissed me...

A groan escapes my lips as I sit up and tug the wet towel from my head before flinging it across the room in frustration. I try to push all thoughts of him away, but his warmth lingers like a ghost in the room.

I should have said something to him. I should have thanked him for defending me. Rosa's words filter back into my head, and I remember my resolve to be nicer to him. Not thanking someone for defending you and buying out an entire store for you isn't nice, now is it?

After what feels like an eternity, I finally gather the courage to get up. My heart beats faster as I approach my bedroom door, each step filled with a mix of anticipation and anxiety. Maybe I should just go back and force myself to sleep. But I'm already twisting the doorknob and pulling it open.

A breath gets caught in my throat as I find Dario standing behind the door, his hand poised to knock. For a moment, we just stand there staring at each other, the air around us thickening. The tension between us isn't awkward anymore... It's electric, chilling even.

His raw gaze pierces into mine, and I can barely breathe. The rational part of me, the one that remembers that Dario is supposed to be my enemy, screams at me to run away, to run as far and as fast as I possibly can from him. But the wild, carnal side that resides deep within my soul screams at me to move forward, to reach for him.

The moment stretches, the air heavy with unspoken words and pent-up desire. I watch Dario's eyes darken as they drink me in, trailing from my face down to my chest and to my exposed legs. My body burns, feeling completely naked under his gaze.

I take him in, too, from his dark, tousled hair to the casual white shirt and faded jeans he's changed into. My throat runs dry at the way his muscles ripple beneath his shirt, reminding me of what else lies underneath.

Then, as if something snaps, we both move simultaneously. One second, he's watching me with heated eyes, the next, he has grabbed my wrist and pulled me into his arms, pressing me against his hard chest and locking his lips to mine.

My lips part beneath his, and the sound he lets out is rough and demanding, sending sparks flying through me.

The weight of everything—the anger, the desire, the unspoken feelings—crashes down on us. My fingers grasp the front of his shirt as his tongue plunges into my mouth. His hands circle my neck, his fingers lifting my chin and tilting my head to kiss me harder with more hunger.

A moan rips out of my throat as one hand slides down

my neck to my breast, squeezing it roughly and cupping the soft flesh through the thin fabric of my shirt. My fingers travel to his hair, tugging on the strands as he pushes me against the open doorframe.

"Dario," I moan as his thumb slips under the fabric of my top through my armpit and caresses the exposed side of my breast.

"Please..."

He groans in reply before lowering his lips to my chest, down the valley between my breasts, and sucking gently. He makes a low sound that is muffled against my skin as his two hands slide under my tank top to grab my waist. The rough texture of his fingertips against my bare stomach sends waves of pleasure throughout my body.

He takes one clothed nipple between his teeth, biting softly. My breath hitches as I close my eyes, feeling the wetness of his tongue through the thin fabric. But I want more.

Grabbing his head, I kiss him again, sliding one hand over his crotch to squeeze.

"Oh, Ginny," he growls, his voice a low, rough hiss against my lips.

My fingers trace a slow, teasing path up over the waist-band of his pants, skimming past his navel before sliding over the firm ridges of his abs. I pull his bottom lip between my teeth, nibbling and flicking my tongue against it, savoring the warmth of him until a deep, guttural groan escapes his throat, and he jerks away, eyes dark and hungry.

We're both panting, our breath mingling in the heated space between us as I meet his gaze—intense, smoldering with barely restrained desire.

"Thank you," I whisper, my lips brushing his, the words trembling on the edge of them.

His hand trails down, possessive and deliberate, until it grips one cheek of my ass, squeezing firmly. His mouth curves into a wicked smile. "I haven't even given you a real reason to thank me yet, Princess," he murmurs, his voice full of promise. "But by the time I'm finished with you...you'll have one."

26

DARIO

I steal Ginny's next breath by kissing her again, my hands roaming all over her soft body. Her moans are music to my ears. Her taste is so intoxicating that I never want to stop. My hands squeeze her ass again, my hips pressing harder into hers.

"Fuck, you feel so good," I groan, lifting her by her ass against my body. She immediately wraps her legs around me and grips onto my shoulders as I press her harder against the doorframe and grind against her body.

"Dario," she makes a sound between a moan and a whimper, tugging my hair harshly as she rolls her hips against mine. I feel the heat of her clothed pussy against my crotch, and it drives me fucking crazy.

"Please..." she begs, her hand fisting in my hair as she kisses me hungrily. I don't even think about it before I'm carrying her into the room, closing the door with my legs, and leading us to the queen-sized bed in the center of the room.

I lay her on top of it, kissing her hard on the lips again before moving down to kiss the curve of her throat. She gasps when I run my teeth along the sensitive skin. I drag my kisses farther down as my hands simultaneously tug her tank top over her stomach.

She sits up to let me pull the fabric over her head, and my throat bobs at my first sight of her bare breasts. They're an ideal medium size, perfectly shaped, and perky—created to drive a man mad.

She sucks in a sharp breath as my thumb traces over the dark pink skin of her areola.

Then, I lean in, my tongue tracing the path my thumb has just taken. Her back arches, and I open my mouth, taking one nipple into my mouth. My second hand pinches her other nipple between my fingers. While my tongue works her, I look up to see her face, her head thrown back with her mouth slightly open.

She looks almost ethereal, her dark hair spread out everywhere like a halo against the white sheets. Her eyes are closed, and her eyelashes fan across her cheeks, making them appear like wings. Her pink lips hang slightly open, and my cock throbs as the image of fucking her mouth again flashes in my head.

Giving her breast one last bite, I trail kisses down her toned stomach. Her back arches as my tongue flicks over her bellybutton before moving farther down. When I tug the waistband of her shorts with my teeth, she leans up on her elbows to look at me with hazy eyes.

Impatient, I grab the material, pulling it down together with her panties until they are at her ankles. She kicks the material off, her round tits bouncing against her pale chest with every movement she makes, making my dick twitch at the sight.

She's completely naked before me, and I stare at her for what feels like an eternity. My throat goes dry at the way her golden brown locks spill across her breasts and cling to her skin. The fullness of her lips. The curve of her hips. Her plump thighs. Her glistening pussy...

"Fuck, Ginny," I say hoarsely, running my hand over her knee. "Did you get this wet just from me kissing you?"

She bites her lower lip and nods, looking at me with a hooded gaze. I run a hand over my face in an attempt to control myself.

"Spread your legs, baby," I order gruffly.

A blush spreads across her skin as she complies. She pulls her knees up, exposing her wet, glistening folds. I smile as I trace a finger over them. She moans as my fingertips caress and tease her until her hips are rolling and she's pushing herself against my hand.

"Dario," she whines, slipping her hand down to touch herself.

I grab her hand before it makes contact with her wet pussy.

"Mine," I growl before leaning down and giving her one long, wet lick. She moans, spreading her legs even further and burying her hands in my hair.

I groan at her taste, my tongue working in circles while two fingers slip inside her. She pants as my tongue moves in perfect sync with my hands, alternating between slipping inside her and slowly massaging her clit. Her hips rock forward as if begging for more.

I slide my shoulders under her knees, lifting and spreading her legs to further open her to me. Her heels hit my shoulder blades as my mouth returns to her pussy. She moans louder, one hand clutching the sheets beside her while the other tugs painfully at my hair.

I work her faster and deeper now, my tongue thrusting

deeper each time, circling her clit, sliding my fingers through her wetness.

Her hips jerk upward, her moans getting louder as her orgasm builds. When I curve my fingers inside her, she comes hard, moaning loudly as her wetness trails down to her ass while I slurp the rest out into my mouth. She clutches my hair tighter as she collapses, her breathing hard and heavy.

My heart pounds as I stare down at her, my cock throbbing against my thigh. An involuntary smile plays on my lips as I notice the slight tear dropping from the corner of her eye. Dark pleasure ripples through me as I move my face closer to her and lick the salty liquid away.

"I haven't even fucked you yet, Ginny." I chuckle roughly.

She bites her lower lip and stares up at me, and fuck, the sight of her like this makes me want to do the most savage things to her.

"Then fuck me," she whispers, before adding, "Please."

Something snaps inside me.

"Get on your hands and knees."

Something flares in her eyes at my command, and I realize that my Ginny loves being dominated in bed. She obliges, twisting onto her hands and knees in front of me. Seeing the curve of her naked ass and the wetness between her legs makes my dick throb painfully.

With a low growl, I hastily unbuckle and unzip my jeans. Pulling them off and throwing them aside, I crawl onto the bed and kneel behind her on the mattress, spreading her wide apart. She gasps when I press two fingers into her, my thumbs rubbing softly against her entrance from behind. Her hands grip the sheet tightly, her fingernails digging into the thin material. I hold still as I watch her pussy clench around the tips of my fingers.

My dick twitches at the sight, and I grab the soft globes of her ass, pulling her back toward me. A low hiss escapes my lips as she rolls her hips against my dick.

I squeeze her ass, letting my thumb graze very close to her center as she continues to grind against me. A soft whimper slips past her lips, followed by a soft moan of pleasure as my fingers slowly pump her again before replacing them with my dick.

She stills, letting out a low groan as I sink inside her slowly, inch by inch, until I'm buried deep inside her. A low groan escapes my lips at the feel of her warm heat clenched around me.

I pull out slowly, holding her in place as I thrust inside her again. She falls on her stomach, her ass lifting off the mattress and pressing against me. Holding her waist, I move into her again, in and out until I find a steady rhythm.

Slapping sounds intertwined with our moans and grunts fill the room. Her hands are firmly clutching the sheets as I slam into her from behind, her moans buried into the soft pillows. My breathing is labored as her ass moves up and down in time with my hard thrusts, creating an addictive feeling that spreads through every fiber of my being.

"Do you like being fucked by me, Ginny?" I grunt, meeting my question with a hard stroke. She responds by giving another small whimper as I slam into her.

With my hands, I gather her hair together before wrapping it around my right wrist and pulling her body up.

"Oh!" She moans as I pull her back against my front. My free hand slides to her front to grab one breast roughly.

"I asked you a question, Princess," I growl, continuing to pound into her. "Do you like it when I fuck you?" I slide my hand up to circle her neck and whisper into her ear, "Use your words."

"Yes," she moans, her hand covering mine around her neck. "It feels so good."

I thrust harder inside of her and grin against her ear. "That's what I thought, sweetheart."

I push her down against the bed again before slamming down hard into her. Her moans are loud, and so is the sound of me pounding into her. Her ass is angled upwards, making my thrusts hit her deep and hard as she writhes underneath me. Her pussy clenches around me again, and I feel my balls tighten.

My hand slips between her round ass cheeks, my thumb rubbing around her asshole.

"I'll fuck here next," I growl, slipping the tip of my thumb in.

Her body bucks against me as her orgasm hits her hard. I feel mine starting to build as I continue my relentless movements even as her body spasms beneath me. I continue to fuck her until I reach my climax, my dick twitching as I release into her.

A deep groan rips out of my throat as I collapse against her, our bodies slick with sweat. My chest heaves, trying to catch my breath as I turn to pull her into my arms. Our sweaty bodies lie tangled together in bed, the sheets a mess around us.

When she leans up to look at my face, I see the streak of tears on her cheek. Something dark and twisted wells up in my chest at seeing her this way for me. But when she smiles at me before a tired yawn rips out of her throat, the feeling in my chest is replaced by something warm and fuzzy.

I chuckle as she snuggles against my chest, her head settling right below where my heart lay. I bury my nose against her hair, inhaling deeply. She smells like flowery shampoo, vanilla, and the lingering scent of sex.

The warmth that spreads through my chest grows stronger, making my heart beat faster and louder. Blood rushes to my ears as I press a long kiss against her hair. A soft sigh escapes her lips, causing goosebumps to rise on my skin.

As her breathing becomes slow and steady, I feel my eyes drift shut. And the only thing I can think about as I slip into a dreamless sleep is how I don't want to wake up from this moment. I just want to remain in her arms, away from everything else.

Forever.

27

GINEVRA

I slam the refrigerator door shut with a thud, gripping the bowl of cookie dough I made earlier. A rush of cool air brushes my face, mixing with the warmth of the kitchen, but it does nothing to cool my frustration.

My gaze flicks to Lorenzo, still leaning casually against Dario's marble countertop, arms crossed, a small, smug smile tugging at his lips.

"You can't ignore me as if I'm not here, Ginny." He sighs, his voice laced with a weariness I don't care to acknowledge.

I do exactly that—I ignore him. Dropping the cold bowl onto the countertop with a sharp clink, I turn my back, focusing entirely on the dough in front of me. It's a Friday morning, and surely Lorenzo has somewhere to be. Work, perhaps. He'll get tired of standing here soon enough. He'll leave once he realizes he's wasting his time.

I press my fingers into the soft dough, testing its texture, acutely aware of his eyes on me, waiting for some reaction. But I won't give him the satisfaction.

"Come on, Ginny. You can't seriously stay mad forever,"

he persists, his voice teasing now, the lightness of it grating against my nerves.

I roll my eyes, biting back a response, and move toward the pantry, searching for chocolate chips. Lorenzo showing up this morning wasn't exactly a surprise. I've ignored every one of his calls and texts ever since he signed that contract —the one binding me to a marriage with Dario.

The last time I saw him was at the charity gala last week, and despite things not being as strained with Dario as before, I'm still furious with my brother.

Because of him, I've been shoved into this uncomfortable, humiliating mess. I've been insulted, judged, and cornered, all thanks to his actions.

And you've had mind-blowing, animalistic sex with the man you're supposed to hate. Twice.

My inner voice taunts, a hypocritical whisper I've tried —and failed—to silence. I ignore it, just like I ignore Lorenzo.

When I reenter the kitchen, Lorenzo fixes me with a determined look, arms still crossed, a familiar stubbornness etched into his features. "I'm not leaving until you talk to me, Ginny. I mean it. You know I do."

"That's your problem," I snap, the words sharper than I intend. There's a crackling tension in the air, despite my brother's attempts to dispel it.

He steps forward, his tone softening just a fraction. "You know I'm sorry, Ginny. I never wanted this for you. I know you're stuck with a man you can't stand." His lips curl into a teasing smile, but there's an undercurrent of sadness in his eyes. "But I've also noticed you've been doing a lot of baking lately. And if there's one thing I know, it's that you only do that when you're happy."

He's right about that. I've baked every day since Dario

and I last slept together, trying desperately to distract myself from the desire that keeps bubbling up whenever he's around. And since Dario's been home more often, the temptation has only grown harder to resist.

I roll my eyes, unable to suppress the flicker of warmth at his observation. "Baking is my escape, Lorenzo. It doesn't mean I'm happy about this mess," I lie.

Guilt flares as I realize I've let Dario, the very man who orchestrated this situation, touch me while I'm still furious with my brother. A brother who, admittedly, had little say in the matter. But I can't shake my disappointment in Lorenzo. I expected more from him.

"I've been baking because Rosa's not here," I lie, focusing intently on the dough.

"Rosa?" he asks, eyebrow raised.

"The cook and head housekeeper," I reply curtly, irritation bubbling up again. My hands pause their movements as I glare at him. "Stop talking to me."

A low chuckle escapes his lips. "We haven't spoken since all of this went down. Aren't you even a little curious about how I've been?"

I turn to face him, arms crossing defensively. "And what exactly do you want me to say, Lorenzo? That I'm thrilled to see you? That I've missed you even though the mess we're in is entirely your fault?"

His smirk widens, a glint of amusement flashing in his eyes. "You're just as charming as ever."

I scoop up a spoonful of dough, rolling it into a ball, ignoring the sarcastic edge in his voice. But his steady, probing gaze follows me, making my skin prickle. He's waiting for something—waiting for me to crack.

"I'll scoop out your eyes with this," I mutter, waving the spoon at him in mock threat.

Lorenzo chuckles again, but this time his smile falters, a flicker of sadness in his eyes. "You sound just like Papa," he says quietly.

The mention of our father hangs in the air, heavy with unspoken memories. I pause, the dough resting in my hands as I think back to the way he used to push us, beyond our limits and to the point of exhaustion.

My memory of him was that he was always angry, and I often bore the brunt of his anger. However, whatever I suffered was nothing compared to what Lorenzo faced, especially since he was much older. He was also the expected heir to the Bianchi Empire.

"I don't think I'm like him," I huff, and that earns me a small chuckle from him.

"Yes, you are, at least right now," Lorenzo teases. "You're being extremely difficult, unforgiving, and grumpy."

I roll my eyes again, but a small smile teases the edges of my lips at the fact that he's not wrong. Children often take little bits of traits from their parents, after all.

"Papa wasn't a bad man," Lorenzo says after a few beats of silence. When I look at him, he has a serious expression on his face. "You know he only wanted the best for us."

I don't say anything because, well, I don't have anything to say. I liked my Papa as much as liking parents went, but that's where it ends.

Lorenzo continues, something distant flickering in his eyes. "He did some terrible things, but he wasn't a bad person."

Why does it sound like he's trying to convince himself of that?

"Right, tough love and all that," I reply, my tone sarcastic. "Was it worth it, though? Your children having to think very hard before they remember good moments with you?"

Lorenzo sighs before taking a step closer. "Maybe he didn't care about that. All he wanted was for the family legacy to continue, and to an extent, that happened. The company was thriving...before everything went wrong."

"And how's the company doing now?" I ask, suddenly aware that I haven't heard anything about it since my engagement to Dario. The only time I've seen Lorenzo lately was at the gala to which Dario took me.

To my surprise and pleasure, Lorenzo smiles. "The company is doing great, actually, thanks to Dario's help. He's really stepped up."

I raise an eyebrow at his words, shocked that he's giving Dario credit.

"That's unexpected coming from you. Thought he was the bane of your existence."

Lorenzo chuckles, and I can see a genuine happiness radiating from him, even brighter than the last time we spoke. Despite my earlier annoyance, that thought brings warmth to my chest.

"Dario may be everything I've said, but he's kept his promise since..." He trails off, clearing his throat before continuing. "Even though he's responsible for us getting back on our feet and owns the majority of the stock, he lets me run things as I always did. He's not interested in over-throwing me or taking control as I initially feared," he adds, a smirk creeping back onto his face. "Although he's still a jerk and we definitely don't see eye to eye."

I chuckle as his words do something to my chest. The thought of them no longer being sworn enemies warms my heart in a way I hadn't expected.

A deep sigh escapes his lips, and he runs a hand through his hair, a gesture I've come to recognize as a sign of his inner conflict. "But I'm partly to blame for that," he admits, his voice low and earnest. "And I want to make things right."

Before I can push him further or ask what exactly he means by that, he swiftly changes the subject, catching me off guard.

"So, what's got you all chippy today? I know you only bake in your happy moods. If you really hated Dario and this house as much as you say, I don't see how you'd be in such a good mood. Is there something you want to tell me?"

A flush of heat rises in my cheeks.

Well, I've been experiencing an abundance of pleasure lately. As in, black-out orgasm after black-out orgasm. Who would've thought my enemy would be the only man capable of making me *feel* this much?

"In a weird turn of events, Dario seems to have that effect on people now," I reply dryly, hoping the sarcasm covers up the truth hiding behind my words.

"That's good," Lorenzo says, his expression softening. A flicker of relief passes through his eyes, barely noticeable but enough for me to catch it. It's the kind of relief that tells me maybe, just maybe, he believes I'm not as miserable as he once feared.

A thought strikes me then—Lorenzo would never let me get involved with a man he couldn't vouch for. Despite their bad blood, they were once friends, and deep down, I know that's not something he's forgotten. He must be assured that I'm in good hands to have allowed this whole arrangement to go this far. Even if he's not thrilled about it, the fact that he hasn't fought harder against it says more than his words ever could.

As much as I want to stay mad at him for the contract, I know my brother. He wouldn't have let this happen if he didn't believe, on some level, that Dario could take care of me. And that realization makes something twist inside me —something a lot more confusing than I'm ready to admit.

"Since things are almost normal now, at least for you, I think it's high time you start dating." I smirk, shaping the dough with a deliberate casualness.

"Not this again, Ginny," he groans, rolling his eyes, but I can tell he's not entirely dismissive.

I stop mid-roll, my hands stilling on the dough. "It wouldn't kill you to put yourself out there. You'll be thirty-seven this year, Enzo. I want to be an aunt so bad. You know, take my little pumpkins to the park, bake them the sweetest tooth-rotting confections, and just be the badass aunt I've always dreamed of but never had."

Lorenzo chuckles, grabbing an apple from the bowl on the counter. He tosses it into the air, catches it effortlessly, and takes a bite before leaning back against the counter with his arms crossed, a teasing smirk on his face.

"Well, you can still do all those things, Ginny. Just with your own kids. I'm sure Dario wouldn't mind helping out by, you know, *pumping* you full of some little Ginny mini-me's."

I groan in disgust. "Oh my god. I *so* do not want to discuss Dario pumping me with babies right now. Especially with you."

He laughs, clearly enjoying how flustered I am. "Like it's not going to happen eventually. I mean, if you weren't my sister, and I was in the exact same position as Dario—living in a house with a beautiful woman, with the whole marriage thing looming—I'd make sure she was pregnant before we even reached the altar."

"Enzo, please *stop*."

"Just telling you—you have my blessing to screw my ex-best friend, little sis. Am I not the coolest brother ever?"

If only he knew I already was.

"And that ends this conversation," I say firmly, trying to hide the heat rising to my cheeks.

Lorenzo laughs again, but the sound softens, the teasing ebbing away. He takes another bite of the apple, his expression turning more serious as he leans against the counter.

"But, in all honesty, Ginny, I'm glad you're not totally hating being here. And I need you to know...I'm still here for you. Anytime. The minute anything goes wrong, or Dario crosses the line—even by an inch—you tell me. I don't care if it's business or for the company. I'll get you out of here. The company be damned. Okay?"

His words hit me like a wave, stirring up a mix of gratitude and a painful reminder of how much he cares. There's that protective side of him, the brother who won't let anything or anyone hurt me, no matter what's at stake.

"Okay." I nod, my throat tightening. "I know."

I hesitate for a second before meeting his gaze again. "And you too, Enzo. Promise me you'll put yourself out there more. You can't hide forever. I'm not going to be around the house much anymore, and I don't want *you* to be lonely, either. Just...think about it, okay?"

"I don't have the time for that right now," he says with a sigh, exasperation creeping into his voice. "With the company getting back on track, I've got a lot on my plate."

I raise my eyebrows, not buying it. "And when business keeps doing well? You'll just get busier and busier, making more excuses."

"I just can't commit to anything serious right now—"

"Then when will you commit? When you're forty? Fifty?" I challenge, cutting him off. "You've never even introduced me to a single woman you've been serious about. Don't you think it's time?"

He shakes his head, a small, reluctant smile playing at

his lips. "Fine. I'll think about it," he concedes, though there's a teasing lilt to his voice. "But I'm not promising anything."

I chuckle softly, satisfied for now and making a mental note to keep reminding him of it. But as I finish shaping the dough, I can't help but feel the shadow of our earlier conversation lingering in the air—what he didn't say, what he's still hiding.

Whatever happened between him and Dario...I need to know.

As I finish rolling the dough and arranging them on the baking pan, I put the pan in the preheated oven before returning back to sit by the island. In a few minutes, delicious warmth surrounds us, and the smell of chocolate chips fills the air.

As soon as I finish rolling the dough and arrange the cookies on the baking pan, I slide it into the preheated oven. A few minutes later, warmth envelops us, the rich smell of chocolate chips filling the air.

But the earlier lightness fades as I glance at the time on my phone and realize Lorenzo may have to leave soon for work. The question I'd asked earlier gnaws at me until I can no longer hold it in.

"So... why did you guys stop talking in the first place? What exactly happened? Every time I ask, you brush it off. I want to know, Enzo." My voice drops, almost pleading.

Before he can protest, I add, "You owe it to me, considering I'm in this situation because of this beef."

Lorenzo's expression shifts, and another sigh escapes his lips. "You really want to know, don't you?"

"Absolutely. I'm in a forced marriage with him for crying out loud," I press, my tone serious. "I need to understand."

A flicker of hesitation crosses his eyes, and he glances

away, as if weighing his words. "Well, everything started on that camping trip when you were just four..."

Thick footsteps echo in the space as Dario strides in, his expression unreadable. The atmosphere shifts instantly, the earlier ease I felt evaporating like steam.

"Don't you have somewhere to be, Lorenzo?" Dario snaps, his voice slicing through the air.

I bristle at his tone while Lorenzo exchanges a tense glance with me." I was just catching up with my sister," he replies.

"You'll have more than enough time for that later. Right now, you need to be at work. I'm not investing so much in your company for you to slack off--"

"Dario!" I interject, stepping forward. "He was just--"

"It's fine, Ginny." Lorenzo cuts me off with a tight smile, the warmth draining from his demeanor. "I was already about to leave anyway."

I'm fuming, barely able to contain my anger as Lorenzo presses a kiss against my forehead.

"I'll see you later," Lorenzo whispers with a small smile before grabbing his briefcase and walking away.

The moment he leaves, I turn to Dario, my cheeks flushed as my frustration bubbles over.

"Why are you such a jerk?" I scream, my voice trembling. "Just when I thought you were starting to show some humanity, you revert back to this!"

Dario's expression hardens as he glances at his wristwatch, not even sparing me a glance. "I'm not in the mood to argue with you," he says coldly, brushing past me as if I'm invisible.

Anger and resentment clog my throat, and I can't hold back. "Asshole," I shout, the words echoing in the now tense silence of the kitchen.

The moment he leaves, my chest feels heavy. Intertwined with my anger is a gnawing suspicion. Dario must have eavesdropped on our conversation, interrupting before Lorenzo could reveal the truth. A tight knot twists in my stomach, and I can't help but wonder just how bad the story really is.

The oven pings, signaling that my cookies are done. I turn it off and pull the pan out, but the sweet aroma does little to lift my mood. I arrange the cookies in a container, placing them by the fridge, and then retreat angrily to my room, the comforting scent fading behind me.

I stay holed up in my room for the rest of the day, having my meals brought up like I'm some kind of prisoner in my own life rather than the soon to be wife in this mansion. The weight of everything presses down on me, and I can't shake the feeling that something's off.

That night, I toss and turn, the bed sheets tangled around me, sleep refusing to come. My mind is a storm of frustration, anxiety, and a gnawing sense of dread. I *need* to know what really happened between Lorenzo and Dario. The more I try to push it away, the more it claws at my insides, demanding answers.

As much as I'm furious with Dario for interrupting earlier, for being so infuriatingly controlling, I can't shake the concern I feel for him. There's this growing, stubborn part of me that worries for his well-being. *Why?* I shouldn't care, not after everything. But I do.

Each passing minute drags out my fears, twisting my stomach into knots. What if the truth is worse than I imagined? What if it shatters whatever fragile peace I've managed to cling to? Worse still...what if knowing the truth makes me fall for Dario completely?

That thought terrifies me most of all.

28

DARIO

The morning sun hangs low in the sky as I jog up the street, the soft glow illuminating the manicured lawns and grand houses that line the way. Each heavy step on the gravel is steady, but my mind races faster than my feet.

I can't shake thoughts of Ginny off my mind. I spent the whole of yesterday trying to forget the disappointment and anger I saw in her eyes. Hearing her ask Lorenzo about the history of our animosity shocked me at first. I thought he'd have already given her a false story painting me as the villain. But he hadn't even told her the root of our falling out in the first place.

I wonder why he hadn't told her? Maybe he was embarrassed about what he'd done several years ago, or maybe she just believed everything he told her so she'd never asked what the root of the problem was.

Regardless of that, I panicked the moment I heard him about to recount that memory. It's something I've buried deep within me for such a long time, and I felt uncomfortable having Ginny hear about it.

A heavy breath leaves my lips as I realize I've spent my whole jog thinking about Ginny, and she's the exact reason I went out to clear my mind in the first place. I try to shake my thoughts off, but they cling to me like the sweat on my skin.

The air is crisp and fresh, scented with the faint aroma of blooming flowers from nearby gardens and lawns. As I approach my house, I quicken my pace, eager to grab a cold drink and cool down.

I enter the gate and jog toward the front door before pushing it open. The faint creak echoes in the stillness of the early hour, and the cool air inside hits me like a wave, a welcome relief from the warmth outside.

The house is quiet, save for the faint hum of the refrigerator in the kitchen. As I walk in, the sunlight pours through the windows, illuminating the dust motes dancing in the air.

My vest clings to my back, soaked from the jog I took to clear my head. Sweat trickles down my forehead, stinging my eyes, and I wipe it away with the back of my hand.

I head straight to the kitchen, hoping for a cold drink to cool down. But as I enter, my breath catches.

There's Ginny, bent over, rummaging through the lower cabinets. Her shorts cling to her legs, accentuating the curve of her hips. And that ass...god, that ass.

I exhale sharply, frustration bubbling up as I mutter a curse under my breath. My plan is to head toward the fridge, but instead, I slam my toe into the counter. A dull pain shoots up my leg, and my irritation rises, spreading like wildfire.

"Ginny?" My voice is rough, a growl, really. "What are you doing up?"

She doesn't rush. Slowly, deliberately, she straightens up, turning to face me with a look that has trouble written all over it. Her front isn't any better. That light pink tank top clings to her, and it's blatantly obvious she's not wearing a bra, her nipples pushing through the fabric like some kind of twisted dare.

"Oh, you're here," she says, feigning surprise with a smug little smile. Without a second glance, she walks straight to the fridge, right where I was heading. "Didn't know you jogged in the mornings."

I clench my jaw so hard it hurts. It's barely 7 a.m., and she never gets up this early. Not without a reason. My eyes narrow—she's doing this on purpose, needling me after yesterday.

"You should probably wear something more appropriate when you're out of your room," I grind out, folding my arms across my chest in a way that's meant to look casual, but really it's just to keep myself from doing something I'll regret.

Her gaze flicks to my arms, lingering a moment before she raises an eyebrow at me. "And what's wrong with what I'm wearing? Is it the shorts?" She cocks her hip, twisting just enough to give me a perfect view of her backside, her eyes dancing with mischief.

I ignore the heat rising in my chest and focus on her next move as she grabs a bottle of water from the fridge. With a flick of her wrist, she shuts the door and makes her way to the cabinet. It's too high for her, and she knows it. As she stands on her tiptoes, her tank top inches up, revealing a sliver of toned stomach and a slim waist that does nothing to help my self-control.

After a minute of struggle, she turns and gives me a hard stare. "Won't you be a gentleman and help me, Dario?" Her voice is soft, almost a purr, dripping with the challenge she's throwing my way.

I run a hand through my damp hair, my breath still heavy from the jog, and try to focus on anything but the way she's looking at me. I walk over to her, standing behind her body as I reach for the glass cup. A different type of heat burns through my body as I tower over her, despite the few inches between us.

"There are other glass cups in the lower drawer," I mutter, retrieving the one she was so adamantly reaching for.

She turns, her fingers brushing mine as I hand it over, her lips curling into a knowing smile. "Yeah but I wanted this one," she breathes, her voice soft but dripping with provocation.

The air around us thickens, every second stretching out. I exhale sharply, stepping back, trying to create distance, trying to control the rising frustration and something far more dangerous. She smirks again, brushing past me, her shoulder grazing my arm.

A spark shoots through me—hot, immediate, and impossible to ignore.

I grit my teeth, willing myself to focus as I move to make a cup of coffee. My hands go through the motions automatically setting the pot to brew. The comforting hiss of the machine fills the space, but I'm acutely aware of her movements behind me, the subtle sounds of her shuffling through cabinets.

From the corner of my eye, I see her bent over again, her hips swaying as she searches for something in the lower cabinets. I force my eyes back to the coffee, watching the dark liquid drip down as if it's the most important thing in the world.

If I just focus on the pot, if I stay busy, maybe I can push her out of my head.

But then I feel it—her body pressing close, the soft curve of her breast brushing against my back, sliding along my arm like a whispered temptation. My grip tightens on the coffee cup, and without thinking, I grab her elbow, spinning her and pinning her against the opposite counter.

She tilts her head, eyes glinting with amusement and challenge. "Stop what?" she asks, her tone innocent but her expression anything but.

"Stop playing games with me," I say, my voice taut with exasperation. "You know exactly what you're doing."

"Maybe I do," she murmurs, her voice taking on a seductive edge that sends a shiver down my spine.

A surge of frustration and something darker courses through me, a heady mix of desire and fury. My heart hammers against my chest, the beat growing louder as she leans in, her lips brushing my ear as she whispers, "But messing with you is so fun."

I tighten my grip around her arm, pulling her closer instead of pushing her away, but the fire in her eyes only flares hotter. She thrives on this, on pushing me to the edge.

"You're driving me crazy, Ginny," I grind out, my voice rough, the heat between us almost unbearable.

"Good," she says, her voice a velvet taunt, daring me, pulling me in deeper. "You deserve that and more."

The air between us crackles, charged with everything unsaid, everything hanging between lust and fury. I step forward, pressing my body against hers, feeling the softness of her curves melt into the hard lines of mine.

"You should know," I growl, my lips inches from hers, "before you start playing games with me... I'm not a gentleman. I always punish those who cross me. And you've just made the list."

Before she can respond, I claim her mouth in a rough,

desperate kiss, every ounce of tension between us exploding in that moment.

Her lips move against mine with equal hunger, her arms wrapping around my neck, pulling me down as she presses her body flush against mine. A low groan escapes me, the sound guttural and raw. This—this is what's been consuming my mind since I fucked her two days ago.

My fingers tangle in her hair, tugging gently, pulling her closer until there's no space left between us. Her lips move feverishly against mine, each kiss stoking the flames. When her tongue slides into my mouth, I suck on it greedily, tasting her like she's the only thing that can quench this fire. We're both breathless when we finally break apart, gasping for air.

"I'm so mad at you," she whispers, her voice low and breathy as her lips trail down my neck, pressing hot, urgent kisses against my skin. "God, I need you."

Her teeth graze my throat, and the sensation sends a shiver straight down my spine. The hunger inside me roars, primal and uncontrollable. Without a second thought, I grab the backs of her thighs, hoisting her up and placing her on the countertop. My hands move swiftly, impatiently, as I yank her shorts down her legs, desperate to feel every inch of her.

The world around us fades. All I can think about is the heat between us, the way her body responds to mine, the wild need coursing through my veins. And I know, in this moment, nothing else matters but her.

When I kiss her again, it's even more rough, desperate, and aggressive. Her small hands travel down to my waist to pull my vest off. With each brush of her mouth against mine, another layer of control breaks apart in me. She's ruining me.

When I pull back again, her entire body is flushed. Her lips are swollen and pink, her dark hair falling down her shoulders in wild waves. I'll never get over how beautiful she is. She's so pretty, it hurts.

And now, my dick is painfully hard, straining against my sweatpants. I want to fuck her so badly that there's no room for foreplay. Without sparing another second, I pull the waistband down to my ankles while she tugs off her top.

"I've thought about fucking you on this counter ever since our first night in this kitchen," I tell her, pulling one beaded nipple between my fingers.

She gasps when I pinch her hard before numbing the pain with a soft caress. Grabbing her knees, I pull her to the edge of the counter and kiss her again. This kiss is slower, hotter, wetter. My tongue slides over hers as I grind myself up against her. Her clit is already hard and swollen in anticipation.

"Please, Dario," she whimpers against my lips, and I hiss as she wraps a hand around my dick.

Stroking it firmly, she guides me to her wet entrance. A low moan escapes my lips as I slip into her wet, tight walls. The sensation shoots straight to my balls as I sink deeper, filling her.

My hands grab her waist, fingers digging into the soft flesh as I begin to move at a steady rhythm. Our breathing becomes erratic as I keep pumping into her, slowly building my pace and taking all that she has to give.

She moans loudly, one hand gripping the edge of the counter while the other one tugs on the hair at the nape of my neck. The action feels incredible, and it's almost impossible to keep my eyes open from the pleasure.

My thrusts become faster, harder, deeper, and my movements become rougher and more demanding. Her fingers are digging into my back now, the sting of her nails sending electric shocks down my spine and through my dick.

Her moans become louder as my thrusts become harder.

"Dario," she moans one last time as her body quakes, coming undone in my arms.

I feel my balls tighten, and with one last deep thrust, I join her, my orgasm crashing into me like a tidal wave. Panting heavily, I collapse against her, resting against the edge of the cool tile. Our foreheads are pressed together, our breathing mingling in the air. We stay like that for a few seconds, letting our hearts slow before turning toward each other.

Her hazel eyes are still wild and filled with lust. Her chest heaves rapidly, and a slow smile spreads across her lips. Then she cups my cheeks and leans down to kiss me again.

Our lips and tongues move lazily against each other for a few minutes, neither of us wanting to do much of anything other than bask in the moment.

When I finally pull away from her again, I catch the hint of anger in her eyes.

"You were an asshole earlier," she murmurs.

I sigh, pressing our foreheads together for the millionth time. "I know I was. I'm sorry."

I see the surprise flicker in her eyes as she looks at me with those golden-green eyes.

"Promise me you'll stop acting like a jerk then," she says softly.

I kiss her forehead. "I promise," I whisper against her skin.

And I realize that I would do almost everything for her, even if it involved the one person that I hate the most—her brother.

29

GINEVRA

The sound of Dario's car engine fades into the distance as I sit up in bed, the remnants of sleep still clinging to me. I stretch like a cat, a yawn escaping my lips as I elongate my limbs.

The sheets are still warm from his body, and my body thrums with the echoes of last night.

A smile creeps onto my face, memories flooding back—how his hands couldn't seem to leave me alone, how we fucked in different positions until we were both spent. And later, when he thought I was asleep, the way he pressed a tender kiss on my forehead, his warm breath fanning across my skin as he whispered, "Sweet dreams, Princess."

Things are undeniably different between us now. We're no longer two people bound by a union steeped in hate and revenge. Instead, we've become entwined, spending every day Dario isn't at work together. Almost every night, our bodies are tangled, lost in waves of intense pleasure and passion.

We always end up sleeping naked, whether it's in his bedroom or mine, never apart.

As the days pass, I can't deny it any longer—I don't hate this life we've carved out together. Living in the same house with him, sleeping in his bed, wearing his ring... With our wedding looming closer, I'm surprised to find that I don't feel as panicked about it as I once did.

The idea of becoming his wife doesn't seem so terrible anymore. In fact, I find myself imagining what it might be like to bear his last name.

Ginevra De Luca. It has a nice ring to it.

I know better than to indulge these thoughts. I understand that I shouldn't get swept away by whatever this is between us. Feelings and emotions aren't supposed to factor into our equation—not for us.

But I can't ignore the truth that's taking root inside me. The flutter in my chest when he presses soft kisses on my skin, the butterflies in my stomach when he compliments my baking, the hitch in my breath when he tells me I'm beautiful. And the undeniable heat that pools in my core when he whispers how he can't wait to be inside me...

A warm, fuzzy feeling envelops me at the thought. Could this be something more than just lust or infatuation?

Could this be love?

A sharp breath escapes my lips at the realization, and I shake my head, dragging myself out of bed, determined not to dwell on it any longer.

As I plant my feet on the floor, my eyes land on the remnants of last night—a sock tossed carelessly near the closet, a tie draped over the edge of the single sofa against the wall, and a crumpled shirt half-hidden under the chair.

A blush warms my cheeks as the memories flood back, vivid and intoxicating. No matter how many times I have sex with Dario, I can never seem to get enough of him. Each encounter only leaves me craving more.

I bend down to pick up his things, a familiar warmth spreading through my chest with each item I gather. I love how sometimes he's frantic and rough, as if he can't get enough of me, while other times he takes his sweet time to touch and tease, driving me to the brink of begging him to fuck me. When he finally does, he moves slowly and passionately, as if he wants to engrain every second of it in his mind.

I like that. I like how it's obvious he wants me just as much as I want him—maybe even more.

Once I've collected all the scattered pieces of his clothes, I slip out of my room and head to his. It's empty, just as I expected. He's off to work and won't return until late afternoon or evening. I've learned his routine by heart, almost as well as I would know my own if I had one—indoor gym, then the office, then home, where we spend the rest of the evening together.

Rosa is the most thrilled about my blossoming relationship with Dario. She never fails to tell me how glad she is that he looks happier, eats more, and comes home early instead of working all the time.

When I step into Dario's room, his familiar scent envelops me. It's so him in here—clean, sharp, masculine, and a touch expensive. The bed is perfectly made, the nightstand clear except for a black-covered notebook and his phone charger. It feels strange to be in his space without him, as if I'm intruding somehow, but find myself lingering anyway.

I drop his clothes into the laundry hamper beside his bathroom door and glance around, a flutter in my chest as I remember the first day I moved in. When Rosa told me that Dario had requested my things be taken to his room, I'd thought he was the biggest prick in the world.

The idea of sharing a bed and space with him had felt like pure torture. Now, it all reminds me of him—his taste, his smell. *Him.*

No matter how much I try to pretend otherwise, I like how our arrangement has evolved. It's as if our bodies and minds were made for each other. I'm excited about what the future holds for us. My thoughts drift back to the contract Lorenzo signed binding Dario and me in marriage for ten years before either of us can pull out.

Ten years is such a long time, but time flies when you're having fun. After ten years—then what? An uncomfortable knot forms in my stomach at the thought of ever leaving Dario. I can't imagine ending it when our time is up.

It's too early for this kind of thinking.

But before I can get lost in those thoughts, a soft buzz pulls my attention. I glance at his sleek black phone lying on the dresser as it lights up with a new message.

I freeze.

I shouldn't. I know I shouldn't.

Yet, something compels me to walk over to the phone. Curiosity—or maybe something deeper—urges me closer. My fingers hover over the screen, my mind racing. He must've forgotten his phone in his office this morning. The lock screen displays a notification with a woman's name. My stomach flips as I stare at it.

I should definitely drop the phone now, walk out of his room, and pretend none of this ever happened. But curiosity and something else I can't recognize twist my stomach.

I hesitate only a second before I guess the password. It's easy—Rosa. The fact that he uses it is almost sweet, like a small gesture of respect toward the woman who's cared for him like a mother for years. But that thought quickly fades when I open the message.

Should I come to your office or will you come to mine?

My breath catches in my throat. My heart sinks like a heavy stone to the bottom of my chest. I scroll up, skimming the previous messages between them. They're casual, not too vulgar, but the meaning is crystal clear.

They used to meet up like this. For sex.

The air in the room thickens, pressing down on me like a weight. I drop the phone back on the dresser as if it has burned me, my hands shaking slightly. What had I expected? That he'd be faithful? That he'd stop sleeping with other women just because he spends most nights in my bed?

My chest tightens, a wave of sadness crashing over me. I don't understand why it hurts so much. I should've known better. Men like Dario don't do commitment. They don't do love. Every decision they make and action they take is either for their business or their own pleasure.

But still, I feel it—a deep, aching sadness I can't shake. I stumble back to my room, feeling hollow, and close the door softly behind me. The house feels too quiet, too empty. My heart feels too heavy.

I try to push the thought away, reminding myself that this is just sex. We were both taking advantage of an unpleasant situation, using each other's bodies for pleasure. But the truth lingers, gnawing at me—this is just an arrangement.

Each thought leaves me feeling increasingly hollow, because deep down, I know I'm lying to myself. It's been more than just sex for me.

The day drags on. I don't leave my room. I don't eat, having lost my appetite. Rosa comes up to check on me, but I don't move or leave my bed to attend to her. My mind keeps replaying that message, the casual tone of it, as if meeting up with other women is just normal for him. As if I'm nothing special.

The sun sets, casting long shadows across the room. I hear the familiar rumble of his car engine pulling into the driveway, and my heart races. I rush to the door and lock it, my hands trembling as I twist the key. I can't see him. I can't face him—not now.

I press my back against the door, closing my eyes as I hear his footsteps approach the house. They're slow, steady, like he's not in any rush. The front door creaks open, and then silence. My breath catches in my throat as I wait, half-expecting him to come straight to my room, to demand to find me. But the house stays quiet.

I know he'll come looking for me eventually. He always does. But for now, he stays downstairs, probably talking to Rosa.

I don't know if I can face him when he finally comes. How can I look at him, knowing what I know now? How can I pretend I'm not breaking inside, and that my heart isn't shattering with every beat? How can I even be mad at him, knowing our agreement is just that—an agreement? Sex and feelings aren't included.

I return to the bed and sink under the covers, my heart pounding with dread.

He'll be here soon, and I'm not sure if I can hold it together when he finally knocks.

30

DARIO

The warehouse is dimly lit, a single bulb swinging gently from the high ceiling, casting eerie shadows across the concrete floor. The air is thick with the stench of sweat and blood, mingling with an oppressive fear that clings to everything.

As I step inside, my footsteps echo, the sound reverberating through the silence like a death knell.

The man tied to a chair in the center of the room looks almost unrecognizable. His arms are bound tightly behind him, and his face is a grotesque mask of swelling and bruises from the beating he has endured. He's already a wreck, but I have every intention of making it worse.

Behind him stands Anton, flanked by two of my men, his expression grim as he meets my gaze. He nods slightly. "Boss, he's been talking, but not enough. All he keeps saying is he's sorry, and that's it."

A smile creeps across my face, but there's no humor in it —only cold satisfaction. I advance, anger simmering within me, rising up my spine like a coiled serpent. He dared to mess with my shipment, to take what is mine, and he has disrespected me in the most unforgivable way.

Does he honestly believe I'll let this slide just because he offers a halfhearted apology? He will suffer for this, and I'll make an example of him, ensuring that no one else dares to cross me again.

I come to a stop in front of him, towering over his pitiful form. His breath comes in sharp, shallow gasps, his gaze averted as his body trembles with fear.

Good. He should be terrified.

"Rafael," I call, my voice cutting through the eerie quiet. "You stole from me." The calmness of my tone is laced with an unmistakable fury. "You know what happens to those who cross me."

His head jerks up weakly, bloodshot eyes filled with despair and pain. He's still shaking, and I watch as he struggles to form words, his mouth opening and closing like a fish out of water. "P-Please, Dario. I didn't mean to..."

"You didn't mean to what? Steal from me?" A harsh chuckle escapes my lips, sharp and mocking. "Do you honestly believe I give a fuck about your apology? Do you think *sorry* will somehow fix this?"

His bottom lip quivers, and he swallows hard, desperation etched across his face. "Of course not...I just—"

"I want one thing from you, Rafe," I interrupt, my voice low and deliberate. "Whom do you work for? Surely, you couldn't have orchestrated this operation on your own."

When he remains silent, only sobbing quietly, I feel my patience stretch thin, fraying at the edges.

"I don't have time for this." My voice slices through his sobs like a blade. I glance at Anton, who moves swiftly to hand me an aluminum bat without hesitation. I grip it tightly,

feeling the cold metal against my skin, its weight a solid reassurance in my hands. The room falls silent, my men watching, their anticipation palpable as they wait for my next move.

Rafe's eyes widen in terror as I step closer, raising the bat
slightly. "Dario, please!" he begs, his voice cracking with
desperation. "I didn't have a choice. I had to—"

I swing the bat hard against his ribs, the sharp crack
echoing around the room. Rafe lets out a guttural groan, his
body jerking in pain. I raise the bat again and swing,
sending him sprawling to the ground, blood gushing from
his mouth.

"Fuck. I really need to take up baseball as a hobby
again," I muse dryly, a cruel smirk crossing my face. "Haven't
played since high school."

A few murmurs and chuckles ripple through the room,
but they quickly fade when Rafe begins to speak.

"I don't work for anyone," he groans, coughing violently,
nearly choking on his own blood. "I carried it out on my
own..."

"You must think I'm a fool," I ground out, but he keeps
talking, words tumbling from his lips in a rush.

"My wife—she's sick. Cancer. I...I needed the money for
her treatment, for the chemo. She's dying, Dario, and I
couldn't watch her suffer anymore."

Cancer.

I pause, my chest heaving with a mix of emotions. The bat
suddenly feels heavier in my hands, and for a split second, my
rage flickers. But no. I won't allow myself to feel sorry for him—
not after he jeopardized my business. "You think your sob story
changes anything?" I spit, my voice low and dangerous. "You
think I'll just let you walk out of here because your wife's sick?"

Rafe's body trembles with fear, his face twisting in

desperation. He struggles to sit up, but it's nearly impossible with his hands bound behind the chair. "No, I...I know it was wrong. I shouldn't have taken the goods. But I was out of options, Dario. She's all I've got. Without the treatment...she'll die."

His words linger in the air, but I feel not a shred of sympathy for him. I didn't climb to this height in the underworld by showing mercy. Striding over to a table propped against the nearby wall, I grab a knife, its cold steel glinting under the dim light. When I storm back toward him, Rafe's eyes widen like saucers, fear etched across his battered face. I raise the knife, tension crackling in the room as I prepare to bring my hand down.

But then his voice, broken and pleading, cuts through the haze of my anger. "Please," he whispers, barely audible through his tears. "I'm begging you. I'll pay back every cent, every ounce of it. I'll do anything. Just...don't let her die because of me."

I freeze, the knife hovering in mid-air.

Don't let her die because of me.

Suddenly, the image of my mother flashes in my mind— her pale face, weak hands trembling as she tried to hold mine. The cold, sterile hospital room we could barely afford, and the helplessness I felt as I watched her frail body succumb to the pain, powerless against the stings that shot through her. I blink, feeling a tightness in my chest, something I haven't allowed myself to feel in years.

I lower the knife, taking a small step back, my anger giving way to something else—something I don't want to acknowledge.

Compassion? Pity?

No. That part of me died the moment I was left to fend

for myself. The Dario I am now is the one people fear, the one who doesn't hesitate, doesn't flinch.

But then there's Ginny.

As much as I hate to admit it, she's changed me. Because of her, I feel things—things I didn't give two fucks about before. Emotions I'd successfully mastered the art of hiding away now refuse to stay buried. And it's all because of her.

I grit my teeth, fighting the inner battle raging inside me. One part of me still wants to finish this, to beat Rafe within an inch of his life, to kill him so that no one dares to cross me again. But the other part—the part that Ginny has softened, the part buried deep under layers of darkness for so long—won't let me. She's unlocked something in me, something I can't quite control anymore.

And it terrifies me.

"Leave us," I order, my voice sharp.

Vito and Gabriel, my other two men, move quickly, but Anton hesitates, clearly confused by the sudden shift in my demeanor. But he knows better than to question me. He nods, following the others out. The door clicks shut, and suddenly it's just Rafe and me in the room.

I stare at him, my chest tight, my mind racing. I should hurt him. I should make him suffer. I should inflict unforgettable pain. But I can't. Not after hearing that.

I crouch down in front of him, grabbing his chin and forcing him to meet my gaze. His eyes are wide with terror, but there's something else there now—hope.

"I'm not going to kill you," I say, my voice low and controlled. "But you're not walking out of here without punishment."

Rafe lets out a shaky breath, his shoulders sagging with the slightest hint of relief. "Th-thank you—"

"Don't thank me," I snap, cutting him off. "You'll pay me

back. Every cent. And if you ever cross me again, you won't live to see your wife's next treatment."

He nods furiously, tears streaming down his bloodied face. "I swear. I won't... I'll do anything. I won't mess up again."

But I'm not done. I lean in closer, tightening my grip on his jaw until a whimper escapes his lips. I bring the knife to the side of his face, hovering just over his skin, watching as he trembles under my touch.

Then, with one swift motion, I drag the blade from the edge of his eyebrow down to his jawline. A deep groan rips from his throat as blood pours from the gash, staining my hands.

"This is your warning," I tell him, pushing his head back so hard it slams into the ground.

His groans and whimpers echo in the room as I leave him there, stepping out into the cool hallway. My men are waiting outside, silent, their eyes locked on me. Anton hands me a white handkerchief just as Timoteo opens the car door. I wipe the blood from my hands, the fabric soaking it up as if it's nothing. Then, I slide into the waiting car.

Minutes later, I'm back in my office, collapsing into the leather chair behind my desk. But my mind won't settle. I run a hand down my face, feeling the anxiety creeping in, that familiar pressure tightens around my chest, suffocating.

Ginny.

Her beautiful face fills my mind, and I close my eyes, imagining her. She's a mix of softness and strength, sass and warmth. I recap the past few days. In the quiet moments, when we're not tangled up in each other, we talk. About everything and nothing.

I've memorized every sound she makes when she laughs —her mocking snicker, her amused chuckle, that soft, sarcastic laugh. And the way she looks at me... like she sees right through the walls I've spent years building. Like she loves the hidden parts of me I've long since buried.

Her eyes... they shine brightest under the sunlight, sparkling with hints of green and gold. But when she's aroused, they darken to a deep forest green, shadowed with brown. And when she looks at me with admiration, they soften, glowing with a warmth that makes me feel... exposed. Seen.

I'm not a saint. But with her, I want to be better.

My stomach churns as my thoughts begin to spiral. They turn darker, sharper. What if she ever gets sick? What if she leaves me? What if I lose her the way I lost my mother?

The image of Ginny in a hospital bed, pale and fragile, shoots through my mind like a nightmare. I can't handle that. I've barely started letting her in, and the thought of her leaving tears me apart.

I close my eyes, and suddenly, I'm seventeen again, back in that cold, sterile hospital room with my mother. The soft, rhythmic beeping of machines fills the room. She's trying to smile at me, but her face is so tired, so worn from the sickness.

We were watching *Friends*, her favorite show. Joey said something funny, and she laughs. But then the laughter turns into violent coughing, so hard I thought she was choking.

Panic flooded me, and the nurses rushed in, her hand squeezing mine, weak and frail. My father burst into the room moments later, alerted to the emergency. His eyes mirrored mine—helpless, broken, afraid.

That same helplessness claws at me now, just like it did back then. My chest tightens, my throat feels like it's closing up. I can't lose Ginny. Not her. I've already lost too much, and I know—I *know*—I'm not strong enough to go through that kind of pain again.

I might not lose her to something tragic or out of my control, but that doesn't mean I won't push her away with my constant hot and cold behavior. The way I keep pulling her close, then shutting her out—it's not fair to her. It's not fair to *us*.

Trapping her in this marriage, forcing her into a life with someone like me... It was never the right step. And if I don't change, if I don't start doing better, I'll lose her.

I'm going to start now. For her. For me. For whatever this thing is between us that's growing stronger every day.

Because losing her? That's a pain I wouldn't survive.

I push away from the desk, unable to breathe. I need to see her. I need to be near her.

The drive back to my house is a blur, my hands gripping the wheel so tight my knuckles ache. I almost told her this morning while she slept. The words were right there, lingering on my lips. But I held back. Fear—a feeling I haven't felt in a long time—clawed at my chest, whispering that I had time. That I could tell her later.

Now? Now, it feels like every second I don't say it is wasted.

I drive into the compound and pull into the driveway, my eyes instantly drawn to her window. The soft glow of her bedroom light spills out onto the garden, casting shadows across the flowers below. My heart pounds hard against my ribs as I cut the engine, but I don't move right away. I sit there, gripping the steering wheel, my breath heavy, my chest tight.

I need to calm down. I need to think. But all I can feel is the urgency building in me, the sense that this moment is different. That *this* is the moment everything changes.

Finally, I step out of the car, and the cool night air greets me, brushing against my skin. As I walk toward the front door, each step feels heavier, like the weight of the past is pressing down on me, trying to drag me back to where I've always been—guarded, distant, untouchable.

But everything in me is screaming that this I should bury it all—the pain, the old wounds, the fear I've carried for too long.

Before it's too late.

31

GINEVRA

I've been lying in my bedroom all day, locked away in my room. Rosa knocked a couple of times, her soft voice filtering through the door, asking if I wanted something to eat. I didn't answer. I couldn't. Except for the breakfast I forced myself to eat this morning, I don't think I can stomach anything else. Even the mere thought of it makes my stomach churn.

Everything feels too heavy. Too painful. Just when I thought what we had was real, just when I let myself fall for this man, I was brought crashing back to reality. There is no us.

Maybe all the sex and spending time with him because he took some days off made me delusional. Or maybe I just fell for his irresistible charm. But I'm back to my senses now. Nothing good, real, or genuine, can come out of a union built on revenge and blackmail.

So why does it still hurt?

I know all these things, so why does it still feel like my heart is being ripped out of my chest? I think about the text again, and I wonder if there are other women other than her. Other women he meets up with in his office, their office, a hotel room, his bedroom...

Of course there are.

The weight of this sham marriage presses down on me, harder now, more than I expected it would. Surely, at some point during our marriage, Dario will get tired of pretending and show his true colors. He doesn't even seem like the kind of man who would pretend, especially not for ten years.

When his flings come here, will I have to act as if nothing is happening? Will I be expected to ignore them and focus on performing my duties as a good wife instead? A shudder wracks through me at the thought.

Yes, I'm committed to keeping up appearances for the sake of the company. I owe my brother that much. But pretending with Dario—pretending this relationship is anything more than a business deal while he fucks other women is something I don't think I'll be able to handle.

Outside, I hear the muffled sounds of the house—footsteps of the domestic staff walking around, the faint rustle of wind against the windows, and above the wall hangs a wall clock that ticks loudly in the silent room.

My body curls deeper into the blankets, wishing the world around me would disappear.

I lose track of time, and I don't know how long I've been lying on the bed when I hear the sound of Dario's car driving into the compound. I tell myself that I've stripped off the effect he has on me, so why does my breathing stop at the knowledge that he is home?

The door downstairs creaks open, and his familiar heavy footsteps echo in the distance. My body clenches even further as I hear him climb up the stairs with a female voice overlapping his deep ones.

I tense as the footsteps stop in front of my door, listening as he speaks to Rosa. His voice is low, but I can still hear the frustration laced in his words.

"She hasn't come out all day?" His tone is clipped, sharp.

"No, Boss," Rosa replies, sounding worried. "I've tried."

A heavy silence follows. It's thick and uncomfortable, curling around my throat. I can imagine the look on his face —those clenched jaws and balled fists he does when things don't go his way.

"I'll deal with it," he says finally, his voice gruff.

For a moment, I think he might come up, bang on my door, and demand that I face him. A small part of me wants him to do that. But he doesn't. The house falls quiet again, and I can almost feel the tension evaporate, leaving behind a strange emptiness.

Maybe he's given up. Or maybe he's just as tired of pretending, as well.

My chest squeezes at the thought. At this point, I don't know what to feel anymore.

I roll over, staring at the ceiling, letting the silence wash over me. My thoughts swirl in endless loops—frustration, confusion, anger, all tangled up with something else I don't want to admit. I've spent so long telling myself this marriage doesn't matter. That Dario doesn't matter. But the truth is more complicated than that.

Minutes pass, or maybe hours, before I hear something odd—a soft bark. I freeze, not sure if I imagined it. But then I hear it again, clearer this time. I sit up slowly, confusion marring my features.

Is that a dog?

Curiosity stirs inside me as I throw my legs out of bed and slowly near the door. I crack it open, just a sliver, peering out into the hallway.

And there, sitting right outside my door, is the last thing

I expected to see—a small, fluffy Norfolk Terrier with bright eyes and a red ribbon tied neatly around its neck.

My heart stutters in shock, then swells in my chest as I take in the sight. Slowly, I open the door wider, stepping out into the hall. The cute brown dog wags its tail, looking up at me with big, expectant eyes.

"Hey cutie," I whisper, crouching down and stretching out a tentative hand toward the little thing. The dog nudges its head against my palm, and warmth spreads through me —something soft and familiar. Memories flood back. Harlow, my dog when I was about twelve. She was the same breed, the same color, and had the same bright expressive eyes. My throat tightens at the thought.

The only person who knew about Harlow was Lorenzo. Dario and Lorenzo weren't even friends when I had her, so there's no way Dario could know about Harlow on his own. Which meant he'd asked Lorenzo about something I loved and had gone out of his way to get it for me.

Harlow was a rare breed, not common in the U.S., which meant Dario must have gone to great lengths to find this dog. I'd cried for days when Harlow had died, and Lorenzo knew how much she'd meant to me. I'd never gotten another pet because my dad had felt I was too old to get attached to something "not worth it."

I glance down and spot a small, folded note next to the dog, tied with the same ribbon as around its collar. My fingers tremble slightly as I pick it up and unfold it. The handwriting is neat and slanted, and tears well in my eyes as I read the words.

You're mad at me for some reason, and I figured you need some company while you sulk. Don't expect this very often. I'm not always this nice. Just wanted to make things less unbearable. —Dario.

I can't help the smile that tugs at my lips. I guess it's typical of him to act like this isn't a big deal, downplaying it with his usual cold and nonchalant attitude. But I know better. He'd gone out of his way to do this. And he most certainly didn't have to.

As I stroke the terrier's soft fur, I feel something shift inside me. The tension I've been holding onto loosens just a little, and I can't stop the warmth spreading through my chest. Dario did this for me.

I stand up, holding the note in one hand, and look down the staircase. And there, at the bottom of the stairs, leaning casually against the banister, is Dario himself.

He doesn't say anything—he just watches me, his eyes unreadable but locked on mine. He's still in his work clothes —a dark, tailored suit that fits him perfectly, his tie loose around his neck. His hair is a little messy, as if he has run his hands through it too many times, and the security lights from outside stream in through the windows, catching the sharp angles of his face.

My heart stutters again, and I hate that it does. Why does he have this effect on me?

I bite my lip, unsure what to say. Unsure if I even want to break the silence. But he's staring at me, waiting, the strain between us thick and crackling in the air. I can feel my pulse in my throat as I take a deep breath, my feet slowly carrying me toward him down the stairs, step by step.

As I get closer, my heart pounds harder. He doesn't move, doesn't say a word, but his eyes follow me, watching every step I take. I don't know what's pushing me forward, what's making me feel this pull toward him, but I can't stop.

When I reach the bottom of the stairs, I stop in front of him. My breath hitches in my throat, and for a moment, we just stand there, inches apart, the air between us charged.

His eyes flicker, something unreadable, yet hot and heavy, flashing in them. I feel my pulse race even faster.

Finally, he speaks, his voice low and rough. "Why were you hiding from me, Ginny?"

His question lingers in the air, hanging heavily between us. I open my mouth, but no words come out. Instead, I just stare up at him, at the lines of his jaw, the way his lips press together, the slight furrow in his eyebrows as he looks at me, as if he's trying to figure something out.

But I don't have answers. Not for him. Not for myself.

My heart pounds heavily, and I don't know what I'm doing. All I know is that the weight of the unspoken tension between us is suffocating. I can't take it anymore.

Without thinking, I step closer, closing the distance between us, and before I can stop myself—before I can even process what I'm doing—I lean in and press my lips against his.

The moment I kiss him, everything stops. The world goes quiet. My pulse roars in my ears as I feel the warmth of his lips against mine, soft but firm, slow at first but quickly deepening. His hands move to my waist, pulling me closer, and the kiss grows more urgent, more intense, until there's nothing else but him.

I lose myself in the feeling—his warmth, his touch, the way he pulls me against him like he can't help it, like he's been waiting for this as much as I have. My mind goes blank, and everything else fades away.

There's no deal, no sham marriage, no pretending.

Just us.

32

DARIO

A low groan rumbles through my throat as I reluctantly pull my lips from Ginny's.

"If you keep kissing me like that, I'm going to fuck you right here," I murmur against her mouth, making sure only she can hear.

Her eyes flash with mischief, and in a hushed, teasing voice, she replies, "I think you're a few days too late to worry about who might walk in. Anyone could've caught us when you fucked me in the kitchen a few days ago."

Her breathy voice makes me hard as a rock, a delicious shiver running down my spine at the memory. But then mild annoyance fills my chest at the thought of someone else seeing her, hearing her moans and cries as I fuck her.

Ginny is mine and mine alone. She's meant for my eyes and ears only, and the thought of someone else getting even just a glimpse of that makes me furious.

Seeing the look on my face, she laughs and slides her hands over my shoulders.

"Don't get all possessive now. I don't think anyone saw a thing. Your domestic staff resume for the day at eight, remember?" she whispers into the space between us, her lips brushing my lips with each word. "Besides, no one else gets to touch me but you."

I bite back a moan as she kisses my jawline before moving downward toward my neck. Her warm tongue traces its way over my beating pulse as I grab her waist firmly, trying to eliminate the space between us.

A soft bark interrupts us from our sex-crazed bubble. My head bends down to the source of the sound, and that's when I remember that we have a new addition to the household.

Ginny gasps, crouching down as if she too just remembered my gift. Her breathless laugh fills the air as the puppy, all shaggy fur and overexcited legs, bounces forward, its tiny tail wagging frantically as it yips again.

"Has she eaten?" She looks up at me, and I grind my teeth. "It's a *she*, right?"

She furrows her eyebrows cutely, running her hand over the soft fur of the little animal. When it licks her hand, its pink tongue darting out, Ginny giggles, a sound that sends a reluctant warmth coursing through my chest.

When Ginny continues to pet the dog for a few more seconds, I groan inwardly. When I thought of buying Ginny a dog, I didn't consider that my girl's attention would be divided between us both. Now I stare at them, my dick painfully hard in my pants, while the reason for my current state makes baby sounds and coos at her new pet. Ginny's head tilts slightly as she gently raises the dog's wagging tail.

I'd almost forgotten I'd asked a question until Ginny gasps.

"It's a girl!" Ginny beams, looking up at me through long lashes as she cradles the dog to her chest.

My annoyance disappears—for a moment though,

because I'm still painfully aroused—replaced by warmth spreading across my chest at the pure joy on Ginny's face. When I promised myself that I would do anything to make her happy, I meant it.

"What should I name her?" Ginny asks, cradling the pup in her arms.

"Anything you want, Princess."

I swallow the thick arousal choking me up before taking a step towards her. With a gentle but deliberate motion, I take the squirming pup from her hands, feeling the warmth of its tiny body against mine as I carry it to the corner of the kitchen where I've set out its food. It sniffs around, tail still wagging, then dives eagerly into the dish, its tongue lapping up the food with little, contented snorts.

Ginny watches, smiling. I can't help but admire the grin on her face and the way her eyes soften. I slip my hand into my coat pocket and whip out my phone.

"Rosa, where are you? Come to the kitchen," I call softly into the receiver the moment she answers. "I just bought Ginny a dog, and I need you to look after it for a while."

Ginny's eyes narrow into slits as she turns to look at me, but I see the unbridled desire beneath those hazel depths.

I end the call with a beep before stalking dangerously toward my girl. "Can I have your undivided attention now?"

I don't wait for her to answer before my lips find hers once more, my kiss insistent and claiming. I lift her off the ground, her legs instinctively wrapping around me as I carry her toward the winding staircase. She lets out a small noise of pleasure as my hand slides down under her short dress to caress her soft ass.

I don't know the exact bedroom I stumble into until the door slams shut behind us. My mouth leaves her lips for a second, and I press her body into the door, grinding against her. She giggles at my impatience, but it quickly turns into a moan when my hand travels under her dress again to pull her panties to the side.

"Wet," I drawl, one finger slipping inside her. Ginny whimpers, her eyes closed, her fingers digging into my hair. I feel her wetness coating my digits as I slide two of them inside her. "Just how I want you."

As my movements get deeper, her hips roll against my hand. I kiss her again, slow and deep, my tongue exploring her mouth. She makes a soft whimpering sound as my fingers continue their careful stroking.

"You feel so good, baby," I whisper, nipping at her jaw and kissing the spot behind her ear. Her skin is smooth and flawless, her hair falling over her shoulder to tickle at my chin. As my lips trail down her neck and collarbone to her breasts, she moans in appreciation. But when I don't increase the pace of my thrusts, she whines impatiently.

"Please, Dario," she says breathlessly, tugging on my hair. I let out a low growl as my dick gets even harder. But I don't increase my pace. I continue to stroke her, wanting to savor every second of this moment. My cock grows even harder, throbbing against the center of her thighs.

The ache makes it hard to think straight, and when I feel Ginny's hand slide down my stomach, sliding under my waistband, I release a painful hiss.

"Bad girl," I groan, pulling her hand away and pinning it against the door above her head. Her eyes flash with desire as she stares at me wide-eyed and flushed.

Deciding to put her out of her torture, I add an extra finger inside her, watching as her body clenches around mine. Her breathing becomes even heavier, and her moans becoming louder as I slide in and out of her. I'm still pumping her slowly, but my movements are deliberate. I want to drive her crazy. I want to watch her come apart right here against the door, trembling as I hold her up by her wrists.

"Dario," she moans again, moving her hips up and down to keep pace with my thrusts.

"Do you want to come, Princess?" I murmur, leaning down to take one earlobe between my teeth.

She nods frantically, her dark curls bouncing off her shoulders. I thrust deeply, curling my fingers inside her. She clenches around me, her hips bucking off the door as her orgasm hits her.

"That's it, come all over my fingers like the dirty fucking girl you are," I murmur, pumping into her a few more times before slipping my fingers out of her. When I raise my hand up, I see that I'm coated with her juices.

"Open your mouth," I order gruffly.

She obeys, moaning softly as I slip three thick fingers into her mouth. Her lips close around them hungrily. I watch carefully as her tongue licks her juices clean, closing her eyes to hum at the taste.

"Good girl," I rasp, my dick becoming impossibly hard.

If I don't get inside her soon, I may explode in my pants.

Ginny presses her lips against mine again as I carry her to the bed. We are in her bedroom, her strawberry and vanilla fragrance mixing with the aroma of her arousal. I lay her against the soft mattress, kissing her body as I pull her dress over her head. As usual, she isn't wearing a bra. She's only in panties now, a pale pink lace thong.

I run my hands lightly across the bare flesh of her legs, making her squirm beneath me. Her nails claw at my shoulders as I lower myself down her body. When her panties are finally gone, I gently push her legs farther apart. Then I lean down and place kisses along the inside of her thighs.

"Dario..." She gasps from the intense pleasure. She still hasn't recovered from her last orgasm. I want to give her more orgasms in millions of ways until she can't take me anymore, but I don't think I can last a minute longer if I don't bury myself inside her.

"I want to make love to you, Ginny."

The words slip out of my mouth before I can stop it. I feel her body freeze slightly, her eyes still on mine. And then, without saying a word, she leans up to kiss me.

Our hands move slowly, taking off every piece of clothing I have on. My suit coat, my tie, my dress shirt—all gone. My body feels hot, my cock throbbing painfully as she runs her hands lightly across my chest. Then she grabs my dick and starts rubbing. I let out a low groan.

She leans back against the soft sheets, wrapping her legs tightly around my waist as I hover over her. Her eyes are on mine, her hands buried in my hair. When I run the tip of my dick over her slick folds, she throws back her head and moans.

"Look at me, Ginny," I say huskily.

She does, bringing our faces even closer as I slowly slide into her. Our moans mix together in the little space between our bodies. Her arms are around my neck, her legs around my waist as she clings to me like she never wants to let me go.

My grip on her waist tightens as my hips press forward, pushing myself all the way to the hilt. Her face is flushed, her eyes shining with arousal, lust, and something deeper. I roll my hips slowly, and she hums in pleasure.

Every inch of her body is pressed against me. Every touch is a caress, each thrust is a promise to be gentle, loving...forever. She lets out another moan, her hands clenching tighter onto my shoulders. The feeling of being inside her has always been intoxicating, but nothing compares to the sheer bliss now. Fucking her hard and fast feels good. But this...this is heaven.

I stare into her eyes as my hips grind into hers. Our bodies move together in perfect strokes, matching each other like two orderly puzzles pieces. There's no hesitation or doubt. Our bodies fit together as one, and for the first time ever, I lose myself completely.

The orgasm that hits me is almost blinding. It comes hard and unrelenting, shaking through my entire body, leaving a tingling, buzzing sensation. I continue to slide in and out of her even as the sensation washes over me, threatening to drown me in my own bliss.

Then she gasps, her body trembling as she clings desperately to me. Her nails dig into my shoulders, sharp and painful, but I welcome the sting. Tears spill from her eyes, and something inside me tightens as I lean in to kiss them away, my chest constricting with a flood of emotions I can barely contain.

The words are right there, teetering on the edge of my tongue. This feels right. More than that—it feels perfect. It's everything I've wanted for so long, everything I didn't know I needed.

"I love you," I confess, my voice thick with emotion as I stare deep into her tear-filled eyes.

Her eyes widen slightly as I continue. "I've completely fallen for you, Ginny. I have for a while now. And I thought it would be terrifying. I used to believe love was this dangerous thing that made people weak, but with you...I feel stronger. I feel alive, like I've become the best version of myself."

Her eyes search mine, tears gathering in their golden-green depths. She's silent for a long moment, just staring at me, as if she's processing every word, every feeling I've just laid bare. And then, without a word, she leans in, her lips pressing softly against mine, the kiss filled with an unspoken tenderness.

But when she pulls back, she doesn't say it back. The absence of those words cuts deeper than I expected, and for a moment, hurt surges through me like a wave, tightening in my chest. I swallow it down, forcing a soft smile as I ease myself back against the mattress, pulling her close, her body warm against mine.

I didn't tell her I love her just to hear the words echoed back. No, I want her to say it when she truly means it, when every part of her heart is in it. And no matter how long it takes, I'll wait—patiently, endlessly—for the day she tells me she loves me, too.

33

GINEVRA

I sit in the bathroom, staring at the little plastic stick in my hand, my heart pounding in my chest.

This isn't happening. It can't be.

But the two lines are there, staring right back at me. I blink once, twice, hoping they'll disappear, but they don't. A shaky exhale leaves my lips at the reality.

I'm pregnant.

One hand clutches the edge of the bathtub till my knuckles turn white. My mind spins without stopping. The second hand drifts to my stomach, and I feel a certain weight I hadn't felt before.

A small sliver of excitement slips in, mixing with the fear swirling inside me. A baby...a life is inside me. I rub my stomach again, feeling my chest swell. We created this child —Dario and I. We made life together.

Except... this wasn't part of the plan.

The sinking feeling returns, this time, deeper and darker than the last. I'm not ready for a baby. Heck! I'm not ready to be a mother. How can I be? I've barely figured life out. I've barely figured out exactly what my relationship with Dario is. Is it just a sham? The meticulous revenge plan Dario thought out? A business deal? Or is it real—what we feel for each other? What I feel for him?

When Dario told me he loved me a few nights ago, I froze. Those were the words I'd been waiting to hear, the words I'd wanted to tell him, but for some reason, I couldn't bring myself to say anything. How can I be sure that he truly loves me? How can I be sure this isn't part of his twisted plan? To get me to fall for him, then break my heart...

You watch too many daytime soap operas, Ginny.

The plastic test kit clatters to the floor as I bury my hands in my hair, a groan slipping out of my lips.

Dario and I are supposed to be getting married in a week, and I can't even figure anything out. I don't know if I should be happy about this baby or not. I don't know if I should tell Dario...*what* I should tell Dario.

You have to tell him.

My hands tremble as I pick up the test from the floor and set it down on the sink beside the tub. No matter how I feel about this, I should at least give Dario the chance to know he could be a father.

I could tell him immediately, but he's been away on a business trip for three days now, unreachable until tomorrow. But even when I can reach him, this isn't exactly something I'd tell him over the phone. I have to tell him in person.

My chest tightens, almost to the point where I can't breathe. I stand quickly, needing air, needing to move. The bathroom feels too small, too close. As I rush out, walking into the room, I hear a soft bark.

Piper—I've named her already—jumps up and down, her tail wagging in excitement. I know she wants to play, but

I'm unfortunately not in the mood for that. As I head out of the room and down the stairs toward the kitchen, she runs after me, hot on my heels as my bare feet slap against the cold marble floor.

The sun is just starting to rise, casting a soft golden light through the large windows of the house. Everything looks so peaceful, so normal, but inside me, it feels as if a storm is raging, like a bomb seconds away from exploding.

The kitchen is empty when I step inside. Relieved, I exhale softly. Even if it's just for a moment, I need to be alone. I need to sit in my thoughts.

I grab a carton of eggs from the fridge and set a pan on the stove. Maybe some food will settle me, help me think more clearly. I add a little butter to the pan, watching it sizzle and dissolve. But as soon as I crack one egg into the pan, the smell hits me, and my stomach churns violently. I clamp a hand over my mouth, fighting the urge to vomit.

"Ginny, *querida*, what's wrong?"

I turn to see Rosa standing in the doorway, her kind eyes full of concern. Piper rushes toward her, and Rosa smiles briefly, carrying the dog into her arms.

"I'm fine, Rosa," I say, my voice shaky as I turn off the stove. "Just...I don't feel great this morning."

Rosa steps closer, her gaze narrowing slightly. "Not feeling great, hmm?" She trails off, her eyes narrowing.

I stiffen. Fuck. Can she tell? I know older women can often tell about stuff like this, but I would be more at ease if no one else knows about my pregnancy for now.

"You're looking a little pale, Ginny. Maybe you've caught something."

I exhale, avoiding her eyes. I don't think she suspects I'm pregnant. God! I hope not.

"I don't think so," I say quickly, but Rosa just raises an eyebrow, not convinced.

She steps closer, touching the back of her hand to my forehead. "Hmm, no fever. A stomach bug, maybe? You've been looking off for a couple of days now. Maybe it's because Dario hasn't been home." Her voice turns playful and teasing, but I feel my heart race at the mention of his name.

I force a laugh. "Yeah, maybe that's it."

Piper makes a whining sound. I absentmindedly reach out to rub her fur.

"You should have waited for me to make you breakfast," Rosa chastises like she always does when she's in full care-taker mode. "Go and lie down. Get some rest. I'll make you some tea later. Do you want some cakes with it?

My heart softens slightly as I nod. She's observed me to the point of knowing the things I like.

"Thanks, Rosa," I sigh, thankful for the escape.

"Come on, Piper. I know you're hungry too," I hear Rosa coo as I walk out of the kitchen.

As I head upstairs, I walk straight to Dario's room without thinking. I may be unsure of what I should feel about him, but one thing I know is that being in his room right now, inhaling his scent and just imagining him with me, will make me feel better.

Or not.

When I collapse into his bed and pull the covers up to my chin, I try to follow Rosa's advice, but sleep won't come. My mind is too restless, my thoughts too loud.

I keep thinking about Dario. What if he doesn't want this baby? What if it's too much for him? For us? And what about the wedding?

I toss and turn, trying to find a comfortable position. The silk sheets feel cool against my skin, not the warmth I wanted. His faint scent lingers in the air, not enough to fill my lungs.

The door creaks open minutes later, and Rosa walks in with a tray in her hand and a smile on her lips.

"I knew I'd find you here."

"Where's Piper?" I ask weakly as she sets the tray down on the bedside drawer.

"She's eating." Rosa smiles before patting my head lovingly. I'm glad when she leaves me alone.

I drown most of the scorching tea almost immediately before taking a few nibbles out of the cake. I know I should eat more for the baby, but I don't think I can stomach anything more than that.

I lie back against the sheets and close my eyes. My thoughts won't quiet down, and the bed feels too big, too empty. I sit up, hugging my knees to my chest, staring at the empty space beside me where Dario should be. I can't do this. I can't just sit here and mope around all day. I need to move. I need to clear my head.

I swing my legs off the bed, walking over to the dresser where Dario keeps his things. My eyes land on one of his car keys, and before I can second-guess myself, I grab them.

Dario no longer keeps me prisoner in the house, and I'm free to go out, so long as I'm escorted. I know I should call Timoteo to drive me, but I don't want anyone with me right now. I just want to be alone.

I change into a simple, casual outfit—a pair of washed jeans, a graphic tee, and my favorite sneakers—before heading down the stairs.

"I'm heading out," I yell toward Rosa, who is still in the

kitchen. I hear Piper bark as Rosa turns to say something, but I don't wait to listen.

As I slip out of the house, the crisp morning air hits my face. Dario would probably lose his mind if he knew I was going out alone, but I'll deal with that when he returns.

I get into Dario's Maybach, the familiar scent of leather and his cologne filling the air. It's comforting, making me breathe easier. I grip the steering wheel tightly as I pull out of the gates, my thoughts still a jumbled mess.

Without realizing it, I find myself driving toward the old building I once dreamed of owning. It's the one thing I wanted to build for myself—my escape from everything else in my life.

I park the car across the street and get out, staring at the building from the sidewalk. It still looks the same. Tall, white, empty.

I'm surprised to find it still in this state. I know Dario purchased the property, and I'd assumed he would have sold it by now since he has no use for it.

I step closer, running my fingers along the brick wall. I can almost see it—what it could have been. The smell of fresh bread wafting through the air, the display of mouthwatering pastries, the quiet hum of conversation. A place where people would come to feel at home.

I can't resist. I push open the door and step inside. The smell of dust lingers in the cold and empty space. I feel a pang of sadness, thinking about how close I came to making this place mine. But it was snatched up by none other than my husband-to-be.

I hear footsteps behind me, and I turn to see the landlord, Mr. Jenkins, coming through the back door. His eyes widen when he sees me.

"Ginny! I wasn't expecting you," he says, wiping his hands on his shirt. "What brings you here?"

I force a smile on my lips.

"I just...wanted to see the place again," I say, my voice faltering. "I didn't know it was still available."

He raises an eyebrow, chuckling. "Available? Didn't Mr. De Luca tell you? This building is yours."

Huh?

"What do you mean it's mine?" I ask, my heart skipping a beat.

Mr. Jenkins smiles softly. "Mr. De Luca bought it for you. He transferred everything into your name the day after..." He hesitates, as if realizing he's about to bring up something sensitive. "The day after the...uh, well, he told me you were in an accident."

I think back to when this must have been, and then it clicks. The kidnapping. I swallow hard, memories of that day flooding back.

"He really did that?" I ask, my voice barely above a whisper.

"He did. Paid for the renovations, too. Said he wanted it ready for you whenever you decided you were ready."

My breath hooks in my throat. He bought it? And never told me? Why would he do that?

"He didn't mention it?" Mr. Jenkins asks, mirroring my exact thought.

I shake my head, still trying to process what he's saying. Why did Dario do this for me? And why didn't he tell me?

"I had no idea," I say softly, my voice thick with emotion.

Mr. Jenkins sighs before walking over to gently pat my shoulder. "He must've wanted it to be a surprise. It's all here for you when you're ready, Ginny."

The emotions hit me all at once—gratitude, disbelief,

confusion. How could he be so thoughtful, so generous, and yet still have someone else in his life? Still see other women?

I bite my lip, fighting back tears. It's too much. The baby, the wedding, the bakery...Dario. How am I supposed to handle all of this when I can't even handle my own feelings?

"Ginny, are you all right?" Mr. Jenkins asks gently.

I nod, wiping at my eyes. "Yeah, I'm fine. Just...over-whelmed, I guess."

He gives me a sympathetic smile. "I understand. It's a big responsibility, but you've got time. No rush."

I manage a weak smile, thanking him softly before heading to the door. The moment I step outside, the cool air slaps my face, and all the emotions I've been holding in come crashing down on me at once. It feels as if everything is closing in, suffocating me. I can't keep it inside any longer.

Tears blur my vision as I slump against the car, my body wracked with silent sobs. How could Dario do something so thoughtful, so kind, and still keep secrets from me? How am I supposed to trust him with a baby, with my heart, when he's still hiding things? His mercurial nature, his hot and cold demeanor—how many more secrets does he have buried away?

And now there's a baby. A piece of him is inside me. How am I supposed to tell him? What if he's not ready for this, just like I'm not? The weight of everything presses down on me, and I feel utterly lost.

I'm still trapped in my thoughts when I sense someone behind me. Before I can turn, a sharp, searing pain shoots through my arm. I barely have time to process what's happening before a hand clamps over my mouth, and a sickly sweet scent invades my senses. My vision swims, and panic rises, clawing at my throat.

No, no, not again...

I try to struggle, but my body feels heavy, my movements slow and uncoordinated. My knees buckle beneath me as the world starts to spin, darkness creeping in at the edges.

The last thing I hear is a voice—low, cold, and unfamiliar.

"Don't fight it, sweetheart."

And then...nothing.

34

DARIO

The moment I step inside the house, I know something is wrong.

It's too quiet. Too empty. Normally, I'd hear Ginny somewhere in the distance—her soft humming as she helps Rosa in the kitchen, the mouth-watering aroma of something baking, her laughter as she plays with her dog... something—but today, there's nothing. Just the eerie silence that claws at my chest.

The air feels colder, heavier, as if the house itself is bracing for something. I pause, listening, but the emptiness presses in on me from every direction. My heart picks up, thudding uneasily as I walk deeper inside. I can't shake the feeling. It's gnawing at me—like something is missing, something vital.

"Ginny?" My voice echoes through the house, but there's no response.

The knot in my stomach tightens. The farther I go, the worse it gets, the silence deafening. Every step makes the dread build, my mind racing through every possible scenario. Where is she? Why is it so damned quiet?

I reach the kitchen, my eyes darting around. It's spotless. No sign of her usual baking supplies strewn across the counters. No flour, no bowls, no Ginny. Panic flashes through me, a sharp, cold wave.

Something's not right. Something's terribly, terribly wrong.

I clutch the small box containing the Harry Winston bracelet tightly in my hand. The moment I saw it behind the glass display—the silver chain adorned with delicate charms, tiny stars, and crescent moons—I thought of her.

I can already picture her smile, that teasing glint in her eyes when I give it to her. She'll probably laugh and call me cheesy, but I couldn't care less. I've fallen too hard for her to worry about that now.

I head upstairs, shaking the feeling that something is wrong. She must be asleep. Ginny goes to bed early sometimes. My little sleepyhead.

But when I check her bedroom and then mine, she's nowhere to be found. My sheets are slightly rumpled, showing that she was here. But it feels cold to the touch.

I drop my briefcase and step out into the corridor. Running a hand through my hair, I wonder if she's somewhere in the house. As I rush down the stairs again, my eyes briefly glance out the window, taking in the night sky. She must be here. Ginny can't be out at this time of the night.

"Boss…" Rosa's voice breaks through the silence as she emerges from the back door. She looks almost hesitant, and her face is pale.

I frown, slipping the box into my pocket. "Where's Ginny?"

Rosa's expression tightens, and she avoids my eyes, a sure sign that something's gone terribly wrong.

"I asked you a question, Rosa. You know I hate repeating myself."

Her breath hitches. "I...I'm so sorry, sir, I—"

"Rosa," my voice hardens, my patience shredding. "Where is she?!"

"She left this morning. Alone. We thought she'd be back quickly, but..."

"She left alone?" I chuckle bitterly, and Rosa winces at my tone. I blow out a tense breath before asking. "But what?"

Rosa's lips tremble. "She...she didn't say where she was going. I was in the kitchen when she said she needed some air, and before I could even get to the front door, she was...gone." Her voice breaks, and guilt weighs heavy in her tear-filled eyes.

Gone. I feel the walls closing in, my throat constricting as panic slithers through my veins.

"Why didn't she take Timoteo? Why the hell didn't anyone stop her? Why didn't anyone call me?" My voice rises, barely controlled, shaking with fear. My heart thuds erratically in my chest.

Rosa shakes her head, her hands wringing together. "I thought she'd be back soon... I didn't know she'd be gone this long."

I'm already pulling out my phone, dialing Ginny's number, praying for her voice to answer—but all I get is the cold, automated tone telling me her phone is switched off.

"Fuck!" The curse explodes from my lips, echoing off the walls. I dial again. And again. But nothing.

My hands tremble as I frantically dial Lorenzo's number next, my pulse thundering in my ears. The phone rings twice before cutting to voicemail.

"Damn it, Lorenzo, pick up!" I mutter under my breath,

dialing again, but the same thing happens. The panic is relentless now, coiling tighter and tighter around my chest.

"Rosa," I snap, my voice coming out harsher than intended, "when exactly did she leave?"

Rosa's eyes well up with fresh tears as she answers, her voice barely a whisper, "Around eight this morning, sir. I thought she was just going for a walk... I didn't think..." She trails off, visibly shaking now.

Eight. It's been *hours*. Too many fucking hours. My blood roars in my ears, and fear sharpens its claws into my gut.

I pace the room, my mind racing through worst-case scenarios. "Has anyone seen her? At all?" I demand, the desperation creeping into my voice.

Rosa shakes her head. "No, Boss. I sent Angelo out to drive around the neighborhood to search for her, but..." A tear slips down her cheek, and her voice cracks. "I'm so sorry."

"Get Timoteo. Now!" I shout, storming toward my home office, my fists clenching at my sides. "Find him. And check the garage. See if any of my cars are missing."

Rosa, Timoteo, the security guards, and the gatekeepers are my only workers that live at the staff quarters behind the main house. The rest come and go. These ones are here because I used to believe that they were useful to have around. But now, I'm livid at their display of incompetence.

Every negligent person who was involved in this will be punished. The maids, Timoteo, Angelo and his fellow security guards, the gatekeepers...

But that's not my main focus right now.

My fingers fly across my phone, dialing every contact I have in the police and underworld. My intel, my resources —all the people I've built relationships with over the years.

It doesn't matter if they owe me favors, if they're old friends or enemies. Everyone is expendable if it means finding her.

"Conduct a search, now!" I bark into the phone. "I don't care what it takes. Use the cameras, check the traffic feeds, shake down every street corner if you have to."

With every call I make, the sinking feeling in my chest deepens, clawing at me. The silence on the other end, the hesitation, the same damned response every time.

No one has seen her. No one knows anything.

I can't rely on these people, not now. Their promises are worthless. *Mere fucking promises.* Ginny could be in real danger, and I have nothing—nothing except my own gnawing fear. My stomach twists as the thought crosses my mind.

Kidnapped.

God, no.

My pulse races, the blood roaring in my ears as the possibility becomes real. Ginny, taken? In *my* city, under *my* watch? I let her leave alone, I let my guard down. If someone has her, they're signing their own death warrant, but I can't think about that right now.

Right now, I have to get her back.

I know this isn't some random disappearance—this has someone's fingerprints all over it. Someone is trying to get to me.

The hours tick by. Timoteo confirms that Ginny took one of the cars, but there's been no trace of her or the car since she left. Rosa says she seemed upset and sick when she went out, but no one knows why.

I don't sleep that night. I can barely even sit still.

I call Mr. Jenkins at the crack of dawn the next day, wondering if possibly Ginny tried to meet up with him.

Maybe she's looking to find a new building for her bakery. Maybe she's tired of staying home all day.

He answers on the second ring, his voice groggy. "Mr. De Luca? Haven't heard from you in a while."

"Have you seen Ginevra, my fiancée?" I snap immediately.

There's a pause. I hear him scratch at something, maybe his beard, as he thinks. "Yeah, yeah, she came by yesterday. She looked upset."

"Upset?" I echo, my heart hammering. It's the same thing Rosa said. "What do you mean?"

"Well, she didn't seem like herself. It looked like she was seconds away from crying, especially when I told her you'd bought the building in her name. I thought she was just emotional over the gesture. Then she just thanked me and left," he narrates as my heart pounds even faster.

"Where did she go?"

"I...I don't know. When she left, I went back to the backyard where I'd been fixing something. She looked like she was in a hurry, though. Haven't seen or heard from her since."

"Around what time was that?" I breathe.

"Around 8 or 9 a.m., maybe?"

"But there's something else... well—"

"Tell me!"

"She didn't take the car she drove here. She left it in the parking lot. I thought it was intentional or something, but now I realize I should have done something. I'm so sorry, Mr. De Luca. If I had known..."

I curse under my breath and hang up. She was there, *right there*. And now she's gone.

My phone rings and my breath hitches when I see Lorenzo's name on the screen.

"I've been trying to reach Ginny since yesterday morning, but she's not answering," he rushes out the moment I answer the call. "Is she by any chance with you?"

"Ginny's missing," I say through gritted teeth.

I hear the sound of his breathing over the line as he stays silent for a few seconds.

"What do you mean by that?" he finally asks, his voice low.

Irritation zings through me. "What you fucking heard, Lorenzo! If you'd answered your call last night, maybe you'd know."

"What do you mean she's missing?" he chokes out again. "You promised me you would protect and take care of her!"

I grind my jaws painfully, my hands balling into fists.

"I traveled out of the state for a business trip. I just got back last night. My workers say she drove off in the morning but never came back," I rush out, my breath coming in heavy pants. "I know you're fucking pissed—"

"Of course, I'm pissed." He interrupts me with a loud voice.

"Well, this is not the time for that. We need to join forces together and find Ginny," I say harshly. "You said her number rang when you called. What time was that?"

"In the morning, around 11 a.m. But when I called later in the evening, her phone was switched off."

I run a frustrated hand through my hair. "If she was taken..." I choke, taking a deep breath. "If she's been kidnapped, they probably switched her phone off or threw it away."

"Or smashed it," Lorenzo exhaled shakily before his voice hardens. "I'll contact my tech guy to track it. There must be a way to find her."

When the call ends, I resist the urge to fling my phone

across the room. I can't be here. I can't be at home while she's missing. Without bothering to shower, I head out of the house. Throughout the day, all my movements are fruitless. All the people I go to meet—private investigators, informants—all tell me the same thing. It'll take a few days to find her.

By the second day, I'm unraveling. There's no positive news. No new leads to where she might have gone and what exactly had happened to her. Dread twists in my stomach as I wonder if she willingly left me. If the idea of marrying me in about a week got too scary and too real for her.

Did she finally have enough of the life I'd dragged her into? The possibility claws at me, eating away at my sanity.

I call Lorenzo again, pacing the length of my office, where I've been staying all these hours.

"Dario, I've been looking everywhere," he says the moment he picks up. "I've got my people on it."

"Your people?" I snap. "She's your sister, the only person she probably fully trusts. You're trying to tell me you don't know where she is?"

Lorenzo's silence stretches across the line before he speaks, his tone clipped. "What are you insinuating, Dario?"

"Are you trying to screw me over, Lorenzo?" I say through gritted teeth. "Did you take her somewhere far away? After all, I've settled all your debt. You've gotten almost everything you wanted from me in the first place—"

"You think this is some kind of sick game? You think I would risk my sister's life, risk everything we've built just a week before your wedding?" Lorenzo asks, his voice hard and sharp as a knife.

I shake my head. I don't believe him. I can't. Not after everything that's happened. Not with our history.

His scoff is bitter, piercing into my ear through the

receiver. "If you think I'd take her just to mess with you, then you need to get your head out of your ass."

His words slice through my anger, but it doesn't calm me. Instead, it just stirs the frustration and confusion further. He sounds sincere, and I know Lorenzo would never put Ginny in harm's way. But still, he could be lying. He could be playing me.

We both end the call without resolving anything.

The third day is a blur of desperation. I drive from place to place, meeting people I know can find anyone for the right price. But each dead end hits harder than the last.

By the time I return home, exhaustion weighs me down, but I can't stop. I find myself staggering toward her bedroom. I push open the door, the scent of her lingering in the air. Strawberry. Vanilla. It feels like a punch to the gut. I stand in the doorway, staring at her things—her neatly folded clothes, her hairbrush on the vanity. It's almost like she never left.

I walk over to her bed, the sheets still wrinkled from the last time she slept there. My hand brushes the fabric, and I feel something crack inside me.

I fall onto the bed, burying my face in her pillow and inhaling deeply. The familiar scent of her hair and body fills my lungs. I can't hold out much longer. I haven't slept. Haven't eaten. I feel like I'm drowning, the fear pulling me under. I squeeze my eyes shut, and finally, exhaustion wins.

I'm twelve again, trapped in that dark, damp room. The stench of sweat and blood chokes the air. I stand in the corner, two henchmen gripping my arms, pinning me against the cold stone wall. My heart races as I watch my father kneel on the ground, beaten and bloody. His face is barely recognizable, a grotesque canvas of bruises and despair.

"Where is it?" Antonio Bianchi demands on a low growl as he grips my father by the collar and shakes him violently.

"I don't know," my father whispers, tears streaming down his cheeks, mixing with the blood that drips from his cracked lips. "I don't have it."

My heart clenches painfully at the sight. I place a hand over my chest and squeeze, struggling to breathe.

Isabella Bianchi stands in the opposite corner, her lips curling into a sneer. "Lies," she spits. "If you didn't take it, then your useless son did. He's a thief. He took it."

Then, a sob breaks out of her lips as she looks at me. "I knew you were trouble when you started hanging around my Enzo. I knew you were a bad influence," she cries, clutching Lorenzo against her chest.

Lorenzo told me his father had a special watch that contained a chip linked to all his business dealings. The shady and legit ones. This was just the day before.

That's what they're talking about. It's madly suspicious that it immediately went missing after he told me about it. But I don't know where it is. I swear I didn't steal it. I try to speak, but my voice sticks in my throat.

"You." Antonio finally acknowledges my presence. His eyes are as sharp as knives as they bore into mine. "Where's the watch, boy?"

I shake my head frantically, my body trembling with fear. "I don't have it. I didn't take it, I swear."

But my words fall on deaf ears. He backhands me, the force of the blow sending me to the ground. Pain explodes across my face, the metallic taste of blood pooling in my mouth.

"You better tell me the truth," he tsks. "Or your father will pay for your lies."

I scramble to my knees, my heart pounding in my chest. "I didn't take it. Please, believe me!"

My father coughs, blood dribbling from his mouth. His blood-shot eyes meet mine, filled with desperation, pleading for me to hold on. "Dario...tell them. Tell them you didn't take it."

"I didn't," I sob, my voice shaking. I look at Lorenzo, standing silently in the corner with his mother. He's my best friend. He knows I wouldn't steal anything. I'm not a thief. "Lorenzo, please. Tell them!"

His eyes meet mine for a brief second before he looks away. His face is expressionless. Cold. As if he doesn't even know me. His mother whispers something in his ear, and he nods, stepping forward.

"He took it, Papa," Lorenzo says, his voice calm and detached. "I told him about it yesterday, and it went missing today. Dario stole the watch."

The words hit me like a punch to the gut. The room spins, and for a moment, I can't breathe. My heart feels like it's being torn apart, ripped from my chest.

Lorenzo's father smirks, satisfaction dancing in his eyes. He turns back to my father, his fist rising—

I jolt awake, my breath ragged, my body drenched in sweat. My heart races, and I remind myself it's just a dream.

I'm not twelve. I'm not in that room.

I'm in Ginny's bed. And she's gone.

My phone buzzes on the nightstand, the sound slicing through the silence like a knife. I grab it with shaky hands, my heart plummeting as I read the chilling message on my screen.

You've stirred the wrath of too many vipers, Dario. If you want to see your girl again, come to the Manor's junkyard behind the old cemetery. Alone. Or she dies.

35

GINEVRA

The floor beneath me is cold, and I can feel the rough concrete through my clothes as I sit huddled against the wall. The room is small, with nothing but bare, peeling walls and a dim bulb overhead. Musky air clings to my skin, smelling like dampness and rotten wood.

It's very quiet here, except for the sound of my shallow breathing and water dripping in the distance somewhere.

It's been three days...or maybe four. Heck! I've been holed up in here for a long time, and the only source of outside lighting is the small, broken window high against one wall in the room. I can't exactly count the days accurately.

My stomach growls in the silence, and a tired sigh leaves my lips as I slide my hand against it. I'm starving. It feels like hours since my last meal was brought.

As if on cue, the door creaks open, snapping me from my thoughts. I tense, my heart pounding. It's the same man as before, his smirk already plastered across his face. He swaggers in with a metal tray, his grin wide and smug as he kicks the tray toward me with his boot. The metal screeches against the concrete, the sound grating on my ears.

"You know the drill, Doll," he drawls lazily. "Eat up. Can't have you dying too soon, can we?"

The contents of the tray are the usual watery soup that barely passes for broth, and a slice of dry, hard bread. My stomach growls in hunger, and even though the sight of the food makes me nauseated, I know I have to eat it. I've been forcing it down since I got here, just enough to keep up my strength, just enough for the baby. I wonder if they know about my pregnancy. If they found out...I think it would be worse for me.

My unwelcome company stands there, watching me with those eyes full of malice and something else, something disgusting. He waits for me to break, to cry, to scream. But I've learned not to give him anything. Not anymore.

On my first day here, I insulted him when he touched me. He slapped me so hard that my ears rang for hours. Since then, I've been meek and quiet. I'll do whatever it takes to leave this place alive and safe.

If I ever leave this place.

I pick up the bread, and crumbles fall into the tray as I bring it to my mouth, chewing slowly. My jaw aches as I struggle to digest the bread, so I bring up the bowl to sip some of the tasteless soup.

He chuckles, and the sound makes my skin crawl. "That's right, sweetheart. You keep eating like a good little girl."

Disgust rolls through my body as I glare at him, resisting the urge to throw the tray in his face. Instead, I drop my head back down and stare at the soup, the pale, lifeless vegetables floating on the dark green liquid.

"You think he's coming for you, don't you?" he asks,

leaning against the doorframe, his arms crossed over his chest. "Dario. Your knight in shining armor."

I stay silent. The first day I was here, after I woke up from my drugged slumber, I screamed at him, demanding to know why I was here. I threatened him, claiming that Dario was going to come save me. That had only made him laugh harder.

Now, I don't give him the satisfaction.

He sighs, clearly bored with my lack of response. "We'll see how long that hope lasts."

He kicks the door shut as he leaves, the loud bang ringing in my ears long after he's gone.

I sit in the quiet, cradling my belly. It's only been days. But it feels like an eternity. I close my eyes and picture Dario panicking, frantically searching for me. I wonder what he thinks and how he feels.

He's looking for me. He has to be. He's coming. For me, for our baby.

Every hour since I got here has seemed like forever, the days blending into each other. I don't know whether it's day or night since the light in the room almost never changes. Sometimes I drift in and out of restless sleep, only to wake up in the same position, the same cold creeping into my bones.

I've dreamt of Dario every night since I got here. Sometimes, I dream of Lorenzo, as well. In my dreams, they find me, break down the door, and pull me out of this nightmare. But then I wake up, and I'm met with deafening silence.

I don't know how long it's been when the door opens again. Hours maybe. This time, it's not the first guy. Instead, it's another man, leaner, with a cruel smile that makes my skin crawl just as much. He never brings food with him, just his presence.

"Getting comfortable, are we?" he asks, pacing the room like a predator. When I don't give him an answer, he chuckles. "You should be grateful. Boss doesn't usually keep people alive this long."

I watch him, my heart pounding in my chest, and as usual, I remain silent. I've learned to read them by now—their body language, the way they circle me like vultures. Like his colleague, he just wants a reaction. He wants to see me cower.

When he becomes annoyed by my lack of response, he crouches down in front of me, his breath hot and reeking of beer and cigarettes.

"You know, I wonder if Dario even cares about you. We sent him a message the moment we captured you, but we still haven't heard a thing from him." A wicked glint flashes in his eyes. His voice drops into a whisper. "Maybe he's moved on by now. Found someone else. Realized you your stale pussy wasn't worth the stress. Happens all the time."

His words cut me like knives, but I force myself not to move or give him any reaction. I won't let him see the fear or doubt creeping into my chest. Dario wouldn't move on. He wouldn't abandon me.

Or would he?

"I'll bet you thought you were special," he continues, his bitter snicker filling the room. "I don't know why you women are always attracted to the bad guys. Men like Dario never settle down. They don't get attached. They don't fall in love."

My heart is pounding as he leans in even further. I resist the urge to pull my face away, and that leaves only a few inches between us.

He smirks. "I see you still have some fight in you. But in time, you'll see that I was right. Men like Dario only want you around for a good time. The moment things get tough, they disappear. It's good thing we have your brother to rely on if your bastard husband doesn't comply. A few million transferred to our offshore account, and we'll send you back to him in pieces. Everyone wins."

The words settle in the air between us, heavy and suffocating. But I don't break my expression—or lack of.

He stands up with a sigh, clearly disappointed that I didn't give him the reaction he wanted. He walks out the door and slams it shut again, leaving me alone with my thoughts.

The only time I ever get a semblance of peace here is when I'm asleep, which is why I rest against the wall and close my eyes, my food long forgotten as I try to shut the world out.

Time blurs as I slip into a dreamless slumber. When I wake up, my body feels weaker, and all my joints hurt. I hear the door open again, and I don't bother getting up from where I'm sprawled on the ground.

"Time for your breakfast, Doll," the familiar voice drawls.

Breakfast? I groan inwardly. It's a new day. Another day of being stuck here.

At the smell of the soup, my stomach growls loudly. The guard lets out a loud guffaw, but I pay him no mind.

"You look pathetic, sweetheart." He squats down in front of me, his eyes roaming over my face, lingering on the exposed skin where my t-shirt had lifted up. His grin widens, making my skin crawl. "You know, if you're real nice to me, I might bring you something better tomorrow. Maybe even some fresh bread."

When I still remain silent, he snarls and suddenly grabs my wrist, pulling me to my feet. I yelp and stumble. My body is weak from lack of food, but I manage to pull away from him, my heart racing.

"Get off me!" I shout, finally breaking my silence.

He laughs, still holding me. "Relax, Doll. Just wanted to see if you can still talk. It hurts my feelings when you ignore me, you know that?"

The air stills as the door is suddenly pushed open.

"Leave her the fuck alone," says a man I don't recognize.

The moment he leaves me, my body crashes into the floor. My body is trembling, tears pricking at my eyes.

"Sorry, Boss," the first guy says in a terrified voice before scrambling out of the room.

The man who just stepped into the room isn't like the others. He walks with a purpose, his eyes scanning my crumpled body on the floor. He's tall, broad-shouldered, with a bandage covering part of his cheek, concealing what looks like a healing scar.

"What the fuck have they been doing to you?" he asks, sounding pissed as he reaches me. "I'm so sorry. I didn't know my men could be such brutes."

"Who are you?" I ask, flinching as he tries to touch me.

He smiles, slow and cold. "My name is Rafeal, but you can call me Rafe. I'm the one who brought you here," he says in a casual tone, as if we're having a normal conversation.

I reel back slightly, my heart pounding in my chest. "Why?"

Rafe's smile widens as he drags an old chair from the corner of the room, sitting down in front of me like this is all a game to him. "Because your man needs to learn a lesson."

"Dario?" I breathe. "What does this have to do with him?"

Rafe leans forward, resting his elbows on his knees as

his eyes lock on mine. His brown eyes look soft, almost sympathetic, before he laughs.

"So you're the reason Dario became weak," he drawls, his eyes trailing over my body. "I can almost see why. You're pretty."

"Who the fuck are you?" I ask through clenched teeth.

He leans back in the seat, a sinister smile creeping across his face.

"Dario spared me once. I stole from him—goods worth billions." He chuckles darkly. "He probably thought he was doing the right thing. I spun him a tale about my pathetic wife, about her having cancer." His smirk widens. "Turns out, he bought it. Let me live. But here's the kicker—that story? Pure bullshit."

I stare at him, the room spinning as his words sink in.

His voice remains calm, almost mocking. "Well, it's not entirely bullshit. My wife does have cancer. I just don't give a damn." He laughs, the sound cold and devoid of empathy.

I remain silent, staring at him as anger and disgust curl into one big ball in my chest.

"You know," he inhales sharply, "I was shocked when Dario only left me this little scar on my face. The Dario I know doesn't let anyone mess with him." His eyes glint with malice as he grins. "I'm sure you know your boyfriend—oh, wait." His gaze lands on my ring, and he laughs. "Your fiancé. I'm sure you know your fiancé is a murderer. Guess you're not as innocent as you look."

"I know Dario has done bad things, but it's because of men like you," I snarl, not knowing the source of the sudden burst of energy. "Men who take advantage of his kindness, steal from him, kidnap people..."

His loud laughter cuts me off, shaking his shoulders as amused tears well in his eyes. Rage simmers within me.

"Either you're delusional or just plain stupid," he finally retorts, the smirk on his face infuriating me further. "Now I see why Dario killed Esteban, broke your ex's nose, and got someone fired for your sake. You basically worship him like a god."

Has he been stalking us? How does he know all of this?

He grins at my shocked expression. "Word travels fast in our world, darling. Dario went soft—spared me because of you. Because he's in love," he sneers. "He wouldn't even let me cash out from a small operation despite being a long-term associate. So I figured, why not hit him where it hurts?"

Dario didn't do anything to this man, and this is how he decides to pay back kindness.

"You're a bastard, I wish Dario had given you what you deserved," I seethe, unable to hold back my anger.

The sudden slap across my cheek stuns me, a groan escaping my lips.

"Despite being a gentleman, I hit women, darling," he says, his tone mocking.

"Gentleman?" I scoff, the pain throbbing in my face. "Is that what you tell yourself to feel better?"

You have a fucking death wish, Ginny, my inner voice whispers as he grabs my chin roughly, raising his hand to strike me again. I close my eyes, bracing for the blow.

"Enough!"

A new voice, one I recognize.

Rafe shoves me aside, and I crash against the wall behind me, but my focus isn't on him. It's on Rinaldo, who has just walked into the room.

36

DARIO

My car engine rumbles beneath me, my hands tight against the steering wheel, knuckles white and tense. The directions were clear. Meet them at the old Manor's junkyard alone, or Ginny dies. I don't care if it's an obvious trap. I don't care what happens to me tonight. I just need to see her.

I need to get her back home safely.

The space is barely lit as I drive in, shadows creeping from piles of rusted metal and broken cars stacked like tombstones. A perfect place for them to kill and dump a body.

If anyone dies here tonight, it should be me and not Ginny.

On getting to the middle, I kill the engine and step out. My breath is sharp in the cold air, but my heart pounds harder than the bite of the wind. My nerves eat me up as I slip my hands inside the pockets of my coat. Waiting. Eerie silence wraps around me. I look around, but there's nothing out of the ordinary.

Just me.

But then, the roar of engines slices through the quiet night. Flaring headlights blind me, and in a split second, I'm surrounded by four, maybe five cars.

Their doors fly open, and men leap out, dressed in black, masked, and carrying various weapons. I count at least ten, maybe even more, as they close in on me like wolves approaching their prey.

There's no sign of Ginny. This is definitely a fucking trap.

My eyes zoom in on them as they get even closer. It's almost impossible for me to fight them off. They easily outnumber me. I ball my hands into fists and raise them to my face. The weight of my gun in my inner coat pocket presses against my skin, but this isn't the time to reveal all my cards.

The door to one of the cars opens, and a figure steps out. The sound of his shoes crunching against gravel reaches me before his face does. My stomach drops.

Rafe.

A bitter chuckle rips from my throat. This can't be fucking happening.

"The one time I decide to spare a man's life, he stabs me in the back," I say through gritted teeth.

His grin is wide, mocking, as he steps closer, his eyes glinting with menace. "Dario, Dario. Long time, no see. Although the wound on my face says otherwise..."

"You should be dead," I hiss, and he smirks.

"That's right, but you were a fool for sparing me," he drawls, shaking his head. "Just as you're a fool now. You really thought you'd just stroll in here and take her back, huh?"

I step forward, not caring about the men around me. "You still owe me a couple of billion, Rafe," I call back, my voice steady despite the thick tension in the air. "Once this is over, I'll get every single penny back before I kill you."

He laughs, but I can see the twitch in his jaw. The men make way for him as he steps into the circle. "Money, Dario? You think I care about that now?"

"Money's all you care about. But you and I both know what happens when people try to screw me over." I glance at the men surrounding us, sizing them up. "This? This is your last resort, isn't it? Kidnap my girl? Rough me up a bit and then what?" My chuckle bites against the night air. "You're still the same coward I remember."

Before he can reply, movement from behind the line of cars catches my eye. My words die in my throat when I see her being huddled out roughly.

Ginny.

She's barely standing, her arms bound in front of her, and her eyes are hollow. Her t-shirt hangs loose on her thin frame, dirty and worn, and the jeans she's wearing are scraped at the knees, smudged with dirt and blood. Her dark hair, matted and tangled, falls into her face as she's hauled out of the car.

"Don't fucking touch her!" I move to step toward her, but Rafe's gun is already out, the barrel pointed right at my head.

"Uh-uh!" Rafe tuts, a smirk playing on his lips. "Stay right where you are. We wouldn't want things to get messy just before the real fun begins, would we?"

My chest tightens as one of the men drags Ginny toward Rafe. Pain grips my heart as her face comes into the light. I see the faint bruise on her sunken cheek, her chapped lips, and the tears glistening in her eyes as she looks at me.

"Let her go, Rafe," I demand, turning to face him. "I'm the one you want, not her."

"True," he replies, a sinister smile spreading across his face. "But first, get on your knees."

With a heavy heart, I drop to my knees, hands raised in surrender. "Now fucking let her go," I growl, the urgency in my voice rising. "I swear to god, if you don't—"

"But where's the fun in that?" He tilts his head, smirking, but the expression quickly shifts to a scowl as he barks, "And you don't get to give orders here."

With a snap of his fingers, his men close in on me.

Fists and boots rain down on my body, and I feel my ribs crack under the relentless assault. Pain explodes in my chest, my back, my head—everywhere. My face collides with the gravel, and I taste blood as it spills from my mouth. Through my blurred vision, I see Ginny struggling against her captors, screaming my name.

"Dario!"

I force out a laugh, broken and raw. "Is that...all you've got?" I spit blood onto the ground, pushing myself up to my knees. My body screams in protest, but I focus on Ginny. I won't break. I have to be strong for her.

The men hit me again, each blow landing with excruciating force.

"Dario... Please stop," Ginny sobs, turning to Rafe and gripping his arm with her bound hands. "Please tell them to stop. We'll cooperate with your demands."

"Don't worry about me, Ginny." I cough up blood and saliva, wobbling as I struggle to push myself back up. "I'm completely fine."

Fat tears stream down her face as she looks at me, completely helpless. My chest constricts as I watch her, as well. Her eyes are heavy with the weight of her emotions and unspoken words. Our souls call out to one another, but the physical barriers keep us apart.

"Aw, a lovers' reunion. How sweet," Rafe's mocking voice cuts into our haze. "Well, this has been fun." He sighs. "But it has to end now."

A whimper leaves Ginny's lips as he grabs her arm.

Don't you dare lay a filthy hand on her!" I scream, forcing myself to my feet.

I swing at the first man who tries to stop me, landing a punch, and then drive my elbow into the gut of the second. But then a metal bat slams into the back of my head, sending me crashing to the ground.

"Relax. I won't kill her." Rafe laughs. "He will."

A figure emerges from the shadows, approaching me with slow, deliberate footsteps.

"Long time no see, Dario."

That voice. I know it.

Rinaldo steps into view, his smug face illuminated by the headlights. His tailored coat stands in stark contrast to the dirty, ruined yard around us. He looks like he doesn't belong here, yet somehow he owns the moment.

My stomach tightens. Of course. It's him.

"Well, look at you, finally finding your family. You fit right in—designer suit and all, but your soul is as dirty and soulless as a trench dog," I spit, my eyes narrowing as my hands curl into fists.

Rinaldo steps closer, his gaze shifting between me and Ginny. His dark eyes linger on her like a predator eyeing its prey, then return to me with a sinister smile.

"Surprised? Did you really think this would play out without me?"

I feel my blood boiling, but before I can respond, he turns his attention to Ginny, his voice dripping with mockery. "Ah, Ginny. You've really made quite the mess, haven't you?" He steps closer to her, running a finger down her cheek, and she flinches. I see red.

"Get your filthy hands off her," I shout, lunging forward, but Rafe's men seize me before I can reach him. Pain radiates through my body as they punch and drag me back, but fury blinds me. "I swear to god, Rinaldo, I'll end you!"

Rinaldo laughs, crossing his arms. "You're not in a position to make threats, Dario. Not anymore." He glances at Ginny, then back at me, his grin widening. "In fact, you'll want to hear what I have to say. You see..." His eyes narrow as he studies me, voice dropping to a whisper. "Ginny's carrying something very important."

I freeze. "What the hell are you talking about?"

"Oh," Rinaldo says, reveling in my confusion. "You didn't know?" He leans in, lips brushing Ginny's ear as he whispers, "She's pregnant. With your child."

The world tilts. My head spins, and I can barely register the words. Pregnant? Ginny? My eyes lock on hers, wide and terrified, and suddenly it clicks. She seemed sick and upset the day she left. This must be why. She'd found out that she was pregnant.

"You bastard!" I growl, lunging again, but this time I'm met with fists and weapons. The men pound into me, sending me to my knees, but I barely feel it. My mind is consumed by swirling thoughts.

Ginny is pregnant. They kidnapped a vulnerable woman. Rinaldo knows she's carrying my child.

A knife slashes into my arm, but without thinking, I grab the hand, twist it, and snatch the knife. A guttural groan escapes as I stab it into his neck. The others recoil, and I stagger up, brandishing the weapon like a madman.

My gun is still in my coat pocket, but I've lost the coat in the fray.

Staggering forward, I spit blood and glare at Rinaldo through swollen eyes. "Touch her again, and I'll break every bone in your body," I hiss, my voice low, dangerous.

Rinaldo's smirk falters for just a second. "You're in no position to make demands," he says, a sharp edge to his voice. "But tell you what," he continues, his fingers trailing down Ginny's arm, "I'll spare her life if she admits she made a mistake. If she begs for me to take her back."

Ginny shudders but stays silent. Her jaw clenches, and she glares at Rinaldo with pure hatred.

"Tell me, Ginny," Rinaldo mocks, grabbing her face in his hands. "You left me for this brute. Do you regret it? Do you regret humiliating me in front of the world?"

I snarl, surging forward even though my body is screaming in protest. Rafe steps right before me, into the large gap between me and Rinaldo. "Not so fast," he mutters with a gun pointed directly at my head.

Gritting my teeth, I glance behind him. "She left you because you're weak. You've always been weak, Rinaldo."

His face twitches. "Is that so?"

"Yeah," I spit. "Remember when I broke your nose? You couldn't touch me then, and you can't now." I laugh, blood dripping down my chin. "You're pathetic. Hiding behind daddy's money, sending thugs to do your dirty work."

Rinaldo's eyes blaze with fury, but he keeps his voice calm. "Your problem is that you like to act so tough. Look at you now." He chuckles. "You look unrecognizable, and I didn't even have to lift a finger."

He takes a step closer, tugging Ginny along with him. "That's the problem with you commoners. Why get my hands dirty when I have men to do that for me?"

"That's exactly why you're weak and no one wants you,"

I snarl. "Send your men away. Face me, one on one. Let's see how tough you are then."

Rinaldo hesitates, his jaw clenched so tight I can see the muscle twitching. But instead of responding, he waves his hand.

"Beat him."

The men rush in again, fists, bats and boots crashing down on me. I swing the knife wildly, not caring who it hits. They land more blows, but the pain is drowned out by one thought--

Ginny.

Amidst the chaos, I hear her scream. Rinaldo's soft, taunting voice cuts through the noise. "Let's end this right now, Dario," he says, fingers trailing over Ginny's face. "I didn't call you here to kill you. I want you to watch while this weak man kills the woman you love, alongside your unborn child, right before your eyes."

I look up, barely able to see through the blood and pain. But I see enough.

The gun in Rinaldo's hand is now pressed against Ginny's head.

37

GINEVRA

I've never imagined how I would die.

Death is something I don't really like to think about. It's inevitable at the end of the day. So why spend all your life thinking about something that's bound to happen?

But now that I'm standing directly in the face of death, the fear I assume everyone feels in this moment is nowhere to be found. Instead, clawing at my chest is pain, digging its fangs into the numbness that has enveloped me.

The cold barrel of the gun is hard and unforgiving, pressing directly against the side of my head. The metallic chill seeps into my skin, and all I can do is stand there frozen. Every nerve in my body is screaming, but my mind seems calm. Terror skirts around my heart, waiting for the right opening. My body trembles uncontrollably from the harsh cold biting my skin.

Everything crumbles when my eyes meet Dario's again.

He's been pushed back to his knees. He keeps fighting to stand, but the men keep dragging him down. His face—god, his face—is bloodied and swollen. And like Rinaldo said, unrecognizable.

But I recognize him. My Dario. His emerald green eyes are wild, locked on me, and I can see him fighting to breathe. He's trying so hard to stay conscious, to protect me, but he can't even stand. They've beaten him so badly, he can barely move.

Helpless. We are both helpless and hopeless.

The tears fall fast, no longer controllable, pouring from me in waves of desperation. The hot liquid streams down my face, mixing with the grime that coats my skin. The gun digs deeper, forcing my head to tilt slightly, my wet cheek brushing against the metal.

A loud sob breaks from my lips unbidden. This is the end. It feels so final now. Rinaldo's hand tightens around the gun, and his laugh—sharp, cruel—echoes in my ears.

"You're scared, aren't you?" He sneers, nudging the gun harder into my skull. I wince from the pain but ignore his taunts. I don't care about that anymore.

This is the moment I die, right here in this godforsaken junkyard, and I'll never get to hold Dario again. I'll never get to say all the things I should've said.

My mind is racing. All I can do is wish, hope, and beg for more time. But unfortunately, that time has run out for me. For us.

"I'm sorry," I'm choking on my sobs. My voice is so weak it's barely audible, but Dario hears me. I know he does. He always hears me, even when I say nothing. "I'm so sorry, Dario."

From the distance, I watch his face tighten. "Ginny, don't..." He tries to move, but they slam him back down. He's helpless. For the first time, Dario is utterly powerless, and I can see the pain tearing through him as he struggles against the men holding him.

To protect me, a woman who is only moments away from dying.

"I love you," I choke out, the words slipping past my lips like a desperate cry. The confession hangs between us, like a final truth I had been too afraid to admit until now. Dario's face crumples, the disbelief and anguish fighting through the pain in his eyes.

This is it. The admission of what I should have said a hundred times before.

"I love you," I say again, louder this time. "I should have told you sooner. I...I thought we had time. I thought..."

"No." Dario shakes his head, his voice breaking as he calls out to me. "Ginny...don't talk like that." His words are slurred, thick with emotion. I can see the tears in his eyes, blending with the blood streaking down his face. "You'll get many more chances to say it to me. This won't be your parting word."

But how can he even believe that? I'm not coming back from this. I feel the weight of death closing in, and it's so heavy, so suffocating. I close my eyes for a moment, just trying to steady myself, to calm the frantic pounding of my heart.

I hear Rinaldo's breath behind me, hot and vile against my neck, and I want to scream. But I don't. I won't waste the limited time I have left on him.

"Well, well," Rinaldo mocks. "How touching. Ginny, confessing her love at the last moment. Are we watching a movie or something?"

The pressure of the gun shifts slightly as he steps closer. He laughs, a low, sickening sound that makes my skin crawl. "Go on," he says, voice dripping with mock sympathy. "Keep telling him how much you love him. Maybe it'll make his miserable life easier after I'm done with you."

"That's if he doesn't move on with someone else the moment she dies," Rafe buts in from where he stands nearby. A few of their men join in the laughter. They're enjoying this. Watching me break. Watching Dario fight to save me.

The mixed sounds of their laughter feel like sharp nails scratching against my skin. More tears pour down my cheeks as I keep my focus on Dario, who hasn't stopped struggling, desperate to reach me.

My heart clenches as my mind drifts to Lorenzo.

God, Lorenzo.

He'll be devastated. He'll be all alone.

I won't get to see him again. I won't get to hug him, to tell him that I'm proud of him. My heart aches, the pain sharp as I picture his face. "Dario...take care of Lorenzo," I murmur, my voice trembling. "Make sure he's okay. Tell him I forgive him, and I love him so much."

And Rosa. The poor woman would be broken. She's lost a son in the past, and she's taken Dario as her son and me as a daughter she never had. The news of my death will break her.

Dario's face is twisted with grief. His mouth opens, but no words come out—just a broken, choked sound that shatters what's left of my heart.

The life I've lived, the moments I've spent with Dario, are all flashing before me—every argument, every kiss, every single moment we spent wanting each other even though we hated each other—the exact moment I realized I'd fallen in love with him. It's right before my eyes, rolling in my mind like the credits of my favorite movie.

I never imagined we would end like this.

My chest tightens as I think about our unborn baby— the life we created. The child I'll never get to hold, never get to see grow. My heart breaks all over again. I press my lips together, refusing to let the sobs overtake me.

Rinaldo shifts behind me, letting out a long sigh, almost bored. "Well," he mutters, "I think that's enough. Time to wrap this up."

I take a deep breath, my whole body trembling as I force myself to speak. "Just pull the fucking trigger, Rinaldo," I say, my voice firmer than I thought it would be. "Kill me now."

He chuckles harshly. "It'll be my pleasure, Sweet Pea."

I squeeze my eyes shut and ball my hands into fists, bracing for the impact. I hear the gun cock, the cold, metallic click that seals my fate.

And then Dario's voice breaks through, raw and desperate. "This isn't fucking goodbye, Ginny!"

Then the chaos ensures.

Something clatters to the ground. There's a sudden hissing sound, and I hear someone yell. My eyes fly open just as thick, white smoke explodes around us, swallowing everything in an instant.

"What the fuck?" I hear Rinaldo growl just as the world around us explodes into a blinding, choking haze of white.

Everything is chaos. Men shout and stumble, blinded by the smoke. There's shouting, cursing, and confusion all around me. I can't see anything, and I can't hear anything but the pounding of my own heart.

Rinaldo and Rafe's voices overlap each other, barking commands and curses. Just then, I feel Rinaldo's grip on my arm loosen. I don't think. I wrench myself free, falling to the ground in a heap. Pain shoots through my body as my knees hit the dirt. But I don't care. I'm coughing, choking on the smoke as I crawl blindly away from Rinaldo, away from death.

"Dario!" I scream, my voice hoarse and desperate. He must be looking for me. My tied hands scrape against the rough ground as I grunt, using my legs to push my body forward.

I can't see him. I can't see anyone, but I hear the shouts and the panic of men stumbling around in the smoke. My body aches, every muscle burning as I struggle to get on my feet. Desperation fuels me as I get on my knees in an attempt to steady my body. I plant one foot forward before propelling the rest of my body to stand up.

Hope blossoms in my chest as I begin to move. I can be with Dario again. We can survive this. But first, I have to find him, and we have to get out of here.

"Not so fast," I hear Rinaldo growl somewhere behind me.

His rough hand grabs my ankle, yanking me back to the ground. I scream as sand and dirt fly into my open mouth. Panic surges through me as I kick out wildly...

And then—BANG.

38

DARIO

The gun slips from my hand, clattering to the ground as I surge forward, desperately searching for Ginny through the thick smoke. I'd heard her scream my name before that cry of fear pierced the chaos.

In a moment of panic, I fired into the sky, hoping to instill terror in her captors. My heart races in my chest as I wonder if any of them had gotten to her again.

The smoke is thick, burning my lungs and stinging my eyes, but all I care about is finding her. I release a sharp, relieved breath as her voice rings out again. She's still safe. She's still here. My heart pounds as I push through the haze, my hand waving the smoke away so I can see clearer.

That's when I see her.

Her body is slumped on the ground, coughing and struggling against the ropes binding her hands together. My breath catches as I rush towards her, dropping on my knees beside her.

"Dario?" she asks as I immediately lift her into my arms. She doesn't wait to see my face before a relieved sob escapes her lips. "Oh my god, Dario. I thought..."

"You're okay, Ginny," I say through gritted teeth, something cracking within me at the sound of her broken voice. "We're okay."

I cradle her fragile body in my arms as I carry her out of the smoke. She rests her head against my chest, and my heart clenches painfully when I feel her tears soaking through the light material of my shirt. We reach where my car is parked. I open the back door, place her in a sitting position to face me by the door, and sink onto my knees before her.

A mixture of anger and pain cuts through my chest as I observe her face. She's pale, her face streaked with dirt, blood, and tears. My hands tremble as I tear at the knots I realize are still tied around her wrists. She looks different—malnourished, weak, broken...

But she's still alive. Relief floods through me, but my anger still burns right beneath it.

I open my mouth to speak, to tell her I'm sorry for having her dragged into my mess and for making her life miserable since the moment we met. But my throat feels heavy, and I'm seconds away from breaking into tears. Because I can't resist, I pull her into my arms again, holding her tight as if she might disappear. She clutches me, shaking, her fingers clutching at my shirt as if she's afraid.

"Dario," she whispers again, her voice weak, but I hear the relief in it.

"I'm here, baby." My voice cracks as a lone tear slips down my eyes. "You're safe now."

I press my forehead to hers, trying to calm the storm inside me, but anger still burns in my chest.

Before I can say anything more, another panicked voice breaks through the smoke. "Dario!"

I look up to see Lorenzo pushing through the smoke, his

eyes wide with panic as he spots us. He hurries over, his gaze immediately locking onto Ginny. As he reaches us, she pulls away from me and turns to look at her brother. There's a fleeting hesitation, a moment where he almost stops, as if unsure how to approach his sister after everything.

"Enzo..." she whispers hoarsely.

Lorenzo's face crumples as he strides over to where she's sitting and pulls her into his arms, holding her close. "I'm sorry," he mutters, his voice hoarse. "I'm so sorry, Ginny."

She shakes her head, her tears mixing with his as she clings to him. "You came. You're here now. That's all that matters."

"Of course I came." He chuckles, then sniffs as he tightens his arm around her. "You're my sister."

My heart squeezes in gratitude and disbelief. Our plan had worked.

It feels like a lifetime ago that we sat down and made it, though it's only been hours. Hours since I showed him the text. Hours since we dug deep and found out about Rinaldo's sketchy movements from all the sources we reached out to.

We'd predicted he was the kidnapper, and we were right. Rafe was the person I hadn't expected to be involved.

I remember the look on Lorenzo's face when I told him everything—the shock, the anger, but most of all, the guilt. The guilt he's carried since the day he'd betrayed me as a child. But this time, I was ready to set aside my hatred.

This wasn't about us anymore. It was about Ginny.

"You owe me, Lorenzo," I had told him, grabbing the front of his chest in desperation. "If anything happens to Ginny...I'll never forgive you."

He didn't reply at first, just stared, the weight of my words sinking in. I could see it in his eyes—this was his chance to make things right, to fix the mess he'd created all those years ago.

And he had.

He'd hijacked the bus with Rinaldo's men and paid them off—triple what Rinaldo and Rafe were offering. Convincing them to switch sides was easy, as was replacing their guns with blanks and setting off the smoke bomb. He'd even joined in my beating, a risky move that could have cost us everything. But for Ginny, I'd take that risk.

And it worked. It fucking worked.

The sight of them reunited should ease the tension in my chest. But all I feel is the boiling rage inside me still waiting for release. This isn't over. Not yet.

I rise to my feet, my hand on the gun at my waist. The first thing I did when the smoke bomb went off was find my gun.

"Stay with her," I tell Lorenzo in a cold voice. His eyes flicker to mine, and for a moment, we exchange a silent understanding.

He nods, pulling Ginny closer. "I've got her."

I turn to Ginny, and she's looking up at me, her eyes filled with fear and desperation. "Dario, don't... Don't go. Please."

I crouch beside her, taking her hand and brushing my thumb over her knuckles. "I'll be back," I tell her softly. "Just one minute."

She grips my hand tighter, her eyes pleading as I try to pull away. "One minute," I repeat, my promise lingering in the air. I turn to Lorenzo again, my voice hardening. "Don't let anything happen to her."

I press a chaste kiss against her forehead before I turn and stride back to the center of the junkyard.

The smoke has cleared up now, and I see the two men

tied up ahead. They're on their knees, their faces twisted in fear with the men that once answered to them standing by the side. The fire in my chest burns hotter at the sight of them, my steps slow and deliberate as I come to stand before them.

They'd tried to take everything from me. They'd put a gun to Ginny's head. They'd laid their fucking hands on her.

Rafe spots me first, and immediately he begins to plead in a trembling voice.

"Dario...wait—please..."

Rinaldo's eyes meet mine, and though he tries to put on a brave front, I can see the fear in his eyes. Rafe is shaking at this point, his breaths coming out in fast, uneven gasps. They both know what's coming.

"We didn't mean for it to go this far, man. I swear..."

My fist connects with his face before he can finish his plea. He falls backward, gasping in pain, blood pouring from his nose.

"You didn't mean for it to go this far?" I spit, standing over him. "You kidnapped her. You put a gun to her head."

Still trying to hold onto some shred of dignity, Rinaldo sneers. "What? You think killing us makes you a big man, Dario? You think this makes you..."

I don't give him a chance to finish. I raise my gun and shoot him in the leg. He clamps down on his lips with his teeth, but a deep groan slips past his throat, echoing in the night.

This makes Rafe even more scared.

"Dario! Please! I swear, I didn't want any of this. He convinced me," he points towards Rinaldo, who is clutching his leg. "He blackmailed me."

"With what?" I demand, taking a step closer, aiming the gun at his hand. "What did he blackmail you with?"

His eyes go wide as he stammers, scrambling for an answer, for a lie.

I aim for his mouth and pull the trigger. The shot rings out, and Rafe's screams become muffled as he cradles his bloodied face.

"You lied to me the first time," I say, reaching over to grab his hair roughly and pull him up. "Did you really think I would believe you again?"

Senseless mumbles mixed with groans escape his lips. His face is a mess, with tears, blood, and snot seeping through the available holes.

Rinaldo's face is pale now, the arrogance gone. "You really think this is going to change anything? You think killing us makes you better than me?"

I crouch down in front of him, gun still in hand, our faces inches apart. "I don't give a fuck about being better," I say in a quiet, cold voice. "This is to make sure you never hurt her again."

I stand up and fire a shot into Rinaldo's arm. He grits his teeth, refusing to scream, but I see the pain etched on his face, the tears slipping from the corners of his eyes. He's trying to maintain control, but it's of no use. He's going to die anyway.

I point the gun at his other hand. "You should have known better," I say softly, my voice almost a whisper. "You should've known better than laying your filthy hands on her."

I fire. Rinaldo finally lets out a guttural cry, his two hands a bleeding mess. But there's no mercy in me. Turning, I raise the gun one last time and aim it squarely at Rafe's head.

Rafe's eyes widen, filled with pure terror as he shakes his head vigorously, unable to speak or beg.

The shot is swift and final. Rafe's body slumps forward, lifeless. Dark red blood pools beneath him, soaking into the dirt.

I turn to Rinaldo. His chest is heaving with labored breaths, blood seeping from his wounds. The fear in his eyes is thick, but he's too proud, too arrogant, to beg for mercy, even in the face of death.

I don't give a fuck about that. Whether he begs or not, he'll still be a dead man in...

I glance at my watch. The one minute I promised Ginny is almost up.

"I'll give you credit," I say, cocking the gun again. "You've got guts. Too bad they'll be spilled all over this very ground by noon when the vultures find your body."

"My father will come for you," he splutters, his body visibly vibrating when I raise my gun to his head. "You won't get away with..."

The gun fires, the bullet piercing into the center of his forehead. His body crumples and collapses beside Rafe.

The silence that follows is deafening. I stand there, breathing heavily, staring down at their bodies. There's no satisfaction in their deaths—only cold, hollow emptiness. The only thing that satisfies me is the thought of reuniting with Ginny, of continuing our lives together without any threats.

"Leave their bodies here," I tell the men hovering around. I meant it when I said they'll be consumed by vultures.

The men have their heads bent down in fear. Their hitting me was also part of the plan. Since their guns were basically useless, we didn't want Rafe or Rinaldo catching on to the deceit.

Plus, I intended to kill these bastards in cold blood—no police involvement.

I turn and stride back to the car. Lorenzo is already in the driver's seat when I arrive. I slip into the back where Ginny waits. Her large hazel eyes scan me as I pull her into my arms.

"I told you, Ginny," I murmur as the engine rumbles to life. "I'll be back in just one minute."

39

GINEVRA

I *hate hospitals.*

The sharp smell of antiseptic and medicine clings to the air, suffocating me. The harsh fluorescent lights glare down from sterile white ceilings, and the pale walls feel like they're closing in. The steady beep of machines is a reminder of vulnerability I can't stand.

But until now, I didn't realize how I'd rather spend my whole life locked in a hospital room than spend a minute in the dingy cell room where I was a couple of days ago.

A heavy sigh escapes my lips. I told myself I would stop thinking about it, but sometimes, especially when I'm alone, those bad memories creep back in.

I shift in the hospital bed, trying to make myself comfortable, but the healing bruises and fatigue are a constant reminder of everything that's happened. A soft knock on the door startles me out of my thoughts, and before I can say anything, Dario slips inside, ignoring the doctors' orders, of course.

I can't help but smile despite the pain that pulls at the corners of my mouth. "You never listen, do you?"

"You shouldn't be surprised by now, Princess," he replies, his grin lighting up the room.

Dario was admitted to the same hospital two days ago. By the time he and Lorenzo brought me here, I was teetering on the brink of unconsciousness from severe malnutrition, a dangerous condition for my pregnancy. Frantic, Dario explained my situation to the doctors, who'd rushed me into the ER.

He'd wanted to stay by my side, but the bleeding and visible injuries from his beating had forced him into a different ward. Since then, it's been a relentless battle. He often sneaks out at odd hours to see me, sometimes skipping his medications and consultations. The doctors are at their wits' end with him.

Today, he enters my room with that mischievous spark in his emerald eyes, and I can't help but feel a flutter of warmth in my chest.

"Hard ass..." I scold half-heartedly as he shuts the door quietly behind him and limps toward me. Without hesitation, he slides into the bed beside me, wrapping his arms around me gently. "I missed you."

"Missed you more, my love."

"The nurse from last night told me you spent the night here." I chuckle. "You only left this morning."

"Yeah. I knew you'd give me a hassle if you woke up and saw me."

"You need rest, too," I remind him softly.

"I wouldn't get it from the stupid ward 100 feet away from you. I will not let you out of my sight again, Ginny. I almost died from worry the last time I let you out of my sight and something happened to you. I'm incapable of staying away."

I smile, my heart swelling with affection. His pining over

me these past few days is both sweet and thoughtful. I love him fiercely, wanting to shout it from the rooftops like the lovestruck fool I feel, but I'm striving to maintain my composure, resisting the urge to let my heart dictate my every move.

"I'm incapable of staying away from you too, Dario." I lean in and kiss him gently on the lips. This is our first kiss since the whole Rafe and Rinaldo incident, the first in almost two weeks, and it honestly feels too long.

Before I can pull back, he tugs me closer and kisses me with more fervor but gentle, conveying everything his words haven't. That he's completely in love with me, just as I am with him.

We breathe each other in after what feels like minutes, the air thick with relief and desire. Finally, we've reached this point where we can love each other openly. We stay like that for a while—no words, just the soft rise and fall of our breaths syncing together. I turn to rest my head against his chest, listening to the steady thrum of his heart.

But there's something nagging at the back of my mind, something I've held onto for too long now. I need to say it, to clear the air once and for all.

"Dario," I murmur, touching one side of his face. "There's something I need to ask you."

His arms tighten slightly around me, and he tilts his head to look down at me. "What is it?"

I hesitate, biting my lip, unsure of how to begin. "I saw a message on your phone...from a woman. It...it sounded like you were meeting her, and I thought..." My voice falters, embarrassment flooding my cheeks, but I push through. "I thought you were cheating on me. Are you seeing another woman?"

Silence hangs between us for a moment as I trace the furrow in his brow, waiting for his response. "What message?" he asks, his expression shifting to confusion.

I pull back slightly to meet his gaze. "It was from a woman asking where to meet. The day before you brought me Piper. I went through your phone, and you guys used to meet up before."

Dario's brows knit together in concentration, and then, suddenly, he lets out a soft laugh. "You mean the day you locked yourself inside and refused to come out? The message you're talking about was from the woman I bought Piper from."

My face heats up instantly. "She's...a dog lady?"

"Yes, a dog lady." He laughs, his amusement infectious. "And while I did have something with her in the past, I made it clear I don't do relationships. She's been trying her luck since. I only reached out to her because of the short notice. Honestly, I hardly remember her name most days. She was just confirming where to drop off Piper. I told her it was a surprise for my wife."

I groan, burying my face in my hands. "Oh my god, I'm such an idiot."

Dario chuckles, gently pulling my hands away from my face. "Ginny, you really thought I'd cheat on you?"

I meet his gaze, a mix of foolishness and relief washing over me. "Well...I mean, I didn't know what to think. Everything was just..."

"Stop," he says softly, cutting me off. "You're the only woman I see. The only one I love."

His words melt the last remnants of doubt in my heart, and I smile, feeling the warmth of his sincerity.

"Speaking of dogs," he mutters, a mischievous glint in his eyes.

Before I can ask him what the matter is, the door opens again, and Rosa walks in with Piper cradled in her arms. The moment I see them, my heart leaps. The little bundle of fur in Rosa's arms wriggles, eager to jump into mine.

"Piper!" I laugh, sitting up straighter in bed to attend to the hyper animal first. Rosa sets her down gently on the bed, and Piper rushes to me, licking my face with excited little whimpers. I laugh, joy bubbling up in my chest as I hold her close and bury my face in her fur.

"I missed you," I whisper to the pup, tears springing to my eyes. I didn't realize how much I'd missed her until now.

Dario watches me with a soft smile, his hand resting on my back as Piper nuzzles into me, her tail wagging furiously.

When I raise my head to look at Rosa, I notice her eyes are red-rimmed, as if she's been crying. She has a soft smile plastered on her face, but I can tell she's struggling to keep her emotions in check.

"Rosa..." I whisper, my heart squeezing painfully.

She hesitates, as if she's not sure if she should come any closer. But then she rushes to my side, her hands trembling as she reaches out to touch me.

"Oh, my sweet girl," she murmurs, her voice thick with emotion. Her shaky hands cup my face gently. Tenderly. "I'm so sorry. I never should've let you leave that day. If I had stayed with you, maybe...maybe none of this would've happened."

Her voice breaks, and as tears start streaming down her face, I feel mine coming in, as well. She wipes them away quickly, but I can see the overwhelming guilt she's been carrying.

"Rosa, stop." I grab her hands, holding them tightly in

mine. "I needed to clear my head that day, so even if you'd been with me, I would have still left the house. I made the decision to leave. Please don't blame yourself."

"But if I had just stayed with you..."

I shake my head firmly. "No. You couldn't have known what was going to happen. None of us could. The only people to be blamed are the men who kidnapped me," I swallow thickly before continuing. "Please...don't carry this guilt. I'm okay, and that's what matters."

She presses her lips together and nods, wiping another stray tear from her eyes. "I just... The thought of losing you..."

"I love you too, Rosa," I whisper, my tears betraying me as I pull her into a gentle hug. She holds me tightly, her arms wrapped around me as if she never wants to let go. "And you didn't lose me. I'm right here."

We stay like that for a few moments. When we finally pull back, her eyes are still wet, but she looks a little more at peace.

"My sweet girl," she says, brushing a hand through my hair and wiping my tears away. "I'm glad you're okay."

Just then, the door opens again, and Lorenzo steps inside. He's in a simple t-shirt and jeans, so I know he hasn't gone to work. He looks around, a little hesitant, and I presume it's because of the visitors in the room. He greets Dario with a handshake, and I notice that the atmosphere isn't as stiff as it used to be whenever they're together. He also gives Rosa a warm smile before finally looking at me.

"Hey, Enzo," I greet softly.

His expression softens as he takes me in. I know what he sees. I look and feel better than the last time he saw me, which was yesterday morning. He's been the only other person Dario has let in over the past two days, but even then, he doesn't stay very long before he gets an urgent call. I don't mind though. If not for Lorenzo coming to our rescue...

Well, I don't want to think about what could have happened.

"Hey," he walks over to my bedside. "How are you feeling? You look like you've been crying."

I chuckle. "Just...emotions," I give him a tired smile. "I'm better now that I've had some visitors."

Lorenzo takes one of the seats beside the bed, putting him in between Rosa and Dario. His presence is calm and comforting. For the next few minutes, we all talk about little things—mundane things like the weather, a new big shot client he got, and how Piper has been adjusting to life at home. It's nice talking about something that doesn't involve danger or violence.

But exhaustion eventually pulls me under, and my eyes grow heavy as our conversation slips to the back of my mind. I feel Lorenzo squeeze my hand before standing to press a kiss to my forehead.

"Get some rest," he whispers. "I'll be back soon."

I nod, my eyelids fluttering shut as I feel him and Rosa leave the room. Sleep takes over—a deep, dreamless rest that I so desperately need. When I wake up again, the room is quiet, the only sound coming from the machines next to me. I blink groggily, and when I turn my head, I see Dario sitting in the chair next to my bed, his green eyes vivid and watching me closely.

He smiles when he sees me stir, and without a word, he reaches for my hand, his thumb brushing over my knuckles. There's a strange look in his eyes—something heavy, something unresolved.

"Hey," I murmur, still groggy from sleep. "How long have I been out?"

"Just a few hours," he says softly. "Everyone left so you could rest. The doctor came to see you, but you were out cold."

"Oh," I murmur, sitting up.

"She told me to inform her when you wake up." He stands to his full height and kisses the back of my hand.

Despite being sick, a flutter rises up my stomach. Apparently, I'm not immune to Dario's touch, no matter what the situation is.

"I'll be right back."

He leaves the room, and a moment later, he comes back in with the doctor.

Doctor Williams is a dark-skinned black woman with kind eyes and the most perfect set of teeth, like the ones you see in toothpaste ads.

"Miss Bianchi. How are you doing?" she greets with a warm smile.

"I'm good. You?"

"Oh, well, other than the fact that your fiancé here never stays in his ward so his progress could be monitored, nor does he even take his medications, I'm wonderful. Thanks for asking."

I laugh at her sarcastic tone. Dario does nothing but smile in satisfaction.

"I'll be out of your hair when we get discharged, Doc," he says, his eyes full of mischief.

She sighs but doesn't argue, turning her attention to me instead. "Ginny, you're recovering well. I'm happy to say that both you and the baby are doing just fine."

My hand instinctively goes to my stomach, and I feel Dario's fingers intertwine with mine. The relief is overwhelming, and I can't stop the tears that well up in my eyes.

"Thank you," I whisper.

She checks a few more things before she eventually leaves after some minutes.

For a moment, the room is filled with the quiet rhythm of the machines. Dario is back on my bed, his hands mindlessly drawing circles on my back. But his eyes are distant, like he's lost in his own thoughts. I can sense there's something he wants to say, and just before I ask him, he clears his throat.

"Ginny," he begins, "I know you've been wondering...about what happened between me and Lorenzo."

The shift in his tone makes my heart clench. I look up at him, searching his face. "You don't have to tell me if you're not ready."

He shakes his head. "No. I want you to know."

He takes a deep breath, and I can almost feel the weight of his words before he even begins. "It was years ago on a trip. Your family was going on a yearly vacation at a resort in Miami. Lorenzo asked me to tag along, and as the excited child I was, of course I said yes." He chuckles humorlessly. My heart pounds in my chest as I wonder the direction the story is headed.

"My father worked as a henchman for your dad, so he was also there as part of their staff. Late one night, I was harshly woken up and called down to this underground room...and when I got there... "

He pauses, and I see his jaw tighten as he struggles to continue. "I found my father. They'd beaten him up so badly, he could barely stand. They accused him of stealing a watch, but he didn't do it. He couldn't have."

I reach for his hand, holding it tightly, but his gaze is

distant. "Your mother..." he chokes, and I see a hint of red in his eyes. "Your mother said if my father didn't take it, that meant I was the thief. Lorenzo was there. My best friend. I thought he'd defend me. I thought...he'd help."

A bitter laugh escapes his throat. "Instead, he claimed to be a witness. He lied. Said he saw me steal it."

My chest tightens with a mix of anger and sorrow. "Dario..."

"They let us go after beating us some more," he continues, his voice low and raw. "But obviously Antonio fired my dad. After that, he had to take odd jobs just to keep my mother's chemotherapy going. We wre already behind as we couldn't make payment. But it wasn't enough. She died. And then, not long after, my father was mugged and killed."

Tears spill down my cheeks as I listen, my heart breaking for him. I had no idea what my parents had done...what Lorenzo had done.

"Lorenzo came to the funeral," Dario continues in a hollow voice. "He admitted that his mother had forced him to lie. But the damage was done. I told him I'd never forgive him."

I can barely see through the blur of tears. "Dario, I'm so sorry... I never knew..."

He shakes his head, turning to me with a sad smile. "It's okay, Ginny. Yes, I was angry at everything that happened, but as I got older, a part of me realized he was just a kid, too. He was just obeying his mother by lying. He didn't know what he was doing."

"But he hurt you so much."

Dario cups my face, his calloused thumb brushing away the remaining tears. "It doesn't matter anymore. You came into my life, and everything changed. I've been in the dark for so long, but you're my light, Ginny. You're the family I never had."

His words send a rush of warmth through me, my heart hammering against my chest.

Dario nods, his eyes filled with love. "I love you, Ginny. And I want to make a family with you. I don't care about the contract, or revenge, or everything else. I just want to have you and our baby for the rest of my life..."

Tears pour down my eyes as he leans down to rest his forehead against mine.

"...If you'll have me."

40

DARIO

I'm still sitting beside Ginny on her hospital bed. The room is suddenly too quiet, tension thick in the air. Her fingers toy with the edge of the pale-green blanket, her eyes staring at mine. I don't breathe, waiting for her to say something...anything.

"I'll be yours," she finally whispers.

It takes a moment for her words to sink in, but when they do, my chest tightens with a flood of emotion. Without thinking, I pull her into my arms, holding her as tight as I can without hurting her. "Thank god." I bury my face in her hair, kissing her lovingly. "Thank god."

I hear her soft sigh as her arms circle around my waist. For a moment, we just hold on to each other. Everything else fades away—the past, the present, and the only thing I can think of as her warm scent fills my lungs is our future together.

I haven't felt this in a very long time.

Peace.

My heart slows into a steady rhythm, joy dancing in my stomach as she clings to me. It's a reassurance that everything is going to be okay. When I pull back slightly, she whines softly.

"I was really loving that hug."

A chuckle slips past my lips as I tilt her chin up with my fingers. Her eyes meet mine. Hues of brown, green and golden dance together, filled with warmth.

"You have me forever now, Ginny. There are millions of hugs to come."

As I brush the pads of my fingers across her cheek, a warm blush appears on her face. "I really love the sound of that."

"You and me," I say, brushing a strand of dark hair from her eyes. "It's for real this time."

Ginny smiles, soft and sure. "I don't want to wait anymore for us to get married."

I chuckle again, though the thought of her being my wife officially makes my chest tighten with emotion. "The wedding is the day after tomorrow. I made sure Rosa went on to take care of everything though it had postponed. Nothing's going to stop us from being together now."

"Promise?" Her voice is teasing, but I sense the edge to it. I know that there is still fear lurking around her chest somewhere. I don't expect her to recover from the trauma of being kidnapped in a short time.

But I've sworn to protect her, to shield her. Nothing like this will ever happen again, I'll make sure of it.

"I promise," I say vehemently before leaning down to kiss her forehead. "I love you, Ginny. More than anything. And I'll spend every day of our lives together showing you just that."

"I love you too, Dario," she whispers, her words wrapping around me like a warm blanket. "I've only said it once, but I promise to keep saying it. I'll never hesitate or waste any second to tell you exactly how I feel."

Emotions clogging my throat, I lean in to press my lips against hers. Ginny immediately hums softly into the kiss, bringing her soft hands to my face as she tilts her head to kiss me even deeper. My tongue slips in, searching her mouth, taking all of her, giving her all of me.

When I pull my lips away from hers, we are both breathing heavily. I press our foreheads together for the millionth time and close my eyes.

And for the first time in a long time, everything feels right.

"WHAT'S your favorite ice cream flavor?" Ginny asks from the passenger seat beside me.

We were discharged from the hospital this morning, and the first thing Ginny requested as soon as I drove us out the gates was vanilla ice cream.

"I don't have a favorite flavor," I say, turning the steering wheel into a corner street.

"I don't think I've ever met someone who doesn't have a favorite ice cream flavor."

"Well, I don't eat ice cream."

Her disbelieving gasp fills the air, and I chuckle when she looks at me as if I'd just admitted to a heinous crime.

"Why not?" She asks, then raises her hand in the air before I say anything. "Let me guess. You think it's unhealthy, and you're obsessed with being fit?"

"Oh my god. How did you know that?" I drawl sarcastically.

She catches on to my tone before releasing an annoyed

huff. "Well, too bad. As long as you're married to me, you will learn to like ice cream. And sweet treats…"

Her voice trails off as if she remembers something.

"Mr. Jenkins told me you bought the store in my name."

I feel her warm gaze on the side of my face, and an involuntary smile pulls at the sides of my lips.

"I hadn't realized I was in love with you then. I just thought I was doing it because I felt bad for taking the building you wanted so badly."

I feel her soft hand slide over mine on the center console before she murmurs a soft, "Thank you."

As we pull into our familiar neighborhood, I glance at her, her eyes fixed on the passing scenery with a peaceful expression on her face.

When we drive into the compound and pull into the driveway, Ginny's breath hitches. She looks at the house as if she's seeing it for the first time. I park, get out, and walk over to her side, opening the door for her. She steps out slowly, taking in the place, her home.

Our home.

Some housekeepers rush to welcome us in, going to the trunk to retrieve a few of our belongings that had been brought to the hospital. I intertwine my fingers with Ginny's as we head toward the front door.

Piper is the first to rush towards us as soon as we step into the house. A pleasant laugh escapes Ginny's lips as she bends down to scoop the puppy into her arms.

"Piper." She laughs as the dog licks her face, her tail wagging in excitement.

I spot Rosa next as she emerges from the kitchen, wiping her hands with a napkin.

"You both arrived just in time. I just finished making lunch."

Ginny drops Piper carefully on the ground before leaning down into Rosa's waiting arms.

"Mmm," Rosa hums with her eyes closed. "It feels so good to have you back, my dear."

"It feels good to be back," I hear Ginny mumble, her face pressed into Rosa's shoulder.

When they detangle from the hug, I watch Ginny's eyes sweep over the space.

I don't say anything, just watch her as she moves from the living room to the dining room, as if she's rediscovering each corner of the house anew. When she steps into the kitchen, she stops, her fingers tracing the marble countertop where she's spent so many hours baking.

"I didn't realize how much I missed this," she murmurs. "I missed being here. The kitchen...everything."

"You don't have to miss it anymore," I say, moving closer to her. "You're home now."

She turns to me, her eyes soft and grateful. "I know," she says, resting her head against my chest. "It just feels good. Really good."

I hold her for a moment, the two of us standing there in the quiet kitchen, the house filled with an odd sense of calm. This is where we belong. Together.

I receive a call later that evening for an urgent, quick meeting. Ginny doesn't mind me leaving, claiming that my business is also important, and I shouldn't neglect it because of her.

I leave, not because of what she said, but because I know it'll be a very short meeting at a restaurant. The whole time I'm away, I can't stop thinking about Ginny. About how unreal everything seems to be.

I chuckle in the middle of the meeting when I remember she's asked me to buy her some ice cream on my way back. I think it may be a pregnancy craving at this point.

My blood is thrumming with excitement when I get home later. I immediately head upstairs and toward my bedroom, where she was when I left. As I push the door open, I stop dead in my tracks.

All of Ginny's things—her clothes, her books, even the little things she keeps on her nightstand—are now in my room. Our room.

I stand there, my heart pounding, and it's as if I'm seeing the future right in front of me. This is it. This is what I've been waiting for.

Ginny is on her knees in the middle of the room, arranging some of her things into a box. When she turns to look at me, I see a mischievous glint dancing in her eyes.

"Surprise."

I walk toward her, my chest tight with emotion. "You did this while I was gone?"

She nods. "I'm tired of us having separate rooms."

A chuckle slips past my lips, one of disbelief, of happiness, of joy. "You have no idea how much this means to me."

"Oh, I do," she drawls.

I chuckle before pulling her body up against mine. "I have to finish unpacking," she whines as I carry her to the bed, laying her back against the mattress as I hover over her.

"You can finish that later." I kiss her neck, and her breath hitches as my kiss goes lower.

"You know pregnant women can't have sex, right?"

I halt, leaning up to look at her face, my eyes searching hers. "You're lying."

"I'm not," she says, but I see a smile cracking through her facade.

A loud laugh bursts out of her lips.

"You should have seen your face!"

I tickle her sides, her laugh turning into gasps as tears run down her eyes, before settling right beside her and pulling her body flush against mine.

"Fine. We won't have sex for nine months," I murmur in her ear.

She giggles, snuggling closer to me and resting her head on my chest.

"We both know that's not possible," she whispers back, her hand tracing lazy circles on my arm. "You'll go crazy."

I laugh. I've realized laughing comes easy to me these days, ever since I met Ginny again. I feel different. Happier. Lighter. As if all the weight of the past is finally lifting.

"The wedding is the day after tomorrow," I say quietly, my fingers brushing through her hair.

She hums in agreement, her voice soft. "I can't believe it's almost here."

I chuckle softly. "Are you ready?"

She tilts her head up to look at me, her eyes filled with warmth. "More than ready."

I kiss her forehead, pulling her closer. "Me too. It's going to be perfect, Ginny."

For the first time ever, I believe it. That everything is going to be perfect. That we are finally getting our happy ending.

And this is only the beginning.

EPILOGUE

Five years later

Loud laughter echoes through the house as we gather around the dinner table, plates scattered with the remnants of Rosa's delicious lasagna.

I still don't know how to cook. I've tried to learn since, well, I'm a mother now, but the kids—brutally honest, those ones—much prefer Rosa's cooking.

They love my baking, though, and won't stop gushing to me about how they've made lots of friends in their kindergarten because I keep sending sweet treats for the whole class. Some of the mothers even come to my bakery, referred by my kids' teacher.

The dining room feels warm, alive, and filled with a kind of contentment I could never have imagined five years ago. Dario sits across from me, his eyes crinkling with amusement as he watches Nicolas, one of the twins, trying to tell a joke he's told a million times.

"Why don't eggs tell jokes?" Nico asks, barely able to contain his giggles as he waits for the punchline.

His twin, Sofia, rolls her eyes, trying to hide the soft smile tugging at her lips. She's quieter, more thoughtful, and already too smart for her age. "Because they'll crack each other up," she answers dryly, beating Nico to it.

Nico's laugh erupts before he can even finish the joke himself. His loud, infectious giggles bounce off the walls, filling every corner of the room with joy. He's always been the loud one, full of energy and mischief, a complete contrast to Sofia, who watches the world with careful, observant eyes.

Dario shakes his head, grinning as he wipes his mouth with a napkin. "That's the third time today, Nico. I think you need some new material, buddy."

Nico pouts, but the mischief gleaming in his eyes shows he's already planning his next joke. "But it's funny, Daddy!" he insists, his mouth full of lasagna.

Sofia rolls her eyes again but doesn't say anything, and I can't help but chuckle at the way she mirrors Dario's calm demeanor, while Nico's wild energy seems to come from...well, me, I think.

Rosa walks into the dining room with that familiar motherly smile on her face. She's been a constant in our lives, and after all these years, I think she loves our children just as much as we do.

"It's a good joke, Nico," she says kindly, ruffling his dark curls before collecting the empty plates. "But tomorrow, I expect a new one."

Nico beams up at her. "You've got it, Rosa!"

As we finish up, Dario stands and stretches, reaching for Sofia and Nico's hands. "All right, bedtime, you two."

Nico groans dramatically, throwing his head back. "Nooooo, I'm not tired!"

Sofia just stands, already making her way toward the

stairs. "Come on, Nico. We have school tomorrow," she says sensibly, her voice soft but firm.

Dario and I exchange a glance—amusement mixed with pride. Our family may not be perfect, but it's ours, and I wouldn't trade this life for anything in the world.

Upstairs, the night settles into a usual yet chaotic rhythm. We've fallen into a routine. Dario tucks Sofia into bed first. She's already half asleep by the time her head hits the pillow. I watch from the doorway, my heart swelling as Dario brushes a kiss on her forehead.

"Goodnight, sweetheart," he whispers.

She blinks up at him, her dark lashes fluttering, and offers him the smallest, softest smile. "Goodnight, Daddy."

In the other room, I struggle to get Nico into bed. He's bouncing off the walls, still full of energy despite it being late. "Come on, buddy," I say, finally catching him in my arms and lifting him onto the bed. "It's time to sleep."

"But I'm..." He lets out a big yawn, "...not tired."

I shake my head, laughing softly. "Sure, you're not."

He grins, his eyes sparkling with the familiar mischief that I know too well. "Mommy, can you tell me a story?"

I sit on the edge of the bed, smoothing his brown locks back. "All right, just one."

Dario joins me, leaning against the doorway, watching us with that same quiet smile he's worn all evening. I tell Nico a quick story—one he's heard a hundred times. It's the tale of the ruthless savage king who trapped a princess into marrying him for revenge, only to fall head over heels for her after rescuing her from two ugly trolls and slaying them.

Of course, I rephrase it, adding some edited parts, but it's still the story of our love, nonetheless. I can't wait for our kids to piece it together one day and ask for the candid story of how we came to be. Well, mostly for Nico to figure it out.

Sofia caught on months ago—like I said, she's way too smart for her age. By the end of my tale, Nico is finally drifting off, his little hand curled around mine.

Just before I pull away, his grip tightens around my hand.

"Are we going to Uncle Lorenzo's house tomorrow?" he slurs groggily.

A sigh escapes my lips. Lorenzo is married now—shocking, I know—with a three-year-old, and my kids treat his house as their second home.

"Yes, buddy. You'll get to play with Fabio after school tomorrow. But tomorrow won't get here if you don't go to sleep."

That does it. He slips his hand from mine, a satisfied smile creasing his lips as I pull away.

When we close the door to the kids' rooms, the house falls into a soft, peaceful silence. However, I'm burning on the inside.

As Dario takes my hand and guides me toward our bedroom. The moment we get in, I'm kissing him, my tongue slipping inside his mouth as his arms wrap around me, drawing me impossibly closer to him.

"Fuck, Ginny," he groans against my lips, lifting me off the ground so I wrap my legs around his waist.

The kisses grow more heated, his hands roaming over my curves, squeezing my ass as he leads us towards the bed. My pussy is already slick with wetness from his touch, but I don't care. His kiss is intoxicating, his taste like a drug. The man of my dreams...my husband.

I moan, running my fingers through his hair as he pins my body to the bed. His hips grind against mine, and I can feel his erection straining out of his silk pajama pants.

My cotton nightgown comes off quickly, and in the next

second, he's pulling my nipples between his teeth, sucking and biting as his hand finds my folds.

"Dario," I moan, spreading my legs farther apart for him to slip two fingers in. I grab his hair, tugging on the strands as I kiss him deeply, passionately.

"You know how much I love foreplay, baby, but I'm afraid we don't have time for that," I murmur against his mouth, reaching down and pulling at his pants. He grunts before shoving them down, leaving himself exposed, his dick erect and gleaming with precum.

He's gorgeous, so fucking beautiful.

His eyes are smoldering, watching as I grab his hard length and guide him to my dripping pussy. With one fluid motion, he thrusts into me, and I moan, arching my back so he goes deeper, faster.

He pulls away, leaning over me and staring deep into my eyes. "Keep your moans low, baby," he says huskily. "We don't want the whole house hearing us."

Dario doesn't care about the whole house hearing us. He's fucked me in more open places around the house than I can count, and there's not a chance that not one of the domestic staff has heard a single noise.

What we care about is the *kids* hearing.

People say that marriage is supposed to lower your sexual libido as a couple, but that hasn't happened in our case. The only change to our very active sexual life is having to be quieter and less spontaneous because of the kids.

I bite my lower lip, nodding as he thrusts in again. Carnal pleasure washes over me, causing every nerve to tingle as he makes love to me. As he moves above me, I roll my hips to meet his thrusts. He loves it when I do that.

His eyes darken as he lets out a low groan before gripping my hips and driving even faster. "Fuck, Gin, you drive me crazy," he hisses in my ear, letting go of one hip to rub my clit with his thumb.

My nails dig into his shoulders as he continues to fuck me relentlessly, wildly yet softly, murmuring dirty phrases to me and promising to fuck me forever. I feel my walls tightening around him, feel the orgasm building as he continues to slide into me. When my climax finally hits me, it takes everything in me not to scream out in release. I bury my face into the pillow beside my head as he fucks me through my orgasm.

Soon, his own release rips through him, and he thrusts into me a few more times before he collapses on top of me with a contented sigh. Our heavy breaths echo around the room as he slides onto the mattress beside me and pulls my body to him.

We lay there in silence for a while, my head over the steady beating of his heart.

"What do you think the kids will be like when they're older?" I suddenly ask, my voice soft as I snuggle closer to him.

"Nico will probably be causing all kinds of trouble." Dario chuckles, his chest vibrating against my cheek. "And Sofia...she'll keep him in line. She's already smarter than both of us."

I laugh, the sound quiet in the stillness of the room. "You're probably right."

We fall into a comfortable silence before I break it again.

"And us?" I ask, propping myself up on one elbow to look down at him. He meets my gaze, green eyes glinting in the dim lamplight.

"We will keep loving each other," he murmurs, his fingers touching my cheek. "Loving our kids, loving our home, our family...always."

I smile softly, leaning forward and capturing his lips with mine. It's a slow kiss, filled with the promise that we are going to make this work, before whispering, "Always."

THE END

If you enjoyed *Dark Mafia Vows,* then you'll also like *Billionaire Daddy's Secret Baby*.

(Click Here to get Billionaire Daddy's Secret Baby)

Mia watches as the father of her child says, "I do" to her best friend in this one night stand off-limits romance that will leave you yearning for more. ***Read Chapter One on the next page!***

41

SNEAK PEAK

Billionaire Daddy's Secret Baby Sneak Peek

I had a one-night stand with a stranger on the worst day of my life.

Five years later, I am at a wedding.

The groom walks in...

And I watch as the father of my child says "I do" to my best friend.

COLIN PRESCOTT, my sexy as sin, yet arrogant protector who disappeared without a trace.

Turns out, he's a hot-shot billionaire.

And my BFF is about to walk down the aisle with him.

SHE HAS no idea I know him, or that he's the father of my child.

. . .

I DON'T WANT to think about him.

But I burn with the memory of that night...when he devoured every inch of my body.

Now each moment with him sparks a carnal desire I can't deny.

UNTIL A SHOCKING TRUTH about their marriage changed everything...

AND WHEN THE drama can't get any hotter with lies and betrayals.

There is one more secret Colin still needs to know.

He's four and has his smile.

(CLICK HERE TO get Billionaire Daddy's Secret Baby)

CHAPTER ONE
Mia

"OH, you've got to be kidding me," I groan as my car slowly sputters to death. My heart pounds hard in my chest as the car stops in the middle of literally nowhere. It's past nine at night—a terrible time for my car to break down.

"Come on, baby," I say, trying to start it one more time. "Come on, you can do it. Just twenty more minutes, please."

I pat the steering wheel, as if I can cajole the car into starting up once again.

It doesn't work.

"Oh God." I rest my head on the steering wheel. This is it. This is my last straw. Tears start to stream down my cheeks.

I get out of the car and pop the hood, praying that whatever's wrong with the car is something I can fix. I scan the car's insides in desperation.

"Come on, come on," I whisper, hoping to find something out of place.

"Hey, pretty lady." I hear a voice call out a few feet behind me.

A cold shudder runs through my body and I remain frozen to the spot, hoping whoever it is will leave me alone if I don't turn.

"Yo. You deaf or something?" the person calls again, this time louder and this time closer.

I shut my eyes tightly, trying to stop a new wave of tears threatening to escape.

Why is this happening to me today of all days?

"Hey!" The voice is angrier now and even closer.

I turn and see a guy in a black hoodie and pair of dark pants slowly approach me. His face isn't visible in the darkness, especially since his back is to the light.

"Look, I don't want any trouble, okay? My car just broke down and I need it to start so I can get out of your way," I say, trying to keep my voice from breaking. The last thing I need is to make this guy think I'm scared of him.

"Well, you should've said so. I'm an expert with cars." He closes the distance between us. "I can fix it but it's going to cost you." He runs a hand over my cheek and I shut my eyes again, desperate to blink back the tears.

"Please," I say, feeling small and helpless.

"Oh, don't be like that," he says, tracing his hands on my face. "I'll be gentle."

"Hey!" a voice calls from a distance.

We both turn and see another man approach us, a wrench in hand.

"If the lady doesn't want your help, the best thing to do is buzz off."

The creepy guy turns back to me. "Whatever. It's not worth it anyway." With that, he starts to run away.

"Hey, are you okay?" the man with the wrench calls out, a little closer to me.

I turn to look at him, and almost like a loose faucet, the tears start to fall freely from my face. I can't do anything to stop them. "Yeah," I say, blinking hard. I don't want to break down in front of this total stranger, but I can't seem to help it.

"Hey," he says as he moves to stand in front of me. "Did he do something to you?"

"No," I say, trying to look anywhere but his face.

"Did he touch you in any way?"

"No."

"Did he—?"

"For the love of God, I'm fine!" I feel the words escape in a jagged whisper.

He takes a step back and I feel a wave of guilt wash over me.

"Look," I say, rubbing my hands across my face. "It's just been one of those days. I'm sorry."

The man nods. "Can I have a look at your car?" he asks.

I nod and gesture to the hood. "Knock yourself out."

He steps over to the car and starts his own inspection.

I feel the cold night air start to get the better of me, so I wrap my arms around my chest.

"Okay, it looks like there's something with the motor coil," he announces after a few minutes.

"Motor coil?" I ask, confused.

"Yeah. It doesn't suddenly go off. You should've been getting some warnings before it broke down. Something on the dashboard, weird sounds."

I slap my left hand over my face, feeling regret for not taking care of things sooner. "Yeah. There were some warning signs. I thought I could do whatever I needed to do today and fix it tomorrow. I planned to take it to a mechanic and everything."

"I'm afraid this car isn't going anywhere tonight," he says, looking at his watch like a doctor pronouncing the death of a patient.

"Great," I say, wrapping my arms around my body once again, feeling the cold come down even harder for some reason.

I watch as a wave of concern grows on his face. Without saying anything, he takes off his coat and hands it to me.

"I'm fine," I say, knowing I'm anything but.

"Take the coat. Please." His voice is firm and deep. Something tells me he's going to keep pushing if I don't take it, so I do, feeling slightly better once I wrap it around my body.

"Thanks for your help tonight. I think I'll just call an Uber or something, and send a tow truck out tomorrow to get my car."

"I could drive you home, if you want."

I shake my head. "The last thing I want to do is trouble you. You've done more than enough. I can take it from here. My house is just thirty minutes away."

"What happened anyway?" he suddenly asks.

My eyes narrow. "What?"

"You said it's been that kind of day. What happened today?"

"I don't think that's any of your business, thank you."

"Please." He calls. That's when I look up at him for the first time. At his deep brown eyes and the calm demeanor on his face. The stubble around his jaw and his dark hair. For some reason, despite the darkness surrounding us, his face has never been clearer. I swallow.

He's hot. He's really hot.

"I don't want to bore you with all of the drama." I try to say it again.

"Try me." He responds.

I swallow and look up at him again. How the hell do I start?

A Few Hours Earlier

I DRAG the tip of my lipstick along my lips carefully, my eyes laser focused on the mirror before me, like the slightest slip could ruin my life forever.

I study my face in the mirror, wondering if there's anything I left out of place. My red hair is brushed out and shiny. I feel unsatisfied with the blush on one side of my face, and grab a tissue, ready to dab some of it off.

My phone buzzes on the dresser, interrupting my work, but I reach for it right away. It's a message from Kevin, my boyfriend.

KEVIN: *We need to talk.*

ME: *After my presentation.*

I place the phone back on my dresser and study myself in the mirror again. I blot at the blush until it's just the right amount. I rise from the chair and grab the pair of shoes I picked out the night before. I bought them solely for this presentation and I just know they're going to bring me luck.

I work for a jewel company in downtown San Francisco and have been trying to get promoted to house director for the past two years. A month ago, an opportunity fell into my lap. I could get the promotion I wanted if I could make an adequate presentation on the ongoing market trends and give even more reasons why I think I can do better as a house director. And for a month, I've been working hard putting everything together and rehearsing everything I want to say.

I am not screwing this up.

The dark green shoes match my pantsuit perfectly. I spray on some perfume and feel almost ready to take on the day.

My phone buzzes with yet another message.

KEVIN: *This is urgent, Mia.*

I shake my head and swipe open the text. I'm trying to get in a calm zone. The last thing I need is a distraction from anything or anyone.

Especially my boyfriend.

ME: *It'll have to wait.*

I grab the handbag lying on my bed and slip my phone inside before heading out of the house, affirming myself almost every step of the way. I've been working on this for weeks. I deserve it. I deserve the promotion.

My phone rings as I get into my car, and I throw my head back, wondering who it could be this time around. I take out my phone and see it's Jessica, my best friend.

"What's up?" I ask, putting the phone on speaker and starting the engine.

"Please tell me you're out of your house already."

"I just got in the car," I say, and stare at the lit-up icons on the dash. I feel a wave of worry snake down my spine.

"I think my car might have a problem," I say, almost absent-mindedly, to my friend.

"What, it's not working?" Jessica asks.

"It is, but I'll take it to the mechanic tomorrow to be safe."

"I hope everything will be okay. But I was just calling to tell you I got the job," Jessica says, her words causing my eyes to widen.

"The VP job?" I ask, feeling my hands falter on the steering wheel.

"The VP job," she confirms. "I'll be leaving for London in a week."

"Oh my God!" I scream excitedly. "I'm really happy for you, Jess. You deserve this."

"I know. We'll talk more after your presentation. For now, hurry up and get to work on time," she says, and hangs up.

With my hands tight on the steering wheel, I finally leave my house and get on the highway. Jessica has been my best friend since college, and we tell each other almost everything. She's been vying for the job she just got for almost a year. I'm extremely glad she was finally able to get it. While I'm certainly over the moon that my friend gets to move up in her company and her career, I'm going to severely miss her. I hope she's going to miss me too.

I get to work with ten minutes to spare and look at myself in the rearview mirror one more time before getting out. My hand is wrapped right around my bag as I walk briskly into the building.

"Hi, Ms. Ravenwood," Holly, the receptionist, greets me, a giant smile on her face.

I return the smile. "Hey, Holly."

"Big day, huh?"

"Wish me luck."

My phone buzzes again as I step into my office and shut the glass door gently behind me. I pull it out of my handbag and see a third message from Kevin.

KEVIN: *This can't wait. Call me.*

I look up at the giant wall clock behind my chair. I only have six minutes. I most definitely don't have time for whatever Kevin wants to talk about. I shake my head and type on my phone as fast as I can.

ME: *You know I don't have the time, Kevin. My presentation is in a few minutes.*

I put my phone down and grab the files in my desk drawer. I take a few deep breaths to center myself, putting Kevin out of my mind for the time being. I've been preparing for this opportunity for a long time. I've got this. I've got every situation mapped out and have prepared for any and every possible question the supervisors could throw at me.

What could possibly go wrong?

There's a soft knock at my door, and I look up as Henry, one of the supervisors, pops his head into my office. "Ravenwood," he greets, his voice warm. "You're on in a few minutes. Are you ready for this?"

I look up at him and smile. "More than I've ever been for anything."

"Good. You're going to crush it. I know that," he says, and walks away.

I smile and grab a few more files before heading out of the office and towards the conference room.

I *am* going to crush it. I've gone through the material millions of times. I know the pages in and out. Nothing can be thrown at me out of left field. Nothing should surprise me.

I stop before the door leading into the conference room and stand for a minute, taking another series of deep breaths. I can see the supervisors inside, all settled at the long table. This is it. This is probably what makes or breaks my desperate need for a promotion, and probably my career.

Henry's eyes shift to the door and he sees me behind it. I smile at him and he returns it, this time with reassurance. My phone buzzes in my pocket as I reach for the doorknob. I shut my eyes in frustration and pull it out. It's Kevin again. What I see on the screen makes my heart skip a beat.

KEVIN: *I think we should break up.*

My eyes blur and I can't help but wonder if misread what was there. But I know I didn't. The words are there, staring back at me like a sleep paralysis demon.

I think we should break up.

I blink back tears. I did not prepare for this.

Like that isn't enough, another text appears on the screen.

KEVIN: *I don't think this is working for me anymore.*

I remain frozen at the door, reading the texts over and over. Why is this happening to me now? Why is Kevin intent on doing this at this exact moment?

I have no idea what I should send as a response.

I look up helplessly, struggling to maintain my composure, and see Henry waving at me to get inside. I nod and push the door open, feeling internally destabilized. The utter confidence I had felt a few minutes ago has completely disappeared. Now I'm just running on absentmindedness and I know, as I walk to the screen, I'm going to screw this up.

(CLICK HERE TO get Billionaire Daddy's Secret Baby)

Made in United States
Troutdale, OR
05/27/2025